HERE'S THE SCOOP

COMING HOME TRILOGY BOOK 2

THE WAY TO A WOMAN'S HEART SERIES

SHERIDAN JEANE

HERE'S THE SCOOP

Sheridan Jeane

First published in the United States by Flowers & Fullerton.
HERE'S THE SCOOP
www.FlowersAndFullerton.com
First published in Medina, Ohio, United States by Flowers & Fullerton.
Library of Congress Control Number: 2023905740

ISBN-13: 978-1-63303-023-7 (trade paperback)

First edition: 2023

To my dear family and loved ones,

Thank you for always being my anchor in the stormy seas of life. Your unwavering love and support have given me the courage to follow my dreams and write this book.

To my family, you have taught me the value of community and the power of love. Your endless encouragement has been the driving force behind this novel, and I am forever grateful for the warmth and comfort you provide.

To Tom, your unwavering belief in me has been the wind beneath my wings. You have been my sounding board, my inspiration, and my biggest fan. Your love has taught me that even in the darkest of times, there is always a light at the end of the tunnel.

This book is a testament to the power of love, the resilience of the human spirit, and the importance of coming together as a community. I dedicate it to you, with all my heart.

Forever and always,

Sheridan

BOOKS BY SHERIDAN JEANE

Contemporary Romances

The Way to a Woman's Heart series - the **Coming Home** trilogy

Slow Simmer
Here's the Scoop
From Bitter to Sweet

———

Coming in 2024
The Way to a Woman's Heart series - the **Destination Wedding** trilogy

Too Much On My Plate
Say Cheese!
Turkish Delight

———

Historical romances

Gambling On a Scoundrel

Secrets and Seduction series:

* Lady Cecilia Is Cordially Disinvited for Christmas
*(only available via Sheridan's VIP club)
It Takes a Spy…
Lady Catherine's Secret
Once Upon a Spy
My Lady, My Spy
Along Came a Spy

ABOUT HERE'S THE SCOOP

It's not every day that a woman has to go into hiding from the online world, but when you're being hunted by the paparazzi because of a rockstar's lies, you do what you gotta do. Sonya knows all too well, but she's tired of running and hiding. That's why when Max Ross, the man who caused her old life to go up in flames, walks back into her life with his niece in tow, she decides to face the music. With a little help from her fifth-grade class and a whole lot of humor, Sonya sets out to prove that love can conquer all - even when the paparazzi are lurking in the bushes.

Max Ross may be a movie promoter, but he's not exactly a master of his own destiny. When he stumbles back into Sonya's life when he walks into her fifth-grade classroom with his orphaned niece, he knows he's got a lot of making up to do. Unfortunately, Sonya's not exactly making it easy for him. With the school musical fast approaching and the rockstar coming back into the limelight, Max has his work cut out for him. But with a little help from the kids and a whole lot of wit, he's determined to show Sonya that love is worth fighting for - even if it means going up against the paparazzi and the online world.

In this lighthearted and laugh-out-loud romantic comedy, Sonya and Max will have to avoid the limelight, avoid the trolls, and survive the fifth-grade musical if they want to find love. With plenty of laughs, a touch of drama, and a whole lot of heart, this book is guaranteed to put a smile on your face.

WELCOME BACK, EMMA

Dear Max and Ford,

I was so sorry to hear about the passing of your sister, Hailey, and your brother-in-law, Barry. I can only imagine how much you are hurting right now. I didn't know your sister well since she was a few years older than us, but her loss hit me hard. My heart goes out to you. Please know that I am here for you if you need anything at all.

—With deepest sympathy, Angelina

SONYA

As the morning bell rang, one of my students darted in and I closed the door of my fifth-grade classroom behind him.

"Good morning," I said in my teacher voice. "Please put your things away and take your places. I have news to share with you."

My students immediately stilled and turned to face me, their eyes as round as saucers. I mentally kicked myself for causing those wary reactions. I should have chosen my words more carefully. They were all still shaken by the horrible announcement I'd had to make a couple of weeks ago. "It's good news," I reassured them. "Nothing to worry about."

The kids unstuck themselves and then started moving more quickly. They stashed their lunch boxes and backpacks in their personal cubbyholes along the wall as they made their way to their assigned seats.

Liam stopped at the Halloween-themed bulletin board I'd decorated yesterday and found his name on one of the orange pumpkins at the base of the tree. The enormous tree's construction-paper branches spread onto the ceiling and held tissue paper leaves in red, yellow, and orange. Next month, I'd replace the pumpkins near the trunk with fallen leaves and a turkey for Thanksgiving, so the display would be up for a while. Between cutting out the leaves while sitting in front of the television, writing the students' names on them, and then stapling them in place, I'd spent a few hours on the project, so I wanted it to last.

A few of my students preferred to use traditional chairs at their desks, but most of them sat on the kid-sized exercise balls I'd provided. The balls helped the fidgety kids move around and stay active without being a distraction to the rest of the class, plus they were great for promoting proper posture. I hadn't expected to be able to raise the money for them so quickly through the crowd-funding program I'd launched when I'd started working here in August, but my kids' families and other people in the community had donated enough money to purchase them in less than a month.

"Principal Goodfriend just informed me that Emma Bachar is returning to school today," I said. "Her uncle drove her to school this morning, and she'll be joining us shortly."

Liam started bouncing up and down on his green yoga ball with a worried expression on his face. "Where will she live? I thought her house burned down. Is it fixed? Is she moving back in?"

Crystal shot Liam a scowl. "Don't be stupid. Her house burned down. I saw a bulldozer there last week. How could she live in an empty lot?" She paused, taking on a pinched, haunted look. "It was a good thing she spent the night at Marley's house, or she'd be dead too."

Marley's lower lip quivered, so she pressed her lips together into a tight line. "The sirens woke us up, but we didn't know they were heading to her house—so we just went back to sleep."

The new girl who'd moved here from Germany bounced gently up and down on her yellow exercise ball, one arm held high.

I nodded at her. "Yes, Ally?"

"Miss Gambit, where will Emma live now?" Her German-accented English was clear and precise.

"I understand she's living with her uncle, but Emma can tell you when she gets here." I'd met Sinan Bachar last month at a school event and he seemed pleasant enough, but I was surprised to hear he'd been chosen as Emma's guardian. He'd mentioned he'd recently moved here for work, and Emma didn't seem particularly attached to him, but maybe she didn't have anyone else.

Ally nodded sagely. "*Das ist gut.*" She flushed. "That's good."

Liam looked thoughtful. "At least she won't have to live in the same house where her parents died."

My chest tightened. That would have been horrible, but with the house demolished, I was grateful she wouldn't have to face that sort of situation.

"Since you're all fifth graders, I'm sure I don't need to remind you to be kind to Emma. Your questions show me you understand how difficult and complicated these last weeks have been for her. She'll need your help and sympathy. I expect you all to be the kind and supportive children I know you are."

Marley sat up even straighter on her ball. "You can count on us." She glanced around the room at her classmates.

They all made sounds of agreement. They were good kids. Restless at times, as were all fifth graders, but I had an unusually kindhearted class this year. Every year, each class developed a sort of group personality. Some became competitive, some rowdy, but this group—they were amazingly kind. Emma's tragedy seemed to have cemented that in them.

A knock sounded on the classroom door, and I spotted the principal through the side window. I waved for her to come in.

The door swung open, and Emma stood framed in the doorway. The adorable, dark-haired girl wore a new outfit I'd never seen before. Of course, she'd probably had to purchase all new clothes after the fire.

Directly behind her stood Principal Goodfriend, and next in line I glimpsed a tall man in a suit. That had to be Emma's uncle, whom I'd met at last month's Family Day event.

Mrs. Goodfriend wore a bright, cheerful smile and a gorgeous melon-colored business suit. She always looked completely professional and competent. Nothing seemed to faze her.

As my eyes focused on the man in the perfectly tailored business suit, my breath caught in my throat. A chill ran through my body, followed by a surge of shock mixed with pulse-thumping anger that left me feeling momentarily lightheaded.

This couldn't be happening.

Emma Bachar was supposed to be living with her uncle, Sinan Bachar. Not this man. Not Max-freaking-Ross—the man who'd singlehandedly destroyed my life.

He was the last person on Earth I'd ever wanted to see again.

Based on his gobsmacked expression, he hadn't expected to see me, either.

2

BEWILDERED

MAX

I stared at the curvy platinum blonde in the white cotton shirt, navy skirt, and scuffed pumps, barely able to believe my eyes. Sure, she'd bleached her hair and used tinted contact lenses to change her eye color, but I'd know Essie Harlow anywhere. Other people might not have recognized her, but everything about the woman was seared into my heart.

What the hell was she doing here? Was she the substitute teacher? An aide? Principal Goodfriend had said Emma's teacher, Miss Gambit, knew we were on our way and was preparing the class, so why was Essie Harlow standing here, staring at me like I was an alien invader?

Mrs. Goodfriend didn't appear to notice Essie's stunned expression. Her attention was focused on the classroom full of students. "This is Emma's uncle, Mr. Ross. He's her new guardian. Can you all say hello to him?"

"Hello, Mr. Ross," the students said in unison.

Creepy. It reminded me of *Children of the Corn*.

The principal focused her laser-like gaze on my niece. "Emma, would you like to put your things in your cubby and take your seat while I speak with your uncle and Miss Gambit?"

I stared at Essie, confounded. Was Essie Miss Gambit? *Miss* Gambit, not *Missus*. That didn't make sense—unless—had she gotten married and divorced in the past five years? The thought that she could have forgotten me so quickly after she'd disappeared rankled. I certainly hadn't been able to forget her.

Emma tightened her hand in mine, pulling my attention back to where it should be: with her.

I squeezed her hand back and followed up with a reassuring wink. A moment later, she took a deep breath and waded into her classroom. Her first cautious steps seemed filled with trepidation, but the welcoming smiles of her classmates made the tension in her shoulders ease, and she began to move more quickly.

A girl jumped up from the yellow yoga ball she'd been sitting on, ran over to Emma, and wrapped her in her arms. "Miss Gambit said you could sit in our pod if you wanted. You want to, right?"

When Emma glanced up at her teacher, *Miss Gambit* nodded her approval. I gave my head a hard shake to clear away my confusion. Clearly, this was Essie. She'd recognized me too. None of this made any sense, but I'd figure it out later.

"I thought you might like that," said the woman who'd broken my heart five years ago. "Go ahead and take your seat. Later today, I'll gather together some of the assignments you missed. I know you won't want to fall behind, but I don't want you to feel overwhelmed, either."

Emma nodded and took an empty chair—or rather, a vacant red ball—next to the girl who'd hugged her. Emma immediately began rocking from side to side on the ball, releasing some of her anxiety.

I cleared my throat as I forced myself to meet Essie's gaze. "I'd like to talk with you later today to discuss bringing Emma back up to speed." I blinked a few times. Had I just suggested a private meeting? Apparently, my mouth was moving faster than my brain.

Principal Goodfriend nodded approvingly. "That's a

wonderful idea. Mr. Ross, I'd like to introduce you to Emma's teacher, Sonya Gambit.

I stared at her blankly. Sonya? She was calling herself Sonya Gambit? No wonder I'd lost track of her. Either she'd married someone, or she'd legally changed her name to hide. I wasn't sure which explanation hurt the most.

"Pleased to meet you," she said, not revealing the faintest flicker of recognition as she met my gaze.

I gave a stiff nod. *Sonya* had apparently recovered from the shock of seeing me. Either that, or she simply wasn't as affected by this unexpected encounter as I was.

"I'll pull together Emma's assignments during my planning period later today," she continued in a crisply professional tone. "Can you stop by after the students are dismissed for the day to review them with me? I'll be free at around three-thirty. Does that work for you?"

"Emma can take the bus to my house after school," said the girl who'd hugged Emma. She bounced up and down on her yellow ball, grinning with enthusiasm.

Emma beamed. "Oh, please, say yes, Uncle Max. I always go to Marley's after school on Mondays and Wednesdays."

So, this was the infamous Marley. "I'd better clear that with Marley's mom first," I said. "I don't want to impose."

"She happens to be on the school premises right now," Mrs. Goodfriend said. "She volunteers at the library every Monday morning. I can introduce you so you can make arrangements with her before you leave."

"Then it's settled." I locked gazes with Essie—I mean, *Sonya*. "I'll see you at three-thirty."

She licked her lips. "I'll be ready for you."

AN UNCOMFORTABLE PARENT-TEACHER CONFERENCE

SONYA

My classroom was too quiet now that my students had left for the day. I checked the clock above the whiteboard. Nearly three-thirty.

I spotted some black grime on the sleeve of my white blouse. It must have come from the whiteboard. I tried to brush it away but only managed to turn it into a gray smudge. I let out a sigh of frustration as I slid my arms back into the jacket of my Old Navy suit to hide the stain.

The classroom phone chirped with an incoming call, and my stomach gave a jolt. I needed to pull myself together. This wasn't the moment for nerves. I needed to be calm. In control. After all, this was *my* classroom. *My* territory. *I* was the one in charge.

"Hi Sonya," the secretary said. "Max Ross is here to see you. Should I send him to your room?"

"Yes, please."

Less than a minute later, a shadow crossed my doorway a split second before he appeared.

My stomach tensed as I rose from my chair. "What are you doing here?"

He stared at me blankly. "I'm here for our meeting."

"I mean, here in Sewickley. You're supposed to be in Los Angeles."

He glanced away. "I was. I mean—I was living there when you and I met, but after you left, I moved back here to Pittsburgh. This is where I grew up. Sewickley is my hometown."

He—what? I sat up abruptly in my chair. He was from here?

"Essie?" He rushed forward. "Are you okay?"

My eyes snapped toward him, and I shot him a glare that could melt steel. "Don't call me that. I don't use that nickname anymore. Call me Sonya. Or even better, Miss Gambit."

"A nickname?" He hesitated, looking confused. "How do you get Essie from Sonya?"

Of all the questions he could ask, this was what he wanted to know? I sighed. "Sonya starts with an S—Essie. My baby sister called me that, and it stuck."

"And Gambit? The last time I saw you, your name was Harlow." He was on the verge of saying more, but when I rocketed out of my chair and raced toward the open door, he stopped abruptly.

"Shush," I hissed. I poked my head into the hallway and looked around for eavesdroppers.

Empty.

I closed the door and faced him. "Harlow was my dad's name. I don't use it anymore. Please don't mention it again. After everything that happened, I'm sure you can guess why I prefer to distance myself from that man. Mom took her own name back after their divorce. After the fiasco he staged, I finally legally changed mine as well."

His jaw tensed and he gave a tight nod.

"Take a seat." I pointed toward one of the small, student-sized chairs.

He ignored it and instead perched on one of the largest yoga balls.

I sat behind my desk and frowned at him. Max didn't look the

9

least bit awkward on the ball, which irritated me. The jerk looked perfectly at ease.

"Was part of the reason you changed your name because of everything that happened with Raven?" His eyes were full of sympathy.

As if he cared. Hah. Crocodile tears.

I knew better than to believe Max Ross. The liar. I'd never make *that* mistake again. Even so, he was a pro at that fake sympathy thing.

I shrugged as I adjusted my gaze and focused on the center of his forehead. Looking into his eyes was too overwhelming. They were too blue. Too expressive. They elicited too many memories. I felt myself wanting to soothe him, idiot that I was. The scandal with Raven was the last thing I wanted to discuss with him. Well, one of the last.

I cleared my throat as I considered my reply. "It was, but I'd been thinking about changing it for years. Once I realized I needed to do a better job hiding from the paparazzi, especially those jackals at *Here's the Scoop*, I finally hired a lawyer to file the paperwork. My father left when Mom was pregnant with my little sister. Mom took back her own name in the divorce, so she and my little sister were both Gambits. I was the only one still named Harlow. It was a relief to get rid of that name."

He held up his hands in a soothing gesture. "I promise not to tell anyone about your former name."

That movement irritated the crap out of me. Who was he to placate me? I scowled at him, and he winced.

He dropped his hands in defeat. "I'm the one ultimately responsible for everything that happened to you." He met my furious gaze and didn't flinch. That sort of impressed me.

"I was a self-centered ass," he said. "It never occurred to me that keeping my ex-girlfriend's identity a secret could hurt you. If I'd told you about her, you'd have been better prepared for the media frenzy after she had that public meltdown and shaved off all her hair."

"Good God, her hair," I said, stroking my own long tresses and tucking a strand behind my ear. A woman's hairstyle could be deeply integrated into her identity, and it had killed me to start bleaching mine. I'd had no other choice. I'd needed to become someone completely different. Five years ago, I'd worn my brown hair in a short, edgy cut. My current long blonde style was the polar opposite.

I couldn't believe I'd forgotten about Raven's hair. I guess I'd blocked it, along with everything else. I had to. My voice turned bitter. "That's what comes from being crucified by all her fans for breaking up the two of you. Oh, and for causing her to attempt suicide nearly a year later. Apparently, that's my fault too."

He winced. "Her fans wouldn't listen to me. No matter how many times I told them, they wouldn't believe you weren't to blame."

My chest tightened. "I know. I saw the first few responses you posted on YouTube and Twitter. Then you disappeared from social media too. I guess the video she put out there was too convincing. It made her look completely pitiable—and sane. Thanks to my dad's interference, I'm the one who came across as a lunatic."

Max shook his head. "Not you. Him. He was unhinged. Unreliable as hell."

I shrugged. "He's my dad, though. There's a saying about apples not falling far from trees." When Max gave that wry grin I'd always loved so much, my heart gave a twinge of pain.

"You're nothing like him," he said, trying to reassure me. "And I know what you mean about Raven. We started dating after her second rehab stint, but when I found out she was using again and hiding it from me, I couldn't take it anymore and broke things off. That's when I met you."

I watched him closely. "She claimed you were still together and I'd seduced you away from her."

His yoga ball came to an abrupt halt. "Lies. I'd broken things off weeks before you and I met."

I clutched my hands together under the desk. "You can't

imagine what it was like for me. The hate mail I got. The nasty tweets. Someone even started the hashtag #EssieIsASlut. It was horrible. Obsessive fans followed me everywhere, recording me on their cellphones. The paparazzi were just as bad as the rabid fans." I shook my head, trying to shake away the memories. "I even received death threats."

His eyes widened in horror. "Death threats? I'm so sorry. That must have been terrifying." He reached out as though he wanted to take my hand, then thought better of it. "I can't imagine what you went through."

I tensed. "I had to get away. I moved to Kentucky and started teaching, but then Raven tried to kill herself and the whole story came back to life. Some idiot took pictures of me at the school and sold them to *Here's the Scoop*. The parents were furious. I don't blame them. I was asked to leave before my contract was up. That's when I finally decided to change my last name."

He rocked forward on his yoga ball. "How did you end up here?"

"I was teaching fifth grade in an inner-city school in Philly. It was close to home, so I got to see my mom and sister a lot before she..." I cleared my throat. "Before Mom died." I swallowed, pushing down my grief. "The kids there were great, but the school wasn't in a safe neighborhood. I felt like prey when I left work after dark. When one of the other teachers got mugged going to his car, I decided to find a new job. I saw the opening here and jumped at it. This is one of the best school districts in the state and I was excited to work here. I knew about it since I'd attended Pitt, but I should have known better. I should have stayed far away from Pittsburgh. You'd mentioned you were from the area, but I didn't know you'd lived right here in Sewickley."

He'd been staring down at the floor, but now he glanced up and met my eyes. "I know it isn't enough, but I *am* sorry for everything I put you through. I wish I could go back and do things differently."

His words infuriated me. "Life doesn't work that way," I

snapped at him. "You can't change the past. You can only learn from it." I reached for a folder of papers on my desk, but my hand shook so much that I snatched it back.

Not good. I needed to control myself better than this.

I TOOK a deep breath and let it out slowly. I picked up the folder of papers, my hand steady this time. "Let's review the work Emma missed while she was gone. She'll get an automatic A because of what happened, so don't let her stress about it. She doesn't need to worry about the smaller assignments, but there are a few important concepts she should master since we're building on them. Her teachers will expect her to know the material next year. I'm particularly concerned about some of the math and science topics we covered during her absence. Before she left, we were learning about electricity, which she was really enjoying. Math is my biggest concern."

Max examined the papers carefully while I spoke. When I paused, he glanced up. "I'm not sure I'll be able to help her with all of this, but I'll do my best."

I'd expected this. "If you like," I said, "I can meet with her after school for some private tutoring to bring her up to speed."

Max shook his head. "I made arrangements today for her to take the bus every day after school to Marley's house. She'll be able to stay there until I can pick her up after work and drive her back to my apartment."

I frowned. "I thought you had a place in Sewickley. The principal mentioned you'd bought a house here."

"I did, but we can't move in yet. I need to make a few renovations first. My friend is the general contractor, and he's pushing hard to get everything done quickly. Emma doesn't want to live there until it's finished—not that I can blame her after what happened to her parents. I'm hoping we'll be able to move in about a month, but in the meantime, I'll be driving her to school every morning. My apartment is in downtown Pittsburgh, so it's a bit of a drive. Kincaid Gillette is the general contractor. He's great to work with."

I stiffened. Courtney Gillette was in my new book club, and I'm pretty sure her youngest brother was Kincaid. How had I ended up smack-dab in the center of Max's life?

He must have picked up on my reaction because he cocked his head and peered at me. "Do you know him?" It was as though he could read my mind. He'd always been able to do that. It was partly why I'd believed we were perfect together. He hadn't just liked the person I was on the surface. He'd known me deep down. We'd connected on such a fundamental level that we could often complete one another's sentences.

"I joined a book club over the summer, and Courtney Gilette is a member."

He gave a faint frown. "Kincaid's her brother. And I think my brother's fiancé is in your book group as well. Mara Stellar."

I inhaled sharply, feeling overwhelmed. Trapped. The world started pressing in on me. I turned to one of the techniques I'd learned when I'd gone into therapy five years ago. I focused on the here and now. The clock ticking on the wall. My hard chair. The familiar woodsy scent of Max's cologne.

My tension eased.

"Let's focus on the two main issues we need to address today: our prior relationship and Emma's situation. Emma is going through a tremendously difficult time, and she needs our support. It's October, and school has only just started." I fixed him with my teacher's stare, the one that always got my students to comply immediately. "Can I count on you to keep our former relationship private? The last thing any of us needs is for an old scandal to breathe new life. It could make my situation here difficult, if not impossible. I'm asking you to be discreet. Your life is much more public than mine is, thanks to your father's movie business. I can't afford to be swept up into your world again. We need to keep things professional between us."

He sat up straight as his back stiffened. "Of course. Anything you want. The school year ends in June. After that, we never have to see each other again."

"Good," I forced myself to say. The ache in my chest didn't ease. Instead, it tightened. "Very good." I stood and smoothed the skirt of my dark, polyester suit. In contrast, his perfectly tailored one probably cost more than what one of my biweekly paychecks could cover. "My school email address is in this folder," I held it out, and he rose to take it. "Please don't hesitate to contact me if you have any questions about Emma or her schoolwork." *Certainly not about anything personal.* I left that part unspoken as I stared at him.

His lips thinned. "Understood."

4

DANTE'S COOKING CLASS

Max

Later that evening, I drove down a tree-lined street toward my brother's house in Sewickley. Some of the leaves were beginning to turn yellow as summer drew to a close, but the season wasn't quite ready to give up yet. The days were still warm, but the nights were pleasantly cool.

A jogger passed me going in the opposite direction. Two girls dropped their bikes on the lawn of an enormous house and ran for the front door as the sun dipped low in the sky.

I parked my BMW in my brother's driveway and stepped out of the car just as the light in a lamppost next to the street winked on.

Seeing Sonya had rocked me. I still wasn't sure how to take it. I was certain she hadn't known I lived here, though. Her surprise was too real to have been faked. What were the odds that she was Emma's teacher? Maybe it wasn't that strange, after all. She would have run as far from me and Los Angeles as possible after the scandal broke. The little town of Sewickley must have seemed like a perfect place to hide.

She looked—amazing. Different, but still beautiful. Even though I'd immediately known who she was, my guess was that unless someone knew her well, they probably wouldn't be able to identify her.

I'd recognize her anywhere. I knew her every movement. Every gesture. All the changes were superficial. At least, I'm pretty sure they were. Five years could change anyone—especially after what she'd gone through.

I headed up the broad flagstone path cutting through the manicured lawn and knocked on the carved wooden door, but no one answered. Ford usually met me at the door on cooking class nights, but tonight I'd arrived early. I pushed open the door and walked inside.

"Ford!" I called out in the echoing foyer. "You here?"

"You're early!" Ford's voice came from upstairs. A moment later, he hurried down the wide staircase carrying his shoes and was trailed by a small brown and white dog.

Zephyr trotted up to me and immediately sat, staring up at me. He wiggled his butt in anticipation but didn't jump up. As I continued to stare down at him, he let out a pleading whine and wiggled even more.

"You need to pet that dog before he explodes from excitement," Ford said.

I leaned down and scratched the dog's head. When I stopped, he ran in circles and darted over to Ford. "I had a meeting at Emma's school and then took care of a couple of things on my to-do list. I came over when I was done."

Ford went straight into the living room with Zephyr at his heels and plopped down on the leather sofa. "A meeting about Emma? How's she doing? How was her first day back?" He wedged a foot into his shoe and started lacing it up.

"Surprisingly well," I said as I sat across from him in a matching leather chair. Zephyr came over and sniffed my shoes. "She's at Marley Zerkowski's house right now. Emma wanted to go there after school today. I was able to set things up with Marley's mom to have her stay there every day after school until our new house is ready."

Ford tied his other shoe. "Are you sure the two of you don't want to move in here? It would make the commute easier on you. We have plenty of space."

I shot him an incredulous look. "Are you crazy? You and Mara are going at it like rabbits." At Ford's scowl, I grinned. "I'm doing us all a favor by staying away. Besides, Emma has had too many changes in her life as it is. We don't need to add anything extra. I met with Kincaid an hour ago, and all the renovations at the new house are on schedule. It looks like Emma and I will only have to do this commute for a month." I scratched my jaw. "She finally slept through the night the past two nights. No nightmares. It was good to get some unbroken sleep. Emma looks better for it."

"That's good to hear." Ford assessed me with that too-insightful gaze of his. "These last few weeks have been rough on you."

"On all of us," I said. "Losing Hailey and Barry has been…" my words trailed off. What? Horrific? Shocking? Inexpressibly sad?

"I know," he said softly. I could feel his pain rolling off him. "It was bad enough losing Mom when we were kids, but at least we had Dad and our big sister to lean on. It must be killing Emma to lose both of her parents at the same time. I have to admit, it hit me hard. I keep having nightmares."

My stomach tightened. "About losing them? Yeah. So do I." I was silent for a moment as a fresh wave of sorrow swept over me. "I try to keep it together in front of Emma. I don't want to make things worse for her. It would kill me if I did something that amplified her pain."

Ford rose to his feet, and Zephyr stared up at him expectantly, watching his every movement. "Don't hide your grief from her too much. She needs to know it's okay to miss her parents."

"I know that. I'm not an idiot," I said, snapping at him and then immediately regretting it. I gave a heavy sigh. "Sorry. That came out wrong. Don't worry about it. The kid isn't suppressing her grief. Not in the slightest. She's seeing a therapist, and that's helping."

"No worries," Ford said easily. "You have a lot on your plate. Now that she's back in school, things should get a little easier for you."

I shrugged. "We'll see. At least I should be able to focus more on work. Sorry I haven't been pulling my weight with your new movie. This isn't how I'd planned for these last few weeks to go…" Grief squeezed my chest, making it hard to speak.

"What are you apologizing for? Emma comes first. Mara and I would have been happy to have her live with us. I'd already decided to put *Ghost* on hold so I could be there for her. Sure, Mara would have helped, but she and Emma barely know each other. I would have needed to be the primary caregiver. Plus with the video game company Mara and her business partner just launched, she would have been stretched thin. It was good of you to step up and offer to be Emma's guardian instead."

I brushed away his praise. "It makes sense for me to be the one. I'm over at Hailey's every week for dinner—or at least, I was —" I closed my eyes and inhaled as I corrected my thinking to adjust to this new reality that no longer included my sister and her husband. Again. I'd done this so many times over the past few weeks that I'd lost count. I simply couldn't get used to thinking of Hailey in the past tense.

I took a deep breath. "Emma and I are close. I want her with me." It was that simple. It was what Hailey would have wanted, too.

"We need to get going," Ford said.

"Shouldn't you let the dog out first?"

"He has a dog door. He'll be fine." He reached down and gave Zephyr a scratch behind the ear. "Be good," he said. "No dog parties while I'm gone."

Zephyr gave a disheartened wag of his tail. He looked forlorn that we were leaving without him.

"Do you know what we're cooking tonight?" I asked as I followed Ford out the front door.

"No idea. Dante will tell us when we get there."

I unlocked the car and slid onto the soft leather seat. After Ford climbed in, I turned to face him. "I got kind of a big shock today. It's about Essie. Remember her?"

Ford shot me one of those *do you think I'm an idiot* glares. "How could I forget the woman who disappeared and broke your heart." He frowned slightly and then cocked one eyebrow expectantly. "Don't tell me you've found her."

"Then I won't tell you." I backed out of the driveway.

Ford's eyes went wide and his jaw dropped open. "Wait—are you saying you found her? Where? How?"

I let out a snort. "Right here in Sewickley." I shifted the car into drive, and slowly accelerated beneath the canopy of trees arching above the brick-paved street. "She's Emma's teacher."

He looked astonished. "No. That's nuts. I thought she was avoiding you. Why would she move here?"

"She attended Pitt," I said with a shrug. "I told her I was from Pittsburgh, but I never mentioned Sewickley. Based on what she said today, she assumed I was still living in Los Angeles. When we were dating, I didn't tell her much about my family. She was as shocked to see me as I was to see her." I pulled to a stop at the light and then turned, heading toward the Ohio River.

"I guess that means you never introduced her to Dad back then."

"Never." I tightened my grip on the steering wheel. "I have to admit, I enjoyed the fact that she had no idea who my family was. She liked me just for me. Back then, she'd have had no reason to link me to Ross Film Productions."

"And now you're second in command. Mara tells me I forget how little the people outside the entertainment industry think—or even care—about the business side of movies. They only pay attention to movie stars. She helps keep me humble. Then again, I know next to nothing about the video game industry, so we're even."

"It's the same in the music industry, but there are still tons of people who do care," I said. "Sometimes too much. Look at how Raven's fans destroyed Essie. That's proof of that." I parked in the nearly empty parking lot at Not a Yacht Club and turned to face my brother. "Listen, Essie asked me not to tell anyone about her. I shouldn't have told you, but there's a good chance you'll see her at one of Emma's school functions, and I couldn't risk you blurting out something on the off-chance you recognized her. You have to promise you won't tell anyone else, not even Mara."

Ford scowled at me. "I don't keep secrets from my fiancée."

"I get it. I do. But this isn't your secret, it's Essie's. She's terrified of being found out. So terrified that she legally changed her name and dyed her hair platinum blonde. She's barely recognizable from the woman I knew five years ago. This is important, or I wouldn't ask it of you. Please, you can't tell Mara."

Ford sighed and rubbed at the faint stubble on his cheeks. "I hate this. If Mara finds out and gets pissed at me, you have to back me up. Tell her you threatened me or something."

I grinned. "I'm not sure she'd buy it, but you're welcome to sleep on my couch if she kicks you out."

Ford let out a groan. "I hope I don't have to take you up on that offer." Finally, he heaved a sigh. "Fine. I'll keep your secret, but this had better not come back and bite me in the ass."

We headed inside Not a Yacht Club. It was closed on Mondays, which was why Dante had offered to teach a men's cooking class on those nights. I'd first started attending to spend time with Ford after he moved home, but now I found myself looking forward to the classes. I hadn't been as inept in the kitchen as Ford had been, but I'd still found the lessons useful. Besides, it was better than hanging out at a bar, and a lot less likely to cause liver damage.

When I entered the kitchen, I spotted my general contractor, Kincaid Gillette, standing next to one of the prep areas.

"Hey, Max," Kincaid called out. "Long time no see."

I checked my phone. "What's it been now, an hour?"

"About. How's parenthood treating you?" Kincaid asked.

"Better. I'm starting to get the hang of it."

Kincaid rubbed the side of his nose. "I spoke with the interior designer after you left the house. She placed her order for the finishes you approved. We're on track to get you in on time."

"Thanks, man. I really appreciate it," I said. "By the way, I've been meaning to ask you about the wedding. It's next month, right?"

Kincaid shrugged. "Yeah. Heather seems more excited about the wedding than the baby. I'm the other way around."

"Do you know yet if it's a boy or a girl?"

He frowned. "Heather wants to wait and be surprised. She's really stoked about a ten-thousand-dollar wedding gown she found yesterday." He shook his head. "I'm still trying to wrap my head around the idea that a dress can even cost that much."

I pretended to ogle him and then shook my head with a smirk. "You might have nice legs, but you sure don't strike me as the 'ten-thousand-dollar dress' kind of guy."

Kincaid glanced down at his legs, then put one hand on his hip and the other behind his head and struck a quick pose. "Thanks, man. They'd look great in a dress, wouldn't they?" He grinned and shook his head. "You're right, though. I'm more inclined to splurge on a house than clothes. After all, you live in a house and use it every day. But a dress you'll only wear once?" He scratched the back of his head. "Doesn't make much sense to me."

"Coming through," Dante said as he shoved open the kitchen doors. His pushcart was stacked with boxes of fresh vegetables. "Help me put these away so we can get started on tonight's lesson. Chicken Piccata."

"That's an easy one," I said, hefting one of the boxes and following Dante into the cold room.

"Chicken Piccata? For you, maybe," Kincaid said, picking up another box. "You already know how to cook."

I set the box on an empty shelf. "I pick up new techniques from our master chef every week. It's what keeps me coming back."

"Admit it," Kincaid said, setting his box next to mine. "You only come to class so you can grab a beer with us afterward."

"With you assholes?" I asked with a grin. We stepped to one side to let Ford pass by with another box. "I'm here because I feel sorry for you. After all, you have to live in the same town as my brother. His ego's gotten so enormous lately, I'm amazed anyone else can stand to be around him."

"I heard that," Ford said as he put the box on the cold room shelf.

"You were supposed to," I pointed out.

"Hey!" Dante said. "Don't give Ford too much shit. He might turn tail and run back to L.A. Then who would we harass?"

"Fine, fine," I said. "I won't drive him away. Besides, his fiancé would have my head."

"She'll use her Wonder Woman moves on you," Ford said with a grin. "That lasso of truth is a killer."

"Shut it," I tossed back. "I don't want to hear about your weird-ass sex life. I'm a responsible uncle living with an impressionable child now. Keep that shit to yourself."

"How's Emma doing?" Dante asked. "I worry about her."

His question brought me back to Earth. "She's doing okay. We're taking it one day at a time."

"Yeah." Dante nodded. "That's all you can really do."

At Dante's somber expression, I recalled the fact that his girlfriend's parents had been killed in an avalanche a couple of years ago. Dante certainly knew about grief—and about how helpless you felt when someone you loved was drowning in it.

"Would it be okay if I bring Emma to cooking class with me sometimes?" I asked. "I think she'd enjoy it."

Dante's face brightened. "Absolutely. I always say the best

way to charm a woman is to cook for her. It's even better when you cook *with* her."

"Good point." Five years ago, when Essie and I had been together—*not Essie, dammit, Sonya*—we'd had a lot of fun cooking together. Our kitchen table had seen a lot more action than it had been built for.

If I was lucky, maybe I could get her to remember how amazing everything had once been between us. Dante could very well be right. Cooking for Sonya could be the way back into her heart.

Is that what I wanted? A way back in?

Perhaps, but—there was Emma to consider. Plus, Sonya and I needed to reconnect. A lot had happened over the past few years and she'd probably changed. I know I had.

I wasn't going to force anything. She deserved better than that, especially from me.

5

BOOK CLUB DRAMA

Sonya

The next day at school, I kept expecting someone to point to me and shout, "Essie!"

As the hours passed and nothing happened, I slowly relaxed.

My disguise was still working. Most people would have only seen photos of me, so my voice wouldn't give me away. Of course, there was that video with my dad, but it was five years old now, and he'd done most of the talking. No one had recognized me back in Philly, so there was no reason to assume I'd be recognized here either.

When I left school for the day I considered ditching book club tonight, but I'd been looking forward to it all month. I needed to connect with adults, and this was my favorite way to do it.

I arrived on time for my fourth book club meeting. This group of women had welcomed me with open arms from the moment I joined them. This month, we were meeting at Lianna Alverson's adorable new home perched high on a hillside near the Sewickley Cemetery.

I climbed the steep steps leading to her front door. At the top, I paused to catch my breath and take in the picturesque little town spread out below me. Sewickley looked absolutely charming.

Lianna's house might be vertically challenging, but it certainly made up for it with this view.

I turned to ring the doorbell and spotted a note taped to the door telling me to let myself in.

The sound of voices drew me to the kitchen. Lianna stood next to the stove and she wore a pinafore apron that protected a positively retro fifties-style dress.

"Hi, Sonya," Lianna said. "We don't stand on ceremony. Make yourself at home and pour yourself some wine. You can find the bathroom at the top of the stairs. That's the only thing wrong with my new house. No first-floor powder room."

"And, no closets, you said," Gertrude reminded her.

"Okay. Two things," Lianna conceded as she wiped her hands on her apron.

"Hello, Sonya. It's lovely to see you again," Gertrude said. The slim, silver-haired, septuagenarian perched on a stool next to Lianna's kitchen counter. She wore yoga clothes that looked way too good on her.

"Hi, Gertrude. I pray I'm as fit as you are when I hit seventy."

"It's easy, as long as you keep up with it," Gertrude said. "I do some sort of bodywork most days. Yoga and Pilates are my favorites."

I spotted an open bottle of red wine on the counter and poured myself a glass. "That sounds simple enough."

"I'm making *boeuf bourguignon*," Lianna said as I stepped closer. She lifted the lid of the pot to give me a peek. "It's almost done. I'll turn down the heat and keep it warm. After we discuss the book, all I'll need to do is toast the baguette."

I inhaled deeply. "Mmm. Smells delicious. I was wondering what you'd cook for dinner. Our book mentioned so many different foods that I was dying to know which one you'd make." A single loose strand of my platinum blonde hair grazed my cheek as I leaned forward to peer into the pot.

A tall redhead strolled into the room; Kincaid's sister, Courtney. She greeted me with a wave, and I smiled back and nodded.

"I miss your cooking," Gertrude told Lianna. "Are you sure you don't want to move back into my guest house? I miss having you there."

"Positive," Lianna said with a grin. "But maybe we should reinstate our weekly dinners. I have to admit, I miss having someone to cook for." She glanced at me and explained, "When my ex and I first separated, I stayed in Gertrude's guest house for a few months."

Gertrude's expression immediately brightened. "It's a deal. I get lonely in that big house all by myself."

I grabbed a spoon from the drawer. "Mind if I taste it?"

Lianna laughed. "Are you *that* impatient? You're worse than Gertrude. She always used to steal a taste when I'd cook for her. Go ahead. Try it."

I scooped a small bite onto my spoon, blew on it, and popped it into my mouth. "Oh. My. God. This is amazing!" I raised my spoon in a mock toast. "Well done, Lianna. Does everyone always try to cook something that was mentioned in the book we read that month?"

Courtney nodded, the light glinting on her auburn hair. "When possible," she said in a soft voice that was at odds with her bold appearance. "Sometimes the books don't mention food, or only mention something like a pig roast. None of us really wants to dig a fire pit, though. When we can't find reasonable recipe options, we get creative."

I grinned. "Food and books. This really is the perfect book club for me."

Courtney turned and gave me a belated hug. "You already fit in like you've been with us since the beginning."

I nodded in agreement. "I feel exactly the same way. I've found my tribe."

"I just came from my brother's place," Courtney said. "He says met with Max Ross about renovating the house he bought."

"Max is Ford's brother, right?" Lianna asked.

I blinked as my stomach tensed. That was quick. I'd been hoping we'd never talk about either of them.

"And Mara's future brother-in-law," Courtney said. "He agreed to be Emma's guardian. He said she went back to school yesterday." She paused in her lightning-speed transfer of information and glanced at me. "She's your student, isn't she? Emma Bachar? How's she doing?"

I froze. The last thing I wanted was to discuss Max or Emma. "Sorry. I'm not at liberty to talk about students. School policy." I took a gulp of wine.

"Oops. Sorry," Courtney said. "Of course, you can't."

The front door opened, and another book club member walked in. Scarlet Smith, the town mayor. She looked perfectly polished with bobbed red hair and a tailored emerald-green dress.

"Any idea what caused the fire?" Lianna asked as she led us into the living room.

"Candles in the bedroom," Courtney said as she claimed one of the chairs. "They might be romantic, but they can be also be dangerous."

"Especially when you're doing renovations and the fire alarms aren't working," Scarlet commented without missing a beat.

"Is that what happened?" Lianna asked, her eyes widening. "How terrible."

"That's what I read in the news. Thank goodness Emma wasn't there." Scarlet turned to me as she sat on the sofa. "She was spending the night with another of your students that night, right?"

I sipped some wine to buy myself some time. It wasn't surprising that Scarlet knew so many details. She took her job as mayor seriously. Besides, the Sewickley Times had mentioned that particular fact as well. "It's a good thing she did," I said briefly.

"And she's living with Max now. Another gorgeous Ross brother," Scarlet commented.

"Max?" Lianna raised an eyebrow. "He's hot, all right." She glanced at me. "One of our book club members is engaged to his brother, Ford. You haven't met Mara yet. She's busy with her new video game company and hasn't been here for a while."

"Mara?" I asked, my voice sounding weak. Suddenly the room felt more like a field of landmines than a relaxing book club meeting. I tensed, waiting for the next tidbit of gossip to explode.

"She owns the comic book shop in town," Lianna explained to me, "and she just started a second business, so her life is kind of hectic. I saw her a few days ago. She says 'hi' to everyone. She's hoping to be back at book club next months."

The front door opened, and a petite brown-haired woman came in. "I'm sorry I'm late. An order of books arrived at the library, and I was the only one there to sign for the delivery." She spotted me and tilted her head to one side. "We haven't met yet. I've missed the few meetings. I'm Rose Oliver. I'm a librarian here in town."

I waved. "I'm Sonya Gambit. I'm the new fifth-grade teacher at Sewickley Elementary."

Rose's smile widened. "Welcome. I've been hearing wonderful things about you from your students. I met with your principal last month about the anti-bullying program the school launched last year. It's already making a difference with my library kids. Have you been through the training?"

"Absolutely," I said, quickly warming to her and one of my favorite subjects. "It's one of the reasons I wanted to move to this district. At my last school, bullying was out of control."

"What's the latest advice you give kids when they're being bullied?" Lianna asked. "Hit back? That's what my dad always said to do."

I smiled and shook my head. "I'm glad we're not talking about Max and Emma anymore. But hitting a bully is a bad idea. It's called assault, and you could get suspended. Stopping bullying is more about creating an environment where it's not tolerated. It's about teaching bystanders how to react. Bullies get their power in two ways: from a system that tolerates it, and from onlookers who do nothing. To put an end to bullying, you have to change the system and teach bystanders how to defuse the situation in safe, non-aggressive ways. One great way to do that is to remove the person being bullied from the situation."

"From what I've heard, the program is working really well." Rose glanced around. "I don't see Mara. Isn't she coming?"

"She can't make it." Lianna said.

Gertrude set her glass of white wine on the coffee table and sat down. "With Mara's new business and Ford's new movie, I suppose they weren't able to take on Emma's guardianship."

I tensed. We were heading toward dangerous territory again.

"You're probably right. Ford is busy getting that movie of his off the ground," Lianna said.

Scarlet cleared her throat. "We need to talk about our book, *Gone Girl*, or we'll never get to it."

I breathed a silent sigh of relief. I needed to avoid any topic pertaining to the Ross family.

"Confession time." Lianna held up both hands in surrender and then hung her head. "I watched the movie instead of reading the book. I couldn't manage to get my house unpacked in time for book club and also read. I tried, though. Then again, that's why I chose *Gone Girl*. I heard the movie stuck pretty close to the book."

Courtney scooted forward on her chair and snagged a carrot stick from the veggie tray on the coffee table. "I loved the book. Nick and Amy Dunne had such a dysfunctional marriage with each one trying to out-manipulate the other. The story really kept me guessing."

"Amy was so much worse," Lianna shook her head. "But I think you're right. They were so messed up they deserved each other."

"I still can't get over the way she just up and vanished. That was cold." Scarlet picked up a stalk of celery from the vegetable tray and waved it as she spoke. "Who just disappears like that? Everything about it was so suspicious." She dipped it in some dressing and then bit it with a noisy crunch.

My chest tightened. If Scarlet ever found out about my past

and the way I'd bolted, would she assume I was cold? Manipulative?

When I'd run, I hadn't only left behind Max and my problems.
I'd also hidden from friends I'd known my entire life and classmates I'd gone to college with at University of Pittsburgh. I'd been
too afraid of the paparazzi and rabid fans tracking me down to
risk contacting any of them. A knot formed in my throat, and I
had to clear it before I could speak. "It wasn't just the fact that she
left. That diary was the really troubling part."

Rose watched me closely as she nodded. "Absolutely."

"The whole thing was cleverly written," Gertrude said. "I love
stories like this one. You never know what's what until the end."

I exhaled as I slowed my breathing and made myself relax.
"Those two had a twisted relationship."

An hour later, the oven timer went off. Lianna excused herself
and slipped back into the kitchen. She bustled back and forth
between the kitchen and dining room setting things on the table.

"All right, ladies," Lianna said, standing framed in the
doorway and looking all nineteen-fifties housewife in that ruffly
apron. "I declare that our book discussion is officially over. It's
time for the dinner portion of the evening."

My stomach let out a growl. "At last!" I said with a grin. "The
aroma of *boeuf bourguignon* has been torturing me all night."

We gathered around the dining room table and passed around
the rich stew, salad, and sliced baguette so everyone could serve
themselves. Silence descended as we ate, but I knew it wouldn't
last.

After we finished eating, I'd make my excuses and leave. I
needed to avoid any more difficult questions.

Scarlet sipped her wine and asked, "Does anyone know if Max
Ross is dating anyone?"

I nearly choked on my baguette but managed to swallow
silently without drawing anyone's attention. I was curious to hear
the answer.

Scarlet glanced around the table, but no one responded. "Now that he's raising his niece, it might be a good idea for him to settle down."

Lianna let out a snort. "Who could measure up after Raven? She's a tough act to follow."

I stopped breathing. They'd gone straight to the old Max and Raven story? Again? Five years had passed, and those two were still linked.

I should have expected it. Mention Max Ross, and Raven's name was sure to come up in the next breath. I picked up my wine glass, closed my eyes, and finished off my pinot noir.

"I don't know about that." Scarlet shook her head in bemusement. "Raven's over the top. I wonder if her whole dominatrix thing is just a put-on, or if she's really into that stuff."

I let out a soft gasp. "Raven's a dominatrix?" My eyes went wide.

Lianna noticed my empty glass and refilled it.

"She went all dominatrixy after their breakup," Rose said. "Before that, she seemed pretty tame. Do you think that's what drove Max away?"

"It was the drugs," I said before I could stop myself. I lifted my glass and took a hefty swallow.

"He seems to have lived a fairly quiet life since the gossip died down," Courtney commented.

"Poor guy." Scarlet shook her head. "It isn't as though he had much choice. Not after the way the scandal gave his dad a heart attack."

What? Why hadn't I known about this? I thumped my glass back onto the table. "A heart attack?" My voice was so faint I wasn't sure anyone had even heard me.

"You can't blame his heart attack on the scandal," Scarlet pointed out. "It's not as if he had a fit of the vapors. Don Ross runs a huge company. He deals with stress and bad news every day. There's no way Raven or Essie Harlow triggered it."

Hearing my name hit me like a blow, and I winced.

"Even so, the man's lucky to be alive," Rose said. Her gaze was fixed on me.

"Maybe Raven's a witch," Gertrude said, waggling her eyebrows and cackling. Her voice was low and raspy, and her eyes glittered with mischief. She looked like she was about to cast a spell.

Rose peered at me closely. A moment later, she raised her voice and said, "Hey, Sonya—has anyone ever mentioned how much you resemble Essie?"

I pushed my chair back abruptly and stood, knocking it backward. I grabbed for it before it fell and I wobbled, nearly losing my balance.

Courtney sprang up and reached out to steady me. "Sweetie, are you okay? What happened? Too much wine?"

I was trying to hold it together as a prickle of unease crept up my spine. My gaze caught Scarlet's, and I recognized the growing comprehension in the mayor's eyes.

"Essie?" Scarlet sprang to her feet. "Good lord. You're Essie Harlow."

"It *is* you," Rose said breathlessly. "You're the '*homewrecker*.' I knew it. You look completely different, but I still recognize you."

My knees went all wobbly, so I tightened my grip on the back of the chair.

Scarlet scowled at Rose. "'*Homewrecker*?' *Really*? Not helping."

Rose's face fell. "I'm so sorry. That was stupid of me. I didn't mean it that way. I was quoting an old magazine article."

Scarlet turned back to face me. "How is it I never noticed the resemblance before?" She moved closer to me, staring intently. "I remember that photo of you from five years ago. The one of you and your dad outside that Los Angles restaurant where you worked. You were mobbed by the press and looked like a trapped animal. Sweetie, you're wearing exactly the same expression right now."

I squeezed the back of the chair as my world crumbled around me. I'd have to start over again. I'd have to leave this new life I'd created—these friends—this community. But how? I needed this job to support myself. I didn't have the money to just up and run —again.

I never should have taken a teaching position in Sewickley. It was much too close to Pittsburgh. I should have realized I might run into Max if I ever moved to this area, but I'd assumed he was still living in Los Angeles. Good God, I'd moved directly to his hometown. How was I supposed to have known he'd grown up here?

I'd done this to myself. I could see that now. At the very least, I should have cyber-stalked Max Ross enough to figure out where he was living and where he'd been born rather than ignoring his existence.

What was I going to do now? Run away? But I needed this job. How else would I pay off my student loans and legal fees? This new position at Sewickley Elementary School had seemed like a dream come true. It had been—until today.

My vision blurred as tears filled my eyes. I let go of the chair and spun toward the front door. I bashed my hip against Lianna's buffet in my rush to escape.

I'd need to pack. I had to disappear before those horrible reporters from *Here's the Scoop* found me again—along with Raven's rabid fans. I couldn't bear being hounded. Not now. Not again. I was terrified of the death threats they'd sent me. I simply couldn't take it.

"Sonya. Stop." Lianna's voice barely registered as I made my panicked dash for the door.

"Sweetie. Don't leave." Rose chased after me. "I freaked you out. I'm so sorry."

An instant later, Courtney was standing next to me. "Sonya. We're your friends. You don't need to run away from us. We can help."

I was reaching for the front doorknob when their words finally started to sink in. I stilled and slowly let my hands fall to my sides as I tried to process it all.

Gertrude wrapped an arm around my shoulders, and her grandmotherly presence enveloped me, soothing my chaotic emotions. "Come back to the table. We'll help you figure this out."

I let her usher me to the dining room, but no one sat down.

"I always thought Essie got a raw deal back then." Rose's voice was calm. Reassuring. "Raven was obviously nuts. Why everyone automatically believed her was beyond me. Especially when Max kept insisting they'd broken up before she left for rehab."

"They had." My voice was soft. Barely above a whisper.

"See?" Scarlet gave a sharp nod and pressed a wineglass into my hand. "Rose was right. Essie had nothing to do with their breakup."

"Sonya, your dad was the one who made a mess of things, not you," Rose said. "I kept saying it over and over to anyone who would listen to me. From everything I read, your father took advantage of the situation and stuck his nose into your life after having abandoned you for years."

Panic started rising again, and I shook my head frantically. "I can't deal with all of this again." My gaze latched onto Scarlet. "What if word gets out that I'm back in Max's life again? That I'm his niece's teacher? *That* would certainly be a juicy story. What if Raven's rabid fans show up at my school, just like they did four years ago?"

Scarlet drew her eyebrows together as I listed my fears, but then she slowly shook her head. "That's unlikely. The only reason you popped back into the spotlight a year later was because Raven had a breakdown. Her suicide attempt was national news. That's why those reporters and fans tracked you down at your school." She reached out and squeezed my hand. "If she isn't part of the story, there *is* no story. I haven't heard much about her in ages."

"I saw a photo of her a few months ago," Lianna said. "She's dating that director now, right? The weird one who makes those horror movies?"

Rose snorted. "As far as I can tell, those two are perfect for each other. Raven seems to have replaced her drug addiction problem with a new kink."

"The whole dominatrix thing?" Scarlet grimaced. "Yeah. I'd noticed that too. I rarely see a photograph of her anymore when she isn't wearing skin-tight leather pants and carrying that riding crop."

Gertrude's eyes became saucers. "Oh, my. Is that normal these days? I never know with your generation."

"Not exactly normal, but not unheard of," Rose said.

I snatched my glass from the table and took a hefty swig of wine.

"And those handcuffs," Courtney added. "Do you think they're just a prop?"

"Nope." Rose shook her head decisively. "Not from what I hear."

"Oh, my," Gertrude said again, looking stunned.

Rose shot me a curious glance. "Was Max into whips and bondage when you were together?"

My mouth fell open and I nearly choked on my own spit. "Definitely not," I managed to squeak out between coughs.

"That fits with what I read in *Here's the Scoop*," Rose said. "According to them, Raven's new boyfriend introduced her to that world."

With my pulse racing, I began to get lightheaded, so I clutched the back of the chair to steady myself.

"I hope you know that none of us would ever reveal your former identity as Essie," Scarlet said reassuringly.

Lianna wrapped her arms around me. "You can count on us."

My throat tightened. I set down my wine glass and grabbed a paper napkin from the table to wipe away my overflowing tears. "You're the best. All of you. I know I freaked out just now, but you have no idea how bad things were. The paparazzi and Raven's fans even came to the school where I worked and took photos of me on the playground. There was one where I was wearing a white dress—"

"I remember that one," Gertrude said. "The wind lifted your skirt and that photographer got a shot of your pink undies."

"I'd worn that dress a hundred times and never had a problem. Then one spring day, a freak gust of wind comes along, and my panties are plastered all over some website's homepage so that anyone with an internet connection can ogle me."

Courtney stroked my shoulder. "I'm sorry you went through all that, but I hope you know you can trust me. There's no way I'll ever tell anyone who you are or what you're hiding from. Your secret won't leave this room." She hugged me and then pulled away, leaving behind a lingering scent of floral perfume.

I took a deep breath and exhaled shakily. "Thanks. That means a lot to me."

Gertrude patted my shoulder. "My kids are all grown now, so my motherly protective instincts need something new to focus on. They're already reaching out to include you. This book group has become like family to me. I'll take on anyone who tries to drag you down."

I smiled at that. Gertrude was adorable. With that protective glint in her eye, she reminded me of a miniature Doberman Pinscher.

"I'm feeling pretty damned protective toward you too," Scarlet added. "I think it's safe to say every one of us has your back."

"I don't know what to say—how to thank you." I looked into the faces of my new friends and realized they were filled with support and sympathy. "You're all so kind to me."

"Could you transfer your student to another classroom for the rest of the school year?" Lianna asked. "That way you wouldn't have to see her uncle."

I shook my head. "I couldn't do that. Emma has already lost so much. I want to keep her school life as stable as I possibly can. I won't separate her from her classmates simply to make my life easier. I'd resign first."

"I hope it doesn't come to that." Rose gave me a sweeping gaze. "You really *do* look completely different. Almost no one would recognize you as Essie Harlow. I just have an eye for that sort of thing. Your hair used to be super short and dark, and your eyes were brown."

"And to think I'd been considering transitioning back to my natural hair color next summer."

"Keep it blond for now," Rose said, "and for heaven's sake, make sure you keep wearing those contact lenses."

One by one, the others departed until Lianna and I were left alone. "I need to get going too," I said. "It's tough to wrangle a roomful of ten-year-olds if you haven't had a decent night's sleep."

"I'll walk you out," Lianna offered.

A moment later, we were heading down the steep steps to the street.

"Thanks again for dinner," I told her.

"We weren't too much, were we?" Lianna asked.

"Maybe a little, but it all worked out."

"You'll be back?"

I nodded. "Definitely."

"I'm glad to hear that." Lianna hesitated. "Last month you mentioned you'd set up a first date with someone. How did it go?"

I let out a sharp laugh. "I'd nearly forgotten." I looped my arm through Lianna's, enjoying this companionable moment more than I would have guessed. "I've had better dates. It turns out he knew the man I'd gone out with one time when I first moved here in July. He felt obligated to recount every complaint the other guy had made about me." I laughed softly. "There's nothing like hearing that the pretentious jerk you wrote off complained that you had no sense of humor." I gave a wry smile. "I guess I was supposed to have laughed at his lame jokes."

Lianna grinned. "Were they that bad?"

"You tell me. This was his best one; a photon checks into a

hotel. The receptionist asks him if he has any bags. The photon says, 'No. I'm traveling light.'"

"Oh, no," Lianna said with a groan. "That's bad. I haven't heard that one since I was a kid."

"It deserves your groan. Maybe even a faint scowl. Definitely not a smile. At least it's clean enough to repeat to a fifth grader."

"Should I assume you won't be seeing him again?"

"Absolutely not. I'm not even sure why he asked me out at all." My shoes crunched as I walked on the splash of gravel at the end of Lianna's driveway. "Maybe he just wanted to see if I was as un-funny as his friend claimed."

When we reached my car, we stopped alongside the door and Lianna looked directly into my eyes. "I know we've only been friends for a couple of months now…" she hesitated, and the weight of her silence pressed down on me.

As the silence stretched, I jumped in to fill it. "I'm sorry my complicated past reared its ugly head tonight."

Lianna waved away my apology. "You're entitled to your privacy. It isn't that." She paused, staring down at the ruffled pinafore apron she still wore. "I apologize in advance, but I'm gonna get nebby for a minute."

I looked at her blankly. "Nebby?"

"Pittsburgh slang. Nebby means nosy." She sighed. "From what you told me last month, you almost never go on a second date with anyone, but—according to the news stories—you and Max were really close. Is it possible that the trauma of the scandal sort of—broke you? Made it hard for you to trust a man?" Lianna bit her lower lip and then met my gaze. "Sorry for being nebby, but I happen to know what that's like. My ex-husband cheated on me, and trust is hard for me now. I'm only mentioning this because I'm wondering if maybe you never really got over Max."

I shuffled back and pressed my key fob repeatedly to unlock my car. "You hit that nail on the head. I have trust issues. Can you blame me? First Max kept that secret about Raven, and then my dad staged a confrontation with me that the entire world saw on

YouTube." I yanked open my car door and climbed inside, eager to get away.

Lianna put her hand on the door so I couldn't close it. "The point I'm trying to make is that Max might be back in your life for a reason."

I let out a snort. "To torture me some more?"

"To bring you some closure. I think you have things you need to say to him so you can move on. Maybe this is finally your chance to say them."

"Could be," I said. "Or maybe he's simply going to ruin my life again."

I yanked my door closed and started my car. Lianna took a step back as I drove away.

Was she right? Could something positive come out of seeing Max again?

My heart squeezed at the thought of any sort of interaction with him. He'd hurt me so much that all I wanted to do was run and hide.

Lianna might be right. This could be my chance to find closure. To finally heal. I wasn't sure I was ready for that, though. I'd have to think about it.

6

TEACHERS' LOUNGE

SONYA

That Friday, I sat alone in the teachers' lounge while I waited for my leftover chili to heat up in the microwave. I loved this new recipe. I'd coaxed Courtney into giving it to me after I'd tried it at our book club meeting at her house last month. The addition of marjoram, dark chocolate, and coffee gave it a deeper, richer flavor. Courtney told me the recipe had come from the chef at the Not a Yacht Club.

The principal, Cindy Goodfriend, came in and stopped dead in her tracks. "What *is* that delicious smell, and what do I need to do to try some?"

I chuckled. "My chili. If you're nice, I'll give you a bite."

"You're a gem. I'll give you whatever you want. Would you like to trade your week of recess duty for a week of front door drop-off duty?"

I gave her a skeptical look. "That's a downgrade, not an upgrade. A week of front door duty means I'd have to get here earlier."

A pair of harried-looking first-grade teachers came in. One headed for the refrigerator and the other claimed the small table next to it and pulled a sandwich from her brown paper bag.

"You'd get to spend recess in your room," Cindy pointed out.

I shrugged. "I like being outside."

Cindy let out a beleaguered sigh. "Natalie asked me if someone would switch with her. Her son broke his leg, and she has to drive him to school for the next few weeks. That will make her too late to cover her shift."

"Ah-ha!" I raised a finger and grinned. "I'm a master of detection. You were trying to pull a fast one on me. Admit it."

"Guilty as charged. Will you swap with her?"

The microwave chimed and I grabbed the potholder hanging from a hook on the wall as one of the other teachers stepped forward to use the microwave the moment I was done with it. "Of course, I will." I pulled the bowl from the microwave and set it on the counter. "All you had to do was ask." I stirred my chili and then tested the temperature by tasting it. "But just for trying to pull a fast one on me, no chili samples for you."

The first-grade teacher slid her prepared frozen meal into the microwave and set the timer. She gave my bowl of chili a covetous glance.

Cindy groaned. "That's brutal. Maybe I should give you both recess duty *and* drop-off duty."

I narrowed my eyes at her. "In that case, I'll need to talk to my union rep about your gross misuse of power."

The first-grade teacher smirked.

Cindy widened her eyes in mock horror. "N-n-not necessary. I see the error of my ways."

"Seeing as I drove you to such extreme lengths in a desperate attempt to taste my chili, I suppose I can relent. You get *one* bite."

"You're too generous," Cindy said.

"I know. It's a weakness. Grab a spoon from the packet drawer." I gestured toward the drawer crammed with ketchup and soy sauce packets as well as plastic cutlery still wrapped in hygienic wrappers.

Cindy returned with a spoon and immediately scooped up

some chili. "Mmm," she said, smacking her lips. "It tastes as great as it smells. I love home cooking."

"I didn't get much of it growing up unless I made it myself," I said. "I'm self-taught."

"That's right. You had a single mom and a younger sister. Did you do most of the cooking?"

"It was either that or heat up a frozen meal." *Or go hungry.*

Cindy leaned back in her chair. "You said you're visiting your sister in New Jersey this weekend, right? Is she still in college?"

"No, and yes." At Cindy's questioning eyebrow raise, I said, "Yes, Kendra is finishing up her civil engineering degree at New Jersey Institute of Technology, but no, I won't be visiting her this weekend. She canceled on me."

Cindy looked genuinely disappointed for me. "That's too bad. What happened?"

"She's job hunting since she graduates next spring. She has an interview in New York City and wants to spend the weekend there with some friends and catch a Broadway show."

"That sounds like fun for her."

"It does. I hope she lets loose and enjoys herself. It hasn't been easy for her to get straight As while holding down a job. She could use a mini vacation. But now I need to figure out something else to do this weekend." I pulled a face. "There's always laundry." I definitely needed to buy my own washer and dryer. Going to the laundromat was a ginormous hassle. I should check out Craigslist this weekend and try to find something used.

Should I, though? What if I had to leave?

Well, I'd cross that bridge if I ever came to it. I was tired of taking my clothes to the laundromat.

"How's the fifth-grade musical coming along?" Cindy asked.

"I'm learning a lot. We already held auditions. Tykera is a whiz at this. How many years has she been the director?" I blew on a spoonful of chili and took a bite.

"Five, I think," Cindy said. "Have the two of you decided which kids are getting which roles?"

"Yep. We haven't cast the understudies yet, though."

Cindy looked impressed. "My, my. Listen to you. You sound like you're catching on fast. You're a lifesaver. I'm sure Tykera appreciates your help this year."

"No biggie. I'm happy for her."

"We all are. She's super excited to finally be pregnant."

Tykera had mentioned that she and her husband had been trying to conceive for a couple of years now. "I'm glad I can take some of the load off her," I said. "It's a good thing she'll still be directing the show, though. I've never done anything like this before, so being a co-director is excellent on-the-job experience for me."

A tentative knock sounded at the door of the teachers' lounge, and I glanced over to see Emma Bachar's slight form framed in the opening. The dark-haired girl had lost weight since her parents had died. Either that, or she was trying so hard to be invisible that she was beginning to fade away. She certainly looked too pale.

"Emma." I waved her into the lounge. "Come on in. What can I do for you?"

Emma nibbled on the corner of her thumbnail as she stared at an empty spot on the table between me and the principal. "Um. I'm having trouble with some of the schoolwork I'm trying to make up."

"I can help you with that." I kept my voice bright and cheerful as I tried to pull Emma along with me into the light.

"It's the math stuff. The one assignment is so complicated, I don't even know where to start."

"Are you talking about the one where you have to calculate discounts and compare prices?" I asked.

Emma nodded, keeping her gaze fixed on the table.

"That one's difficult. You have to do a lot of calculations to get to the answer. Would you like me to walk you through it?"

Relief filled Emma's face and she finally looked into my eyes. "Oh, yes. That would be great."

"How about after school?" I suggested.

Emma shook her head. "I can't. Staying after school doesn't work for me because I have to take the bus to Marley's every day. Uncle Max said we have Saturday afternoon free if that works for you. We can either meet you at the library or you can come to his apartment." Her face took on a pleading expression. "Come to the apartment. Please? No one ever comes to see me there."

Max's apartment? That was the last place on Earth I ever wanted to go.

The principal arched her eyebrows and shot me an expectant *go-ahead and help the kid* look. "It's a good thing your sister changed her plans for the weekend."

I froze. Why had I opened my big mouth and spilled the news that Kendra had canceled on me? Now I was trapped. Not only had I just confessed that my weekend was open, but Cindy also knew how much I cared about Emma's welfare. Refusing to help would look bizarre.

Worse. It would look suspicious. The last thing I wanted to do was draw undue attention to my relationship with Max.

Nope. Not a relationship. That was giving it too much weight. All we had was a *non*-relationship.

Given the choice of being seen with Max in public or visiting him in the privacy of his home, I knew which option was safer.

"I'd be happy to come to the apartment," I said, pasting on a false smile. "How about tomorrow at four?" That would give me time to get my laundry done first and perhaps even track down a washer and dryer of my own. "I'll send your uncle an email to confirm."

7

MAX SETS THE STAGE

Max

On Saturday morning, I pulled my BMW into a parking spot on Smallman Street near the Strip District in downtown Pittsburgh.

Emma frowned at the brick wall the car faced. "This doesn't look like a shopping area. Are you sure this place doesn't have anything to do with strippers? It *is* called the Strip District, after all."

I gave her a sidelong look, wondering if I should quiz her on the stripper comment. What could I even say? At a loss, I chose to let it slide. "I promise. No strippers. Just food markets, unique stores, street vendors, and some absolutely amazing restaurants."

"And sunglasses." Emma's eyes looked skeptical. "You promised me sunglasses."

"There will be lots of street vendors selling them. I'll help you find the perfect pair." I gestured at the nearby loading docks. "We parked along the back side of the Strip District. These big garage doors are where the trucks come to make deliveries."

She stared wide-eyed at the red brick walls and the huge industrial doors. "At least there are lots of people around. This place would be scary otherwise."

I glanced around but didn't see anything to be afraid of on the broad street. Just cars and delivery vans and people going about their business. "Maybe you're feeling nervous because you've never been here before."

Emma looked doubtful. "Maybe."

She tucked her small hand in mine, and I led her around a corner. We skirted around a long line of people waiting to enter Pamela's.

"What's that?" Emma pointed toward the old-fashioned-looking diner.

"A Pittsburgh tradition. Even Michelle Obama ate there when she visited. I'll have to bring you back sometime for breakfast. They make the best pancakes I've ever tasted."

"It smells really good," she conceded.

Emma started dragging her feet as we approached Penn Avenue, pulling on my hand to slow down. "It sure is crowded."

"That's because this is a popular place to be on the weekends." I grinned down at her as I gave her hand a squeeze. "Stick with me, kid. There are lots of cool things I can show you in this city."

She squeezed back and offered me a quicksilver smile that disappeared almost immediately. Even so, she picked up her pace.

As soon as we entered the flow of pedestrians on Penn Avenue with all its shops and street vendors, Emma's face lit up. "Look. Sunglasses."

She dropped my hand and rushed over to a table along the edge of the sidewalk. It held rows and rows of sunglasses. Emma found a pair with large round white frames and slid them on. They overwhelmed her face, making her look like an owl. She looked at them in the mirror mounted on the side of a rack and made a face. "Definitely not."

She put them back and kept searching. She finally settled on a pair of black Wayfarers.

"You look retro. I like it." I handed the street vendor some cash.

Emma looked more relaxed now. "What else do you want to get?"

"I need to pick up steaks to grill for dinner. There's a grocery store on the next block."

Emma slid her hand into mine and I weaved through the crowd. As we passed a store that sold perfumes and candles, she came to an abrupt halt. "This is the best-smelling place I've ever smelled in my entire life." Her grin nearly split her face in two.

She dragged me through the open door, and I happily complied. I hadn't seen a grin light up her face like that in over a month. Not since before the fire. Such a glorious smile tied my heart in a knot. Anything that made the kid this happy had to be good, right? I was ready to buy out the whole store and move it into her bedroom with a single word from her.

"Let's get some of those candles." She lifted one lid after another from the various jars, sniffing them. "They'll make your apartment smell more like a home."

I moved to stand next to her.

Emma suddenly went rigid and abruptly set down the candle she'd been holding. Her face contorted as huge tears streamed down. She turned and threw herself against my chest.

In a panic, I dropped to one knee and wrapped my arms around her, pulling her close. "Emma. What's wrong?"

"I'm a bad person. I can't believe I forgot about what happened to Mom and Dad. I can't believe I wanted to bring a *candle* into your apartment. I *hate* candles. They *died* because of candles."

Emma sobbed even harder, her thin body collapsing against mine. "It's okay. Don't be so hard on yourself. You're still adjusting to them being gone. It's perfectly normal to relax for a while and simply experience the world. Your parents wouldn't want you to grieve for the rest of your life. They'd want you to figure out how to continue on. You don't need to be in a rush to get over the pain of losing them, but you don't need to shroud yourself in grief either."

She pulled away slightly and rubbed at her face with the backs of her hands. A pleasant-faced woman looked at us both and then pulled a plastic packet of tissues from her purse. She pushed a couple of them into my hand, gave us a sympathetic smile, and then turned away to give us some privacy.

I handed the tissues to Emma.

She wiped her face and blew her nose. "What does 'shroud' mean?"

"It means covering yourself or wrapping yourself up in something. A long time ago they'd wrap a corpse in a shroud before burying it." I scrubbed my hand across my face. Had I just said 'corpse' to a grieving child?

"That might not have been a good example, but what I'm trying to say is that you didn't die. You're still alive. Your parents had dreams for you. Lots of dreams. I know they wouldn't want you to stop living just because they died. They'd want you to live a full, rich life. I know you aren't ready to take on the world yet, but I don't want you to think you're betraying them when you're finally ready to start living your life again. They wouldn't see today as a betrayal. I know they wouldn't. They'd see it as a good sign. Your mom was my big sister, and she had a big heart. She'd want you to be happy."

Emma nodded. Her eyes were red-rimmed, but at least she wasn't crying anymore.

"Do you want to pick out a candle?" I asked. "The ones inside the glass jars are pretty safe. They smell good, too."

She shook her head. "No. I don't think I'm ready for candles yet."

Yet. That was a good sign, right? "No problem. Do you want to look around here some more, or should we head to the grocery store?"

"Let's go."

As we headed for the exit, I spotted the woman who'd handed me the tissues. I lifted my chin to acknowledge her and mouthed the word "thanks." She smiled and nodded back before turning her attention to her own daughter.

Back on the crowded street, Emma slid her hand back into mine. I gave it a squeeze and then tucked her hand around my elbow. I liked this kid. In fact, I was crazy about her.

Of all Emma's uncles, I'd always been the closest to her. The two of us clicked. Having her live with me simply made sense.

Not that taking on the responsibility hadn't upended my life. It had, but—in a good way. I liked being needed. It had come as a surprise to me, but there it was, nonetheless. No one had ever depended on me this way before.

I glanced down at her, and when she beamed up at me, I glimpsed Hailey's warm smile on her daughter's face. My heart gave an aching twist of pleasure and pain.

This little girl would always have a home with me—no matter what.

Inside the grocery store, I grabbed a small shopping basket and proceeded directly to the produce section where I surveyed the piles of fresh fruit and vegetables. Maybe a salad?

"Can we have green beans?" Emma asked.

I lifted my eyebrows in surprise. "I think this is the first time you've ever asked for a particular food."

She shrugged. "I like fresh green beans and I haven't had them in ages. Mom cooked them with rosemary."

"In that case, green beans with fresh rosemary are on tonight's menu." I grabbed a couple of handfuls of loose green beans from the open bin in the produce section and stuffed them into a plastic bag. "Our mom used to make them with rosemary, too. That's why Hailey cooked them that way. How about a salad, too?"

She made a face. "You love that stuff. All grown-ups seem to. I guess Miss Gambit will probably like it, so you might as well make it."

That brought me up short. I must have had a strange expression on my face because Emma added, "Don't worry. I promise I'll eat some."

She'd completely read me wrong. "Did you invite Miss Gambit to dinner?"

"Well, not exactly," Emma said, "but if she isn't getting to our house until four, she'll be hungry after we do all that math. We'll need to feed her."

Although her logic was sound, I doubted Sonya would be willing to share a meal with me, but I decided to keep that to myself. "In that case, I'll buy enough of everything for her to join us. Remember though, she might have other plans, so don't be disappointed if she can't stay. *Capiche*?"

"*Capiche*."

I ruffled her hair. "Good girl."

"Woof." She stuck out her tongue and panted like a dog.

I grinned, happy that she was beginning to act more like her old self. I added more salad supplies to the basket alongside the green beans and fresh rosemary. "Let's go pick out those steaks." I led the way to the meat department and chose three steaks for dinner. I tossed them in the basket and headed toward the checkout.

"I really hope she stays." Emma rolled up onto her toes and back down to her heels as we stood in line. "I like Miss Gambit." She stroked the back of her fingers along her cheek in a self-soothing gesture she'd started using a lot recently.

I found myself hoping exactly the same thing. For Emma's sake, of course. Well, maybe for myself as well. "I bet I know a way to tempt her. A special dessert. One that's unique to Pittsburgh." And one I knew for a fact Sonya loved beyond any other dessert. At least, she had five years ago when I'd first introduced her to it.

"Well, it can't be one of those sandwiches that has French fries on it." She shot me a skeptical look. "That isn't very dessert-y. It can't be pierogies either."

I let out a low laugh. "No. I was thinking of something more along the lines of a Burnt Almond Torte."

"Ugh!" She shot me a horrified look. "That sounds ghastly!"

"Ghastly? You crack me up, kid. You have the most impressive vocabulary I've ever heard come out of the mouth of a fifth grader."

"It's a vocabulary word," she said primly. "How many other fifth graders do you know?"

"You make an excellent point."

"Why would someone want to eat a cake with burnt almonds?"

"They don't taste burned. I promise you'll love it. You'll be wishing you could eat it every day."

She gave me a scornful smirk that reminded me she'd be starting middle school next fall. "Fine, but if she hates it, I'm holding you responsible."

"And if I'm right?"

She grinned. "Then I'll pretend I knew it would be delicious all along."

Damn, but this kid was going to be a handful. "It's a deal."

8

SONYA GOES A-TUTORING

SONYA

I hitched my backpack higher on my shoulder, took a sip from my coffee cup, and then pressed the button for the eighteenth floor of Max Ross's apartment building. I still couldn't get over the fact that a doorman had admitted me in the lobby and called up to Max's apartment to announce me. I shook my head. I'd thought doormen like that only existed in New York City.

Well, la-de-freaking-da.

The elevator doors opened onto a quiet, gray-carpeted hallway. Eighteen B was at the end of the corridor.

I pressed the doorbell and was startled when the door immediately flew open.

Despite Emma's bright grin, neat denim skirt, and ruffled top, something about the girl seemed off.

It was her eyes. They looked red, as though she'd been on a crying jag.

"Hi, Miss Gambit. Thanks for coming." She stepped back to let me in.

"No problem." I went inside and came to a standstill as I took in the startling view of the city below. I could see a river in the distance, but I wasn't sure if it was the Allegheny or the Monongahela since I didn't know if I was facing north or south. Downtown Pittsburgh sat where the two rivers converged and formed the Ohio River. I moved closer to the window and realized the sun was to my right, which meant I was facing south. That meant this river had to be the Monongahela.

"We can sit at that table to do our work." Emma indicated a spot just off the kitchen. We'd have a fabulous view of the river and the spectacular autumn leaves on the opposite bank.

I drained my coffee cup as I glanced around Max's apartment. It was nothing like his old place in Los Angeles. Five years ago, he'd filled the place with IKEA furniture and family castoffs. I'd suspected even then that he'd come from a more affluent background because some of those castoffs had been gorgeous antiques.

Now, the only item I recognized was his prized antique wall clock. Oddly enough, its usually loud ticks and tocks were silent, and that felt wrong. The clock's hands pointed downward in a frown. Nine seventeen. Frozen in time. It was strange to see it that way. Max had always been obsessed with winding it. He'd loved that clock. Perhaps his responsibilities as Emma's guardian had taken an even bigger toll on him than I'd realized, and he'd forgotten to wind it.

Or perhaps he'd simply changed.

I didn't see the kitchen trash can, so I set my empty coffee cup on the counter and turned to face Emma. "Let's go ahead and get started." I put my backpack on the table and opened it.

Emma started to pull out her chair but paused. "Can I offer you something to drink?"

"Water?"

"We have sodas, too."

"I prefer water. Really."

Emma nodded and headed into the open kitchen.

Approaching footsteps echoed on the hardwood floor and I turned to see Max walk in.

"Hi, Sonya. Thanks for coming." He reached out his hand as though he wanted me to shake it.

I stared at it a moment before I took it. Smooth and dry. I remembered that hand. Remembered its contours. Its feel. The texture and shape of his fingers. I had to swallow before answering. "Anything for Emma."

He nodded as he let go. "I feel the same way. Anything for Emma." He watched the girl as she filled a water glass. "About that," he said as he leaned closer and lowered his voice, "she had a bit of a breakdown earlier today, but she's better now. Just be careful with her, okay? Gentle."

"Thanks for the warning." I backed away and avoided his gaze by unpacking my laptop and some of Emma's worksheets.

"Do you want the Wi-Fi password?" he asked.

"That would be great."

He leaned over, picked up my pen, and then hesitated. His face reddened slightly as he wrote something on a piece of paper. "The Is are ones," he muttered as he handed it to me without meeting my gaze.

When I read it, I blinked. The password was W1ldTh1ng. That's what he'd nicknamed me five years ago. His Wild Thing. My mouth snapped shut in surprise.

Max dropped the pen and backed away.

Emma joined us and set my water glass on the table.

"Thanks, kiddo," I said.

Max cleared his throat. "Do you need anything before I go downstairs? I was hoping to use the gym for an hour or so. It's right here in the building. You can call me if there's a problem. I can be here in two minutes."

A disorienting combination of relief and disappointment rushed through me. I had to remind myself that having him leave was a good thing. I didn't want him underfoot, distracting me while I tutored Emma. Simply being in his home was already distracting enough. "I'm sure we'll be fine."

I took in his black athletic shorts and gray Under Armour t-shirt. Workout clothes, I now realized. His attire hadn't even registered until now, which showed how off-balance he made me.

Max gave me a nod and then headed out the door. The room felt emptier without him in it.

Emma fiddled with her papers rather than meeting my eyes. "Before we get started, I need to ask you something."

I tensed but forced myself to appear calm. "No problem. Shoot." She hadn't picked up on the strained vibes between me and Max, had she?

"It's about the fifth-grade musical. I missed auditions while I was out, and I know you already cast the leading roles, but I was wondering if I could still help with it."

I relaxed. "Sure, sweetie. Of course, you can. The show is open to all fifth graders." I tilted my head to one side. "What would you like to do? You could be in the ensemble and still be on stage, or if you prefer, you could be a member of the stage crew. You could even work on the set or help with costumes."

Emma's eyes widened in surprise. "Could I still be in the show?"

"Definitely. All the parts have been cast, so I can't give you a speaking role, but if you're interested in being an understudy, Mrs. Warren and I could still consider you. You'd need to audition though. Would you like that?"

"Definitely."

I took a sip of water while I considered my options. "Do you think you could be ready to audition before our first rehearsal this coming Tuesday? I could set it up with Mrs. Warren so you can do it right after school."

"Absolutely. Marley's in the show, so I can stay after with her. I've attended a performing arts camp every summer ever since I was in the second grade, so I've already auditioned lots of times."

I chuckled. "I guess that means you're a pro."

Emma shrugged. "It sort of runs in the family."

I had to stop myself from smacking my palm against my forehead. Of course, it did, considering who her grandfather and uncles were. One producer, one director, one stuntman, and one... what was Max? Was he still a videographer? I knew he worked for Ross Film Productions. He did something in marketing now, didn't he?

Based on the time I'd spent with Max five years ago, I already knew he could sing, dance, and play the guitar. I'd always loved going to a club or some other venue to dance with him. The guy could dip like a professional ballroom dancer. He always made me look better than I actually was.

Back when we'd first met, he'd posted weekly videos on his YouTube channel. He interviewed celebrities out in L.A. Since I hadn't been into YouTube, he'd had to explain what having a YouTube channel meant. It turned out that YouTubers could make some decent money if enough people watched them.

Weird. I still didn't quite get how the whole thing worked. Where did the money come from if people watched YouTube for free?

I'd been oblivious to what those videos meant in regard to Max's notoriety. To me, he'd been nothing more than a guy with a film degree trying to pay off his student loans by working as a barista.

After we'd broken up, I'd finally come to understand how hugely successful Max's YouTube channel had been. Since his dad was a movie producer, he'd had access to loads of A-list celebrities.

If Emma followed in her family's footsteps, talent must be oozing from her fingertips.

"Are you ready to get to work?" I asked.

Emma nodded and pulled out a math assignment. "This is what's been giving me so much trouble. I don't get how I'm supposed to do it."

I leaned in. "You aren't the only student who had trouble with this one. It's challenging."

"I thought that since the entire homework assignment was just one problem, it would be easy."

I shot her a sympathetic smile. "Actually, I only assigned one problem because it was so hard. You need to break it down into steps in order to complete it. Let's walk through the example that's printed on the back of the page first, and then we can apply the same steps to the homework."

An hour later, I finished reviewing Emma's solution and said, "This is perfect. You've clearly grasped all the concepts." Behind me, I heard the front door open.

Emma glanced up. "Hi, Uncle Max."

"Hi, Em," he replied as I swiveled to face him. "I want to take a quick shower. Is there anything you need from me first?"

"Nope."

Max looked way too sexy and disheveled from his workout. This version of him was much too familiar to me. My cheeks heated as I recalled a similar rumpled look after some of our more strenuous lovemaking sessions. His hair curled around his face and sweat beaded his skin. Whatever he'd done in the gym over the past hour had been extremely physical.

I must have been looking at him oddly because he raised one eyebrow. I felt my cheeks flame as I turned my back on him, but not before I saw the look of realization cross his face. Somehow, he knew I'd been picturing him naked.

How humiliating. Could this get any worse?

As Max headed back to his bedroom, I snuck a peek. His calves and glutes bunched and flexed as he moved. He was more heavily muscled than he'd been five years ago. He'd still been youthful back then, but there was nothing boyish about him now.

Max Ross was all man.

"Can you help me with the electricity homework now?" Emma asked.

I jolted back to the present. "You're sure you aren't getting tired yet?"

"Only of math. I love science. It's cool."

"I'll let you in on a secret. I love science, too."

Emma squinted at me. "That's no secret, Miss Gambit. At the beginning of every science lesson, you start off by saying, 'I love science.'"

I grinned. "So, you *are* listening in class."

I could hear the water turn on through the apartment walls. Max must be stepping into the shower. Naked. Just twenty or so feet away from me.

I crossed my legs as I leaned closer to Emma's textbook, scrutinizing the diagram on the page. "This diagram shows how a circuit works." I tried to banish images of Max naked. Of water cascading down his body.

It was a challenge.

A few minutes later, Max sauntered back into the room, hair still damp. His jeans were slung low on his hips, and a charcoal gray t-shirt clung to his slightly damp torso. He headed directly for the kitchen and removed a cloth from a ceramic bowl. I couldn't tear my eyes away as he lifted a ball of dough from the bowl, coated it in olive oil, sprinkled it with salt and dried herbs, and then placed it in a loaf pan.

Well, look at that. The man even knows how to bake bread.

"Miss Gambit, are you listening?" Emma said, obviously not for the first time.

Max glanced over his shoulder and caught me watching him before I turned to face Emma.

I coughed. "Sorry, Sweetie. I was thinking about something."

"What?" Emma asked.

"Just laundry and errands. Nothing special."

The oven door squeaked as it opened, followed by the sound of metal rubbing across metal as Max slid the loaf of bread into the oven. This time I refused to glance up.

That man was entirely too distracting.

When he left the room again, I refused to watch, but that

didn't keep him from invading my thoughts. I tried to stay focused on Emma and her science homework, but my own brain kept distracting me.

Five years ago, we'd usually picked up prepared meals. I was clueless in the kitchen, and Max only knew how to make a couple of things. It looked as though we'd both learned some kitchen skills since then.

He'd probably changed in lots of other ways, too. I started drawing circles on my notepaper, circling the Wi-Fi password, and turning it into a flower. Then I added a bee buzzing around it.

That bread was beginning to smell amazing. "Does your Uncle Max bake bread often?"

Emma shrugged. "I guess so. I've been living with him for three weeks and he's made it a couple of times." Emma's chin wobbled and she pressed her lips together hard. The grief that swept over her face tore at my heart.

I reached over and stroked Emma's back. "Do you want to take a break?"

Emma shook her head. "Definitely not. I'm better when I stay busy."

It had been the same way for me when I'd been five and my dad had suddenly disappeared from my life. Momma had been angry that he'd left, and somehow, I'd known it was all my fault he was gone. It was easiest not to think about it at all and pretend everything was normal. Maybe that was what Emma was doing now. "Then let's do some science."

Emma opened the textbook and turned to the chapter on electricity.

At six o'clock, the alarm on my phone chimed.

I stretched my arms over my head. "We got a lot done in the past couple of hours. Did I wear you out?"

"Only a little, but I think I'm mostly caught up now. I hate it when I don't understand what's going on in class."

I closed my computer, set my backpack on the table, and slid it inside.

The oven timer went off and Max came in from the back of the apartment. He removed the bread and set it on the stove. "Are you two finished for the day? You've been hard at work." He opened the refrigerator and pulled out a plate bearing three steaks.

Three. He must be expecting a guest for dinner. Was it another woman? A date? Could it be his girlfriend?

I felt that betraying flush creep up my neck again. "I didn't realize it was so late." I zipped my backpack shut. "I'll get out of your hair."

Emma put her hand on my backpack, stopping me from picking it up. "But you have to stay and eat with us. Please, Miss Gambit. We even bought a steak for you."

"For me?" I repeated, halting mid-motion.

Max cleared his throat. "Emma mentioned she wanted you to have dinner with us, so when we were shopping, we bought enough for all three of us." He stared down at the granite countertop as though it might do something fascinating.

I hesitated. This was a bad idea. The last thing I needed was to spend more time with Max Ross, but when I glanced at Emma and saw the pleading expression in her still-reddened eyes, my resolve wilted.

"I have a secret weapon," Max added, risking a glance at me.

Other than Emma? I tensed and gave him a hard stare. What on earth did he think he was up to?

He grinned that broad, sweet grin that always made my heart flutter. "Burnt Almond Torte."

My jaw dropped. "Get out of here."

"Ugh. See?" Emma put her hands on her hips and scowled at her uncle. "She hates it."

I shook my head. "Not at all. You've obviously never eaten a Burnt Almond Torte if you can say that. It's pure goodness. Nectar of the gods. A Pittsburgh bakery makes them. People order them from all over the country and have them shipped directly to their homes." That's how I'd first tasted one. Max had ordered one and had it shipped to Los Angeles.

Emma rolled her eyes, completely unimpressed. "Does that mean you'll stay for dinner?"

I gave a slow blink and then said, "Of course. Who could resist the lure of Burnt Almond Torte? I'm only human."

9

OF MEMORIES, CLOCKS, AND PHOTOS

Sonya

Emma practically vibrated with excitement. "That's awesome. While Uncle Max grills the steaks, you can come and see my bedroom." She grabbed my hand and started dragging me toward the back of the apartment.

I willingly followed along, relieved to see Emma being a bit more lighthearted. I'd do just about anything to keep this expression on her face. Plus, spending time alone with her would give me a few minutes to mentally prepare myself.

I was nervous about having dinner with Max, but a part of me was oddly expectant. Tonight felt inevitable. Lianna had been insightful. She was right. I had lingering issues I needed to resolve. Perhaps tonight would be the first step down that path.

When Emma pushed open her bedroom door, I was struck by the room's sophisticated decor with its pale gray walls and darker gray carpet. It was way too somber for a child. Someone had tried to personalize it for Emma by adding a pink lamp and bedspread. A poster adorned one wall of a girl standing under an umbrella that was reminiscent of the Morton Salt girl, but more modern. Rain fell around her in vibrant streaks of color.

Emma picked up a framed photo from her nightstand and

handed it to me. "Uncle Max gave me that. All my stuff was ruined in the fire, but he printed that one for me. It was here on my nightstand when I moved in."

I stared down at the image of Emma and her parents in front of a snow-covered mountain. They stood grinning together in the bright sunlight wearing matching green ski jackets.

Emma held out a small, square book that I took. "We made this together on his laptop." I flipped open the photo book and found images of Emma with her parents. There were a few with Max as well, along with her Uncle Sin and some other people I didn't recognize.

"We picked out the photos from the ones Uncle Max had taken with his cell phone or that Mom and Dad had sent him, and then we used a website he knew about to make this book."

My heart gave a hard thump. "What a lovely idea. That's a thoughtful gift."

"Uncle Max is more sentimental than he lets on. He's weird that way. He has this old clock on the mantel that doesn't even work, but he won't get rid of it."

Emma must be talking about the clock I'd recognized when I'd arrived. No wonder it had been silent. "It's old. Maybe that's why he keeps it."

"Nope. I asked him. He said he keeps it for sentimental reasons. It broke the night his girlfriend walked out on him. He said the clock reminds him to be more careful in the future."

My throat tightened as my heart gave another hard thump.

I recalled every detail from the evening I'd stormed out. After I'd slammed the door, there'd been a loud crash a moment later. I'd assumed Max had thrown something in anger but had I been wrong? Maybe I'd slammed the door so hard it had knocked the clock off the wall. I swallowed to ease the tightness in my throat. "That's a sad story." I tried not to say anything more, but…"Did he care about her a lot?" I asked. The question slipped out before I could stop it.

"I think he loved her." Emma shrugged. "Grampa Don had a

heart attack the very next day. Max says the broken clock symbolizes lost time and bad choices. *I* think he keeps it because she broke his heart."

The words hit me like a punch to the chest and I couldn't breathe for a moment. Had I really broken Max's heart?

"You know we bought a new house in Sewickley, right?" Emma asked. "We'll be moving there in a month or so—I hope. Uncle Max hired some people to make changes to it. They're going to fix up my new bedroom to be exactly the way I want it. An interior designer is helping me pick out furniture and paint colors. Uncle Max is even installing a sprinkler system to put out fires." Her eyes filled with sudden tears. "I wish my mom and dad had thought of that. None of my friends' houses have sprinkler systems, but this apartment does." She pointed up at the sprinkler head above her bed. "It probably would have saved their lives. When I saw it, I told Uncle Max I'd never live anyplace that didn't have them."

Emma may have been right about a sprinkler system saving her parents. They'd fallen asleep during a romantic evening at home with a bottle of champagne and candles, and hadn't woken up when the fire broke out. The fire alarm hadn't been working because they'd been renovating their house.

"If I'd been there, I would have woken up." Emma closed the photo book and tightened her grip on it, turning her knuckles white. "I would have saved them."

"But you weren't," I stated the fact simply. "You also could have died if you'd been there. Listen, sweetie. You can drive yourself crazy with 'what-ifs.' It's impossible to go back and change what happened, no matter how much you wish you could. All you can do is move forward." I stroked her soft hair and tucked a strand behind her ear. "Don't torment yourself with wondering how things might have been if you'd done something different. All you'll do is drown in worry and doubt. It's not as though someone is offering you a ride in a time machine to go back and change everything. That will never happen. If you keep questioning the decisions you made, you'll only end up trapped in your past, unable to create a future for yourself. You need to live in the present."

Emma frowned, then sighed. "I guess that makes sense."

I winked at her. "Just don't think that means you can skip reviewing your tests when I hand them back to you in class. I still want you to *learn* from your mistakes. What I mean is that once you've learned what you can, you have to move on. Like you did with the sprinklers your uncle is installing. You learn, you make corrections, you move on."

Emma's small shoulders sagged. Suddenly, she threw her arms around my waist and squeezed tight. "You're my favorite teacher ever," she mumbled into my shoulder. "I'll miss you when I have to go to middle school next year. I don't want things to change." Her little body was a tight ball of tension.

I stroked her back. "You're welcome to come to visit me, even after you move on to the sixth grade. Would you like that?"

Emma nodded against my chest. "I guess that could work," she said, her voice muffled.

I could feel the tension ebbing from Emma's body.

Eventually, she let go of me and sat back, rubbing the heels of her hands against her eyes.

"Better?"

She nodded, then opened her photo book and turned to a picture that showed her sandwiched between Marley and Liam. "Liam's in the play, right?"

"He has the male lead."

Emma let out a soft sigh. "The night of the fire, Marley and I were practicing for the auditions. I was hoping Liam and I would get the lead roles."

My heart tightened in my chest. This poor kid had lost so much. "He's really talented. I bet you would have been great together on stage."

Emma nodded. "He and his friends are always making movies and putting on shows in the summer." She faced me. "I thought it would be fun to do some scenes with him and run lines together." She shrugged. "Now I'll just be lost in the ensemble."

"At least you'll be in the show, though. That's something."

"And something is better than nothing," Emma agreed.

Max knocked softly on the door. I glanced up to find him holding a glass of red wine as he leaned one shoulder against the door jamb. "You two look cozy. I'm sorry for interrupting, but the steaks are ready."

Emma jumped up from the bed. "I'm starved."

"Go wash up," he said.

Emma hurried from the room.

As I moved to follow her, Max handed me the glass of wine. "This is for you. If you like, you can wash your hands in the kitchen. Emma tends to leave a pond around the sink after she's done."

"Thanks." I took a sip as I followed him back to the kitchen.

"We're also having green beans," he said over his shoulder, "at Emma's request."

I glanced at the dining table and stopped short. Everything looked beautiful.

Max had turned down the lights and pulled open the drapes to let in the view of the river and the city below. It was a stunning sight.

My heart beat a staccato rhythm. If not for the fact that *three* plates sat on the table, I'd think he was trying to seduce me.

MAX REMEMBERS

Max

I found myself transfixed by Sonya as she stood silhouetted against the setting sun. The physical details she had altered to hide from the world disappeared in the orange glow. Her blonde hair, her tinted contact lenses—all of it faded into shadow. Right now, she looked exactly as I remembered her.

She was my Essie once again.

Emma rushed into the room, knocking me loose from the momentary spell. "What did you do in here, Uncle Max? Everything looks different. *Fancy*." She said that last word with a posh accent.

"Thanks. Since we have a guest, I thought I'd make a special effort." As I adjusted the dimmer switch for the chandelier above the table, I watched my niece's reaction. I didn't miss the frown that crossed her face when she spotted the unlit candles in the center of the table. Damn. I should have removed them sooner.

She stared at them as she licked her lips. "What about those?"

I whisked them off the table and stashed them in the buffet drawer. I'd need to go through the apartment and get rid of any others I had sitting out. "Candlelight is a bit too romantic for dinner with your teacher, don't you think?"

When Emma's tense shoulders relaxed and she took her seat, I knew I'd done the right thing.

Sonya's chair faced the window, but she barely paid attention to the view. "Everything smells delicious. You shouldn't have gone to so much trouble." Her eyes were fixed on the small philodendron in the center of the table. Her stiff smile didn't fool me for a second. She'd recognized exactly what I'd done. I'd recreated the essence of one of our dates when I'd first cooked dinner for her—and had ended up burning the steaks.

My old apartment had been small and cheap. Nothing like this high rise. When I'd first moved out of the place I'd shared with Raven, I'd found the best apartment I could afford without dipping into the trust fund my grandparents had set up for me. I'd managed to scrape by on the income from my YouTube channel and my job at Starbucks.

That YouTube channel had been my passion back when I'd attended film school in Los Angeles. I'd met Raven because of it. Come to think of it, maybe that was part of the reason I had abandoned it. If not for the videos I'd made, I probably never would have met her.

Back then, I'd relied on Dad's connections in the film industry to land celebrity interviews for my channel. Raven had been an up-and-coming music star back then. She'd been living in L.A. when someone introduced us at one of the many industry parties my dad had hosted while I was living with him. I'd found it easy to lasso rising talent for my YouTube channel. They always wanted free publicity.

When I'd reached out to Raven to interview her about the new album she was about to release, she'd agreed to be my guest. I'd done the interview in the recording space at Dad's place up in the Hollywood Hills, and Raven and I had immediately hit it off.

Our attraction must have shown up on camera as well because my viewers had filled my feed with comments about it. Raven sent me tickets to her concert along with a backstage pass. When I'd arrived, she'd filmed us together and put it on her own

YouTube channel. I'd loved every second of it, and both our channels had exploded with new subscribers.

If asking Raven out had been easy. Falling for her had been even easier. Raven was amazing. Exciting. I never knew what would happen next when I was with her.

Our fans had been thrilled as they'd watched our relationship unfold. Raven had frequently mentioned me in her videos and often included clips of the two of us together. She occasionally complained that I didn't mention her on my channel, but my channel focused on interviewing people involved in the movie industry, whereas hers was about current gossip and personalities in the entertainment world. After I interviewed someone, I always moved on to my next subject.

I moved in with her, but after we'd been together for a few months, her mood became volatile. She would swing from being relaxed and lackadaisical to being manic and focused on some new goal. When I tried to talk to her about it, she blamed it on the strange hours she kept as a singer and her stressful schedule.

Then I discovered she'd been taking drugs.

That had been a rude awakening. She knew how I felt about drugs. A bit of pot was okay. After all, it was legal. But the other stuff she was taking? The oxy? The coke? That was bad news.

She promised to stop taking drugs. She even checked herself into one of those spa-style treatment facilities. The problem was that she only stayed the minimum amount of time, complained that they wanted her to stop drinking and smoking pot, and immediately started doing both again the moment she got out.

Things didn't go well between us after that. Even though she was off the harder drugs, she'd still have those manic phases that had gone along with her former addiction to coke. Her behavior baffled me. If her illegal drug use was all in the past, as she claimed, her continued bad behavior simply didn't make sense.

And then I'd found her stash. I watched it for a couple of days just in case it had been left over from before she'd gone through rehab. When the drugs disappeared and then were replaced the next day, I knew the truth.

She was using again.

When I confronted her, our argument unfolded exactly the way I'd feared it would. She'd claimed it was an old stash she'd forgotten about. When I told her I knew she'd replenished it in the past twenty-four hours, she'd gotten angry with me and accused me of spying on her. Of not trusting her. She'd yelled and kicked and thrown things at me, including her cell phone which had shattered against the wall.

I'd told her I was done. I'd had it with our relationship and with all her lies.

We were over.

I'd walked out and never looked back.

She'd checked herself into rehab that night, and I'd stayed at my dad's house. The very next day, I'd found a new apartment and moved everything I owned out of her place.

I'd needed a clean break from that former life. I was done with the Hollywood scene. The parties. The drugs.

I'd needed to reinvent myself.

Within two days, I'd found a job at Starbucks, and less than a week later, I'd met Essie.

She'd been everything Raven wasn't. Stable. Kind. Thoughtful. Joyful. Nothing like the manic, self-obsessed rocker I'd walked away from.

One of my friends messaged me that Raven planned to stay in rehab for at least six months. I took that as a good sign. With luck and hard work, she might manage to kick her habits this time. I didn't hate her; I simply couldn't be with her anymore.

She'd checked out as soon as she hit the six-month mark, and what was the first thing she'd done? She'd contacted me, wanting to pick back up where we'd left off.

I'd been on my break at Starbucks sitting on a stool near the storage area when my phone had rung. I didn't recognize the number but answered anyway.

"Max-man!" Raven cooed. "I'm out, I'm clean, and I'm all yours."

"Raven?" I said, stalling. All mine? This conversation couldn't go anywhere good. I wished I hadn't answered. "Have you been out long?" I asked, trying to buy some time.

"I got out yesterday. I went home, but you'd moved out. I'd have called sooner, but I broke my phone, and the rehab center wouldn't let me get a new one. It seemed like I stayed there forever! Where are you? I want to see you."

I rubbed my hand along the cool stainless-steel shelving unit next to me. "That isn't a good idea."

"But I miss you."

"I broke up with you." I closed my eyes. "You can't have forgotten."

"That was just a fight. We always make up after fights." Her voice was husky.

I let out a heavy sigh. "We've never broken up before. That was a breakup, not just a fight. I wasn't kidding. I told you after you came back from rehab the first time that if you ever started doing drugs and lying to me again, I was out the door. Don't pretend you didn't know that. It was why you lied to me when you started doing them again. You knew I'd leave."

"Max," she wailed. "Addiction is a disease. You can't blame me for being sick."

I tightened my grip on the phone as I rose to my feet. "I can't do this. I can't be with someone who lies to me. Who sets out to systematically deceive me and gaslight me. If we were together again, I'd always be checking up on you. I'd never be able to trust you. I don't want to be that person. I don't want to live that kind of life. We aren't good together. We have to accept the fact that we simply aren't right for each other."

She was breathing heavily on the other end of the phone, and I could tell she was crying. "You can't mean that. I went to rehab. I worked really, really hard. I'm done with drugs. I have my life back again."

"I'm happy for you." My voice softened. "Honestly, Raven. I'm proud of you. I know it can't have been easy, but I'm not part of your life anymore. I've moved on."

"What do you mean you've *moved on*?" Her pitch was rising, making her voice sound shrill over the phone, but even so, she managed to imbue those last two words with seething scorn.

I sighed. "I moved into my own place. I found a job as a barista while I try to figure out what I want to do with my life."

"You make *coffee*? You've got to be kidding me." She let out a harsh laugh.

"It's a good job. An honest living."

"But you're in the movie business."

"I'm taking a break. I need time to think things through." When I'd left her, I'd left that entire life behind. Her betrayal had poisoned everything for me. Although, perhaps it was time for me to consider reclaiming certain aspects of my former life, though. Not everything about it had been bad. I'd loved working with my dad and learning how Ross Film Productions worked.

After working as a barista for the past six months, I'd gained some perspective. I was on more solid footing because I wasn't mired in the quicksand that was Raven. "Things are falling into place for me."

"'*Things are falling into place*?' Is that right?" Her voice dripped with sarcasm. "Do you have some new girl on the side too? Some sweet little nothing? Someone the complete opposite of me?"

I immediately thought of Essie. She wasn't a sweet little nothing, although Raven was right—the two of them had almost nothing in common. Essie was a savvy New Jersey chick. She could be sweet, sure, but she had an inner resilience that Raven lacked. I could never imagine her dulling her pain by taking drugs. That wasn't who she was. She was the type who'd go down fighting.

I needed to deflect Raven, though. That little bomb she'd lobbed had landed too close for comfort "We broke up, Raven. Who I date is none of your business."

"You son-of-a-bitch. You're already fucking someone else."

Clearly, I'd said the wrong thing. "Who I see has nothing to do with you. We broke up six months ago. We're over."

"We'll see about that. We're not over until *I* say we're over." She ended the call.

Looking back now, I realized that was the moment when I'd made my biggest mistake.

I should have taken her seriously. I should have known better than to antagonize her. Raven was determined and tenacious. That's what drove her success. I should have known she wouldn't let me go. I should have seen it coming.

Should, should, should... at the very least, I should have told my girlfriend, my amazing Essie, about my relationship and breakup with Raven.

Less than a week later, Raven had retaliated loudly and publicly. She'd posted what she'd entitled her "Maximus Love Letter" on her YouTube channel—a montage of clips of the two of us together. At the end of the video, she'd begged me to forgive her.

The video had swept through the social media landscape like wildfire. Raven performed her coup de grâce a few hours later by naming Essie Harlow as the woman who'd stolen Max from her and wrecked our love story forever.

That's when her fans turned into a virtual mob.

That's when the hashtag EssieIsASlut started trending.

That's when the reporters and the fanatics—and Essie's estranged father—had tracked her down to the restaurant where she worked.

That's when both our lives had gone to shit.

A HEARTFELT APOLOGY

MAX

"I made an enormous mistake five years ago," I said as I sprinkled salt on my steak. I glanced up in time to note Sonya's startled reaction. "I should have found a house in Sewickley rather than renting this apartment in downtown Pittsburgh. I liked the building's security, but I've spent way too many hours on Route Sixty-Five driving back and forth to Ross Film Production meetings or visiting my family."

Some of Sonya's tension eased, but I could tell she was still on edge.

Emma frowned. "And now you have to drive me back and forth to school every day."

I winked at her. "At least I have you to keep me company, even if you don't like my taste in music."

"Seriously?" Emma scowled "That electronic stuff you listen to is gross. There aren't even any lyrics."

"That's why it clears my mind. We'll be in our new house soon, and then you won't be tortured by my music any longer."

"It won't be soon enough," Emma muttered.

"Would you like more wine?" I asked Sonya. The woman really looked like she needed to relax.

She glanced at her glass and seemed surprised to find it empty. "No, thank you. I don't feel comfortable having a second glass of wine when I came here to tutor Emma."

"That's silly," Emma said.

"Maybe so," Sonya said as she placed her napkin in her lap, "but I can't help feeling that way."

I poured myself a glass. "Tell me how the tutoring session went. Are you all caught up?"

Emma shrugged. "I think so."

"I know so," Sonya said. "You caught on quickly and you're a hard worker. That's why you're in the advanced math and English classes. Your work habits make you an excellent student."

Emma sat up a bit straighter in her chair. "Don't tell anyone I told you this, but I like school. At least, most of the time. I don't like all the time we spend standing in line, but at least you make it a bit more fun with your chants and songs."

"What chants?" I asked, intrigued.

"Miss Gambit has us do this silly song that lists all the presidents in order. And there's another one that has the periodic table. And one with the planets. They're fun."

"They sound educational," I commented.

"Shush," Sonya said. "Don't spoil it. If they think they're educational, they won't want to do them."

Emma rolled her eyes. "Of course, they're educational. It's school."

"When you're in your high school honors history class and you have to list the presidents in order, you'll thank me," Sonya said.

There was a lull as we all ate, and then Sonya asked, "So, Max, what exactly do you do for a living?"

I paused with my fork in the air, surprised by her question. "I assumed you knew. I'm the chief communications officer at Ross Film Productions."

Sonya narrowed her eyes slightly as she gazed at me over a forkful of steak. "That's strange. For some reason, I thought you were involved in the coffee industry rather than the film industry." She neatly placed the bite into her mouth.

Coffee? The little minx. She was baiting me. "Funny you should say that. I worked for Starbucks right after I graduated from college." I said that for Emma's benefit, not Sonya's. "I had to hang up my barista apron when my father got sick."

Sonya set down her fork. "Someone at book club mentioned that to me a few days ago. I was so sorry to hear about it. He had a heart attack five years ago, right? How's he doing?"

"Much better. They had to replace a valve in his heart. I helped him run Ross Productions while he was recovering. I didn't realize how much I knew about Dad's business until I had to fill in for him. Don't get me wrong; his executive team was top-notch. I couldn't have done it without them. Dad guided me as well, but I found out I had a knack for the work. I ended up staying with the family business even after he recovered."

She watched me closely. "It must have been hard for you to step down after being in charge."

"Not at all. I was working long hours and traveling all the time. I can see how Dad ended up having a heart attack. Fortunately, after he came back to work, he cut back on how hard he pushed himself. Now he usually sends me as his proxy for his out-of-town shoots. For the most part, he only makes movies he can film here in Pittsburgh or along the east coast. He even sold the house he owned in the Hollywood Hills."

Sonya bit into a green bean. It popped open and sent a squirt of liquid onto her cheek.

I grinned as she shot me a self-conscious glance. She wiped her face with her napkin and rolled her eyes.

Emma's fork clattered as she set it on her empty plate.

"Done with dinner already?" I asked. "Do you want more, or would you prefer dessert?"

"Burnt Almond Torte? No thanks." Emma rose from the table and carried her plate to the kitchen. She flipped on the faucet and rinsed off her plate. "I'm kind of tired. I think I'll get ready for bed and read for a while."

"You're out on missing something delicious," Sonya said. "You should at least have a taste."

"I'll come back after I take my shower and try some. A 'no-thank-you' serving."

I tipped back my wine glass and finished it. "Your mom taught you that, right? The 'no-thank-you serving' thing? Our mom used it on us too. We had to take a no-thank-you serving of anything we said we hated." I shook my head. "It might have worked with some things, but I'll always hate liver and onions."

"Ghastly." Sonya grinned. "I can't say I blame you."

Ghastly? Is that where Emma had picked up the word?

"Mom loved liver," Emma said, "but she didn't make me eat it after the first time. I spit it across the room."

I tipped my head back and let out a hoot of laughter. "You're smarter than I was. I should have tried that trick with my mom. Too bad I didn't know you back then. You could have taught me that."

Emma loaded her dishes in the dishwasher and headed back to her bedroom. "I'll come to say goodnight when I'm ready for bed."

"And you can try the cake," I said, "but no spitting."

Emma heaved a fake sigh. "Fine. I promise. It can't be as bad as liver and onions."

"Nothing is as bad as liver and onions," I agreed.

A minute later, I heard the shower turn on. I glanced up and caught Sonya watching me. "Thanks for coming to tutor Emma. I wasn't sure you would."

She waved away my thanks. "Emma's been through a lot. I can't imagine losing both of my parents at once."

"I guess you know that Emma's mom was my older sister. When I think about her—about both her and Barry—it shreds my heart." I felt some of the tension in my chest ease simply because I could speak openly to her. "I have to keep it together, though.

Emma has enough to deal with without me burdening her with my own grief."

Sonya's eyes softened. "I'm so sorry. I know what it's like to lose someone, too. My mom died of cancer not long ago. Figuring out how to live without someone you care about is a painful adjustment to make. I'm sorry your sister died so suddenly. That has to have been hard."

I could see the grief and sympathy shining in her eyes. "I'm sorry for your loss. It's hard to lose a parent. I don't know if I ever told you, but my mom died of cancer when I was a kid. Losing a parent means losing someone who knows you inside and out. From what you told me about your mom when we first met, she sounded like an amazing woman."

"She was. Frustrating, but amazing." She cleared her throat. "I'm sorry about your mom."

I shrugged. It was an old wound. One I'd gotten used to. I cocked my head and listened for a moment. I could hear the sounds of Emma moving around in the shower. The hollow squeak of feet against the tub.

It was time. I took a deep breath and dug down deep. "I owe you an apology for what happened between us. It's overdue. I'm sorry I didn't tell you about Raven. I'm sorry I left you vulnerable to that media storm. I simply never thought she was capable of something so cruel."

Her expression fell. "It would have helped if you'd been honest with me from the beginning and told me you had a girlfriend."

"I didn't *have* a girlfriend. We'd already broken up when you and I met. Things had been bad between us for a while, so the breakup was more of a relief than anything else."

Sonya shook her head, looking frustrated. "But you dated *Raven*. She's huge."

"She wasn't quite as huge when we started going out."

She flashed me a scathing look. "Seriously?"

"Fine. She was a big deal. But you dated other guys before we met. You didn't tell me about them either."

"I didn't date a rock star with an axe to grind," she pointed out.

"I didn't know she'd react that way. How was I to guess she'd go all *Fatal Attraction* on me?"

Sonya stared at me blankly. "Fatal Attraction?"

I grinned as I shook my head. "I keep telling you, you need to watch more movies."

She waved his comment away. "I'm not much of a movie buff."

"Sacrilege," I teased.

"We live in different worlds."

"Ones that happen to intersect."

"Intersect? I'd say they collided," she snapped back. "My life was nearly destroyed after it came into contact with yours."

Her words pierced me, wounding me deeply. I hated that she believed we were incompatible. "Was it that bad?"

"It brought my dad back into my life, which was bad enough on its own. You saw for yourself what a treat *that* was."

My stomach knotted. "He ambushed you. I still can't wrap my head around a parent acting that way. The whole thing was a train wreck."

"One that still gives me flashbacks. I was finally getting over all the backlash from it a year later when Raven made her suicide attempt and all those nuts descended on me in full force." She blushed. "The school where I was working decided I wasn't worth the trouble and let me go."

My jaw tensed. "I heard. I tried to track you down after I got back to the States from a shoot in Indonesia, but you'd already gone into hiding. I'm so sorry."

She shook her head. "It was for the best. I changed my name that summer, and I've been able to live anonymously ever since." She stared down at her plate. "I'm not sure how long that will continue now that you're back in my life."

"We're old news," I reassured her. "There's no reason for your story to resurface."

"Someone recognized me the other day," she said softly.

I stilled. "Who? What happened?"

"It was someone in my book group. Rose. She works at the library. She recognized me, and then the others did, too. Now even the mayor knows who I am."

"Scarlet?"

"You know Scarlet?"

"Of course, I do. I grew up in Sewickley. So did she. Everyone knows her. Her uncle is a senator, after all." I paused and narrowed my eyes. "Is that the same book club Courtney is in?"

Sonya slumped. "I hate that you know so many of my new friends."

"It gets worse. My brother is living with another of your book club members. Mara. They're engaged."

"You mentioned that already." She heaved a sigh. "Someone from book club has probably told her who I am by now."

I'd better let my brother off the hook about keeping Sonya's identity secret from Mara. I didn't want to get Ford into trouble with her.

"It looks like your secret is out. I'd like to point out, that scandal rag *Here's the Scoop* still hasn't descended on our little town to hunt you down. The world doesn't seem to care. I think you're safe. We're old news."

Sonya scrubbed her face with her hands. "I hate that tabloid." She met my gaze. "Am I stupid for wanting to believe you?"

"Not at all. I'm a pro when it comes to PR and marketing. I think you'll be safe."

"But you're not certain." She slumped back in her chair. "I wish none of this had happened to me."

I looked directly into her eyes. "If I'd told you about Raven from the beginning, your dad might not have come traipsing back into your life at the worst possible moment. Everything might have turned out differently. I'm sorry I was so slow when it came to dealing with the media circus, but I had to help my dad when he had his heart attack. By the time I was able to deny Raven's claims about our breakup, her version of the story had already taken hold. No one wanted to hear my side of things."

Sonya sighed, relaxing slightly in her chair. "I'm surprised she backed off and stopped blaming me for destroying her life. I haven't heard a peep from her in four years. I admit it's been a huge relief. I wonder if she finally decided she'd punished me enough."

I wished that had been the case, but I knew better. "That wasn't it. I flew out to see her after you were fired. I told her she needed to stop blaming other people for her bad choices, get her life under control, and start taking responsibility for her own actions."

Sonya looked stunned. "You did that?"

"I didn't know how else to get through to her."

"That's all it took? A simple face-to-face request from you?" She sipped her water nonchalantly, but her white-knuckled hand gripped the glass.

"There's nothing simple with Raven. I'd made that same request many, many times. No, it was because this one had some teeth. I threatened to expose her two previous rehab stays."

Sonya's eyes went wide as she set her water glass down with a forceful thump. "You didn't."

"I did. I don't know if I would have gone through with it or not, but she certainly believed I would. It's too bad I didn't threaten her sooner. I'm sorry for that. I'm sorry for all of it. I should have told you years ago about all the things I did to try to fix that mess."

Sonya shrugged. "I told you not to contact me. You did as I asked."

"I didn't intend to stay away from you for so long. If my dad hadn't had a heart attack, I would have started calling you the very next day. Instead, I waited a week, only to find out you'd canceled your phone."

"Someone posted my number online and people started harassing me." She shook her head. "It was horrible. They'd say the most hateful things. Calling me a whore, threatening to hurt me... I lost my temper one day and threw my phone into the ocean." Her face was pinched.

"I tried to track you down through your social media accounts," I said, "but you shut them down. I decided to give you some time and let you reach out to me when you were ready. Weeks went by. I kept myself distracted by pouring every ounce of energy into running Ross Film Productions. Weeks turned into months. I told myself I'd give you a year before tracking you down, but you were back in the news that following spring. I was in Indonesia at the time working on one of my dad's films. I came straight back as soon as I heard and tried to find you, but you'd disappeared again."

She frowned in embarrassment. "The district brought in a long-term substitute for the rest of the year and asked me to leave."

"That's what the principal there told me," I said. "I hired a detective to search for you after that, but you'd simply vanished. No one at your old school would say a word about where you'd gone. I began to think you'd left the country. Left everything behind."

She gave a tight smile. "Nope. Just my name. I moved back to New Jersey with my mom and had it legally changed to her last name, Gambit. The hard part was getting my college to change the name on my diploma. I ended up finding a teaching position not far from where my Mom lived, across the river in Philly, but it was in a rough part of town. When the job here in Sewickley was posted, I jumped on it. You know the rest."

Maybe if I'd hired that detective sooner, before Raven's suicide attempt, I'd have found her. There were so many things I wished I'd done differently. So many regrets. "Sonya, I know I keep saying I'm sorry—"

The bathroom door opened with a squeak.

"It's okay," Sonya said softly.

Our eyes locked.

Bare feet padded along the hardwood floor. "I hear a mouse," I called out. "A very big mouse."

"I don't believe you," Emma said as she entered the room. "I sound absolutely nothing like a mouse."

"Time for cake!" Sonya announced gleefully as she rubbed her hands together.

"You got it," I told her as I stood.

We all pitched in. I gathered the dirty dishes from the table. Sonya rinsed while I loaded. Emma set out three plates and forks and then opened the cake box. "At least it smells yummy," Emma said. "Not burned at all."

I closed the dishwasher and grabbed a knife from the magnetic strip on the wall. "You'll love it." I sliced three pieces, slid the first one onto a plate, and handed it to Emma.

"We'll see." Emma stared at it skeptically, but she still picked up a fork and broke off a decent-sized bite. She put it in her mouth and closed her eyes as she concentrated.

Sonya and I exchanged glances, then we both watched Emma for her reaction, but she kept her eyes shut and her expression unreadable.

"Do you hate it?" I prodded.

"Not exactly." She opened one eye and peeked at me. "I think I should try another bite." She took a larger forkful this time and popped it into her mouth. A blissful smile spread over her lips. "This is really good."

"See? What did I tell you?"

Sonya nudged me. "My turn."

I handed her the next piece of cake and then served myself. The three of us stood in the kitchen eating in silence.

Finally, Sonya declared, "This is absolutely the best cake in all of Pittsburgh."

"Can I have a second piece and eat it in bed while I read?" Emma asked.

"Sure thing," I told her, reaching out for the knife to slice off a piece. "Just remember to brush your teeth before you go to sleep."

"Okay. Love you."

"Love you too."

Emma bounced out of the room. When I turned back to Sonya, I found her watching me.

"You're really good with her," she said.

"She's a great kid. It's easy."

Sonya shook her head firmly. "No, it isn't. She's under a lot of stress these days, and you're giving her a loving, stable home. It's exactly what she needs."

I met her eyes, feeling truly seen and appreciated by her. "Thanks."

Sonya rinsed off her plate and set it in the dishwasher. "I should go home now. Thank you for dinner."

I took a small step closer to her, not wanting to crowd her or make things awkward, but also not wanting her to leave. "You're welcome. I'm glad we had a chance to talk tonight."

"Me too. Tonight has helped clear the air between us."

"I still have one question." I took another step closer to her. "Do you forgive me? *Can* you forgive me?"

It took a moment for Sonya to meet my eyes. "Forgiving and forgetting are two different things. I can forgive you. I believe you weren't being intentionally deceitful or malicious, but I can't forget what happened. I can't forget the way our worlds collided. I can't forget the way your secrets destroyed my life."

She glanced around my home, her gaze catching for a moment on my broken clock, and I saw everything the way she must see it. The perfectly decorated executive's apartment filled with high-end leather furniture and expensive electronics. The spectacular view of the city sprawling below us. It bore no resemblance to my old place. The one where we'd first made love.

The one where I'd given her my heart.

"Your mistakes were unintentional," she said. "I can forgive you for being young and thoughtless."

I took her hands in mine and brushed my thumbs along her knuckles. "That's a start."

I edged closer, and her gaze dropped to my mouth.

Her body canted toward mine.

I closed the distance between us, dropping her hands and wrapping my arms around her, pulling her closer as I lowered my head to hers.

She was exactly where she belonged. Exactly where I needed her to be. Her soft, pliant body melted against mine. Her arms crept up my sides until she held my shoulders.

We kissed. The touch jolted through my body, making me lose myself in the moment. There was only us. Only our intermingled breath.

I opened my mouth, teasing her lower lip with my tongue, and she immediately opened to me. Our mouths devoured one another. They fit together in exactly the right way.

Tongues, lips, warm skin. The taste of almonds and frosting. She moaned into me and the sound drove me wild with wanting.

I cupped her bottom, pulling her firmly against my groin. "God, Essie. I've missed you so much."

She stiffened and jerked back, tearing her mouth away from mine.

I opened my eyes and found myself gazing directly into her startled face.

She shook her head. "I can't do this. Not again." She tried to pull free of my embrace, but I was slow to release her, not quite comprehending. "I need to go," she insisted.

The thought of her leaving again broke me. "Essie, stay," I pleaded.

Her forehead furrowed. I could feel her drawing away both physically and emotionally. Her mouth pressed into a thin line and the corners of her lips turned down. "Essie's gone. She was young and foolish, and Raven devoured her. I'm Sonya now." She stepped back, and I dropped my arms to my sides. "Even better,

I'm Miss Gambit to you." She spun her back to me and grabbed her purse and backpack. "Thank you for dinner."

I let her go. She needed time. I could see that. She had responsibilities keeping her here now, though. Not like last time. It wasn't as if she could completely disappear again.

"Goodnight," I said.

She shook her head. "Goodbye."

The word pierced my heart. She said that the last time she walked out on me too.

Now, she opened the front door and slipped out, closing it firmly behind her.

12

DITCH THE GUY

Sonya

I sat down with my latte at a small table at the Loco Mocha coffee shop late Sunday morning, ready to start grading a stack of tests. As I sipped my drink and settled in with the first paper on the pile, memories of yesterday's kiss invaded my thoughts.

I hadn't expected to kiss Max, but that didn't mean I hadn't also enjoyed it. In fact, I'd loved it. Part of me longed to return to those blissful weeks we'd spent together. We'd forged a deep connection, both emotionally and physically. I hadn't experienced anything like it, before or since.

"Sonya, don't you look lovely this morning," Gertrude said. "I could swear you're glowing!"

With a start, I glanced up from the stack of tests to find our oldest book club member smiling down at me. I felt my cheeks flush. Just my luck that someone would walk up as I daydreamed about kissing Max.

"You caught me thinking about my new washer and dryer," I lied. "It'll be nice to have them in the house I'm renting. I'm getting tired of going to the laundromat all the time."

"How exciting!" Gertrude shifted her purse strap farther up her shoulder. "I remember when my first washer and dryer were delivered. I literally did a happy dance in my laundry room. My husband thought I'd lost my mind."

Her obvious delight in the memory brought a smile to my face. "He must not have been the one hauling all the clothes back and forth to the laundromat."

Gertrude gave a rueful smile. "You're right about that. Will they be delivered soon?"

"I have to pick them up myself. They're used. I found them online and drove out to see them this morning. They're in perfect condition, so I bought them on the spot. Now I just need to wrangle a truck so I can pick them up later today. You don't happen to have one, do you?"

"No, but I have connections." Gertrude plucked her phone from her purse. "I'm sure I know someone who can help." She paused and peered at me. "I can't tell you how happy I am to see you putting down some roots here. I was afraid we might have scared you off, but if you're buying large appliances, that's a sure sign you plan to stick around. I'm glad." She flashed a quick smile. "So, when do you need the truck?"

I cleared my throat. I hadn't thought of my purchase that way until now. Apparently, I'd made a decision to stay put. Color me surprised. "Later this afternoon. I need to have them out of the seller's house by five. She's moving across the country and the movers are coming tomorrow."

"I'm on it. You go ahead and grade those papers," Gertrude said, glancing at the stack of tests on the table beside my coffee cup.

"Thanks. You're the best."

Gertrude waved away my thanks and then tapped away on her cell phone as she went to stand in line for coffee. The seventy-something woman's thumbs flew over the screen like a preteen as she rallied her troops in search of a truck.

I shook my head and turned back to the next test on the stack.

I finished two more before my phone rang. I answered it without thinking. "Hi."

"Hi, Sonya. Lucas here. How are you today?"

Lucas Morehead? My last bad date? I wished I hadn't answered. "Fine." I hesitated, then decided on the direct approach. "I didn't expect to hear from you again."

"Sorry I never messaged you. I've been busy. If you're free this Friday night, I'd like to take you out to dinner."

I frowned in confusion. "You said I had no sense of humor. Why would you want to go out with me again?" I placed the paper I finished grading face down and grabbed the next one.

"Not at all," Lucas said. "That was what Perry said about you. I happen to think you have a delightful sense of humor. Don't let it bother you. Perry's jokes often go over people's heads."

I pressed my lips together in irritation. Was that supposed to be an apology? "It wasn't that they went over my head. They were puns. My sister calls them 'groaners.' Your friend Perry happens to be under the mistaken impression that he's hilarious, but most of his jokes are older than I am." I breezed through grading the multiple-choice test—easy, since it had a perfect score —and drew a smiley face in the top corner. I wrote "Good Job!" just below it. I checked the student's name. Tyler. I should have guessed. That kid nearly always earned a perfect score on the social studies quizzes.

"I'm glad I decided to meet you. I couldn't believe you were as bad as Perry said you were, and I was right. You aren't."

"How charming," I said, letting a touch of sarcasm show through.

"That came out badly."

"You think so?" My irritation with the guy grew stronger. "I don't have time to chat right now. I have papers I hope to finish grading before my meeting with another teacher, and then I have errands to run." I glanced at the clock. "She'll be here shortly, so I need to get back to work."

"Nothing like putting things off until the last minute. Teachers have so much free time, I can't believe you need to work on the weekend."

The sudden bite of my anger took my breath away for an instant. "You really know how to sweet talk a woman." I hoped the sharpness of my tone sliced into him, but it was probably too much to ask. "I'll have you know that most teachers arrive around forty-five minutes before their students because they have responsibilities in the morning. I'm at work most days between seven and seven-fifteen. Lunch is always rushed since I only have thirty minutes and can't leave the school grounds. I create lesson plans. I'm an adviser for an after-school club that meets once a week. I'm the co-director of the school play that also meets after school. I frequently have bus duty. I meet with students to tutor them when they're struggling in my class. I attend most of the school events. Concerts. PTA events. Math night. The annual 5k Turkey Trot. The Fall Festival. The Spring Fling. This job doesn't end at three-thirty when the bell rings. I get sick and tired of ignorant people who think that teachers don't work hard."

"Huh," Lucas said, sounding surprised. "I didn't realize you worked such a long day, but you have to admit, you get three months off in the summer."

"I get more like two months off in the summer, from mid-June to early August. Teachers continue to work for about a week following the students' last day of school. Plus, I start back in early August to get ready for my new students. I also teach summer school classes. Are you telling me you don't get vacation days at work? I could have sworn you said you usually take off the entire month of August so you can go to Italy."

"That's different. It's taken me five years to start earning a month's worth of vacation days each year."

"And I don't earn my vacation days?" I snapped back. "You probably make five times more than I do, and when I add in all the school events I attend, I doubt you put in more hours each week than I do."

He cleared his throat. "It all comes down to experience and education level. I happen to have an MBA…"

"And I happen to have a master's in education. Don't talk

down to me. I won't tolerate it." I glanced up and noticed a few people eavesdropping. *Fabulous*. "Don't get me wrong. I love my job. I love teaching. It just sticks in my craw when someone like you is dismissive about what I do."

"I'm sorry, babe. I didn't realize you felt so passionately about the subject."

I squeezed my eyes shut as I counted to three. "Don't call me babe. In fact, don't call me anything at all. We're done here."

"Whatever," he snapped back. "You're no prize."

"Goodbye, Lucas." I ended the call and then blocked his number.

Why were so many men complete jerks? Lianna was wrong; it wasn't that I was hung up on Max. It was that something had happened to the dating pool in the past five years. All the men I went out with had at least two significant flaws. Perry was pretentious and self-inflated. Lucas? He was a manipulative, over-privileged jerk. He had all the hallmarks of being emotionally abusive as well. I wouldn't go out with him again if someone paid me. The guy was toxic. I'd had no better luck when I'd been living in Philly.

Max made an unwanted appearance in my thoughts once again. Everything had been wonderful when we'd been together. We'd fallen hard and fast for each other. That was the happiest I'd ever been in my life—up until the moment Raven had burst our idyllic little bubble with her sharp accusations.

With a frustrated sigh, I grabbed the next ungraded paper and tried hard not to think about my disappointing dating life. I especially tried not to think about Max.

A couple of minutes later, a shadow fell across the page I was grading. When it didn't go away, I looked up into the expectant face of one of my students. Tyler—the history buff. I gave him a broad, welcoming smile. "Hi there, kiddo. What are you doing here?"

"I'm with my parents." He pointed them out across the room. "We just came from church."

The couple was watching us and waved hello. I waved back and noticed Gertrude sitting at a table wearing a satisfied expression as she texted.

"I saw you here and I thought you looked lonely, so I bought you this." Tyler held out a frosted cookie shaped like a jack-o-lantern.

My heart twisted in my chest. "That's so thoughtful. Thank you," I said, taking it. "Do you want to share it with me?"

Tyler glanced at his parents, but they were engrossed in a conversation. "Sure. Thanks."

I broke the bright orange cookie in half and handed a piece to him. The almond scent made my mouth water. This place really did have the best cookies.

Tyler gestured toward the papers I was grading. "Is that the social studies test?"

"Yep. I already graded yours."

"How did I do?"

I grinned at him. "Take a guess."

He grimaced. "I thought I might have missed the extra credit one."

"You thought wrong. Your test was perfect, as usual."

He grinned, showing off bits of orange frosting stuck between his teeth. I sipped my latte to wash away any similar evidence. "Thank your parents for me. I'm sorry. I'd ask you to join me, but I really need to finish grading the rest of these."

"See you tomorrow then," Tyler said. He darted between the tables back to his family.

Five quizzes to go. I glanced at my watch. Tykera was already late. Would I be able to finish the rest? Lucas had been right. I should have graded these yesterday rather than waiting until the last minute. But I hadn't. Instead, I'd gone to Max's apartment in Pittsburgh to tutor Emma so no one would see me in public with him and remember the scandal. Then I'd had to stay and have dinner with him.

Then I'd had to kiss him.

I dropped my forehead to my hand.

I was such a fool.

Focus. I needed to stay on task and finish grading these.

The moment I finished the final test, another shadow crossed my table. This one was larger than the last.

"Got one," Gertrude crowed.

"A truck?"

"A truck. It belongs to Courtney's brother, Kincaid. She said she'll meet you with it at your place later today."

I beamed up at her. "You're a lifesaver."

Tykera Warren came to stand next to Gertrude.

"Tykera. Thanks for meeting me. This is my friend, Gertrude Rachesky. Gertrude, this is Tykera Warren. She's also a teacher. I'm co-directing the fifth-grade musical with her."

Gertrude held out her hand. "Pleased to meet you, Tykera. I don't want to keep you from your meeting. Does two o'clock work for you, Sonya?"

I glanced at the wall clock. It was a little after twelve-thirty now, so I should have plenty of time. "Yes. And tell her thanks."

"Ta for now," Gertrude said, waggling her fingers in a goodbye as she left.

Tykera pulled out the chair opposite me and dropped into it. "I'm sorry I'm late. I don't know what's been wrong with me lately. Do you think it could be the pregnancy, or have I come down with some bug? It seems like I'm exhausted all the time." She took a long sip from her cup. "It's probably because I stopped drinking caffeine. This herbal tea isn't doing it for me."

I peered into Tykera's face a bit more closely and noted the worn expression and the shadows under her eyes. Was her pregnancy taking a toll? "I'm sorry you aren't feeling well. You're usually so full of energy. Have you asked your doctor?"

"I have an appointment tomorrow."

"With luck, she'll be able to help. If you like, I can put together a rehearsal schedule by myself and email it to you for your input."

"That's all right," Tykera said with a shrug. "I'll be okay. Besides, I'm already here." She took another sip of her tea and pulled out her tablet.

We reviewed the school's calendar of events, checked our personal schedules, and finalized a rehearsal timetable.

"With the show less than two months away, we don't have much wiggle room here," I said. "Everything needs to go smoothly."

Tykera sighed. "I know, but you can see from the schedule that other groups already reserved the spaces we need after Thanksgiving, so there's no changing it now. We have to have the show the Friday before Thanksgiving break or we can't have it this year. At least we're doing a short musical. The runtime for the performance should be only about forty minutes."

I peered at my now heavily booked calendar. "What about everything else? We have the rehearsals scheduled, but we still need to figure out sets and costumes and tickets and—"

"No worries," Tykera interrupted. "Congratulate me. I found a student in the theater program at Sweetwater University who wants to be our producer. She can handle all that stuff. One of her professors already agreed to supervise her and provide backup."

Relief flooded me. "You should have led with that," I said, relaxing in my chair. "That's excellent news."

Tykera gave a wry smile. "You're right. I should have. I'm not firing on all cylinders these days. The student's name is Prisha Nathanson. She's excited about the opportunity." Tykera handed me a sheet of paper. "She compiled this list of parent volunteers who agreed to head the committees for the props, sets, and costumes. She says she'll get everything organized."

"You and Prisha have my everlasting gratitude," I said. "Now I'm not as worried about this tight timeline. Having a producer will free us up."

"My thoughts exactly," Tykera said.

By the time I left the coffee shop at one-thirty, Tykera and I had a solid plan in place. The rest of my day could be devoted to picking up my new-to-me washer and dryer and setting them up.

I smiled to myself. With luck, I'd be doing a load of laundry tonight in the comfort of my own home.

As I headed back to my house to meet Courtney, I briefly imagined how happy Max would be about my appliance purchase. When we'd lived together, we'd always hauled our baskets of clothes to and from our building's laundry room together. We'd said over and over that we'd make sure our next apartment had a washer and dryer in the unit.

I shook my head, clearing the memory away. Those days were behind me, so it was best not to dwell on them—or on Max, either. Even if the man still made my toes curl when we kissed.

13

POINTED QUESTIONS

Max

The next morning, Emma and I waited in the drop-off line. After a week of following our new daily routine, I was getting the hang of how things worked at the school.

As I inched my car closer to the front of the line, I spotted a blonde-haired woman with her back to me.

Sonya.

From what I could tell, she was supervising the drop-off line. As each kid exited a car, she greeted them, and when necessary, offered assistance.

As soon as the car in front of me moved forward, I closed the distance. In another minute, I'd be face-to-face with her.

The moment I pulled to a stop next to Sonya, Emma gave me a quick wave goodbye from the back seat and scrambled out of the car. As she shut the car door behind her, she only seemed to have eyes for Sonya. Not that I could blame her. I could hardly look away myself.

Sonya looked picture-perfect in her bright blue fall coat and matching hat. She didn't seem to notice me. She kept all her attention focused on Emma. They chatted briefly and then Emma headed for the front door. Sonya didn't even meet my eyes as she waved my car forward.

As I eased away from the curb, I felt oddly forlorn. It was all a bit of a letdown.

For the rest of the day, my thoughts kept drifting back to her. To that kiss we'd shared on Saturday evening. To the way she'd pointedly ignored me this morning.

She'd kissed me exactly the way I'd hoped she would. The way I'd imagined, over and over. That woman had graced dozens of my dreams these past five years, but ever since I'd walked into her classroom, hardly a night had gone by where she hadn't made an appearance.

That was strange on its own. I didn't often remember my dreams, but the ones featuring Sonya managed to stick with me. They weren't all erotic, either. Some were downright mundane. For some reason, those were the ones that haunted me the most. Dreams of standing on a beach together or holding hands on the sofa. Dreams that left me with a lingering sense of longing.

Later that afternoon I pulled up to the Zerkowski house to pick up Emma. Last week, I'd always had to knock on the door to let her know I was there, but today she was waiting for me on the front porch. The moment she spotted me, she darted for the car.

"Hey, kiddo," I greeted her through the open window. "Is everything okay?"

Emma ignored me as she yanked open the back door and tossed her backpack onto the seat. Then she opened the front door and sat next to me without a word.

"Buckle up," I said when she didn't move.

She reached over her shoulder and yanked on the seatbelt, causing it to lock up. She jerked on it a couple more times with mounting frustration. "What's wrong with this stupid thing?"

"It's designed to lock up when it's jerked like that, so you don't go flying into the dashboard when the car comes to a sudden stop. Pull it gently."

She let out a long-suffering sigh but did as I asked, managing to latch the seatbelt this time. "I knew that," she grumbled.

"I know you did. I think you might be having a bad day. Do you want to talk about it?" I pulled away from the house.

"No," she said, her lower lip jutting out, "but that therapist you make me see says I need to talk to you about my feelings or you won't know what's wrong."

"She's right."

Emma crossed her legs, jamming her shoes up under her knees crisscross style on my leather seats. I decided to let it go, this one time. At least her shoes looked relatively clean.

"It's Mrs. Zerkowski."

I lifted my foot off the gas pedal. "Do I need to go back and have a talk with her?"

"No!" Emma's eyes filled with panic. "It's nothing like that. She didn't do anything wrong. It's just—" She turned to face the passenger window, and I had the distinct impression she was trying not to cry. "Being there makes me miss my mom *so much*. Mrs. Z always has a snack after school. Cookies or chips or something like that. Mom used to have a snack ready too, but she always gave me fruit or hummus or something healthy. It's weird now. You know? It's like Mrs. Z both reminds me of her and doesn't, all at the same time. It's confusing."

I wasn't sure how to respond. I had the feeling there were tons of wrong things to say right now. "Do you like Mrs. Z?"

"Definitely. She's nice. She just isn't Mom. You know?"

I knew. I suddenly found my footing here. I'd been in exactly the same position years ago. "No one will ever replace your mom. There's enough room in your heart to let other people in, but there will always be that special place just for Hailey."

She stared down at her crossed legs. "It's weird to think you knew her as Hailey. That you've known her since you were born." She faced me. "Just like me."

"Since we were six years apart, your mom practiced her parenting skills on me. When she was your age, I was only five. I

99

remember coming home from kindergarten and Hailey giving me apple slices or melon balls that Mom had left for us in the refrigerator." I pulled onto Ohio River Boulevard, heading toward downtown Pittsburgh. I could catch occasional glimpses of the Ohio River outside Emma's window.

"I guess that's where Mom learned it."

"Your grandma always gave us fresh fruits and vegetables whenever possible. There was a place in Wexford where we'd go pick strawberries every June."

Emma's expression brightened a little. "You did that too? Mom took me there every year. I really loved it." She turned her face away from me again and looked out the window at the trees whipping past.

"How about we go next spring? We could continue the tradition together."

Emma seemed to relax into the leather seat. "I'd like that," she said. She turned to face me. "You could invite someone to come with us if you wanted. That way we'd have even more strawberries."

"Do you want to bring Marley?"

Emma shook her head. "She's allergic to strawberries. I was thinking you could invite your girlfriend." Her gaze flickered toward me as she faked nonchalance. "You do *have* a girlfriend, don't you? I mean, you don't have to stop seeing her just because I'm living with you now. The only woman who's come to your apartment in the past month is Miss Gambit."

I tightened my grip on the steering wheel as I changed lanes. "I don't happen to be dating anyone right now."

"Oh." Emma rubbed her lower lip with her thumb, just like Hailey used to do when she was thinking hard. I couldn't help smiling at the memory. That is until Emma spoke again. "Do you think you'll ever get married?"

I shot her a sidelong glance. "Since I'm not seeing anyone, that's kind of tough to do." When I saw Emma's forlorn expression, I added, "But, I always assumed I'd get married once I found the right person." The problem was that I'd met her five years ago, and now she didn't want to have anything to do with me.

Where had that thought come from? I barely registered the satisfied smile that slid over Emma's face. I was too busy trying to understand this rush of emotion. Was I still completely hung up on Essie—Sonya?

Having her walk out on me five years ago had been devastating, but I'd given her the space she'd asked for. I'd never guessed at the time that she'd be able to disappear from my life so completely.

What if losing her was what I'd deserved? I hadn't protected her when the maelstrom had hit, and that had ended up being the worst failure of my life. I'd been overwhelmed by my father's illness and had completely disconnected from the world for three days. Three brutal days that left Sonya running from reporters and rabid fans, facing down her own father, and trying to deal with all those questions and personal attacks—alone. When it came to disconnecting from everything, I couldn't have had worse timing.

"Miss Gambit is on front-door duty this week," Emma said. "I was thinking I might bring her a treat tomorrow. Something to keep her hands warm."

I glanced at her, but she looked completely innocent. I wasn't sure I trusted that look but decided her request seemed simple enough. "Why don't we stop by the Starbucks drive-through tomorrow morning and pick up her favorite coffee?" I suggested. "A skinny vanilla latte."

Emma's eyes narrowed. "How do you know what her favorite coffee is?"

I froze as I scrambled for a plausible explanation. "I saw her empty coffee cup on our kitchen counter last Saturday. It had SVL on the side. That means skinny vanilla latte. You knew I used to be a barista, right?"

"What's a barista?"

"Someone who prepares coffee and other drinks at Starbucks."

"Oh, that's right! That's so cool! So, you know the codes they write on the cups?"

"I do. But don't you think your Uncle Ford's job is way cooler? He makes movies. And your Uncle Sean is a stuntman."

"Yeah, I know. And Uncle Sin is a surgeon. But I never get to see any of them work. I love watching the baristas make those fancy coffees. Will you make me one of those frozen lattes with whipped cream on top when we get home?"

I cocked one eyebrow at her. "I might be new to this parenting thing, but even I know better than to give an eleven-year-old coffee in the evening. You'd be awake all night."

"Pooh."

"I'll make you a cup tomorrow morning, how's that?" I conceded.

"Better. But we'll still stop to get a cup for Miss Gambit, right? That way it will be hot when I give it to her."

"Will do. Anything for you, Emma, my love."

I found myself smiling as I imagined Sonya's surprise when Emma handed her that latte tomorrow morning, and I was still smiling as I pulled into the parking garage.

14

ONE WEEK OF FRONT-DOOR DUTY

SONYA

The next morning was another chilly one. I kept my hands tucked in the pockets of my bright blue jacket as I watched the line of cars approaching the drop-off point in front of the school. Max Ross's BMW moved forward a few feet at a time, but I was careful not to make eye contact with him. It was hard enough knowing he was only a few yards away from me.

When his car stopped between the two orange cones, the rear passenger door flew open, and Emma scooted out. She shouldered her backpack and reached back inside the car through the open front window. Her uncle handed her something.

As Emma turned and grinned at me, I spotted the Starbucks cup in her hand. Wasn't that just like Max to treat his niece to a cup of hot chocolate before school? Five years ago, when we'd been a couple, he'd always brought a cup of decaf coffee home to me after his shift.

Emma stopped and held the cup out to me. Her grin lightened my heart.

"What do you have there?" I asked.

"It's for you. A skinny vanilla latte." I must have looked

surprised because Emma chuckled. "Uncle Max read SVL on the side of your cup and knew you liked them."

"They're my favorite." Maybe he really read it on the cup, but I bet he simply remembered since he'd brought so many home for me. "Let your uncle know I said thank you. He really shouldn't have." I hesitated. "Better yet, I'll give him a call tonight and speak to him myself." I needed to tell him he shouldn't be doing things like this. Even so, I wrapped both hands around the cup, enjoying its warmth in the crisp morning air.

Emma grinned as she turned away.

"Don't forget, you need to stay after school today for your audition," I reminded her.

"I'll be there," Emma said, not bothering to turn around.

Later that day, I moved silently down the hallway in my comfy, low-heeled shoes. Since I stood all day long, I bought my shoes with an eye toward comfort, not fashion, although shoes that were both pretty and comfortable were always a nice bonus. The black ones I wore today were both. I felt like I'd hit the lottery when I found them on the sale rack at DSW.

Tykera's classroom was close to the multipurpose room. As I approached, I spotted the rows of desks and haphazardly placed chairs. The exodus following the end-of-day bell must have been chaotic.

When I entered the room, I spotted Tykera sitting slumped in her chair at her desk. The woman looked completely exhausted.

"You okay?" I asked.

"I'll live. I hope. Pregnancy isn't for the weak-willed."

"You look like you could use a nap," I said as I started straightening up and pushing chairs back in place.

"I'll get a second wind in a few minutes, then I'll be okay." Tykera moved to stand. "You don't need to do that."

I waved away her help. "No worries. Sit. You need your rest."

Tykera didn't need to be told twice and flopped back into her chair.

Emma knocked on the door. "Are you ready for me?"

"Come on in," Tykera said, her voice brightening considerably. I could tell she was forcing the cheerful tone, though. "Did you prepare a scene for the audition, or would you prefer to read the one we provided everyone?"

"If it's okay with you, I'll do something from the show I was in last summer," Emma said.

"That sounds perfect." Tykera's encouraging smile could put anyone at ease. "Relax and have fun."

Emma took a breath and then immediately started performing her audition piece. It was as though she transformed into a completely different person. I didn't recognize what show it was from, but Emma did an amazing job. Halfway through, it was obvious Emma would excel in any of the roles we could cast her in.

When she finished the scene, Tykera and I applauded enthusiastically.

"That was wonderful," Tykera said.

"It certainly was. Thank you, Emma," I added.

Tykera stood. "We need to get to the auditorium to relieve Principal Goodfriend so she can get to her meeting. Mrs. Gambit and I plan to announce the understudies tomorrow, so you won't have long to wait."

"Thanks," Emma said and hurried away.

"Too bad we already announced the leads," Tykera said as soon as Emma was out of earshot.

"I was thinking the same thing. I'm glad she'll still be a part of the show, though."

Later that night, I stared at Max's contact information on my phone, trying to work up the courage to call him. I didn't like the idea of initiating contact, but if I didn't, he might send in another of those coffees with Emma, and that simply wouldn't do.

It was time to set him straight regarding gifts—especially at school. That cup of coffee had been over the line.

I closed my eyes and pressed the call button on my phone.

"Hello?" he answered.

"Hi. It's me."

"Sonya?" Max said, his voice full of surprise. "To what do I owe the pleasure?"

"I wanted to thank you for the coffee. You really shouldn't have."

"I was glad to do it. Emma wanted to get you something to keep your hands warm, so coffee seemed like a good choice"

"Emma?" That threw me off my stride. I'd assumed the drink had been Max's idea.

"She's always looking out for the people she cares about. She reminds me of her mother that way."

I swallowed. I wasn't sure how to proceed, and the silence stretched between us.

"Did I say something wrong?" Max asked.

"No. It's just that I called to ask you not to bring me any more coffee, but now that I know it was Emma's idea, I'm not sure what to do. My students give me little things from time to time, of course, but I thought—"

"You thought it was from me." He paused. "I guess it's more traditional to bring the teacher an apple, is that it?"

I laughed. "I guess so. I remember giving one to my first-grade teacher."

"Message received. No more coffee."

"Thanks." I waited a beat. "Did Emma tell you she auditioned today to be an understudy in the school play?"

"She mentioned it. How did she do?"

"She was wonderful. I only wish she'd been able to audition before we'd assigned all the parts. She'll be the understudy to the lead."

"Did you tell her yet?"

"We'll let her know tomorrow at rehearsal. Mum's the word."

"Got it. Mum."

The next morning, Emma climbed out of the BMW clutching a brown paper lunch bag. As she approached, I noticed her bag was decorated with an outline of a smiling orange flower in a pot. She grinned as she handed the bag to me. "This is for you. A healthy treat. Also, I wanted to let you know I had fun at rehearsal yesterday."

As I accepted the bag, I could tell it held something small, round, and solid. I peeked inside and couldn't help grinning when I spotted the shiny red apple.

"An apple for the teacher? How did you know I was hungry?" I plucked it from the bag and bit into it. A spray of apple juice squirted out the corner of my mouth.

Emma gave me a pert smile and headed inside.

I realized this particular gift was most definitely from Max, which lifted my spirits. It had our conversation from last night written all over it. I glanced up to look for him, and our eyes immediately locked. He stood at his open car door at the front of the drop-off line. After a moment that probably lasted only a heartbeat too long, he gave me a jaunty wave, jumped into his car, and drove away, freeing up the cars behind him.

The mom driving the minivan that pulled into his vacated spot glared at me. Yeah, that little exchange had definitely lasted too long.

On Thursday, Emma climbed out of Max's BMW clutching a bouquet of white chrysanthemums. They were stunning.

I glanced toward the line of cars to find Max watching me again. At least he didn't climb out of the car this time. I nodded my thanks, and he gave me another casual wave as he drove off. Should I call him again to put a stop to this? Not that it had helped last time. I had to give the man credit. He certainly was determined.

"Thanks for letting me be the understudy for Crystal's part," Emma was saying.

I dragged my attention back to the girl. "You earned it. Mrs. Warren and I were impressed with your audition."

Marley stepped forward from where she'd been waiting near the school's front entrance. "Hi, Miss Gambit. Emma, can you bring some money tomorrow so we can go to the School Supply

Shop before school starts? I want to buy some of those Halloween erasers."

The pair headed through the doors, their heads nearly touching as they kept talking.

On Friday, Emma seemed a bit more subdued as she climbed out of the car. She came directly over to me. This time, she carried a larger brown paper shopping bag with twine handles. "Good morning, Miss Gambit," she said as she passed me the bag.

"What's this?" I glanced into the shopping bag. Inside was a small white bakery bag and a larger flat rectangle in wrapping paper that was covered with images from the children's book Where the Wild Things Are.

"We got you one thing for the classroom, and one thing just for you."

"Thank you," I said.

Marley spotted Emma and broke into a run.

"Walk, Marley," I cautioned.

Marley abruptly slowed. "Yes, ma'am."

I set the bag by my feet. "You two should go inside. I just felt a raindrop."

Emma frowned as she glanced up at the sky.

"We need to go to the Spirit Shop," Marley said.

Emma hesitated, but when a raindrop hit her cheek, she said, "Let's go."

Marley took her by the arm and pulled her into the flow of kids entering the school.

I watched them leave. By the time I glanced back out at the parking lot, I didn't see Max's car. I felt a twinge of disappointment to realize I'd missed seeing him today.

Fortunately, the rain decided not to make good on its threats. Five minutes later, the last car drove away. I picked up the gift bag and let it swing from my arm as I collected the orange cones marking the drop-off zone and stowed them near the main entrance.

I surveyed the parking lot, but no one was in sight. All the parents had left, and all the students and teachers were in their classrooms. My own teacher's aide was handling my classroom right now, so I had a moment to myself before I needed to go inside.

I finally let myself examine my gifts.

First, I opened the white bakery bag. I let out a little "Oh," of surprise when I found a chocolate-filled croissant inside. Just like the ones Max had once fed me in bed. I blushed at the memory of him licking croissant flakes off my naked breasts.

I closed the little bag, wanting to quell the rush of emotion it brought, and turned my attention to the flat, square package. It was slightly smaller than one of those old-style LP record albums. The moment I touched it, I realized it must be a book—or perhaps a calendar.

I tore open the wrapping paper.

I stilled when I saw what I held—a copy of Where the Wild Things Are. My breathing hitched in my throat.

Max used to quote lines from this book. He'd said his big sister had read it to him over and over when he'd been little.

I opened it and noticed his bold handwriting on the title page. It read, "Here's hoping that Miss Gambit's students never begin a wild rumpus in her classroom. —Max, King of the Wild Things."

"What game are you playing?" I murmured to myself. I could still remember how he'd loved that book, claiming it was written about him. He'd quote lines from it, pulling me into his arms, kissing me senseless. He'd claimed we were one another's wild things. He'd said I was untamable—until he finally captured my heart.

A heart that now ached with loss.

15

THE OLD HOMESTEAD

Max

The sun was setting later that evening as I drove through Sewickley. "After we're done at your Grampa Don's house, we'll head home."

Emma shrugged.

I wasn't sure if taking her to see that therapist yesterday had been a good idea after all. Emma had been moody ever since. The therapist warned me that might happen. He had explained that finally talking about some of the things bothering her could dredge up some buried emotions, but that once she'd dealt with them, I'd see steady improvement.

In other words, she'd probably get worse before she got better.

I pulled up the long driveway leading to my dad's house up in Sewickley Heights. It backed up to the golf course and had spectacular views of the manicured emerald lawn surrounded by the richly hued autumn forest.

I could almost feel Hailey's presence welcoming us—as though she approved of us coming here today. I probably should have brought Emma to see her Grampa sooner. She'd always loved it here.

I knocked on the door and then walked on in with Emma right behind me. "Hi, Dad, we're here," I called out.

He hurried into the foyer carrying a laundry basket filled with neatly folded clothes that he set on the floor. He held his arms out. "I need a hug from my best grandchild," he demanded.

"I'm your only grandchild," Emma said, stepping into his embrace.

"Why have more, once perfection has been achieved?" Dad said, holding her tightly.

Her satisfied smirk looked just like Hailey's.

Dad held her at arm's length, looking into her eyes. "Your uncle tells me you want to pick through your mom's old costumes to find something to wear for Halloween."

"That's okay, right?" she glanced up at me, giving me a hopeful look.

"Of course, it is. Just remember, not all her costumes are appropriate for someone your age. Once you choose something, you need to run it past me."

Emma's face pinched into a scowl. "As if I'd go dressed as a sexy witch. Give me a break, Grampa Don."

I grinned. Such a smart-aleck.

My dad said, "Exactly what I wanted to hear. Speaking of breaks, can you run this basket up to my bedroom and give my poor old knees a rest?"

"No problem." Emma picked it up and bounded up the stairs.

I glanced at Dad's knees and raised an eyebrow. He shrugged. "They're fine. Sending her upstairs gives us a chance to talk."

He led the way to the kitchen. As soon as we stepped through the doorway, he asked, "She doing okay?"

I waggled my hand from side to side. "She saw her therapist yesterday. I think talking about everything was hard on her. She's been a little off-kilter today."

"When do you go back?"

"Next week." I paused. "I also wanted you to know I'm going

to cut back on my work hours for a while longer. I need to get more involved in Emma's life."

Dad nodded. "That's a good idea. Thanks for stepping up with the whole guardianship thing. You're doing a great job." He opened the refrigerator. "What do you want to drink? Beer? Juice? Wine?"

"I'll have water."

Dad poured me a glass from the pitcher in the refrigerator. "I need to talk to you about the soundtrack for *Ghost*," he said as he handed me the glass. "I've been going back and forth with Ford on this, and we just don't see eye to eye."

"It's his movie, Dad. You agreed to give him complete creative control if he'd make the film with us. Do you really want to pick this fight?"

"Believe me, what I'm suggesting is in everyone's best interests. I think he should choose existing pop music and get the rights to use it in the film, but he's set on the idea of having an original soundtrack, including one big breakout hit. I keep telling him he needs to go with what works. All the other superhero movies use old hits. He should too. But Ford has it in his head that this is one of the ways to differentiate Ghost from the rest of the pack."

I nodded slowly as I considered Ford's vision. "I think it sounds like a great idea. I really don't see the problem."

"He wants to go with someone *new*."

"Then he should. Listen. If it doesn't work out, the worst that can happen is that we'll have to rethink the music."

Dad scowled at me. "Don't dismiss my concerns. A bad soundtrack could be catastrophic. The scenarios range from tanking the movie to delaying its release while we find someone new to score it."

I shot my father a skeptical look. "Ford won't let the score tank the movie. He'll be on top of things. This isn't his first rodeo. You're worrying too much."

Dad opened his mouth to say something and then stopped. He

dragged his hand down his face as he let out a frustrated sigh. "Do me a favor and talk to Ford about this. His idea has a lot of risks."

I shrugged. "I can do that. It doesn't mean I'll try to change his mind, though."

"Just talk to him."

Emma came in. She now wore a faded black Nirvana t-shirt that had seen better days, and her long hair hung forward, hiding her face.

That shirt looked extremely familiar. I recognized it as Hailey's. She'd worn it constantly as a teenager. I'd never forget that black shirt with the weird rainbow splash of colors and the seahorses. Those were seahorses, right? Or snake skeletons? Or both? I'd never been able to decide.

Kurt Cobain had died about a year after my mom had died, and it had nearly destroyed Hailey. She'd taken to wearing that t-shirt every day and listening to Nirvana while she moped around the house.

Emma looked exactly like her right now.

That therapist had been right. Emma had gotten worse. I just hoped he was right about the getting better part.

"Did you find that with your mom's stuff?" Dad asked. "I haven't seen that shirt in years. Your mom cried when she splashed bleach on it. You're welcome to keep it if you want."

I scowled at him. The last thing I wanted was for Emma to mope around even more.

Dad seemed oblivious to my annoyance. "It's nice for you to have something your mom cared about so much."

Emma's eyes brightened with some deep emotion. "Really? You don't mind?"

"Of course not." Dad rested his hand on her shoulder. "You have more right to it than anyone."

"I've never listened to Nirvana," Emma confessed.

"It's good stuff," I said. "It's different from what you usually listen to, but I think you'll like it."

It would certainly suit her mood.

"Did you find a costume?" Dad asked.

Emma shrugged. "I found a cool corpse bride one."

Dad nodded approvingly. "I remember that one. Creepy. Your mom made her face all white and then used black and gray makeup to make her eyes look like empty sockets."

"Cool." Emma grinned.

"I have an old photo I can show you," I offered.

"You can also find makeup tutorials on YouTube," Dad suggested. "I'll send you a link for one of the makeup artists from a film I did a few years ago. I'm pretty sure she had some skeleton makeup videos posted."

Emma nodded, looking a bit more enthusiastic than she had a moment earlier. "I'll do that. Thanks, Grampa Don."

Wonder of wonders, she actually looked a bit more cheerful. Maybe this trip to see Grampa had been a good idea after all.

16

HALLOWEEN PREPARATIONS

MAX

The following Monday evening, I pulled into the driveway of the Zerkowski house. Cemetery headstones filled the front lawn, and a partial skeleton hung from the tree near the door. Halloween wasn't for another three weeks, but the decorations were already in place.

When Emma didn't come out right away, I turned off the engine and headed to the front door. At least this was an improvement from last week when Emma had nearly bolted for my car.

I stepped onto the front porch and noticed the rocking chair held a gruesome-looking, desiccated inhabitant. Its head drooped at an awkward angle.

Creepy. All this place needed was one of those fog machines.

I rang the bell and a witch cackled instead of the door chime that usually played. Nice touch.

I waited.

And waited.

I pressed the button again, and this time a ghost wailed. Finally, I heard feet thumping down the staircase. The door swung open revealing Emma and Marley wearing—were those red and green monstrosities elf costumes?

I crossed my arms. "What are you two doing?"

"We're elves," Emma shot back. "Isn't it obvious?"

"It's October."

Emma rolled her eyes. "They're for *Halloween*. Did you forget it's coming up?"

I grinned and then rolled my eyes right back at her. "How could I when you keep changing your mind about what costume you plan to wear? Does this mean you aren't planning to go as a corpse bride?"

"This is my pre-Halloween costume," she said primly. "That's my Halloween costume."

"Of course." I scanned her outfit. "Do you plan to wear that to the cooking class tonight?"

Emma's eyes widened. "I totally forgot about it. I meant to call to see if I can stay for dinner. Marley says all the food will be black or orange."

I grimaced. "I can't say that sounds particularly appetizing. What's on the menu?"

Renee Zerkowski stepped out of the kitchen, wiping her hands on a dishcloth. "Sweet potatoes, mangos, oranges, and black chicken ravioli. The pasta's made with squid ink. Plus, a special dessert. It's a secret. Dinner's nearly ready. Want to join us?"

"It's nice of you to invite me, but I'm heading to my cooking class now."

"Is it okay if I stay and eat here?" Emma asked, spearing me with her soulful, pleading eyes.

I immediately folded. "Absolutely. I'll stop by after I'm done to pick you up."

"You're welcome to join us for Beggar's Night on the 31st," Renee told him. "I'm making a big pot of chili for everyone. Some of Marley and Emma's classmates will be joining them. The dads are taking the kids around. Steve plans to offer a variety of adult beverages for your trick-or-treating pleasure, or you can bring your own. I'll stay home and hand out candy."

"Sounds like fun. I'll take you up on that." I must be getting domesticated. For Halloween last year, I'd gone to a costume party at a bar and hadn't made it home until after four A.M. This year would be dramatically different.

The sun was dipping low in the sky as I drove down Ford's street. Most of the houses I passed wore their grotesque and tattered Halloween glory. One front lawn looked as though it had been overtaken by a swarm of enormous spiders.

When I pulled to a stop in front of Ford's house, I spotted my brother striding down the flagstone path.

"*Hola, hermano*," I called out to him. "How was Mexico?"

"*Bueno*," Ford said as he opened the passenger door and climbed in. "Where's my favorite niece?"

"She's hanging with Marley tonight, prepping for Halloween."

"Crap. I totally forgot to warn Mara that it's a big thing in this town." He pulled out his phone and sent a text. "Kids descend on Sewickley in droves."

"I bet she already knows. After all, she owns a comic book shop."

He blinked at me, then grinned. "I guess she probably does. I keep forgetting she's lived here for two years."

"There are decorations everywhere. It'd be hard not to notice." I pulled away from the curb.

Ford took note of the elaborate displays along the street and seemed surprised. "So there are. I must have missed them when I drove back from the airport last night. When I woke up, I headed straight for my home office in the attic. I barely left it all day."

"Did you pin down your locations for the movie?"

"I did." Ford tucked his phone into his jacket pocket. "Wendy's working on the film schedule. That woman's an organizational genius."

I'd met Wendy a couple of years ago. She'd been Ford's assistant for ages now. "You struck gold when you hired her."

"Who'd have thought a stay-at-home mom who'd been out of the workforce for twenty years would be so talented?" he mused. "It turns out raising five kids and running a household takes major organizational skills. Mara already threatened to steal her from me. It's a good thing she's loyal."

"Speaking of Mara, Sonya told me her book club friends already figured out she's Essie, so there's no reason you can't go ahead and tell Mara. Just ask her not to mention it to anyone else."

"Thanks, man," Ford said, a slow smile crossing his face. "You have no idea how much that's been weighing on me. You just made my life a million times easier. Like I said, I hate keeping things from her."

"I get it." I flipped on my turn signal. "Secrets have a way of coming back to bite you in the ass, no matter how well-intentioned they are."

"Don't I know it."

I parked in the empty lot at Not a Yacht Club for our Monday night cooking class. As we stepped inside the quiet building, Ford spun off toward the restroom saying, "See you in a minute."

I pushed open the swinging door leading into the kitchen and spotted Conner.

"Good to see you, Max," Conner said, rising from his perch next to a stainless-steel counter. "Is Ford coming?"

"He'll be here in a minute," I said.

"Kincaid's running late," Conner said. "It'll just be the four of us tonight."

"Reed and Eric can't make it?" I asked.

"Reed's busy studying tonight. He has a biochemistry midterm tomorrow."

"And Eric?"

Conner looked grim. "He isn't feeling well. Reed told me the chemo is kicking his ass."

Reed's older brother had been diagnosed with stage four lung cancer a few months ago. He'd been coughing and thought he was suffering from allergies or a cold he couldn't shake. When it wouldn't clear up, his doctor sent him in for an x-ray. By the time they'd diagnosed cancer, the disease had already spread throughout his body. The poor guy had never smoked a day in his life.

"I'm sorry to hear it." I decided to stop by to visit the Pierce brothers over the weekend and see what I could do to help. Those two were on their own, and Reed probably had his hands full taking care of Eric.

Ford pushed through the kitchen door. "Hey, Conner. How's the restaurant business?"

"Booming. The construction crew is putting the final touches on our new river path."

"Your empire is growing," Ford said.

"Did you end up using those embedded glow stones in the walkway?" I asked.

"Sure did. The entire riverfront project cost us a pretty penny, but it'll be worth it. We'll have additional outdoor seating during the warm-weather months. The crew poured the asphalt and added the glow stones earlier today, but I haven't seen the path at night yet. Want to check it out when we take a break?"

"Absolutely," I said.

"I'm in," Ford added.

"Ready to get cooking?" Dante asked as he came into the room. He thumped a large, round wooden bucket onto the counter.

Conner crossed his arms and planted his feet wide. "Don't tell me you're putting us to work scrubbing floors tonight."

Dante smirked. "Actually, that isn't a bad idea. Keeping a kitchen clean is hard work, but I'll save that lesson for some other time. This, my friends, is a good old-fashioned ice cream maker. I have another one just like it that I borrowed for tonight, so you won't have to take turns making your ice cream. After you prepare the ingredients, I'll put the mixture in my blast freezer to firm it up and then," he pulled a tall silver cylinder from a nearby freezer and removed the lid, "you can pour it into this. Next, you'll fill the layer between the cylinder and the bucket with ice and salt. Once you turn it on, the electric ice cream maker will work its magic. The machine needs to run for about a half-hour. When it's done, your ice cream will be the consistency of soft serve. If you want it to get firmer, you can put it back in my blast freezer for a while."

Conner scowled. "Since I don't have a blast freezer at home, how am I supposed to ever make this again?"

"Just use your home freezer. It'll probably take an hour or so to freeze, but the result is the same," Dante said. "The one essential tool is the ice cream maker. You'll need it if you want to give your ice cream that smooth, creamy texture."

Ford sorted through the ingredients. "What's this?" He held up a package of powder that was blacker than night.

"Activated charcoal," Dante said. "That's what turns the coconut ice cream black. This particular kind is made from black coconut ash. The more you add, the blacker your ice cream gets, but it doesn't take very much."

I did a double-take. "Seriously? You're having us make black food? Is it a Halloween thing?" Had I stumbled onto some weird new Sewickley tradition?

"Why not?" Dante shrugged. "Halloween is coming up and I wanted to have us make something festive. It was either this or pasta made with squid ink."

I just stared at him. Maybe Dante and Renee Zerkowski should swap recipes.

"Is charcoal safe to eat?" Conner asked.

"This kind is." Dante patted a foil bag sitting on the counter. "This is food-grade activated charcoal. It's different from those briquettes you use to start a fire. Those things are loaded with toxic chemicals. Pure activated charcoal has lots of health benefits. It's even used in emergency rooms to treat certain types of accidental poisonings."

Dante opened the foil bag and used a spoon to dip out some of the powdery stuff. It was perfectly black. "As a warning, you shouldn't eat it if you're taking meds because it can stop them from working. Even birth control, so be careful who you make this for. Angelina says it binds with toxins and flushes them from your system. I was going to have Eric make his without the activated charcoal so it wouldn't mess with his chemo. I pick up some interesting facts, dating a doctor and all." He slapped his hands together. "Now, let's get cracking."

I read through the rest of the ingredients and was relieved to discover we were making Black Chocolate Coconut Ice Cream. "This actually sounds like it will be good," I said as I handed the recipe to my brother.

"How's Emma doing?" Ford asked. He read the first line of the recipe and then poured coconut milk into a measuring cup.

"She had a rough day about a week ago. We stopped at a shop in the Strip District that sold candles and she broke down. Started crying. It turned out to be a good thing, though. Got some of it out of her system. It seems to have helped."

"Have you taken her to a therapist yet?" Ford asked. "It'll help if she wants it to. If she doesn't, it won't."

"She's been a couple of times. She has another appointment this Friday. I think it's helping, but I'm not sure yet. Emma still seems kind of nervous about opening up to her." I poured the vanilla extract into the saucepan.

Ford swirled a spoon through the coconut milk, and the thread of brown liquid disappeared. "Tell her it's like having a conversation with a friend who gives the best advice."

"You've been to see one?"

"Sure. Doesn't everyone?" Ford asked with a laugh. "If they don't, they should."

I measured the activated charcoal and added it to the bowl, and then shook my head. "That is blacker than black."

"Don't forget the best part," Ford said, handing me the measuring cup with the cocoa powder.

"Forget chocolate? That'd be sacrilege." I dumped it in.

"Don't let it boil," Dante said. "As soon as everything's well-blended, we'll put it in the blast freezer."

"It looks like ours is ready," Ford said.

"Ours is done, too," Kincaid said.

I glanced up. "Hey, Kincaid. I didn't see you come in." The poor guy looked exhausted. Judging from the bags beneath his eyes, he hadn't gotten much sleep last night.

Dante grabbed both saucepans. "I'll bring these back in a few minutes. Grab one of the ice cream machines now and start setting it up. Just don't pour the ice in yet." He headed over to a large stainless-steel box that looked like an industrial freezer and set our saucepans inside, then adjusted the controls. "I don't actually want to freeze these—just chill them quickly. This won't take long."

It didn't take long for Ford to set up the ice cream maker on the floor. Once he plugged it in, I filled a bowl with ice from the restaurant's ice maker. By the time we had everything ready, Dante was back with our chilled saucepan of chocolate and coconut.

"Grab one of the cylinders from the freezer and pour this into it," Dante said. "Then make sure the lid is on securely so none of the saltwater gets into your ice cream and ruins it. Then set the cylinder in the ice cream maker and layer the ice and salt around it."

"Check," I said.

Once we added all the layers, I asked Dante, "What next?"

"Turn it on and wait for twenty to thirty minutes," he said. "You'll probably need to add more ice and salt in ten minutes or so."

"This sounds like the easy part," I said.

Soon, the ice cream makers were churning away.

Conner crossed his arms and stared at the machines. After a moment he said, "This is a lot like watching paint dry. Anyone want to check out my new glowing sidewalk while we wait?"

"Definitely," Ford said.

We all headed out the back door and into the night.

I grinned when I caught sight of Conner's new path. It really did glow. The pebbles embedded in the asphalt path gave off a soft blueish light, like a pale, glowing river. The trail skirted the rear of the restaurant's patio and disappeared into the trees.

I immediately stepped onto the surface. "It's like standing on the Milky Way," I said. "How did they do it?"

"First, they poured a normal asphalt path, and then they tossed the special glow-in-the-dark pebbles on top. After that, they went over the path with a big roller again to press the pebbles into the surface. Quick and easy. I just had to wait until tonight to see the full effect. During the day, they just look like white flecks."

"How many years will these chips keep working?" I asked.

"I picked a top-of-the-line product. They lose about one to two percent of their glow each year, so in twenty years, worst case scenario is that they'd be down to about 60 percent of what you see today."

"That's not bad. You could always add a new layer of asphalt and stones to freshen it up."

"My thoughts exactly. I'll probably need to redo the asphalt before then anyway."

I suddenly wanted to be the one to bring Sonya here. She'd love the idea of walking on a trail of stars. It was sort of like lassoing the moon, à la George Bailey in *It's a Wonderful Life*.

"You should bring Emma here after you pick her up tonight," Conner said. "I bet she'd love to see it."

"She would, but it'll be kind of late and she has to get up early for school. We'll stop by later this month. Maybe on Halloween after she goes trick-or-treating."

"Just listen to you. You're even starting to sound like a dad." Conner grinned as he gave me a friendly nudge on the arm. "Have you thought about adding a mom into the equation? Insta-family."

I crossed my arms over my chest and narrowed my eyes at him. "Somehow I don't think it's a good idea to marry someone simply to have some parenting help."

"Not what I meant," Conner said, raising his hands in surrender. "I'd be the last person to suggest you marry someone just to have a wife." He shot his brother a pointed look. "Or just because someone knocked up someone. That never works."

Kincaid turned an angry glare on his brother. "You just had to give me shit about Heather, didn't you?"

Conner shrugged. "What can I say, man? I'm only human. I told you she was bad news. At least you aren't gonna marry her anymore."

I glanced at Ford. "Did I miss something?" I murmured.

"A shitstorm," Ford said just as quietly. "Kincaid found out Heather lied about being pregnant."

"You know what? You're an asshole," Kincaid told his brother. "I'm going inside. It's time to add more ice to the machine." Kincaid spun on his heel and headed for the door.

Ford gave Conner a sidelong glance. "Knowing you, I'm surprised you held your tongue as long as you did. You aren't exactly tactful."

"Life's too short for bullshit," Conner said. He tilted his head up and stared at the stars above us. "He's better off waiting for the right person instead of settling for the person right in front of him. Heather is selfish, and a complete liar. She was never any good for him. I can't say I was surprised to find out she'd made up the story about being pregnant."

"Shut your mouth, Conner! I can still hear you!" Kincaid shouted from the door as he stepped inside.

I shook my head. "Damn. That must have hit him like a ton of bricks."

Conner let out a heavy sigh and kept staring at the stars. "That guy hates hearing, 'I told you so,'" he muttered.

"Who doesn't?" I asked with a snort.

Ford nudged me with his elbow to get my attention, then took a few steps away from Conner. I followed.

"What about you?" Ford asked. "What if the right person disappears from your life for years and then shows back up on your doorstep?"

I clenched my jaw. "I fail to see the parallel. She never lied to me."

He stared at me steadily. "I'm simply asking if the right woman is right in front of you."

I stared back in blank confusion. "You think she's the right woman for me? You've never even met her."

"Isn't it obvious? You've been hung up on her for five years. Now you finally have the chance to fix everything. The question is, what do you plan to do about it? Will you step up and admit your mistakes so the two of you can have a future together, or will you maintain the status quo?"

Was I that transparent? I wasn't sure if I liked having my brother echo my own thoughts.

17

ROUGH REHEARSAL

Sonya

Tuesday after school, I hurried to the school's multipurpose room. I might not know much about the theater, but I could already tell it wasn't the perfect space for a stage show. Even so, it was a lot better than what most elementary schools could offer.

The room served as the school's gymnasium when the bleachers were folded up against the wall as they were now. When they were open, the room could seat the entire student body. It also boasted a stage with an actual curtain and lights. The backstage area and wings were minuscule, but the fact that we had a stage was a huge bonus.

One of the room's negatives was apparent from the moment I walked through the door. "Get off the gymnastics equipment," I shouted.

Emma jumped off the balance beam, and Liam dropped from between the parallel bars and landed on the mat beneath it. Emma had braided her hair and wore a faded, vintage-looking black t-shirt with a bleach stain. Its rainbow-colored design looked familiar, but I couldn't remember where I'd seen it before. Was it a Nirvana t-shirt?

"I didn't get a turn!" Sean yelled.

"Then you won't get in trouble for being on the gymnastics equipment without permission," I called back to him. "You kids know the rules. We share this space with Mr. Klein, and we aren't supposed to touch any of the gym equipment when we have after-school rehearsals. Where's Mrs. Warren?"

Tykera Warren came into the big room, followed by a younger woman carrying two folding chairs. Tykera moved like a zombie creeping along on its last shreds of energy. "I'm here. I'm late."

"Sorry, Miss Gambit," one of the kids said.

"We forgot," Liam added.

"Don't forget again. I'm not joking about this," I said. "I don't want someone to get hurt. The next time I find someone using the gymnastics equipment without specific permission, I'll remove that person from the show. I don't care if you have the lead and it's the night before we open. You've all been warned."

Tykera wore a stricken expression. "That's my fault," she said. "I should have been keeping an eye on them. I stepped out to show Prisha where to find some chairs."

That wasn't like Tykera. She'd been a teacher for five years and knew better than to leave kids unsupervised. "No one was hurt," I said.

Tykera shook her head, clearly frustrated with herself. "I don't know what I was thinking."

I didn't recognize the younger woman standing next to Tykera. My curiosity must have shown.

"Oh," Tykera said. "I forgot to introduce you. This is Prisha. She's the student intern from Sweetwater University I mentioned. She'll be our producer and parent wrangler."

Prisha held out her hand. "I'm pleased to meet you," the petite woman said in precise, clipped tones. When she smiled, it lit up her face.

"I can't tell you how happy I am you'll be helping us with the show," I said, shaking her hand. "I've never been a co-director before. This is all new to me."

"I emailed the parent volunteers from the list Tykera sent me,"

Prisha said. "They know they should contact the committee heads or me with any questions rather than bothering the two of you. That should free you up to focus on directing the show. I'll be the main point of contact for all communication, and I'll run all major decisions past you."

"Sounds perfect," I said. "Having you manage all that is a huge relief."

"That's why I'm here," Prisha said. "Although I have to admit, it's intimidating to order around a group of parents. They were the ones telling me what to do just a couple of years ago." Prisha unfolded the two chairs she'd brought in and set them facing the stage. "These are for you."

Tykera immediately collapsed onto one.

I nodded at Prisha. "I know what you mean. All new teachers go through a similar adjustment."

Prisha handed us some papers. "Thanks for getting that prop list to me so quickly. I typed it up and these are your copies to keep. I need to leave now to kick off our first prop committee meeting. I plan to assign specific volunteers to track down items for the show. I'll meet with the costume committee in an hour and come up with a plan with them as well. I've also scheduled meetings with the set builders and stage crew for tomorrow." She glanced at her watch. "I'd better hurry or I'll be late."

I stared after her as she hurried for the exit. "I'm astounded. You found us a dynamo," I said.

"It was pure, dumb luck," Tykera admitted. "She pretty much fell into my lap."

"Chalk one up to good karma." I turned my attention to the students. "Okay, everyone," I called out. "It's time to start rehearsing. We're focusing on the pantomime scene today, so Mrs. Warren will be directing you."

Tykera spun to face me and grabbed my arm in panic. "I completely forgot we were doing this scene today."

My mouth dropped open, and then I snapped it shut. I'd only known Tykera since the beginning of the school year, but even so, forgetting something this important seemed completely out of character. "Can you wing it?"

Tykera's shoulders sagged. "I only have a vague idea of how I want this scene to work. I know I told you I had it covered, but I have baby brain. I'm a mess."

I took in Tykera's damp forehead and slumped posture. "Are you sure you're feeling okay? I'm worried about you."

Tykera shook her head. "Pregnancy has fried my brain. This fetus is sucking away every last ounce of energy and leaving me with nothing. How do women survive this?"

"I have no idea. You're the first pregnant person I've ever spent much time with. Have you asked your doctor?"

Tykera sighed. "She says I'll feel better and most of this brain fog will lift once I'm in my second trimester, but that's not for another three weeks."

I gripped the seat of my chair as the full import of Tykera's words sank in. We had less than six weeks until the show. My stomach somersaulted. How would we get through this?

I glanced at the kids sitting on the edge of the stage, restlessly swinging their feet and giggling. They wouldn't stay this calm much longer. We needed to get started. "Do you want me to take over running through the scene?" I offered. I immediately regretted my words. I had no idea how I'd stage it. Not even the slightest idea of how to begin.

A sudden welling of determination seemed to strengthen Tykera and stiffen her spine. "No. I got it covered."

I smiled tightly.

She visibly forced herself to her feet and then clapped her hands for attention. "Let's get this party started." The kids stopped fidgeting and focused on her.

"Imagine the scene," Tykera said, framing the stage with her outstretched hands. "Some of you will be tourists in Washington D.C., looking at all the sights. We'll have photos of landmarks projected on a screen behind you, and you'll be pointing at them and chatting with each other. Others will be workers, senators, or reporters. Crystal and Liam will be the main focus of the scene as they go sightseeing." Tykera glanced at me and lowered her voice. "That's as far as I got. I'd planned to pick out specific photos and have the pantomime reflect the images, but I forgot."

"I assume we'll have the Washington Monument, the White House, and the Jefferson and Lincoln memorials," I said. "Let's start with those for today. We scheduled another rehearsal for this scene the day after tomorrow. You can change it or add to it then."

Tykera heaved a sigh. "That works." She glanced up at the stage, biting at her dry bottom lip. "Don't worry. I got this."

She split the cast members into groups of three or five tourists and directed them on how to move across the stage. It was obvious Tykera's energy was nearly spent. Despite her brief flash of determination, she was practically dead on her feet and her focus was completely gone. After a half hour, she was speaking so softly that the kids could barely hear her when she tried to tell them what to do. I stayed next to her onstage and helped by repeating her directions, hoping she wasn't about to pass out.

When it became obvious we weren't making any progress, I murmured, "You're exhausted. Take a seat, and I'll review the upcoming rehearsal schedule with everyone."

Tykera smiled gratefully and wobbled toward the staircase at the side of the stage. I darted after her and helped her down the steps. As soon as we reached the folding chairs, she collapsed onto one. "I'm wiped out."

A loud thump on stage made me whirl around to see Paige scramble up from the stage floor. When Emma tucked one side of her faded black t-shirt into her jeans and did a cartwheel, I realized Paige must have just done one as well. Apparently, I couldn't take my eyes off these kids even for a second.

"Great rehearsal, everyone," I called out. "Emma and Paige, let's think of a way to incorporate your cartwheels into one of the scenes, but for now, I need you both to stop." I glanced at Tykera to get her opinion, but she'd closed her eyes and had missed everything.

I turned back to the students. "Come down off the stage and gather your things while I run through the schedule for the rest of the week with you."

Some kids jumped noisily from the stage, landing with loud thumps on the gym floor, while others took the stairs. Their rubber-soled shoes squeaked across the glossy floor like a stampede of mice as they rushed to the bleachers.

I spotted a group of parents waiting outside the door and waved them in to join us.

"Tomorrow and Wednesday, you'll meet in here to work on the music for the show with Mr. Wendel. You'll need to learn the lyrics by heart. On Thursday, we'll finish blocking the pantomime scene. Everyone with lines needs to memorize them. Don't put it off. Start now and add a few more lines each day. It won't be long before you know them all."

I spotted Max among the parents, and I suddenly got tongue-tied. Good thing I was done. "That's it. You can all go home now."

The swarm of kids grabbed their backpacks and rushed toward the door.

"Whose sweatshirt is this?" I called out as I picked up a gray, zip-front hoodie with a Pittsburgh Pirates logo.

"Mine," Liam called out. He ran back to take it from me. "Thanks."

As Max sauntered toward me, our eyes locked. I clutched my hands together and edged closer to Tykera.

Emma grabbed her things off the bleachers and joined him.

"You had a short rehearsal today," Max commented as they both reached us. "Did everything go okay?"

"The kids were a bit squirrelly," I said, not wanting to throw Tykera under the bus and tell him about our lack of any real progress. We couldn't afford more wasted days like today.

"It was fun," Emma said. "We were doing cartwheels."

"I saw. You're full of energy." Max tugged at the end of Emma's braid, and she beamed up at him. At least her mood seemed to have lightened a bit. Being part of the show was good for her.

"I wish she could bottle up some of that energy and give it to me," Tykera said as she struggled into her coat. "I'm wiped out." She shook her head. "I don't think I'm up for this. I can't believe how exhausted I am. I thought I'd be excited and energetic when I got pregnant, not dead-tired and forgetful." She looked me in the eye. "I'm sorry, Sonya. This isn't going to work."

Panic swelled in my chest. "Are you saying you can't direct the show?"

Tears welled in Tykera's eyes, and she sniffed. "If I try to push through this, I'll end up failing you again—just like today." She pulled a pack of tissues from her pocket and blew her nose. "I'm sorry. Everything makes me cry these days. I know I'm dumping this all on your shoulders. Maybe if I make a clean break of it, you can find someone else to help you."

Panic squeezed my chest, making it hard to breathe. "How on earth am I supposed to find a replacement co-director? The principal begged me to help because no one else volunteered. She promised all I'd need to do was assist you. Now you want me to take over the entire show? I've never directed anything before."

"We'll put out a request. Someone's bound to help…" Tykera's voice wobbled with doubt.

I slumped. "Yeah. Right." This was going to be a disaster.

Should we cancel the show? But, what about the kids? I glanced at Emma's worried expression. I couldn't do that to her. Not when she'd finally found something to help her overcome her grief. I'd have to find a replacement.

Max cleared his throat. "I can do it."

My jaw dropped. Had he really just volunteered? "Direct the show?" A refusal jumped to the tip of my tongue. I might be in a jam right now, but I wasn't that desperate, was I? The thought of letting Max Ross back into my life on a daily basis sent me into a panic, and with Emma and Tykera's hopeful eyes on me, I tried to come up with a rational reason to reject his offer. "Won't that interfere with your job?" A knot of tension in my neck tightened, and I pressed my fingers into the base of my skull.

"I cut back on my hours for a while so I could spend more time with Emma. She's my number one priority." He glanced down at her, and she smiled back at him. "This is a perfect way for us to spend more time together." He looked back at me, his too-blue eyes entreating me. I'd never been able to resist him when he'd looked at me that way.

Emma threw her arms around his waist and buried her face against his chest. "Thanks Uncle Max. You're the best."

How could I possibly say no? "Thanks. I really appreciate the help. Welcome to the show."

18

PANTOMIME PREP

Max

I was elated. I couldn't have orchestrated this situation any better if I'd tried. Not only would I be able to spend time with Emma, but I'd also get to see Sonya on a regular basis.

Tykera gave a tired smile. "Thanks, Mr. Ross. I can't tell you how relieved I am."

I beamed at her. "It's me who should be thanking you. I've been trying to find something Emma and I could do together. This is perfect."

I avoided meeting Sonya's gaze. She might have needed help, but I knew she couldn't be happy that she'd had to accept it from me.

Tykera peered at me more closely. "You're involved in the movie business, right? With the state I'm in, this show will be much better off with you and Sonya in charge." She waved lethargically and trudged toward the door.

Sonya followed Tykera with a worried gaze. "Thanks for volunteering to help," she said distractedly.

"Not a problem. If you have some time right now, I'd like to run through some ideas I have for that pantomime scene you were working on today."

"You saw it?" she asked, surprised.

I shrugged. "I watched from the door. I read through Emma's script the other night to help her run lines. We could talk about the rest of the show now if you like."

She glanced at her wristwatch and frowned. I could tell she was looking for an excuse to bolt.

"You probably have some reservations. Give me a few minutes and listen to my ideas, then let me know if you agree that we can turn this show into something amazing."

Emma let out a heavy sigh. "I'll wait on the bleachers while you two talk." She trudged away.

Sonya finally returned my gaze. I'd always been able to read her, and time hadn't changed that. She was nervous, but behind that, I spotted a glimmer of reluctant relief.

"It isn't your directing ability that has me worried." She hesitated. "Are you certain you're up for this? Wrangling twenty fifth-graders can be daunting."

I grinned and cocked one eyebrow. "Have you seen the egos on some of the actors I work with? A bunch of fifth-graders will be a walk in the park."

Sonya finally cracked a smile. "You might have a point there."

Emma sat for a moment, but something out in the lobby caught her attention. She sprang up and darted for the door.

"Give me a second," I said. "This discussion could take a while. Marley's mom might still be here. Let me try to catch her so Emma can go home with her while we talk."

I headed to the front lobby and spotted Renee Zerkowski entering from the parking lot as Emma disappeared down one of the hallways. I quickly explained what I needed.

"She's welcome to come over," Renee said, checking her watch. "I need to start dinner soon, though."

"I'll go get her," I said.

"Have her meet me out front. I'll pull up."

I hurried down the nearby hallway Emma had taken. When I

rounded the first corner and approached the open staircase, I found her sitting on a bench chatting—with a boy.

Their heads bent toward one another, and Emma's attention was focused entirely on him. Was this Liam?

I cleared my throat. I had to suppress a grin when the pair jumped as if startled. Emma caught my curious gaze and blushed.

"I need to stay for a while to work on the show with Miss Gambit," I explained. "Mrs. Zerkowski said you can go to her house. I'll pick you up in about an hour."

"Okay," Emma said. She and Liam rose to their feet.

"Hi," I said.

"Hi," the boy echoed. He moved restlessly on his feet, but Emma didn't even glance at me.

"You're Liam, right?" I asked. "I've seen you on stage."

"Yes, sir."

I lifted my chin. "Emma is the understudy for the role of Jane. Do you think you could run lines with her to help her learn the part?"

Liam's eyes widened. A hint of a smile tugged at the corners of his mouth. "Sure thing, Mr. Ross."

"But not today." I turned to Emma. "You need to hurry. Mrs. Zerkowski is waiting for you out front."

"Thanks, Uncle Max," Emma said, shouldering her backpack and heading toward the front of the building.

Liam and I followed her. When we reached the school entrance, a harried mom called out, "Liam! There you are. If you aren't going to answer your phone when I call, maybe you don't need one."

"Sorry, Mom."

Liam and Emma studiously ignored each other as they headed out the front door.

Back in the multipurpose room, I found Sonya sliding her laptop into its bag. "Do you have everything sorted out with Emma?" she asked.

"Yeah." I scratched the back of my head. "Do you happen to know if there's anything going on between Emma and Liam?"

Sonya cocked her head to one side. "Interesting that you'd ask. I've been wondering the same thing."

I let out a groan. "I don't know if I'm up to this parenting thing."

"Said every parent of a preteen." She grinned devilishly.

I had the sudden urge to kiss her. I cleared my throat. "Somehow, that doesn't make me feel any better."

Her smile broadened. "You'll figure it out. Emma's a good kid. You're a good uncle. The two of you will be fine."

I was surprised at how much her words helped. "You think so?"

"I know so. All a kid really needs is someone who loves them and has their best interests at heart. She's lucky to have you."

I hoped she was right.

"Back to business," Sonya said.

"Right." I glanced up at the stage. "I think I understand what Tykera was going for in the scene when I watched the rehearsal. It's a great idea. Is it okay if I come up with my own list of tourist sites in Washington?"

"What did you have in mind?"

"We could start with some iconic images," I said as I climbed onto the stage. "The Washington Monument, the White House. The Senate. Then, we could have them visit the Jefferson Monument. I'm toying with an idea, and I hope you'll go for it. It could be visually stunning."

Sonya climbed the stairs and strode across the stage to join me. "That sounds intriguing. Tell me more."

I glanced away, not meeting her eyes. "I haven't quite decided on the specifics, but I'd like some sort of confetti to fall onto the stage. Maybe a parade."

Sonya held up one hand, stopping me. "We have a problem with that idea. Look up."

I spotted the problem immediately. There was no fly loft where someone could drop confetti from above. There was barely enough room for the lighting. "It's a bit limited. I don't think we'll be putting anyone up there."

"Nope. Since this is a multipurpose room, we have quite a few limitations. Tykera said we can't use large set pieces. There's barely any room backstage as it is, and with such a huge cast, space is an issue."

I scanned the stage. "Then let's try this." I picked up the park bench and carried it from center stage to stage left. "If we put the bench here, we can have the hero and heroine sit with their backs to the wings. Then a stage crew member can turn on a fan and fling handfuls of confetti. It won't be quite as impressive as having it drop down, but it'll still look great."

She nodded appreciatively. "That would make a pretty picture. But what about all that confetti? Won't it make a mess?"

I grinned. "I'll put some kids in custodian uniforms. They can be sweeping the floor here and in the next scene at the Smithsonian. We can also have a senator and some journalists snapping photos of a new exhibit."

"I love that idea!" Sonya said. Her eyes gleamed with excitement.

"It'll be great. We'll have the kids moving on and off stage. They can do some simple costume changes. A fedora hat with a press card in the brim can be swapped for a camera and a folded map to turn a journalist into a tourist."

Her enthusiasm dimmed a bit. "How will the kids manage to learn a complicated scene like that?" She shook her head. "I don't think you have enough rehearsal time to make it work."

"Let me see your rehearsal schedule before I answer that," I suggested.

"It's on my computer. Let me get it."

I followed her as she headed down the steps and sat on a folding chair to pull her computer out of her bag.

"How is it you know so much about staging?" she asked as she opened her laptop. "I thought your degree was in business."

"With a minor in theater arts." I sat next to her. "Competition was fierce out in California. If you wanted a part in one of the college productions, you had to commit wholeheartedly. I'm an okay actor, but not on par with the people I was competing with. Besides, it wasn't what I was interested in. I prefer working behind the scenes. I excel at solving problems like these."

"Handsome *and* talented," she said teasingly. "I suppose that's why your dad relied on you to be his right-hand man after his heart attack."

A sudden burst of affection for her hit me hard. "I can't say nepotism didn't help, but he never would have trusted me to run my business while he was sick if he hadn't believed I could do the job. I've been involved in almost every aspect of movie production. I got my start when I was still a kid, listening to my dad problem-solve. I deal with these sorts of issues all the time. This? It's child's play." I grinned expectantly.

When she furrowed her brows, I nudged her again. "Get it? Child's. Play?"

She groaned and then a laugh burst out. "No puns. Please."

I just laughed harder. "Puns are the highest form of humor."

"Nope. They're the lowest."

I shook my head. "The lowest form of humor would be bawdy jokes. 'There once was a girl from Nantucket—'" I intoned.

"Stop!" She brushed her hand over my lips and then jerked it away. "I don't think I've ever heard a clean version of that limerick. Certainly not one suitable for an elementary school."

She turned back to her computer and opened the calendar.

I leaned in to see it, and the scent of her shampoo and body lotion invaded, bypassing my defenses, and sliding directly into my heart. She wore a soft scent that brought to mind fresh grass and spring meadows. "I remember your perfume," I murmured before I thought better of it. "I mean, I remember you always used this scent. What's it called?"

"Rain Kissed Leaves." Her whispered words sent a vibration

down my spine. I tried to ignore my reaction to being so close to her.

"It's—" my voice turned husky. That scent was messing with my head—or maybe it was messing with my heart. Letting her get to me like this was a bad idea. I needed to keep myself together, or I'd scare her away.

I cleared my throat. "The rehearsal schedule for the pantomime looks fine." *Focus. Think. Speak.* "I'll pick out a specific piece of music we can use to accompany the scene; that way, they can learn the cues based on the music. It'll make remembering everything easier."

Sonya licked her lips. When she noticed me gazing at them, her cheeks turned pink. "That's an excellent idea. Using different modalities of learning allows students to remember new information using different parts of their brain."

"Yes. Modalities." I blinked, trying to get my sex-obsessed brain to remember the word. "I remember reading something about that. Using reading, lectures, movement, and music to learn something new."

"I use chants, too." Her gaze fixed on my lips, letting me know she wasn't immune to what was happening between us. "They're learning all the presidents by reciting them in order whenever we wait in line. I taught them a silly poem." She blinked her eyes rapidly, then licked her lips. "They recite it whenever…"

Sonya surged closer, pressing her mouth against mine, her hands reaching for my chest. The touch of her lips, the soft caress of her hands, the warm sighs of her growing desire—I'd dreamed about all these things—dreamed about them for five long years.

I responded, kissing her exactly the way the dream version of me had. She moved closer, but I felt something shift and begin to slide off her lap.

Her laptop.

I made a grab for it before it could crash to the floor.

Sonya jerked away. Her hand flew to cover her mouth and her eyes went wide. "I'm—I'm so sorry," she stammered. "I never should have done that. It was completely inappropriate." She plucked her laptop from my hands as she sprang to her feet and then shoved it into her bag.

She glanced around as if searching for anyone who might point an accusing finger at her, but no one else was there.

She'd kissed me, which meant she still wanted me. Knowing this changed everything.

Sonya whirled to face me, then scowled. "Don't look so pleased with yourself."

"I can't help it. I know you told me you forgave me, but until now, I didn't quite believe it. If that wasn't a clear sign of forgiveness, then what was it?"

She jerked her coat on. "A momentary lapse of judgment. It won't happen again." She held her arm up, ushering me toward the exit.

I grinned. She was wrong. If I had anything to do about it, which I did, a kiss would absolutely happen again.

19

CHERRY BLOSSOMS

SONYA

On Thursday afternoon, the multipurpose room echoed with the shrieks and squeals of boisterous kids burning off excess energy. I glanced at my watch and then back at the entrance. Max was due any minute.

I wasn't quite sure how I felt about seeing him today. About working with him.

Well, that wasn't quite true. I was nervous. Excited even. That's what had me worried. I was looking forward to this a little too much.

Last night, he'd emailed me his ideas for the show. I almost called him to discuss them, but I chickened out. I was about to see him face-to-face for the first time since that kiss.

When I thought I heard him, I jumped as I glanced toward the entrance again.

Empty.

This was getting ridiculous. How was I going to handle being in the same room with him when waiting to see him had me freaking out? I needed to keep our relationship professional. I could do it. I had to.

A moment later, Max sauntered in juggling a computer bag

while he tugged off a lightweight jacket spattered with rain. As he arched his back to shrug out of it, the fabric of his dress shirt tightened, giving me an excellent impression of his muscled chest. The man made a pair of belted khakis and a pale blue shirt with its sleeves rolled up look positively erotic. I couldn't tear my eyes away as he strode toward me.

Damn. The blue of the shirt even brought out the color of his eyes.

Come on, Sonya. Keep it professional.

He came to a stop next to me, spoke, and grinned.

"What?" I couldn't hear him because of all the noise the kids were making. For all I knew, he'd just propositioned me.

Wouldn't that be nice?

I pointed at my ear and shrugged. "Say that again. I think I'm going deaf."

Max grinned as he leaned closer and raised his voice. "Did you load them up with sugar just for me?"

This was a safe topic. Twenty boisterous children worked as preeminent passion killers.

"This is what happens when it rains all day and they don't get to go outside for recess," I said, raising my voice to something close to a shout. "Most of them spent that time either playing board games or reading. They stayed dry, but they didn't burn off much energy. From what I hear, yesterday's rehearsal with the choir director went well. I guess we were due for a bit of chaos."

Max widened his eyes in mock horror. "Where are those well-behaved kids I saw on Tuesday? I'm genuinely terrified. I'm not sure if I should bring in the boxes of props and hats I brought for the pantomime bit."

I glanced at the scene before us again. A few of the cast members were tossing basketballs. Some were doing cartwheels, others were playing a game of tag. A group had found a long jump rope. Two girls were swinging it and some others were standing in line to take turns jumping over it. It was noisy but orderly. "This isn't all that bad. Everyone's happy. Having fun. Getting along."

Max's eyes seemed to dance with good humor. "That's a relief. Do you think we'll be able to get them to settle down and rehearse?"

"Absolutely. Let me show you a teacher's trick." I turned my head to one side, stuck my fingers in my mouth, and produced a shrill whistle.

The decibel level in the room plunged as the students turned to stare at me.

"All right, you hooligans," I said. "Now that you've burned off most of that excess energy, I need you to put away the basketballs and jump-ropes. After that, we'll have a quick race around the gym. My first, second, and third place winners get to help Mr. Ross carry in some things from his car."

They responded with whoops and cheers as they scurried to put everything away.

Marley raised her hand. "Do we have to run?" She shook a foot clad in a slick-soled shoe. "I'd probably fall and break my neck."

"It's completely voluntary, but you can't win if you don't run."

"I'll just watch." Marley climbed onto the stage and sat with her legs dangling over the edge.

Emma joined her, not bothering to glance in my direction. She didn't even acknowledge her uncle, which was unusual.

As Max watched Emma, he wrinkled his brow and then shot me a questioning glance.

"She's been feeling sad today," I murmured. "I hope rehearsal lifts her spirits."

Two other girls joined Emma and Marley on the sidelines while everyone else lined up at the starting point.

"Two laps around the gym," I called out to them. "No cutting corners. I want you to loop around on the far side of the gymnastics equipment. Mr. Ross will be over there—" I pointed to a line on the floor near the exit "—at the finish line to declare the winners."

The kids formed themselves into a ragged line next to me.

I lifted my arm into the air. "On your mark. Get set. Go!" I dropped my arm in a slicing motion.

The thunderous sound of squeaking, thudding feet filled the gymnasium. The kids initially started racing in a clump, but quickly spread out.

I went to stand next to Max at the finish line. "Thanks again for agreeing to direct the show. The ideas you sent me sounded inspired."

"No problem. I had fun planning it." His gorgeous blue eyes flashed at me, and his voice dropped, becoming more intimate. "Besides, it gives me a chance to spend more time with Emma."

My heart hiccupped. For a moment, I'd thought he was about to say it gave him more time to spend with *me*. The thought made me feel ashamed. *Of course,* he should focus on Emma. "I noticed she wore her Nirvana t-shirt again today."

Max glanced toward the stage where Emma sat. "It was her mom's. She found it at her grandfather's house last week."

I swallowed the sudden lump in my throat. "It probably makes her feel closer to her." I kept my eyes fixed on the runners as they passed behind the gymnastics equipment. "I'm looking forward to seeing what you have planned for the pantomime scene today."

A charmingly boyish grin curved Max's lips. "So am I. It's still a work in progress."

Emma and the others sitting on the stage began cheering as the runners started their second lap. Six kids were in the lead, with Ally at the head of the pack, easily maintaining her lead. Liam and two other boys were in a clump a few lengths behind her, but another boy and girl weren't far off pace.

Sean, who'd been vying for second place, began to lag. Justin, who was just behind him, surged forward to try to secure one of the top three spots. An instant later, Ally flew across the finish line, immediately followed by Liam in second place. Third place was—a tie between Justin and Sean.

"I did it!" Ally exclaimed in her German-accented English. It sounded more like, "I deed eet."

"Great job!" Max said. "Congratulations!"

Justin and Sean glanced at each other, not sure which of them had come in third.

Max waved them both forward. "Since you two tied for third place, you both get to help. Follow me." He led the way outside, and a couple of minutes later the group came trooping back inside. Justin and Sean carried a large cardboard box that probably could have been carried by just one person, Ally carried a huge black plastic bag stuffed with something lightweight, and Liam carried a bulky electric fan.

"Put that stuff up on stage," Max told them. "Right along the edge." He joined me next to the chairs Prisha was unfolding.

"Is it still raining?" I asked, looking for any telltale raindrops on his shirt. At least, that's what I told myself.

"It stopped." Max jabbed his thumb toward the students. "You did an amazing job calming them down. It's like you do this sort of thing for a living."

I flashed a pleased smile. "I learned that particular trick during my on-the-job training as a student teacher. Kids are much more amenable when they've had a chance to burn off some of their excess energy."

"Is it okay if I start the rehearsal now?" Max plucked his computer from his bag.

"Absolutely."

He approached the stage, laptop in hand. "Alright, everyone. We're going to finish staging the pantomime piece today, but this time, we'll do it to music."

Justin let out a groan. "Do we have to dance? No one told me we'd have to dance."

Max set the laptop on the edge of the stage. "Nope. No dancing. But as a side note, you really need to change your thinking on that point. I know it doesn't matter much to a fifth grader, but there will come a time in your life when you'll want to impress someone you like, and nothing does it better than being able to step onto the dance floor with them and not look like a fool."

Before I realized what he was up to, he grabbed hold of my hand and pulled me close. "Remember this?" he asked softly, his breath brushing my ear and sending a tingle down my spine. He spun me away from him in a practiced dance move I remembered all too well, pulled me back in, and then expertly dipped me.

I froze in place with Max supporting me as I arched my back, extended my leg, and gazed up into his eyes. My students applauded enthusiastically as my ears grew hot from embarrassment.

When Max finally lifted me to my feet, I let out a shaky laugh. Max bowed, so I curtsied. It felt so natural to dance with him again. It was as if we'd never been apart.

"I want you all to remember that dancing is fun," Max said. "It's simply another way to express yourself. You won't be dancing in this scene, though. Instead, you'll use the music to help remember your cues." He clapped his hands. "Everyone on stage. Let's get started."

He told each of them where to stand, when to move, and how to behave on stage. The opening part of the scene quickly started taking shape. Max had them run through it a couple more times as he played the accompanying song on his laptop."

"Now for the next part," Max said as he rubbed his hands together. "Marley, since you're tall and have such excellent posture, I want you to play the senator in this scene." He pointed to Justin and Sean. "You two can be reporters trying to take photos."

The newly formed group ran through the additional bit of scene work, hamming it up. Those kids amazed me.

"Let's start working on the end of the scene," Max said. "This is where our two leads—Liam and Crystal—visit the Jefferson

Memorial." He ushered them over. "I want you to cross over here to the park bench."

He snapped his fingers as if remembering something. "This is the part where we'll use the items we carried in from my car." He ran backstage, and from my vantage point, I could see him plug in the electric fan. He came back on stage and handed Ally the black plastic bag. "You're in charge of this. I'll tell you what to do in a minute."

He turned to address everyone. "The Japanese government gave our country some Japanese Cherry Blossom trees early in the twentieth century, and we planted them around the Jefferson Memorial and the Tidal Basin. In the springtime, the trees are all in bloom. It looks amazing. Tourists come from all over the world to see them. I thought we could recreate the feel of that spring day there."

Ally opened the bag to peek inside, and a profusion of pink and white silk flower petals spilled onto the stage floor. A huge grin spread over her face. "*Das ist wunderschön.*" Her cheeks turned pink. "I mean, these are beautiful," she said. She immediately dipped her hand into the bag and let petals drift between her fingers.

Max pointed at Liam and Crystal. "I want the two of you to sit on the bench."

They plopped down.

"Now, I'm not sure how we'll stage this next part. If you were adults, I'd have you kiss."

Liam and Crystal's eyes went wide as their mouths dropped open in horror. Crystal rose to her feet as though she might bolt.

Max held up his hands placatingly. "That obviously won't work in a fifth-grade show. How do you feel about handholding?"

Crystal frowned, but she didn't run. She and Liam exchanged doubtful glances. A moment later, they both shrugged apathetically. Crystal sat back down, but she didn't look happy about it.

"Our other option is to have you stare lovingly into each other's eyes."

Liam grinned and gave Crystal a puppy-dog expression, complete with enormous, soulful eyes.

She giggled and went cross-eyed, pulling a face.

Max let out a sigh. "We'll work on that. You'll need to give the audience the impression that you're crazy for each other, otherwise the scene won't work."

No matter what Max tried, Crystal and Liam continued to look entirely uncomfortable together. Max kept running his fingers through his hair, a sure sign of his growing frustration.

"Maybe you can show them what you want them to do instead of explaining it," I suggested. "Act it out for them."

Max snapped his fingers and pointed at me with a grin. "Excellent idea." He held his hand out to me. "You can stand in for Crystal, and I'll be Liam."

Uh-oh. "Um—"

"Come on, Miss Gambit," Crystal said as she jumped to her feet. "After all, it was your idea." She took me by the arm and escorted me to the bench.

Me and my big mouth.

I pasted on a smile as I sat in Crystal's spot.

As Max joined me, he reached out and took hold of my hand. "If you simply hold hands like this, you don't even need to look at each other. You can pretend you're too shy."

I pretended to be embarrassed and turned away. That wasn't much of a stretch.

"Another option is to show how you feel using only your facial expressions." He turned to me. "Go ahead and look into my eyes."

When I did, he gave me a look of such intense longing that it felt like a punch to the heart. I inhaled sharply and leaned forward slightly, gazing into his eyes, once again finding the love I'd always found there whenever I'd looked into them five years ago.

"Holding hands looks easier," Liam commented. "I'll be pretty nervous on stage."

I licked my lips as our eyes tangled. I was trapped—wrapped up in overwhelming memories of us together. The intensity of this moment nearly undid me.

Finally, Max wrenched his gaze away and faced Liam. "There's a difference between being nervous because you're on stage with everyone watching you, and being nervous because you like someone and are afraid of being rejected. Remember, you'll just be acting. None of this is real."

None of this is real.

The words echoed in my head, punching me in the heart. I know they hadn't been meant for me, but they were the reminder I needed.

I had to stay focused on the here and now. On the kids and the scene they were learning.

I grounded myself in time to see Liam glance at Emma across the room. He slid his gaze away and then nodded. "I think I can do that," he said.

"We should just hold hands," Crystal said. "It looks easier." Five minutes later, she and Liam had managed to pull together a decent-looking pantomime.

Max had been furiously jotting down scene notes as we ran through everything. When he noticed me watching him, he shrugged nonchalantly. "Mind like a steel trap. A rusty one. If I don't write down the cues and the blocking, I'll forget it all and then we'll have to stage the scene all over again."

"That would be a tragedy," I said. "You've shaped this scene into something special. It's on our schedule again for next Thursday."

"We're nearly done blocking it. We'll use next Thursday to review everything." He moved to the front of the stage and opened the cardboard box Justin and Sean had carried in from his car. "Gather around," he called out. "I want everyone to go through this box and find a hat that fits the character I assigned you." He glanced at Marley. "There isn't an official hat for a senator, but I was thinking you could wear one of those pillbox hats like Jackie Kennedy used to have. There's a pink one in there."

The kids descended on the pile of hats. Soon, they were posing on stage. Max had been right; hats immediately defined the various characters.

Liam handed Emma a rainbow-colored hat someone might wear to church on Easter. "Here, this goes with your t-shirt."

Emma blushed as she took it from him. After she put it on and adjusted it, she pulled her phone from her pocket and used the camera as a mirror to see how it looked. When she saw herself, she grinned in delight.

"Is it time to use the petals in the bag now?" Ally asked.

"Absolutely," Max said. "Sean, go turn on that fan. Set it to the highest speed."

Sean scrambled to the side of the stage and flipped the switch. A blast of air ruffled Ally's hair. She immediately grabbed two handfuls of flower petals and threw them into the air.

The result was extraordinary. The silk petals fluttered into the air, swirled around the bench where Liam and Crystal sat, and then drifted in the current before slowly falling onto the stage.

The kids all seemed entranced. I couldn't blame them. I turned my face up and smiled at the cloud of petals surrounding me. It made me feel as though I were standing inside a pink and white snow globe.

Max's warm, smooth hand slid into mine, and he tugged me into the wings and then behind a black curtain. "What?" I asked, looking up into his eyes.

He didn't say anything. He simply pulled me into his arms and kissed me.

I melted. I might have told myself that this was a bad idea, but deep down, this was exactly what I had wanted. To be in his arms. To hold him close. I slid my hand over his firmly muscled forearm, marveling at the heat coming off him. At the smoothness of his skin. At the pure joy I felt at being in his embrace.

When our tongues touched, a bolt of heat shot through me as

memories of other kisses like this flooded my mind. Max had always been able to make me melt with his touch. This time was no different.

Too soon, he pulled away. Losing his supporting embrace made me sway on my feet.

Max dragged his hand through his hair. "Maybe I shouldn't have done that, but I couldn't resist. You looked irresistible." His gaze fixed on something just above me, and then he reached up and plucked something from my hair.

A pink cherry blossom petal.

He took my hand and turned it palm up, then placed the petal into it. He plucked a second petal from my hair, stared at it for a moment, and then tucked it into the pocket of his shirt.

"Miss Gambit?" Emma called out. "Where are you? Prisha brought us some brooms. Do you want us to sweep up the petals?"

With a start, I hurriedly smoothed my hair into place. "How do I look?" I asked Max.

"Perfect," Max said, his eyes drinking me in. "Not a hair out of place."

I took a steadying breath and then stepped out from behind the curtain. "Thanks, Emma. Let's get this stage cleaned up."

Ally was already sweeping with the broom Max had brought, but petals were everywhere. Liam and Justin grabbed the push brooms Prisha had found and started helping. A few of the other kids started picking petals up, one by one, and then Sean grabbed his coat and used it as a broom to sweep a large section of the stage. Within a couple of minutes, all the petals were back inside the plastic bag.

"We're done for today. You can all go home," I announced. "Our next rehearsal is Monday after school. See you then."

Emma ran forward and grabbed Max by the hand, pulling him toward the door. "The flower petals are awesome, Uncle Max! I love them."

"Thanks, kiddo." He ruffled her hair as he glanced back at me.

"I thought it was pretty great, too." He slid his hand over his heart, and then I realized he was touching the shirt pocket where he'd tucked away the flower petal. I smiled as I tucked my own petal into my pocket.

"Night, Miss Gambit," Emma called out.

"Good night," I replied, watching as Max gave me one last lingering look and then turned away.

A FORGOTTEN BACKPACK

Sonya

Max and Emma left as soon as rehearsal ended, but I stayed to supervise the rest of the students while they gathered their things. They left one-by-one or in small groups.

Finally, only Crystal Falls remained.

Crystal was a nice girl. Quiet. I hoped having the lead role would help her gain a bit more confidence. She certainly had talent. She just needed to believe in herself.

I spotted a lone backpack sitting on the bleachers. "Is that yours?"

Crystal glanced at it. "No. I think it's Emma's."

I picked it up and slung it over my shoulder. I'd drop it off in my classroom before I left today. I just hoped Emma had already finished her homework and didn't need anything in her bag.

A moment later, relief swept over Crystal's face. She jumped up from her spot on the bleachers and pulled on her coat. A woman, presumably her mom, came striding across the multipurpose room, not to meet Crystal, but instead on a beeline for me.

"Rehearsal was fun today," Crystal announced as she hurried over to her mom.

Mrs. Falls patted her on the shoulder, but her gaze was fixed on me. "That's good, sweetie, but can you give us a second?" She pressed her lips together in a thin line. "Miss *Gambit*," she said, her tone sharp and unfriendly. "I spotted you out in front of the school every morning last week. You were hard to miss, what with Emma Bachar bringing you a gift every single day. I must say, her extravagance caught my attention. Especially with her uncle holding up the drop-off line to watch your reaction."

I blushed. "I'm so sorry it was an inconvenience. I contacted her uncle and tried to stop her, but he said she was set on the idea."

Mrs. Falls shook her head. Her mouth looked as though she'd just sucked on a lime. "Taking advantage of someone that way. You should know better. Especially after everything that happened."

The sting of her rebuke startled me. I blinked. "That's a harsh accusation, Mrs. Falls. I assure you, I'm not taking advantage of Emma. I'm only trying to help her. That's all I can say, though. I hope you understand I can't talk about another student with you. It violates the school's privacy guidelines."

"I wasn't talking about what happened to Emma. I was talking about Raven. *You should be ashamed*."

I stilled even as my heart started pounding. She knew? Panic squeezed tight around my chest, making it hard to breathe. I opened my mouth to speak and then closed it again. What could I even say?

Darcy took a step closer, her expression filled with fervor. "Raven is a wonderful human being. She's talented, passionate, and genuine. Her voice is amazing and she has a gift for writing songs that connect with people on a deep level." Darcy blinked as her face contorted with emotion. "She's a true inspiration to me, and I am grateful for her music and her message. She helped get me through some difficult times."

Then, her face twisted with anger. "You, on the other hand, are a terrible person. The way you sneaked around behind her back while she was trying to get better was despicable. That woman's been through more than anyone should have to bear, and she didn't deserve your cruelty. I hope you're happy with yourself for what you did to her."

"But I—"

Mrs. Falls leaned in close, her eyes narrowed. "You stay away from Max Ross, and keep your trashy ways to yourself. I don't want this school to turn into a madhouse like the last one you were in. If you so much as step out of line, I'll make sure you're fired." She grabbed Crystal's hand and stormed out of the multipurpose room.

I noticed a movement at the door and spotted Emma, her eyes wide as Darcy and her daughter swept past her. How long had she been there? Had she heard anything Mrs. Falls had said? Would she ask about it? What should I say? How could I explain?

When Emma realized I was looking at her, she broke into a run, heading directly toward me. I tensed, scrambling to come up with answers to the questions she must have.

"I forgot my backpack," Emma said, her hands extended toward me. She didn't look me in the eye. Instead, she glanced over her shoulder at the exit as if she was in a hurry.

I let her backpack slide off my shoulder and held it out. "Thanks," she said, taking it. She turned and darted toward the door.

I stood in the middle of the now-empty multipurpose room, still in shock. At least Emma hadn't overheard. That was a relief.

Even so, Mrs. Falls's words kept ringing in my ears.

Raven. I was talking about Raven.

It had happened. My past had finally caught up with my present.

21

EMMA INVESTIGATES

MAX

Emma opened the passenger door and dumped her missing backpack on the floor before getting in next to me.

"You found it?" I asked.

Emma pulled one of those long-suffering expressions. "No. The backpack by my feet is simply a figment of your imagination."

"Smart aleck." The kid was growing up way too fast.

I glanced in the rearview mirror as I drove away, hoping to catch one last glimpse of Sonya, but I didn't spot her.

That kiss. It had been amazing. She'd looked completely trans-fixed while she'd been watching those silk petals swirl around the stage. I hadn't been able to resist her, so I'd pulled her behind the curtain for that kiss. Everything about that moment had been perfect.

Emma pulled a folder from her backpack and began working on what appeared to be a spelling list. When I stopped at the next light on Ohio River Boulevard, I glanced down at the page in front of her. Sure enough, I found her writing something while referring to a list of words.

"It looks more like you're writing a story than working on a spelling list," I commented.

"Miss Gambit lets us write stories with the list of spelling words if we want. We have to use ten of the words in our story and then underline them. They have to be used correctly for us to get credit for them, but the story doesn't have to be a good one. I've included seven words so far, but I'm having trouble coming up with an ending."

My pulse pounded a little bit faster when Emma mentioned Miss Gambit. I couldn't seem to get her out of my mind. "Want some help?"

Emma sighed heavily. "Sure. Might as well. Here's what I've come up with." She lifted the paper and peered at it. "The middle son suddenly burst into excited laughter. 'I figured out how to memorize each and every element on the periodic table,' he declared. 'I'll create a series of words as a mnemonic and memorize them, like when you memorize speeches.'"

"Impressive. Which words are from your spelling list?" I asked.

"So far I've included: middle, suddenly, excited, memorize, element, declared, series, speeches, and laughter." She peered at the paper. "Oh. I have more than I thought. That's nine words. I only need one more." She bit down on the side of her pencil as she read through her list of words. "I know," she said, plucking it from her mouth. "He'll say, 'I'll celebrate with a cup of hot cocoa.'" She glanced at me. "Cocoa is one of my words too."

"Chocolate as a reward? Sounds motivating."

"A cup of hot cocoa sounds really good right now. Can we make some when we get home?"

"Sure. I have milk, sugar, and cocoa, plus some whipped cream to go on top. That's all we need. I'll make you a cup after we have dinner."

Emma clamped her pencil between her teeth as she tucked the spelling homework into her backpack and pulled out a math worksheet.

"You have math today, too? Don't you usually finish up all your homework with Marley after school? You need to let me know if rehearsal is getting in the way."

She extracted her pencil from her mouth as she glanced at me. "Don't worry; this is the last thing I need to do, then I'm done with today's homework."

Ten minutes later as I pulled through the gate into my building's parking garage, Emma stashed her schoolwork in her backpack.

"Can I use your computer when we get upstairs? I wanted to look something up for school." She jiggled her leg up and down.

"I thought the math paper was the last thing you needed to do. What are you researching?"

She stopped jiggling. "Something about the underground railroad. I need to decide what piece of it I want to research for a project I'll be doing."

I pulled into my assigned parking spot. "I'm making Italian Wedding Soup for dinner. It won't take too long. You can use my laptop while I cook. I'll need it back after dinner. I have to work on the media plan for *Ghost*."

She looked disappointed. "I'm excited about *Ghost*, and all. It's pretty cool that Uncle Ford is filming it right here in Pittsburgh," she said with a frown, "but you work too hard, Uncle Max. Don't you ever get tired of having to work at night?"

"It doesn't feel as much like work when you enjoy what you're doing." But I had to admit, I'd prefer to kick back tonight and spend some time with Emma. I got out of the car and then leaned into the back seat where I grabbed my laptop bag. "I have an idea. Let's do something together after dinner before I start working." I could always focus on the media plan after Emma went to bed.

"Do you have any board games?" she asked.

"No, but I have a deck of cards. How about if you have that cup of hot chocolate while I teach you a game? Do you know how to play Gin Rummy?"

Her eyes widened as she trotted over to the elevator and

pressed the call button. "I love Gin Rummy. Mom and I used to play it when we went camping." She frowned, and I wondered if I'd brought up a tender subject. "I think I remember the rules. I haven't played it since last summer."

"I'll explain them after dinner." The elevator pinged and the doors opened. A minute later, we entered the apartment. I pulled my laptop out of its leather bag and handed it to Emma before heading back to my bedroom to change.

I'd have to look into getting her a computer to use at home. Once she started middle school next year, she'd really need one since she'd be writing more papers. I tugged on a pair of well-worn jeans and a gray t-shirt and then headed back to the kitchen.

I passed Emma as she sat cross-legged on the sofa with her back to the big window overlooking the city. The laptop rested on her legs, and she frowned in concentration.

A bright white light started flashing on the hillside across the river from the apartment. Was someone having a party over there? I'd never noticed that light before. I hoped it wasn't going to become a permanent fixture. It was kind of annoying.

I pulled soup supplies from the cabinet. I cheated a little by starting with a soup mix. After boiling some chicken stock, I added the mix along with some mini meatballs. Then I wrapped a fresh loaf of bakery bread in some foil and slid it into the oven to warm. While everything was cooking, I rinsed some fresh spinach. As soon as the soup began to boil, I added the spinach leaves to the pot and turned the heat down to low.

"Soup's almost done," I called out to Emma. She was so involved in her research that she didn't even react.

That light across the river caught my attention again. Rather than getting annoyed, I should probably simply close the curtains. As I crossed behind the couch, a video on Emma's screen caught my attention.

She was watching Raven's YouTube video. The one where she'd accused Essie of stealing me away from her. There was no sound, and I realized Emma had plugged her earbuds into the audio jack.

Well, damn. That cat was obviously out of the bag. In fact, the damned cat was currently racing around my apartment and ripping my life to shreds.

I rounded the end of the sofa and plopped down next to Emma.

She let out a squeal as her eyes went wide. Her hand darted out to close the laptop, but I stopped her by holding it open.

Her expression fell as she pulled her earbuds from her ears. "I know I'm being nosy, but Uncle Max, why didn't you tell me? You knew Miss Gambit all along and you never said anything."

"She asked me to respect her privacy, and not tell anyone." Even to me, the words sounded like a poor excuse. "She wants to keep her past in the past. Besides, you're kind of young to be exposed to this kind of ugliness." I dragged my fingers through my hair and rubbed at the back of my skull with my fingertips. I wasn't prepared to deal with this. I should have been. I guess I'd been hoping this would never happen.

"Seriously? It's too late for that now. Just tell me, Uncle Max. I'm not a baby."

I sighed. She was right. I should explain. At least that way she'd know the real story instead of what the internet would tell her. "What do you know?"

She flushed. "Just what I found on the internet in the past fifteen minutes. Who is this Raven chick anyway? She's so mean." Emma scowled at the paused video. Raven's normally beautiful face was contorted with anger in the middle of her rant. "She was majorly pissed off. And the things she says about Essie—well, they don't match up with what I know about Miss Gambit, but apparently, they really are the same person." Emma pressed her lips together as she shook her head. "None of this makes sense."

I let out a heavy sigh of frustration. "It's a complicated story. I'm afraid some of the details aren't suited for someone your age."

"I'm *not naive*. I know more about the world than you think I do," Emma snapped. "I know about drug addiction and suicide and pregnancy and alcoholism and lots of things."

I stared at her, dumbfounded. Who was this kid? How did she know those things? Had I known about all that stuff when I'd been in the fifth grade? I wasn't sure. Maybe.

Emma just rolled her eyes at me. "Most kids my age know all that and more. It's all over TV and the internet. We aren't stupid, you know."

"You clearly know a lot more than I gave you credit for. I tell you what, why don't you tell me what you've found out about the whole Essie-Raven mess, and I'll help you separate the truth from the lies."

"Well, there's this." Emma clicked over to another video that immediately started playing.

Seeing this particular clip again made my mouth go dry. Essie's dad stood in front of the restaurant where she'd worked, surrounded by reporters. His collared shirt and khaki pants looked brand-new—they still had the creases in them from their store packaging. His beard had been freshly trimmed, but his hair was overdue for a cut. The man looked as though he'd assembled a costume for the express purpose of making himself appear responsible and sober.

"My Essie always was a looker," Mr. Harlow said, "even when she was just a little girl. She's the spittin' image of her mama. That woman got her claws into me, and I fell for her hard. Bled me dry, she did. You can't blame that Max Ross guy for being taken in by her daughter. I was lucky to get away when I did."

"Mr. Harlow." a reporter held out a microphone, "Are you suggesting that your daughter intentionally seduced Max Ross?"

"I'm not suggesting it, I'm saying flat out. It'd be nothing to someone like her. She was always looking for ways to make her life better. Nothing was good enough for that kid. Every time I turned around, she or her mama were after me for more money."

Another reporter asked, "Mr. Harlow, when was the last time

you spoke to your daughter? Did she tell you about her plans to seduce Mr. Ross? Did you ever meet him?"

"No, I never met Max." Harlow scratched at his neat gray beard. "I can't rightly say how long it's been since I saw Essie. She was about five or so when I left her mama. I guess that means it must have been, what, seventeen years ago?"

"You haven't spoken to her in all that time?" The reporter looked disappointed.

"Nah. Once you escape a snake pit, it's stupid to come within striking distance again."

Emma stopped the video. "He doesn't seem very nice."

I let out a bark of laughter. "That's an understatement. From what Sonya told me, he walked out when her mom was pregnant with their second child. Things were pretty rough for her and Sonya after that. She worked two jobs, so Sonya had to grow up fast and keep an eye on her baby sister."

Emma frowned. "Her dad made it sound like her mom took all his money."

"Not from what Sonya told me. They got a quickie divorce, and then he just disappeared and skipped out on paying child support. Her mom changed her name back to Gambit before the baby was even born."

"So that's why she's called Miss Gambit. I'd wondered."

"Her name was Harlow when I met her, but I think having her dad attack her like that convinced her to change it and sever that one last tie to him."

"I don't blame her." Emma bit her lip nervously. Her leg started bouncing up and down again.

"Anything wrong?" I asked.

"There's something else you need to know." Emma closed the laptop, took a breath, and looked straight into my eyes. "I accidentally eavesdropped on Crystal's mom when I went to get my backpack. She was being really mean to Miss Gambit."

I listened, appalled, as Emma told me what she'd overheard.

"She threatened to get Miss Gambit fired," Emma said. "When

I got home, I found this video of Raven from a few years ago." She frowned at me. "I can't believe you used to date that nut job."

I laughed, relieved that Emma's loyalty to Miss Gambit was still solidly in place. "In my defense, she wasn't a nut job back when we first started dating."

"Did the drugs and the alcohol change her?"

How should I answer that? My stomach tightened as my inadequacy as a guardian for an eleven-year-old girl hit me yet again. I wasn't equipped to talk about this.

When I didn't speak, Emma let out a frustrated sigh. "I know Raven went into rehab, the two of you broke up, and when she came out, she made that horrible video. According to people on the internet, she was 'coked-out' when she made it. What does 'coked-out' mean?"

I closed my eyes, trying to decide how to answer that question. Maybe a bit of divine guidance? Nope. It eluded me. Apparently, I was on my own.

I let out a resigned sigh. I'd answer her questions truthfully, but minimally. "'Coked-out' means high on cocaine. It's a stimulant."

"Like coffee?"

"A million times stronger. It's illegal and it can kill you." I gave her a stern look. "It's highly addictive and very, very dangerous. According to Raven, it's also very seductive." Seductive? Had I just used that word with my eleven-year-old niece? I coughed. "Stay away from it. The stuff is bad news."

Emma rolled her eyes. "*Obviously*." She waved her hand toward the screen. "Look at what it did to *her*."

"It nearly destroyed her career. She's only just now starting to make a comeback, and that's only because she's finally kicked her drug habit." I swallowed. I only hoped Emma hadn't done any recent research on Raven. I sure as hell didn't want to be bombarded with questions about Raven's new BDSM lifestyle. Hell to the no! That's where I drew the line when it came to openness and honesty with my niece.

"Did you break up with her because she took drugs?"

"We broke up the day she went into rehab five years ago. When I found her stash of drugs, she tried to lie her way out of it." I shook my head and let out a deep sigh. "It was the second time she'd lied to me about doing drugs, so I ended things with her."

Emma tugged at her lower lip with her thumb and forefinger.

I scrubbed my hand over my face. "I have to admit, the breakup shattered me, mostly because I felt like a complete fool for believing her lies. I couldn't leave Los Angeles fast enough. I packed up my stuff and moved back here to Pittsburgh. I'd just graduated, and I'd always planned to get a job in the film industry out in L.A., but after I left Raven, all I wanted to do was get as far away from that lifestyle as possible. I used to have that YouTube channel where I did celebrity interviews. I had a pretty big following, but I abandoned it after Raven and I broke up. I did everything I could to make it a clean break from my past life. I even backed away from the film industry for a while and took a job at a coffee shop while I tried to figure out what I wanted to do next."

"That's right. As a barista. That's why you knew about the code on Miss Gambit's coffee cup." She narrowed her eyes. "Wait. No. You knew her favorite coffee drink because you used to date her."

"Clever girl." I grinned as I ruffled her hair. "I still owe you that hot chocolate."

She ducked away and smoothed her hair back in place. "And a game of Gin Rummy."

I rose to my feet. "Can we continue talking over dinner? The soup is ready."

She nodded, and while I served the food, she filled their water glasses.

I set the soup and bread on the table with a flourish, like a waiter, and Emma giggled when I clicked my heels together.

"Dinner is served, *mademoiselle*," I said, using my best French accent.

"*Merci*," Emma replied.

I used a spoon to sprinkle Parmesan cheese on my soup, then passed the bowl of cheese to her.

"What happened after you left Raven?" Emma asked just before she took a bite of bread.

"That's when I met Essie. It turns out that Essie is a nickname for Sonya. Sonya starts with an S—Essie."

Emma tilted her head to one side, considering. "Essie. I like that. So, you met Essie back in Los Angeles and started dating?"

"Yeah." How much did I want to tell her? Enough to let her know Essie—or rather—Sonya hadn't been just a fling, but not so much that she'd think we might still end up together. I didn't want Emma to get any ideas about where things stood between me and her teacher. She'd already said I should date someone. I didn't want her to start pushing me and Sonya together.

"We hit it off." I didn't say that I'd fallen head over heels in love. That was too private to share, and it might give Emma false hope. "Things were great between us. We ended up moving in together." Remembering how we used to be was both sweet and painful. Our immediate, deep connection. The way we'd laughed together. I'd never felt so close to anyone. I'd thought I'd found my soul mate.

Raven's video had put an end to all that.

"Six months after we started dating, Raven attacked Essie on her YouTube channel, and the whole story went viral."

Emma gently blew on her spoonful of soup. "That's how her dad tracked her down, right?"

I set my spoon down. "I think that might have been the worst part for her—to have her dad come back into her life. She'd told me she'd assumed he was dead."

"He's a crappy dad."

I shrugged. "After that, Essie ran. Disappeared." I scooped up a spoonful of soup, but then just stared at it. "I deserved everything she said to me the night she walked out. I should have told her about Raven from the beginning. I kept it from her because I enjoyed being an ordinary guy. Not the son of Don Ross, Hollywood producer. Not a minor YouTube celebrity with a huge following. Not Raven's boyfriend. Just me." I'd been shortsighted to keep it from her. Shortsighted and selfish. "I have to admit, I loved the anonymity. I was used to people wanting to get to know me so they could get an introduction to Dad or Raven. Essie was completely different. She didn't care about who I knew. Having her want me just for myself felt amazing."

I looked up to find Emma's gaze focused on me. Her expression was more knowing than I would have expected from someone her age. "You fell in love with her," she said.

I looked down at my soup. "I don't know about that." Except that I did. I *knew* I'd fallen head over heels for Essie. I'd tried to purge her from my system after she'd stormed out of my life. Tried to honor her request to leave her alone. Even now, that last conversation from five years ago was seared into my brain. If I'd just handled things differently. If I'd just been more understanding. If I'd just been more open and honest from the beginning.

But I hadn't.

I'd done everything wrong, and then I'd let the wound I'd inflicted on our relationship fester and turn into something even worse. Something that ate into my heart and scarred my soul.

22

FIVE YEARS AGO

Max

Five years ago

I was thoroughly frustrated by the time I was finally able to head home from work. Thanks to Chuck, I'd had to stay late to close the store—again—even though he'd been on the schedule to do it. The guy always had some excuse or another for leaving early, and this time had been no different. I told him I couldn't stay because I had plans, but Chuck simply flipped me off and walked out the door.

So much for a romantic evening with Essie. With luck, I could still salvage it, because I had something special planned.

I called to let her know I'd be late, but she didn't pick up. Maybe she was in the shower getting ready. I sent her a text, explaining, and promised to make it up to her.

Still, she didn't reply.

I called again. No answer.

When I finally walked into our apartment, I was nearly two hours late.

Essie didn't look up when I came in. She just sat on the sofa, staring at her laptop.

I could tell she hadn't gotten ready for our special night together. She still wore the same thing I'd seen her in this morning. So, why hadn't she answered? "Is your phone okay? I called and texted, but you didn't respond. I was worried."

She didn't look up. Instead, she clicked her mouse and Raven's voice came out of the speakers.

My stomach dropped. She'd found out I used to date Raven.

I should have told her myself. Having her figure it out on her own and then confront me about it was the worst way for this to happen. She'd caught me in a lie. My only defense was that I loved what we had together and I was afraid to ruin it.

But that's exactly what I'd done by keeping my past from her. Ruined it.

Maybe it wasn't too late. Maybe I could still fix things. Yes, I was clutching at straws, but straws were all I had right now.

This was the very last thing I wanted for tonight. Everything was supposed to be perfect. Special. A night to remember.

Apparently, I was about to get part of what I wanted, just not the memories I'd planned for.

"What are you watching?" I asked as I drew nearer.

A moment later, Raven spoke Essie's name, and I stopped cold. What was she saying? That Essie had wrecked our relationship? That she'd come between me and Raven?

That didn't even make any sense.

Essie finally lifted her gaze to mine, and the pure devastation in her eyes destroyed me. My vision tunneled. I couldn't tear my eyes away from her shattered expression. My entire world began collapsing in on me.

"You're Raven's boyfriend?" Essie's hand moved over her keyboard and Raven's voice halted.

Essie stared at me, pain and betrayal radiating from her in waves. "Is what she says true? Am I just some fling? Some cheap homewrecker?"

I fell to my knees in front of her. "Of course not. You're everything to me. Yes, I used to date Raven, but I broke things off with her months ago—before I ever met you."

I slid the laptop onto the cushion next to her, then wrapped my hands around her bare calves. From my spot on the floor, I pressed my abdomen against her knees and gazed up into her eyes. The agony in them tore my heart in two.

"You have to believe me. I'd never cheat. I'd never hurt anyone that way. Everything is over between me and Raven. They have been for a long time now."

Essie's lower lip trembled. "That isn't what *she* says."

I slid a panicked gaze to the screen where Raven's video was still playing with the sound muted. "She's on drugs again. I can tell by her eyes. Coke, I bet. See how she keeps rubbing her nose?"

Essie didn't spare the screen a glance. Instead, she pressed her lips together, hard, trying not to cry. "Just because she's on drugs, doesn't mean she's lying."

"Actually, it probably does. Those two things always go hand-in-hand with Raven. It's why I couldn't stay with her. Her addictions were bad enough, but her lies were what finally drove us apart."

"Lies? You're one to talk." Essie brushed a tear away from her cheek with the back of her hand. "Why didn't you *tell* me about her? I thought we told each other everything. What's true between us and what isn't? Is our entire relationship built on lies?"

I wilted. Those questions pierced into my heart as sharply as any knife. She was right. By withholding information, I'd been lying to her all along. I'd known it even as I did it, of course—but at the beginning, I'd desperately needed a clean break. A fresh start. I didn't want to talk about Raven, or even think about her. I'd done everything to pretend my past had never happened.

Then, as time went by, the lies and evasions started building on each other. I'd dug myself into a hole. One I didn't know how to get out of it. What if I told Essie and she got angry that I'd been lying to her all along? What if she left me?

"I'm so sorry. I should have been honest with you."

"When I asked you about your life in L.A., you lied. You never mentioned you'd been living with one of the top rock stars in the country. That you'd traveled with her. That you made videos with her. What else did you hide from me? Was anything you told me the truth?"

I dropped my head. She was right. There was more. I needed to get this all out in the open now. "My dad is a movie producer," I said, meeting her gaze. "He has a house in Beverley Hills and regularly hosts parties. Lots of celebrities would come. I met a lot of famous people and I'd interview them on my YouTube channel. That's how I got to know Raven…I interviewed her."

As I spoke, her eyes seemed to harden into balls of granite. "You've got to be kidding me. Are you telling me you're some spoiled rich kid? Your family is loaded? No wonder I couldn't figure out how you were able to spring for some of our expensive dinners out, or the new washer and dryer you bought. You lied and said you worked overtime. It didn't add up, but I let it slide. I trusted you."

I didn't have an answer to that, so I stared at her mutely.

My silence seemed to make her angrier. "What are you doing hanging out with me?" she snapped. "Slumming it?"

She rocketed to her feet. "You know what? I've heard just about as much as I can handle for tonight. I'm out of here." As I scrambled to stand, she shoved her laptop into her backpack and tossed it over her shoulder.

She glared at me. "I'm furious with you, but I'm even angrier with myself for believing all your lies even when I knew things weren't adding up." Her eyes sparked with pain and rage. "Don't call me. Don't text me. Just leave me alone. If—and that's a big if —I'm ever ready to talk to you again, *I'll* call *you*."

She stormed out our front door and slammed it behind her.

I stared at it, stunned. What had I done? How could I fix this?

I couldn't. Not now. Maybe not ever. Essie had excised me from her life.

Anger and self-loathing flooded me. How had I been so self-deluded as to think things could have gone any other way after I'd lied to her for so long?

I snatched up the television remote and sent it hurtling across the room. It hit my antique clock, knocking it to the floor with a loud crash.

I stared at the door. At the broken clock. At the empty room. The silence was deafening.

Our apartment felt cold and empty.

Forlorn and forsaken.

Just like me.

"YOU DIDN'T GO AFTER HER?" Emma asked after she heard how Essie had stormed out that night. "Why not?"

"Because I was stupid?" I forced myself to meet Emma's gaze.

She scowled at me. "That's pretty obvious."

I let out a sigh. "So much came down to horrible timing. She asked me not to contact her, but after I saw that interview with her dad, I called anyway." I scrubbed my hand down my face. "She wouldn't answer, and she didn't reply to my texts. Your grandpa had his heart attack the very same night.

"Your parents and my brothers were all out of town, so I had to handle everything at the hospital on my own. I practically lived there for the next two weeks. Hailey and you and Baris came back from your vacation in Japan and helped, which was a godsend. Your mom took over taking care of Dad's health. He had multiple film projects in the works, so I had to throw myself into running the business. There's nothing like being dropped into an over-whelming job to make you disconnect from the world. Even so, I desperately missed Essie. I tried to give her the time she needed, but then she canceled her phone. I didn't have any other way to contact her."

"You said you lived together. Was that here? In this apartment?"

I shook my head. "That was a couple of apartments ago. Back in Los Angeles."

"What about all her stuff? Didn't she come back to get it? Didn't you see her then?"

"She packed up and moved out the next day while I was at the hospital. The landlord at our old place said the paparazzi were lurking outside to get shots of her, but he helped her get in and out of the building without being seen. I went to the restaurant where she worked to try to see her, but she quit after her dad showed up. No forwarding address. She disappeared, and I couldn't find her. She finally answered one of my texts and asked me to give her space. That was the last time I heard from her.

"Between my dad almost dying and Essie vanishing, I was barely holding on. It had to have been a million times worse for her, though. Her life had been destroyed by Raven and her fans... and I blamed myself.

"Months passed. I tried contacting her, but her number didn't work anymore. I finally had news of her the following spring after that second scandal erupted, but by the time I was able to fly back from a film location in Indonesia to talk to her, she'd already run off again."

"The second time? Raven went after her more than once?"

I closed my eyes, and my shoulders slumped. "Yeah. Raven went off the deep end a few months later. Cut off all her hair. Blamed Essie for everything. Some idiot with a camera recorded Essie on the playground at the school where she worked and posted it. The parents were furious when they spotted their kids in the video, and the principal asked her to leave because she was 'too much of a disruption.'"

"Wow." Emma tugged at her lower lip again. "Why didn't you make Raven take it all back? Why didn't you fix it?"

"I tried, again and again. Nothing I said made a difference.

Sometimes a lie takes on a life of its own." When Emma looked unconvinced, I sighed. "Come on, let me show you something."

I dried my hands on a kitchen towel and led her back to the laptop. Raven's face was still frozen in the paused image on the screen. I pointed at the number displayed below her image. "See this? It shows the number of people who've watched her video. It has over ten million views."

I opened a new screen and brought up a different video. The one I'd made. "Here's the one where I tried to clear Essie's name by setting the record straight. How many views does it have?"

Emma frowned. "Thirty thousand."

"Most people believed Raven's version of the story and thought I was lying. The only people who believed me were my regular followers, and I didn't have all that many compared to her. Face it: I'm a nobody. Raven's a celebrity."

Emma let out a derisive laugh. "Not anymore. No one listens to her music."

"Five years ago, she was at the top of the charts. She still has fans. Still goes on tour. In fact, she's poised to release a new album that might end up putting her back on top."

The kid glared at me. She was clearly team Sonya. "Don't tell me you're a fan!"

"I liked her music, but I don't listen to it anymore. Too many bad memories. No, I'm not a fan, but I do keep track of her career." When Emma's scowl deepened, I chuckled. "Think of it as keeping an eye on your enemy. She did a huge amount of damage when she spiraled out of control. It would be stupid to turn my back on her."

Emma gave a reluctant nod. "That makes sense." She tugged at her bottom lip, pinching it between her thumb and forefinger. "It's been *years* since the last scandal. Do you think anyone still cares? I bet Miss Gambit's safe now."

"Maybe. Maybe not. It's hard to say. I've put a lot of thought into this. If Raven was still hiding from the world, having someone reveal Essie's new identity wouldn't be much of a problem. That isn't the case, though. Raven's about to release a new album. She's creating a lot of buzz in the entertainment industry. If a story about Miss Gambit being Essie was to come out now, it could really take off."

2 3

FRANTIC JOB SEARCH

Sonya

It had been two hours since Mrs. Falls had threatened me, and I still couldn't calm down. Between the woman's accusations and Max's kiss, I was an emotional mess.

I slid a frozen lasagna into the oven, poured myself a glass of chianti, grabbed the rest of the bag of Hershey's minis I'd bought to hand out on Halloween, and unwrapped a Mr. Goodbar.

Hey—it had nuts, right? Protein.

Finally, I'd had it with myself. I needed to stop freaking out and take action. That usually helped calm me down.

First on the agenda? Figure out where I could disappear to.

I opened the browser on my laptop to my favorite site that listed open teaching positions. I doubted I'd find a permanent position as amazing as the one I had now, but I wouldn't know if I didn't try. I needed an escape plan.

Philly should be far enough, right? After all, no one had found me there during the past three years.

My heart ached. I didn't want to leave Max again. Or my students. I was already so attached to them—especially Emma. Having yet another adult disappear from her life would be a blow.

I scrolled through the openings, but I couldn't find any fifth-grade teacher slots. Maybe I could teach middle school?

I sighed with frustration and shut my laptop. I hated having to go through the job-hunt process again, especially when I'd thought I'd found my forever job.

Maybe I should look for something overseas.

I opened my laptop to launch a new, broader search when my phone rang. I checked the display.

Max.

My heart leaped and my lips suddenly tingled with that remembered kiss.

Slow down. It could also be Emma.

The girl could be using her uncle's phone to call for homework help. Or maybe she wanted to talk about whatever had been distracting her in class lately, or—she might have overheard what Mrs. Falls had said.

I took a gulp of wine, took a calming breath, and then answered.

"Hi, Sonya." The low rumble of Max's voice sent reverberations through my body.

"I didn't know if it would be you or Emma on the line. I was just about to pull my lasagna out of the oven." The oven timer went off, and I reached for my potholders.

"I won't keep you." He sounded tense.

I cleared my throat as I set the pan on the stove. "The lasagna has to cool before I can cut it, so I have a few minutes. How can I help you?"

"A couple of things. I need to ask you about Emma first."

I inhaled sharply. "Emma? Is something wrong?"

"I'm not sure. I was hoping you could tell me. She's gotten even more moody and depressed recently. Have you noticed the same thing at school?"

"Actually, I have. She's been quieter than usual, and she wore that Nirvana shirt the last two days in a row. She likes to wear it when she's feeling blue."

"Any idea what's bothering her?" he asked.

"Other than missing her parents, you mean?" I winced. That sounded flippant, which was the last thing I wanted.

Max didn't seem to notice. "I think something happened to trigger this."

I thought back and recalled something. "Earlier this week, our class was talking about Thanksgiving plans. You know—visiting grandparents, favorite foods—that sort of thing. I shared that I'd be having dinner with Lianna and some of my other friends. Emma asked to leave to go to the bathroom. I didn't think anything of it at the time, but that might have been what upset her."

"I bet that was it. Hailey always hosted Thanksgiving dinner at her place. She made a big deal about it. She said Thanksgiving was her favorite holiday because it was all about family, food, and spending time together."

My chest tightened. Poor Emma. No wonder she'd become withdrawn. "I should have called. I didn't realize how much it upset her."

I should try to stick it out in my job a while longer—at least until after the fifth-grade show. Surely things wouldn't blow up in my face that quickly. I hated the idea of abandoning Emma, but I was trapped between two untenable choices. Being publicly outed as Essie Harlow, or abandoning Emma—and Max.

"Don't blame yourself," Max said. "You couldn't have known. I'm glad you were able to help me figure out what triggered her. I'll talk it over with the rest of the family and come up with some Thanksgiving plans."

"You should have Emma help with the planning too."

"Good idea."

I poked at the tray of lasagna with my fork. It still wasn't cool enough to cut.

Max cleared his throat.

I stilled, recognizing the nervous habit. My heart thumped hard in my chest. Was something else wrong?

"I also wanted to check in with you about the show," he said. "Are you happy with today's rehearsal?"

My cheeks warmed. I'd certainly liked the kiss, not that I'd admit it to him. A knot of tension in my stomach unwound. "Three more weeks until the performance," I said. "We still have a lot to do, but if today's rehearsal was an indicator, I think we'll be fine. You were amazing."

"Piece of cake. This is a simple show. It'll be great."

"I'll have to trust you."

He was silent for a moment. "I won't let you down. Not this time."

Suddenly, the weight of the past five years pressed down on me. "I didn't mean it like that. I meant—I just don't have any experience with directing a show. I'm depending on you."

"No worries. I have it covered. I promise. I have a favor to ask, though."

"You do?" I inhaled deeply as some of the tension in my body ebbed. Why did the idea of helping him make me feel better? "What do you need? I really owe you for pitching in."

I heard the scraping sound of his hand rubbing against his five o'clock shadow. "Emma and I are moving into our house next weekend."

I leaned my hip against the edge of the counter. "I bet you're relieved. Getting rid of that daily commute will make life a lot easier on you."

"Emma wants to know if you'll give us a hand."

Emma. Not Max. The shine on my good mood tarnished a bit. "Of course. I'd be happy to."

After we hung up, I sighed and pushed myself away from the counter to check the lasagna and found it cool enough to cut.

Instead of reacting and panicking, I needed to stop and think. What did *I* want? Did I want to leave? Did I want to stay and fight? If I could stay and be assured I could have a life outside the spotlight, I'd never even consider leaving.

The question was, was I more afraid of public opinion, or losing Max again? Of losing this life I'd built for myself.

I wasn't sure. If I stayed—if I tried—were we still a possibility? Could I ever really let go of my hurt and anger at all his lies? Holding onto it meant poisoning our future, but I couldn't simply forget what he'd done.

But—maybe I could forgive and move on.

I caught myself humming as I cut the lasagna and served myself a piece. It wasn't until I took a bite that I realized Taylor Swift's *Love Story* was running through my brain.

Lovely. Just lovely. Just what the heck is wrong with me? Why am I envisioning a happily ever after with Max?

Well, hell. If Taylor Swift, the leader of the 'f-you for betraying me' movement, was going to turn into an earwig and sing to me about love and happily ever afters, maybe I should give the entire concept more thought.

24

A NICE NIGHT FOR DUCKS

Max

Next Monday evening, the rain came pouring down and made driving to the Not a Yacht Club a challenge. I parked as close to the entrance as possible.

"I left my umbrella somewhere," I told Emma. "I'll have to buy a new one. We're going to get soaked going inside. Watch your step. There are puddles everywhere."

She just shrugged. "It doesn't matter. My shoes are already wet from stepping in that puddle in front of Marley's house."

"Ready to make a run for it?" At her nod, I pushed open my door and darted for the entrance, getting soaked in the process. Emma moved more slowly. By the time she stood next to me beneath the overhang, her hair dripped with water.

"I bet it'll rain like this on Halloween," she said as she stared glumly at the parking lot.

"I checked, and the weather forecast says the rain will be gone by then." I pushed open the front door and ushered her in ahead of me.

One of Emma's shoes squelched as we headed toward the kitchen.

"Hi, Emma," Dante said, catching sight of her. "You look half-drowned. I'm glad you made it."

She shrugged. "It was either that or sit in the car," she said in a monotone.

Dante frowned. "I'm glad you chose us." He raised a questioning eyebrow at me in a what's-wrong-with-the-kid sort of look.

I shrugged.

"Come sit on this stool next to the stove," Dante told her. "It's warmer here. You'll dry off faster."

She nodded and trudged after him.

"Hi, Emma," Conner said as he entered the kitchen. "Have you had a chance to check out our new glow path by the river?"

"Not yet," she said as she settled onto the stool. "Uncle Max and I were going to look at it tonight, but it's raining too hard."

"We'll stop by later this week after trick-or-treats," I said. "It should be more fun that night anyway. Spookier."

"Spookier?" Conner repeated, confused.

"A glowing path that disappears into the forest?Sounds ghostly to me."

Conner didn't reply. When Dante announced we were making Lamb Kebobs, Conner didn't even react, which was odd since he'd been the one campaigning for us to learn how to make them. He was lost in thought.

While Ford and I started prepping the ingredients, Emma dragged her stool over to sit next to us. "I'll supervise," she said. She started tapping her heels rhythmically against the stool legs as she watched.

Once I added the breadcrumbs, eggs, and spices to the meat in the stainless-steel bowl, I plunged my hands into it and started mixing everything together.

"That's gross," Emma said.

"The meat?" I asked. "Don't you like lamb kebobs?"

"No. Your hands. Did you even wash them first?"

"Of course." I grinned and stretched a meat-flecked hand toward her.

"Uncle Max!" Emma shrieked. She jumped off her stool and backed away. "You're disgusting."

"It's a talent."

She stalked over to Dante. "Can you make him behave?"

"I doubt it."

"Hey, I got a call from your Uncle Sinan today," I told her.

She flew back over to me, worry pinching her face. "Uncle Sin? Is he okay?"

It took an effort to keep my smile steady. It tore my heart to realize Emma automatically assumed she was about to hear bad news. "He's fine. He says he arranged to get Thanksgiving off at the hospital this year and wants to spend it with us."

Emma's tension evaporated and her eyes brightened. "He can? That's excellent."

"Your Grampa is hosting Thanksgiving at his place," Ford said, "and he's putting me and Mara in charge of planning everything. We could use your help. You up for it?"

Emma settled back onto her stool once again. "I guess so. What kind of help?"

"First, we need a menu. What are some must-have foods?" Ford asked. "We need to make sure we don't forget anything important."

"Turkey," she told him.

Ford gave her a do-I-look-like-an-idiot look. "Check," he said dryly. "What else?"

"That orange-cranberry relish. The homemade kind."

Ford gave her a delighted smile. "I love that stuff. That was my mom's recipe."

Grief passed its shadow across Emma's face. "Mine too."

"I have the recipe," I told her. "We can make it together. What else?"

"Stuffing," she suggested. "Three kinds of pie. Apple, pecan, and pumpkin. Whipped cream. Green veggies. Mashed potatoes. Gravy."

Ford glanced around as if looking for something. "Can you write all that down for me? I don't want to forget anything."

Emma pointed at a pen attached to the wall next to a pad of paper on a counter. "Sure thing," she said and scooted off the stool.

I kept an eye on her as she started writing. "While she's gone, I wanted to tell you about what happened last week." I told him about the conversation Emma had overheard and what I'd ended up telling her about Raven.

Ford winced. "Those must have been some awkward topics."

I rolled some of the ground-lamb mixture into a kebab shape and skewered it down the center with a bamboo stick. "Do you have any idea how hard it is to discuss drug abuse with an eleven-year-old?"

Ford gave a shudder. "Better you than me."

I watched as Dante set a slice of chocolate cake and a glass of milk next to Emma.

She smiled and said something to Dante before flipping to a fresh page on the pad. She started drawing as she took a huge bite of cake.

"She looks content," Ford commented.

I watched her for a moment. "She does. I won't even bitch at Dante for giving her dessert before she's had dinner."

I stretched my stiff neck from side to side. I hadn't been sleeping well. "I'm worried the old Raven scandal could erupt again. Any ideas on how I might be able to control it?"

Ford considered the question. "The way I see it, your biggest threats come from Raven and her fans."

"I agree, but Sonya also seems worried that *Here's the Scoop* will target her again."

"I can't say I blame her. They were downright malicious." Ford slid the baking tray of lamb kebobs into the oven. "You know, there can't be a story if Raven shuts it down before it gains traction."

"What do you mean?"

"She might be as unhappy about having that old scandal resurface right now as you are. Why don't I reach out to her—you know—assess her state of mind? I'm looking for someone to do the soundtrack for my movie. I could contact her to see if she's interested."

"Have you lost your mind?" I stared at him incredulously. "You want to *collaborate with Raven*?" I had to lower my voice when saying those last words, but I'd wanted to shout them.

Ford hesitated. "When I suggested it, I meant it as a pretense, but on second thought, would it really be such a bad idea? Think of it from a public-relations point of view. It would certainly prove to her fans that the two of you have buried the hatchet."

"That's the worst idea I've ever heard. Raven's an unpredictable nut-job. We need to keep her far away from your movie as possible."

Ford raised his hands in surrender. "Enough said. I still think we could use the movie as a pretense to contact her, though."

I hesitated. Ford's idea might help us figure out Raven's current state of mind with regard to me and Essie. It was possible she was as eager to leave that story in the past as we were. Finding out might make contacting her worth the risk. "Okay. You can go ahead and call her—but you need to be careful. Don't even breathe Sonya's name."

"Of course not. I've got your back on this," Ford promised.

25

HALLOWEEN

MAX

I arrived at the Zerkowskis' house an hour before trick-or-treating was scheduled to begin and found Emma crunching away at the remnants of a sucker.

"Is your tongue supposed to be black?" I asked her. "It looks sort of cool."

"Is it?" Emma's eyes went wide. "You're teasing." She scrambled for Marley's first-floor powder room. "Ew!" She said from its depths. "It is!"

"You just finished off a black sucker," I pointed out. "What did you think would happen?"

"Not this! How do I make it go away?"

Hell if I knew. "Brush your teeth and your tongue?"

"Mrs. Z," Emma stuck her head out of the powder room, "can I borrow a toothbrush?"

"There are unopened ones in the top drawer under the sink. Toothpaste, too. Grab one. You can take it home with you."

"Are you sure you want your tongue to be pink?" I asked. "Aren't you a corpse bride? I think the black tongue works."

She stared at me, then headed back into the bathroom. "You're right," she called back to me. "It's perfect with the costume."

I headed out the front door and found Marley's dad, Ted. The man opened a bottle of beer and handed it to me. "You'll need this to make it through the night," he said. "All the shrieking can wear you down."

I glanced at the label. Modelo. I took a swig. "Do a lot of the houses play those recordings with spooky noises?"

"What?" Ted asked, confused. "Oh. No. I meant the girls. You get them together in a pack like this and they'll shred your eardrums."

I raised my bottle in a toast. "Thanks for the heads-up."

Ten minutes later, the girls all stampeded out the front door. A corpse bride, a corpse groom, a giant piece of poison candy corn with Xs for eyes, and Wonder Woman. Tonight, Emma and Marley had Ally and Paige in tow. The four of them led the way, and I followed along with the other dads.

"Can they maintain this pace all night?" I asked Ted as we trotted to catch up with the girls.

"The only reason we'll be able to keep up without running most of the way is that the kids have to go up the path to each door," Ted explained. "If not for that, we'd be at a dead run all night."

The first few houses were spread far apart, and most of the homeowners had elaborate decorations. Around a half-mile down the street, the houses grew smaller and closer together. When Emma knocked on one of the doors, she let out a shriek of excitement. "Miss Gambit! It's you! I didn't know you lived here!"

"Happy Halloween," Sonya cackled. She wore a witch costume with black tights, a purple tutu, a pointed hat, and a hairy wart on her chin. She glanced over Emma's head. Was she searching for me?

I stepped forward into a pool of light. Her eyes caught mine, and she smiled and waved.

When I waved back, Tom Zerkowski caught my eye and gave a sly wink. "You've met the teacher?"

"Yeah. We're co-directing the fifth-grade musical." I said it matter-of-factly, so he wouldn't read too much into it. "I wanted to spend more time with Emma, and helping with the show was the perfect way to do it."

"Right," Ted said, the mischievous light in his eye fading. "How's Emma doing?"

"As well as can be expected. She has good days and bad ones."

"What happened to her parents really sucked. I liked them. They were great people." Tom took a long swallow of his beer.

"Yeah, they were. Thanks."

When Emma came back down the path, she stopped next to me rather than running off to the next house. "Here," she said, passing me a Hershey's Special Dark Chocolate mini. "This is for you. From Miss Gambit."

I grinned as I opened it. I glanced up to see Sonya watching me and waved as I popped the candy in my mouth. "I love dark chocolate," I told Emma.

"I wonder how she guessed that?" She winked and ran off with her friends.

By the time we finally made it back to the Zerkowskis' house, Emma's bag bulged with her Halloween haul.

"Come on," Tom said. "The girls will sort through their candy and trade away the stuff they don't like. That's your chance to snag a couple of your favorites. They're always more willing to share when their enormous piles are spread out in front of them."

The giggling girls stormed into the house and started shedding costume pieces. They all plopped down in the dining room and dumped their loot on the table. Intense negotiations ensued, but soon everyone was happily munching on candy.

"We should head out soon," I said. "We have a drive ahead of us and you have school tomorrow."

"Just a few more minutes?" Emma wheedled.

"Your choice. Do you want to stop to see the glowing path at Not a Yacht Club, or stay here longer?" I glanced at my watch. "One or the other."

She grabbed her bag and swept her arm across the table,

dumping her candy into it. "The glow-in-the-dark path. I'm dying to see it, and tonight's the perfect night."

Five minutes later, I pulled into the parking lot at the Not a Yacht Club. Apparently, I wasn't the only person with this idea. A steady stream of people headed around the building toward the path.

"Do you think they put up some Halloween decorations?" Emma asked.

As we followed the crowd, I heard one of those spooky Halloween recordings playing.

Skeletons crawled out from beneath tombstones and a corpse hung from a tree. Deeper in the forest ahead, I spotted a headless horseman perched on a skeletal horse. Smoke machines made the entire landscape eerie.

"This place is awesome, Uncle Max. Why didn't you tell me?"

"Because I didn't know." I spotted Conner standing beneath a skeleton dressed in tattered clothes hanging from a noose on a tree. He was talking with Reed. "Let's go find out why no one ever mentioned it."

I caught Conner's eye and gave him a what-the-hell look.

Conner just grinned. "When you mentioned bringing Emma here tonight, you inspired me. I've been working on setting this up since then. Reed and some of his friends in nursing school offered to help."

"We've had a blast pulling this together," Reed said. "Almost everyone was able to contribute something to the cause, and Conner filled in the gaps by making some strategic purchases. We were even able to grab a few items from the hospital that were being decommissioned."

My eyes widened as I peered up at what I'd assumed was a fake skeleton hanging from the tree. "Don't tell me that's real."

Emma shrieked in terror and scuttled back.

Conner barked out a laugh. "No, no. That'd be truly horrifying. Not to mention illegal. That guy came from a Halloween store. Resin."

"The grim reaper over there," Reed indicated a tall woman dressed all in black, "just moved to a smaller house and had to put tons of Halloween decorations in storage. She didn't put any of them up this year because she's been so swamped with course-work. She let us use whatever we needed."

"This place is awesome," Emma told Conner.

"You think so?" He asked, looking extremely pleased.

"Let's follow the path," Emma said, tugging on my hand.

"Talk to you later," Conner said.

As we headed into the woods, I spotted a mad scientist tableau. There was an old stainless-steel operating table that must have been borrowed from the hospital along with some ancient-looking lights. Two women, probably Reed's friends, bustled around the table wearing bloody surgical clothes and cackling in delight as they harvested the bloody corpse's organs.

"Look, Uncle Max." Emma pointed down the path.

I spotted a familiar woman in a purple tutu. Sonya.

"Go say hello," I told Emma.

Emma waited, but when I didn't move, she gave a huff of impatience and then quietly scurried down the path. When she was directly behind Sonya, she yelled, "Boo!"

Sonya let out a shriek and whirled on Emma. When she recognized her, she grinned. "You stinker. Just for that, I'm holding a pop quiz tomorrow morning."

Emma just grinned at the empty threat.

Sonya looked up, meeting my gaze. "Is this corpse bride yours?" she asked.

"That all depends. Is she causing trouble?"

Sonya shook her head. "Never."

"Then I'll claim her."

"You know Rose, right?" Emma said, indicating the smaller woman next to her, dressed as that quirky blonde girl from the Harry Potter movies. Luna Lovegood.

I held out my hand. "Actually, I don't think we've met yet."

"You're Ford's brother, right?" Rose asked as she shook it. "We keep missing each other. It's nice to finally meet you." She stared up at me through a pair of quirky, star-shaped eyeglasses. One lens was pink, and the other was blue.

"When did you find out this was going on?" I asked. "Conner told me they threw it all together in just a couple of days."

"One of my teens at the library mentioned it to me this afternoon," Rose said. "They always know what's going on around town. I'd be totally out of the loop if it weren't for them."

"Rose keeps me up to date on all the town gossip," Sonya said. "She's always tuned into it."

I'd been about to confirm tomorrow's plans for Sonya to help us move, but that comment made me look at Rose more carefully. I should take Sonya's comment as a warning and be careful what I said.

"There's Liam," Emma said.

"Let's say hi." I nodded at Rose. "It was nice to finally meet you."

As I followed Emma, I could feel Rose's eyes on us.

26

PACK IT UP

SONYA

I pulled into Max's parking garage the next morning with a light heart. In the week-and-a-half since Darcy Falls had cornered me after rehearsal, I'd been bracing myself for the next attack, but nothing happened. Even the rehearsals had gone well. Amazing, in fact.

I'd been worried Emma might have overheard something, but I guess I'd dodged that particular bullet. Neither she nor Max had mentioned a word about it.

Overall, Emma seemed to be handling everything well. I'd noticed a steady improvement in her mood ever since Max had started taking her to a therapist. Sure, she had bad days, but they'd been happening less and less often. Emma seemed to be healing.

I passed Max's car and took the elevator up to his floor, then knocked on his door.

No one answered. After knocking a few more times, I began to wonder if I'd screwed up. Was I supposed to meet them somewhere else? But that couldn't be right. Max's car was in the garage. They had to be here.

I banged on the door one last time.

An instant later, Emma yanked it open.

A wall of sound hit me. I spotted the booming radio on the kitchen island, amazed I hadn't heard it from the hallway.

Max's living room was already being dismantled. The bookcase was still full, but flattened boxes leaned against it, ready to be filled. A sofa was missing, and the other one was wrapped in quilted blankets and webbed straps.

"How's it going?" I asked, shouting to be heard.

"So far, so good!" Emma shouted back.

I spotted some men in the kitchen, wrapping the dishes in paper and loading them into boxes. "Do you still need help with your room?"

There was a pause between songs, giving my eardrums a break.

"Uncle Max says all our things won't be unpacked for a while. I'm supposed to put everything I need for today and tomorrow in a bag, plus anything special I'll want right away."

"That makes sense. I didn't realize the movers would already be here."

As I stood in the doorway, the freight elevator at the far end of the corridor opened and two men came out. I moved to one side to let them into Max's apartment. They headed for the sofa, lifted it, and headed back toward the elevator.

Emma darted toward the rear of the apartment. "C'mon," Emma said over her shoulder. "You can say hi to Uncle Max and help me figure out what I need to pack."

Before I realized where she was leading me, I found myself in Max's bedroom. He had a suitcase open on his rumpled, unmade bed. I spied his toothbrush, toothpaste, and phone charger on the nightstand.

Max turned, gray boxer briefs in hand. I'd always had a weakness for boxer briefs—that is, for *Max's* boxer briefs.

He spotted me, and a smile brightened his face. "You're here. Thanks for coming." His gaze trailed over my body like a caress. "You look perfect."

I wore a pair of jeans and an old athletic top, perfect for helping someone move, but the way Max looked at me made me realize my snug-fitting top left nothing to the imagination.

"Your purple tutu last night was even better, though." He dropped his boxer briefs into the suitcase.

"I could go home and change," I offered.

"I just might take you up on that."

"I take it back." I'd fallen into our old teasing banter without even thinking about it. It was hard not to. "Sorry for barging into your bedroom."

"No problem. The movers have been in and out of here all morning. At least I wasn't naked." When I blushed, his grin grew broader.

"Don't tease me."

"Why not? It's hard not to."

I gave him the side-eye. "It's inappropriate. If you're not on your best behavior, I'll start treating you like one of my misbehaving students."

"That doesn't sound good." He glanced at Emma. "What does she do when someone misbehaves?"

Emma shrugged. "Lots of different things. It really depends on who it is and what they did. Maybe she'll make you write her a letter of apology."

Max's smile dimmed the tiniest bit.

Emma shuffled her feet. "Is there a suitcase I can use? My old one…"

Struck again by her loss, I rocked back on my heels. Of course. Emma's old suitcase would have been destroyed in the fire.

"I'm way ahead of you, kiddo," Max said. "Go look in my closet."

Emma walked in and immediately let out a squeal of delight. "A pink suitcase! With wheels! Uncle Max, I love it! Thank you!" She abandoned the bag and tore across the room to tackle him with a hug. She buried her face against his chest. He didn't waver under her attack, but simply wrapped his arms around her and kissed her on the top of her head.

"I'm glad you like it," he said.

"It's perfect." A moment later, she grabbed the suitcase and raced toward her bedroom.

"I love kids at this age," I said, smiling fondly. "They go back and forth from being worldly and blase to completely thrilled. So many experiences in their lives are still novel. Ten years from now, she won't be so easy to impress."

"I know what you mean. She has me seeing the world in a different light. With fresh eyes and a new perspective." His eyes bored into me. "Just like when we were together."

I swallowed, at a loss for words.

"Sonya—"

"I should get to work," I said. I backed out of his bedroom and scurried away.

That rumpled bed of his had been an unexpected intimacy. It brought back memories of all the time we'd spent there together.

Of course, our romps hadn't taken place in this particular bed. His old one had been much smaller than this king-sized behemoth. Squeezing into it together five years ago had been both challenging and intimate, but his new one was sending vivid carnal thoughts scampering through my mind. Oh, the things we could do.

I pictured him bare-chested, clad in nothing but those gray boxer briefs he'd been holding just a moment ago, prowling toward me as I lay sprawled across his bed, watching him. When my imaginings had him sliding his thumb beneath the waistband of his briefs as he prepared to strip them off, I banished them. I couldn't think about him like that. Not if I wanted to maintain some emotional distance.

That thought stopped me. Is that what I wanted? Distance?

Perhaps it had been true a month ago, but now? Taylor Swift's earwig started running through my mind again.

I wasn't quite ready to face Emma yet, so I headed into the hall bathroom to give myself time to gather my thoughts. Since I was there anyway, I started loading one of the empty boxes I found in there with items from under the sink.

Yes, I'd fallen for Max five years ago. I admitted it freely. When Raven accused me and Max of having some sort of illicit relationship, I'd been furious with him for hiding their relationship from me.

But hadn't I done the very same thing with every man I'd dated since then? With every parent and student I'd come into contact with? How were my secrets any different from Max's?

They weren't.

I froze with a can of sea spray-scented Febreze in one hand and a box of Band-aids in the other when that particular bolt of truth hit me squarely in the forehead.

⸻

HAD it really taken me five years to recognize my own hypocrisy? I'd been so busy being angry that I hadn't tried to look at things from a different point of view.

I finally understood why someone might not want a piece of their past to color their present or shape their future. All I wanted now was to be judged based on my character rather than an overblown news story.

I finished loading the box, labeled it, and set it down in the kitchen next to the boombox.

I spotted a paper with the words "do not pack" sitting next to some items on the dining table. Max had set aside some oil paintings, framed photos, and the antique clock he'd loved so much.

The broken clock.

Guilt pricked me. If I hadn't stormed out on him that night, his clock wouldn't have been broken. I touched the hands that still marked the time when I'd walked out of his life.

Nine seventeen.

Max might have hidden his relationship with Raven, but I'd been the one who'd left. I'd been the one who'd broken his heart.

It was past time for me to try to mend what I'd broken between us. Time to stop acting so aggrieved and superior, and start being understanding.

As I stared down at Max's clock, I knew exactly how to start. I carefully started packing it into an empty box.

A few minutes later, I found Emma sitting on her bed next to her pink suitcase. She was pinching her bottom lip between her thumb and forefinger, distracted.

"Did you pack your toothbrush?" I asked. "Toothpaste? A phone charger? Pack your soap and shampoo too, so you won't have to open every box labeled 'bathroom' just to find them."

"It's all in there." Emma zipped her bag shut, then stared down at the floor. She opened her mouth like she was about to say something, then closed it again.

"Is something on your mind?"

Her shoulders dropped, and she scooted over to make room for me on the bed. I sat down next to her.

"I need to tell you something." Emma kept her eyes glued to the floor as if a hole were about to open up in it. "It's about Mrs. Falls." She inhaled deeply. "I overheard what she said to you the other day. When I got home, I looked stuff up on the internet. Raven's YouTube video. Your dad. Uncle Max's video. I know everything."

My stomach began churning. Was she upset with me? Angry I'd kept it from her? "I'm sorry you found out that way. I should have told you myself, but I didn't know how, or when, or if it was even my place to do it."

When Emma met my eyes, her eyebrows were pulled together in a deep frown. "That's not the problem. I'm not upset you didn't tell me. What Raven did to you was terrible. If it had happened to me, I'd have wanted to forget about it too."

I exhaled sharply, surprised. "Believe me, I tried."

"I'm upset that Mrs. Falls is being so mean. I know Raven lied about everything. You aren't the kind of person she said you were. She was wrong about you."

Tears sprang to my eyes. Emma's loyalty overwhelmed me. "It means a lot to me that you said that."

Emma patted my arm, soothing me. "I'm just glad you and Uncle Max are friends again." She hesitated. "I talked to my therapist about it. I told her that maybe that's why my parents died—so you and Uncle Max could make up."

"No!" The word burst from me as Emma's confession pierced my heart. I gently took hold of the girl's arms and looked deep into her eyes. "I'd never want that. Emma, you have to believe me. Don't even think it."

"My therapist says life doesn't work that way. None of us has the power to influence things just through our thoughts or wishes. She said it was important I didn't start believing it because I might end up blaming you and Uncle Max for my parents' deaths." She shook her head, hard, frowning. "I'd never want that to happen."

"Oh, Emma." I pulled her in for a hug.

Emma curled against me, a warm bundle in my arms. "She said that since you're my teacher, Uncle Max would have met you at the school play anyway, so you still would have met." She sniffled.

I took a shaky breath. "I bet she's right. Max is so involved in your life, I'm sure he would've come to the show."

"So, now you know I know." Emma sat up straight again and looked me in the eyes. "There's something more. You should also know I think you and Uncle Max are great together. I know you're my teacher and all, but I don't think you should avoid seeing him just because of me. That would be really crappy. Because then, my parents dying would be the thing that keeps you apart instead of the thing that brings you together." She frowned. "See? My therapist is right. Trying to say my parents died for this reason or that one is just stupid and pointless." She grimaced. "She didn't use those words, but it's pretty much what she said."

I smiled as I pulled Emma into another hug. "I think your therapist is giving you some excellent advice."

Emma pulled free and gave me an impish grin. "Just so you know, if you decide you want to be Uncle Max's girlfriend, I won't take advantage of you. I'll be cool about the whole thing."

"Oh, really?" Such a precocious child. "You wouldn't be tempted to find out about pop quizzes or change your grades in my grade book?"

"As if." Emma rolled her eyes, still grinning.

My heart gave a thump of affection. I could really grow to love this girl. "Thanks for letting me know."

"Hey there, kiddo," a man said.

I glanced up and did a double take when I spotted a tall, muscular, well-dressed man standing in Emma's doorway.

"Uncle Sin!" Emma ran across her room and threw herself into her uncle's arms. He picked her up and she wrapped her legs around his waist, hooking her feet together in the back like a monkey. "Are you here to help us move?"

"Sure am. I'll supervise things and answer any questions the movers have while you and Max take a load of stuff over to your new house.".

Emma glanced over her shoulder at me. "This is my teacher, Miss Gambit. She's helping, too."

I held out my hand. "Call me Sonya. We met at Family night."

He shifted his hold on Emma to shake it. "We did. Did I introduce myself? I'm Sinan Bachar. Emma's dad was my brother." The man had dark hair and an olive complexion. I recognized the family resemblance to Emma.

"Sinan is an unusual name. I don't think I've ever heard it before."

"It's Turkish," he said with a smile. "My brother's name was Barin, but he went by Barry. I go by Sin."

Emma slid to the floor, grabbed his hand, and led him down the hallway. "Uncle Max is back here."

"No, he isn't. I just talked to him in the dining room," Sin told her.

Emma did a quick about-face and started dragging him in the opposite direction. "Let's go see him," she insisted.

As soon as Emma spotted Max, she said, "Can we go to the new house now? "I'm all packed and ready to go."

Max finished wrapping a painting in bubble wrap. I spotted three more he'd already wrapped and propped against the wall. "Are you sure you didn't forget to pack anything? Toothbrush? Toothpaste?"

"Why does everyone keep asking if I packed my toothbrush?" Emma asked. "Of course, I did. It isn't as though I've never been on a trip before."

"Ah-ha. There's the smart-aleck girl we've all come to know and love," Sin said. "I've been wondering when I'd get to hear her spout off again." He reached out and ruffled her hair.

Emma batted it away. "Stop it. You're messing up my hair."

"And so, it begins," Sin intoned.

Emma scowled at him.

I hid my grin. I loved seeing this side of Emma. She obviously loved her uncles. She was lucky to have so many people in her life who loved her. Neither of my parents had any siblings. After Dad had ditched us while Mom was pregnant with Kendra, there'd been no one to help us. Times had been tough for a while. Dad never sent any money, and we'd moved in with one of Mom's high school friends until after Kendra was born.

I remembered when Mom found a house where we could live. It was outside a little town an hour north of Philly. I loved having my own room. Even more, I loved the horse pasture down the road. I'd feed the horses handfuls of fresh grass, their soft, velvety noses tickling my palms.

I'd only been six when we'd moved in—eight when we'd moved out. Mom had cleaned houses back then. According to her, it was decent money. All I remembered was that it left Mom exhausted at the end of the day.

Looking back now, I realized the house we lived in wouldn't have passed a building inspection. Of course, that was why we'd been able to stay there. The owner had inherited it, but it was in bad shape. She'd let Mom stay there free for two years in exchange for cleaning the junk out, scrubbing the place, and painting it. According to Mom, there was no way the new owner could have sold it in the shape it had been in, so it would have been sitting empty if Mom hadn't moved us in.

When we'd first got there, the house had been so full of junk that Mom had blocked off sections of it. She'd been afraid I'd wander in, knock something over, and get buried under an avalanche of newspapers or broken toasters.

Now I knew the previous owner had been a hoarder, but back then, Mom had made up all sorts of crazy theories about why the house was full of stuff. Maybe the former owner worked for Santa and got all the rejects. Maybe she thought there'd be a toaster shortage. Maybe people kept sending her broken things to fix for them, but there was too much stuff to repair, and she fell behind.

My mom was one of the bravest, most resilient people I'd ever met. I missed her every day. She'd had a hard life, but she'd always stayed positive—even all the way to the end after she'd been diagnosed with cancer. After Dad left, Mom refused to be dependent on anyone else, and she'd instilled that same belief in me and Kendra. Stand on your own two feet. Invest in your future. Have a career you can count on.

I had to admit though, it would have been nice to have had a big family like Emma's. She didn't know how lucky she was in that respect. Her family would be there for her no matter what, especially Max.

"How many uncles do you have?" I asked Emma.

"Four. You've met Sin. Uncle Max has two other brothers, Sean and Ford."

"Any aunts?"

"Nope. Not yet, but Uncle Ford is engaged to Mara. She's cool. She owns the comic book shop in Sewickley."

"Mara is in my book club, but we haven't met yet," I told Emma.

"Uncle Sin just got engaged to another doctor, like him, but I haven't met her yet."

"Congratulations," I told Sin.

"Thanks. Miranda and I both just started our residencies here in Pittsburgh. I live up on Mount Washington."

"You're a doctor?"

He nodded. "Neurosurgeon. Miranda and I were lucky enough to get residencies at the same hospital."

"My other uncle, Uncle Sean, is a stuntman. He's doing a zombie movie right now," Emma said. "He sent me a photo of one of the actors all done up like a zombie. His skin looked like it was falling off his face. It was sick." She grinned.

"Awesome," Sin said, grinning back at her.

"O-kay," I drew the word out. *Gross.* I gave a shudder and then glanced at Max. "I already loaded some of your boxes in my car. We can drive separately."

"That works." Max glanced at Sin. "Can you help carry stuff down to the car?"

Sin shrugged. "That's why I'm here. To do what I'm told."

Twenty minutes later, I was pulling out of the parking garage. Since Sewickley was a small town, I already knew which house Max had bought. At the next light, I turned right when Max turned left. I had a stop to make first, and it would be easier to do it now since the shop I needed to visit was only a block away.

27

MOVING DAY, ER... NIGHT

MAX

My phone chimed, letting me know I'd received a text message. Emma picked it up and checked the screen.

"It's from Miss Sonya."

"Miss Sonya? Don't you mean Miss Gambit?"

"She said I could call her Miss Sonya when we aren't at school." She waved the phone at me. "Do you want me to read it to you?"

"Sure." I could have had my car read it aloud, but Emma loved doing this particular task for me.

"She says, 'I had to make a fifteen-minute pit-stop.'"

"Text her back and say, 'No problem. Do you need my address?'"

"No problem," Emma said, grinning as she typed the message into my phone.

It chimed again.

"She says, 'It's a small town. I know where you live.' There's a winky-face at the end."

I tried not to wince at the reminder. Sewickley was the kind of place where everyone knew everyone and saw everything.

Goodbye, big-city anonymity. Hello, small-town life.

A half-hour later, I pulled up the driveway of my huge turn-of-the-century home. The wrap-around front porch, stately trees, and white picket fence reeked of domesticity... exactly what Emma needed.

I'd purchased new furniture since my apartment was a lot smaller than this place. The kitchen barstools and Emma's new bedroom furniture were already in place, and more pieces would arrive over the next couple of weeks.

I pushed the opener for my new garage door and pulled in, my car almost touching the built-in workbench at the back. I bet Emma and I could figure out how to build a birdhouse. She'd probably like that.

"C'mon, kiddo," I said as I opened the trunk. "Let's get this stuff unloaded." I removed her pink suitcase, setting it by her feet. "Grab something else too, so we don't have to make as many trips."

Emma grabbed a black duffel bag from the trunk and draped the strap across her chest, and then she picked up my computer bag.

"You can leave those bags in the kitchen and then take your pink one up to your room."

Dry leaves whispered across the driveway as I headed toward the back door, reminding me I needed to buy rakes.

I inserted my key into the lock on the back door and unlocked it. Emma set my two bags on the kitchen floor. "I'm going to my room," she announced as she headed for the stairs.

I brought in the paintings I'd wrapped and stashed them out of the way in my bedroom closet for now. I'd deal with them later after all the furniture was in place.

As I was heading to my car, I spotted Sonya pulling up out front, so I made an about-face to greet her.

"The movers will need to unload the van here. Go ahead and park in the driveway." I indicated the spot in front of the second garage door.

She gave me a jaunty salute and climbed back into her Rav4. A minute later she was lifting the rear hatch and grabbing a box. "This one has the moving-day supplies I gathered."

I picked up another box from the back of her Toyota and led the way to the kitchen door.

"Your house is beautiful," she said. "I love the fire pit out back. And that archway with the vines climbing up the side is gorgeous. Is that clematis?"

I shrugged. "Your guess is as good as mine. Actually, it's better since I have no idea what clematis is."

She grinned. "You have hostas back here, too."

"Hostas. Got it." Maybe I should write this down.

As we walked inside, my phone started buzzing. Sin was calling, so I answered. "What's up?"

"There's a problem with the freight elevator."

That didn't sound good. "What's the problem?"

"It's on the fritz. They can't bring down any more big items. They only loaded the two sofas from the living room before it stopped working. That's it."

"You've got to be shitting me. How long until someone fixes it?

"Hard to say. I called building maintenance. For now, they'll bring down some smaller boxes using the passenger elevator. If the freight elevator isn't working by the time they're done, they'll bring you what they have and come back after it's working again."

"Ask them to start with the kitchen stuff—just in case something else goes wrong. I'd really like to get the kitchen squared away."

"Will do."

I hung up and explained the situation to Sonya.

"That stinks," she said.

"The movers might arrive here with those boxes sooner than we expect. Let's finish unloading the cars and put everything away."

Fifteen minutes later, the cars were empty.

"I'm done," Emma said as she bounced into the kitchen. "What can I do next?"

"This place has four bathrooms, right?" Sonya asked.

"Sure does. Prime seating. No waiting." Emma grinned.

Sonya pulled a four-pack of toilet paper and four bottles of hand soap from her move-in day box and handed them to Emma. "Put a roll and a soap container in each bathroom." She dug into the box and pulled out some hand towels. "These too."

My phone rang.

"Bad news," Sin said. "Building management just told the movers to stop using the passenger elevator. They got complaints. They're trying to get the freight elevator repaired, but it's going to take at least three hours. Could be longer. The movers are heading to your place to unload now."

I rubbed my forehead. "From bad to worse." I stashed my phone in my pocket and told Sonya the bad news.

"We'll adapt," she said.

"Uncle Max, did I tell you how much I like my new bedroom?" Emma said as she slumped into the kitchen.

I cocked my head to one side as I stared at my melancholy niece. "Yes, but somehow those words don't match your mood. What's up, buttercup?"

Emma grimaced. "Buttercup? Really?"

"Would you prefer, what's the deal, banana peel?" I asked.

"That's even worse."

"What's bothering you?" Sonya asked.

Emma frowned and glanced away. "The new bedroom is pretty and all, but I really miss my old one. I kind of feel like a jerk for complaining."

"It's okay, sweetie. I get it," Sonya said. "You have mixed feelings, and that's to be expected. After all, you've been through a lot of changes." She patted one of the barstools. "Why don't you have a seat? Do you want one of the drinks I packed from your Uncle Max's fridge? I have mango juice, Coke, and black cherry sparkling water."

"Mango juice," Emma said, settling onto the stool. "It's my favorite. Thanks, Miss Gambit."

I shot Sonya a look of gratitude. She'd handled that like a pro...which incidentally she was, as a teacher.

The doorbell rang, startling me with the deep, rich sound it made. I liked it. When I opened the door, I found Emma's friend Marley there holding a foil-covered plate.

"Welcome to the neighborhood, Mr. Ross. Mom sent these over. We just finished baking them." Marley handed me the plate.

I caught a whiff of vanilla and chocolate. "Cookies?"

"Yep. Chocolate chip. They're Emma's favorite."

"Mine too," I said.

"Mom says she'll drop off dinner for you tonight at around seven if that's okay. Is it okay?"

I was stunned. "It's more than okay. It's fantastic. Tell her thanks."

"Is Emma here?"

"She's in the kitchen," I balanced the cookie plate on one hand and waved her in. "Follow me."

The moment Emma spotted Marley, her eyes went wide. "You're here!" She said, her voice squealing in delight. "Come see my room! It's ginormous!"

They both started shrieking and jumping up and down, then they went tearing toward the stairs, nearly bowling Sonya over as they flew past.

Was I supposed to do the parent thing and tell her to calm down? I didn't want to. I much preferred her like this over the way she'd been just two minutes ago.

"She's feeling better," I said in a somber voice.

Sonya's eyes gleamed as she grinned. "Are you sure? It's hard to tell."

"I could be mistaken. I'm new to all this."

She smirked and then glanced at the plate I still held. "What do you have there?"

"Nothing you'd be interested in," I said, twisting my arm and hiding the plate behind my back.

"What?" Her eyes lit up and she stepped closer. "Don't make me use my teacher voice on you."

"Will you? I think I might like that. But there are other forms of persuasion that work much better on me."

She mock-scowled at me. "Don't be a tease."

I raised one eyebrow. "But I love it so. Especially when I try to tempt you."

Her scowl deepened.

"With a cookie, I mean. Chocolate chip."

Her face softened. "Are they still warm? I have a weakness for freshly baked cookies. Are they chocolate chip with walnuts?"

I lifted the foil. "Hot out of the oven. And you're in luck. Half with walnuts, half without."

She snatched one from the plate and bit into it.

"Grabby," I said. "I like a woman who knows what she wants."

"Mmm," she moaned. "I think I've died and gone to heaven." She bumped her hip against mine playfully. "Since we're waiting for the movers to get here, why don't you show me around and tell me where the furniture goes? That way I can help direct the movers."

"Good idea." I set the plate on the kitchen counter. She grabbed one more and shot me a devilish grin.

I led her through the house, pointing out the butler's pantry where I'd want some of the kitchen items to be stored, the living room where the sofas from my apartment should go, the family room with the new furniture already in place, and the large, empty master bedroom.

"The bed goes against that wall," I told her, but she'd already walked into the adjoining bathroom.

"I never would have guessed a house this old would have such a huge master bedroom suite," she said, her voice echoing off the tile. "The jacuzzi is big enough for two. And that glassed-in shower is enormous." She came back into the bedroom and came to an abrupt halt. "Oh. My. God. Check out the walk-in closet."

"A previous owner converted the bedroom next door into a master bathroom and closet."

"The ceilings are so high. Fifteen feet?"

I glanced up. "Thereabouts."

She pointed out the bedroom door at another staircase leading up to the third floor. "Is that the attic?"

"Nope. Former servants' quarters. It's a guest suite now. There's a sort of man cave up there too, with a television and built-in speakers. I haven't decided what to do with it yet. Let's check it out. You can give me some suggestions."

"I'll try to get creative."

She led the way up the narrower staircase, and I followed, watching as her perfect ass swayed from side to side right in front of my face.

I stifled a groan.

Amazing.

When we reached the top floor, she poked her head into the vacant room on the right. "Is this the man cave you mentioned? Those rich brown walls give it away. They're like milk chocolate." She crossed the hardwood floor and peered out the window. "You can see all the way to the Ohio River from here. What an incredible view."

I moved behind her and looked over her shoulder to take in the same vista.

Maybe I stood too close. Maybe her hair smelled deliciously captivating. Maybe having my chest brush against her back set my senses on fire. All I knew was that Sonya overwhelmed me—in the most perfect way imaginable.

She glanced over her shoulder at me and smiled. Thank god, she didn't move away. In fact—she leaned back against me. The heat of her body was intoxicating. It took every ounce of self-control not to pull her into my arms.

God, she smelled delicious. I could swim in her scent. All I wanted to do was bury my face in her hair and breathe her in. She was irresistible. I inhaled slowly, silently. She was intoxicating.

When I couldn't resist her any longer, I set my hand on her waist and curled my fingertips in, pressing along the edge of her hip bone in that spot where she'd always loved to be touched.

This was the moment she'd pull away. This was when she'd put a stop to this.

But she didn't.

Instead, she turned to face me and pressed her entire body against mine.

I dipped my head—our lips just inches apart.

Sonya's breathing quickened. I gazed into those amazing eyes of hers—the ones that should have been green but were blue because she wore tinted contact lenses. Her pupils dilated and grew darker, more intense.

I couldn't move. I didn't want to ruin the moment. Didn't want to push her. Whatever happened now had to be her decision. She had to be the one to take this next step.

She lifted up on her toes and pressed her lips against mine.

Holy hell, Sonya was kissing me.

I responded immediately. No hesitation. No second thoughts. This was exactly what I wanted. *She* was exactly what I wanted. *Had* wanted for these past five long years.

I cupped her face with my hands and then slid my fingers into her hair, savoring the touch of her, the feel of her lips against mine, the slide of tongue against tongue.

Her hands moved up my back, stroking my spine, my shoulders. Touching. Teasing. Her caresses turned my entire body into an electric current. I was ready to jump out of my skin.

I let out a deep moan. "Sonya. I've wanted you for so long." I trailed kisses down her neck and along her collarbone. Her head lolled back, that gorgeous blond hair brushing against my arms. Her tight-fitting athletic top showed off every curve. I grazed my thumb across a nipple that jutted against the fabric, and she let out a moan. I kissed lower, moving toward that tempting bud. I almost licked her through the fabric, but instead, I tugged the stretchy garment to one side to expose her breast to my gaze…and my tongue.

The elastic of her top cupped it, lifting it and pressing it toward me. I dragged my tongue across her nipple, reveling in Sonya's startled moan of delight. She dug her fingers into my hair, holding me in place as she arched her back. As I licked one breast, I ran my thumb in circles around the other one, causing its nipple to grow taut as well.

As I began to tug at the other side of her top to expose the second breast, the doorbell rang.

I ignored it. Instead, I changed tactics, dropping my hands to her ass and sliding them down the back of her jeans, pressing her against me. I cupped her bottom and then slid one hand between her thighs, running my fingers along the seam covering the center of her sex.

Sonya gave a shudder of delight at my touch. "Max," she hissed. "Oh, my—What—what are we doing?"

"I can't speak for you, but as for me, I'm seducing you. Is it working?"

Her eyes were glazed with want. She spread her legs and rubbed her hips against my thigh as she let out a whimper. "Can't you tell?"

The doorbell rang again, breaking my concentration. "Shit."

She let out a shaky laugh. "I have the worst timing in the world. When do I finally decide to kiss you? Moments before the movers arrive."

She pulled back and slipped her breasts back inside her top. Aside from her disheveled hair and swollen lips, my sexy teacher looked mostly presentable.

Too bad I couldn't say the same for myself. I glanced down and she followed my gaze. I had one hell of an erection.

Sonya let out a husky laugh. "Poor guy. I guess I'd better get the door. Come down as soon as you're able."

"You're killing me, Sonya."

She grinned wickedly. "What a way to go."

"This isn't over. I promise. We're going to pick this up where we left off."

She froze. A shadow of doubt flitted across her features. "Maybe we should slow down. I'm still Emma's teacher. I don't want to complicate things. This is a small town. People are bound to talk."

She looked so forlorn, it made me want to pull her back into my arms, but I knew better than to do that right now. "We'll be careful," I promised, "both with Emma and the town gossips."

She rubbed her neck and took a half-step toward the staircase. The woman didn't look convinced. In fact, she looked like she was ready to bolt.

"Don't run away from me again because you're afraid of what other people think."

She stilled. "I—" she cleared her throat— "I don't think it's that simple."

"Maybe it is."

She looked doubtful.

The doorbell rang again. And again. Whoever was down there was getting impatient. Sonya whirled away and pounded down the staircase.

When I finally made my way downstairs, I found Emma and Marley had joined Sonya. They were watching as movers carried a sofa through the front door.

A few hours later, the house was quiet. The movers had come and gone, and I had unpacked the few boxes they'd managed to deliver. Fortunately, they'd been able to get all the kitchen items moved before they'd been barred from using the elevator.

The doorbell rang.

I glanced at my watch. "It's seven already. I didn't realize it was so late. That must be Marley's mom with dinner."

"Mrs. Zerkowski is one of the nicest people I know," Sonya said. "She always volunteers to help with class parties and is a pleasure to work with. Nothing seems to bother her."

I answered the door and led Renee Zerkowski back to the kitchen.

"Hi, Miss Gambit," she said.

"Please, call me Sonya."

Renee waved her hand dismissively. "It's easier just to call you Miss Gambit. That way I won't slip and call you Sonya one day when I'm asking Marley if you assigned any homework."

I glanced around the kitchen. "I'll grab some dishes." I opened the upper cabinet next to the dishwasher where Sonya had placed my white plates.

"Don't bother. I brought disposable stuff. That way you won't have to worry about washing up. One less chore." She removed a foil container from her wicker basket. "Don't worry about returning the pan to me. You can just recycle it when you're done." She pulled back a corner to show us the beef stroganoff she'd made.

"That smells delicious," Sonya murmured. "I'm starving."

"The only thing you need to supply is a serving spoon," Renee said.

"That, I can manage," I said, pulling one from a drawer.

"I also brought a surprise," Renee said. She plucked a bottle of wine from the basket and set it on the table along with a corkscrew and two plastic wine glasses. "*Bon appétit.*"

"You only brought two?" I asked. "You're not joining us?"

"I have dinner waiting for me at home. In fact, if you'd like some peace and quiet, Emma is welcome to spend the night."

"I heard that," Emma said as she came into the room. "Say yes, Uncle Max. Please?"

"Are you sure?" I frowned. "I thought you were excited about sleeping here tonight."

"Where? No mattress. Besides, do you have any idea how great it is to live just a few doors down from Marley? It's a dream come true. This house is totally freaking awesome!"

"Glad I could accommodate," I said.

"It isn't just the house, though. It's the life I get to live here. I can visit friends or ride my bike to the ice cream shop or hang out at the comic book store. Freedom."

"Go. Have fun," I told her.

Emma turned to Mrs. Zerkowski. "Thanks for inviting me. Should I eat here or at your house?"

"Either place is fine," Renee said. "Your choice."

"I'll just eat with you. Let me go pack my bag." She turned toward the door.

I watched her leave. "Don't forget your—"

"—toothbrush and toothpaste," Emma finished for me. "I know, Uncle Max. Geez."

Sonya and I exchanged glances and then burst out laughing. "I've just been schooled by an eleven-year-old," I told her.

"I'm heading home now," Renee said as she headed for the door. "Send the girls over when they're ready."

As I pulled the cork on the wine, Emma and Marley tromped down the stairs. They shouted their goodbyes and then stormed out the front door like twin hurricanes.

The sudden silence was startling.

"Wow. When the two of them are together, it's like a force of nature," I said.

"Welcome to my world," Sonya said. "Although I have to say, it's been a while since Emma has been this exuberant." She slid onto a barstool and took a bite of the beef stroganoff. "This is delicious." She let out a sigh and slumped. "I have to admit, my feet are killing me. I haven't sat down since I got here."

I topped off her half-empty wine glass. "We should stop for the night."

"You don't want to finish the kitchen first?"

"I'll finish it in the morning before the movers get here. Sin texted me that the freight elevator is working again."

"That's a relief."

"You know, the movers managed to load the television before they had to stop using the passenger elevator. I set it up in the family room. If you like, we could watch a movie."

She hesitated. "How about if we listen to music, drink some wine, and talk instead?"

"I like the way you think, Miss Gambit." I glanced at her empty plate. "Are you done? Would you like more?"

She held up her hand. "I'm good."

"No; you're amazing. Go on into the other room and put your feet up. I'll put the leftovers in the fridge and meet you there."

A couple of minutes later, I settled onto the sofa next to her. I stretched my arms wide, draped one behind her, then leaned my head back and closed my eyes. "This is the life. A full stomach, a bottle of wine, and you by my side. I'm pretty sure this is the definition of bliss."

Sonya let out a low chuckle and nestled into my side.

I kissed the top of her head. "I've missed you these past five years."

She let out a heavy sigh. "I've missed you too."

INEVITABLE

SONYA

Thank goodness we had the sofas to sit on. We'd been on our feet most of the day. Sitting here with my head resting against Max's shoulder was exactly where I wanted to be. It was as though I'd been running in circles for the past five years and had found myself right back where I'd started. With him.

Lianna had been right when she'd said I'd never gotten over him. Maybe she was also right when she said I needed to get him out of my system. If nothing else, I needed to find my way through this maze of emotional confusion. When I'd run off five years ago, I'd left our story unfinished. I'd stopped in the middle. I'd always wondered how our story might have ended if Raven hadn't interfered.

This was my chance to find out.

I tilted my head to face Max and found him gazing at me. His shoulder muscles tensed an instant before he leaned in and kissed me.

This was like falling into a dream—or maybe the fantasy that had haunted me for so long. This felt right.

I suddenly realized Max's kiss was the standard against which I'd measured every other kiss over the past five years—but it wasn't just his kisses. It was the man himself. No one else could compare with Max Ross. Not in my heart.

Maybe the two of us were inevitable. Maybe I'd been running from my destiny all this time.

Max wrapped his strong hands around my waist and pulled me over him, grabbing my leg and drawing it across him so I straddled his lap facing him.

He broke the kiss and simply gazed into my eyes. His were filled with passion. With longing. I'm sure mine had to be, too.

We sat with our foreheads pressed together, and he stroked his hands up and down my spine, making me tremble with need.

"This is the first time we've had real privacy," he murmured. "We've always either been in a public place or Emma's been nearby. It's driven me crazy—to be so close but not able to touch you."

Heat seared through me, my entire body growing hot. Straddling him like this was doing insane things to me.

The bulge pressing between my thighs told me he was as aroused as I was. When I shifted my weight, pressing into him, the length of him against the seam of my jeans was indescribably erotic.

Max gasped. "You're killing me."

"Sorry."

"No, you aren't."

"Okay, maybe I'm not."

He arched his back a little, pressing our hips together. "You always did enjoy driving me crazy."

I shifted again. Playfully. Teasingly. He grabbed my waist. "None of that. Not unless you plan on doing something about it."

I gazed into his eyes—and shifted my hips again.

Max let out a shaky breath. "Does that mean what I hope it means?"

"It depends on what you were hoping for." I ground my hips against him. "If it's hot, overdue sex that will melt your brain, then yes."

He nearly went cross-eyed. "God, yes. Stay with me tonight. All night."

My breath caught in my throat. That was a big step. "I—"

"Stay, Sonya. Please, stay."

He pressed his hips against mine again and I nearly came right then. Every thought evaporated from my brain. I moaned and managed to say, "I'll stay."

"Thank God." He kissed me, sending me reeling.

I melted into his kiss, but then my one remaining functioning brain cell fired, and I pulled back. "Wait. Do you have condoms?"

He gave a slow smile. "Upstairs. In my suitcase." He quickly rolled to one side, flipping me so I was beneath him on the sofa. "Stay right here. Don't move a muscle."

He darted up the stairs, and less than a minute later, he came back carrying an unopened box of condoms and a plush, gray blanket. He handed me the box and gestured for me to stand. As I tore the plastic wrapper off the box, he draped the blanket over the sofa.

"'Ribbed for her pleasure?'" I read aloud.

"Only the best for you." His eyebrows bounced up and down.

I gave the box a shake and shot him a playful sidelong glance. "Are you implying you had me in mind when you bought these? That's awfully presumptuous of you, Mr. Ross."

"Hopeful. Not presumptuous."

"And exactly when did you make this particular purchase?"

"Um—" He scratched the back of his head and gave me a sheepish look. "Remember the day you came over to tutor Emma?"

"No!" My eyes widened in shock. "You did *not* think I was going to sleep with you that day, did you?"

"Hope springs eternal." He smiled softly, endearingly, and pulled me into his arms. "Can you forgive me for being a hopeful romantic?" He asked, those entrancing blue eyes boring into mine. "For believing we were always meant to be together? For having faith that we'd find our way back to each other?"

My heart gave a hard thump. "When you put it that way—" I wrapped my arms around his waist, "—what else can I do but swoon and fall into your arms?"

"I'm glad you're beginning to see things my way." He pulled me down onto the sofa with him as he skimmed his hands up and down my sides.

When his thumbs grazed my jutting nipples, I inhaled sharply. "You're making an excellent argument. How could I find fault?"

His hand moved to my hip, and he looped one finger into my waistband, tugging me closer. "You're wearing too many clothes." He thumbed open the button of my jeans.

I undid his button as well and then slid down his zipper. I cupped the familiar length of his erection, eliciting a low moan of pleasure.

Max slid his hands inside my jeans and cupped my rear end. As he pulled me closer, I lifted up his shirt. He released me just long enough to let me slip it over his head before pulling me close again.

I grazed my hands up his back, caressing warm, velvety skin.

He felt familiar. Right. The sensation of touching him...my overwhelming emotions—my long-suppressed longing for this man...made tears spring to my eyes.

I'd missed this, so very, very much.

I blinked them away. I was here. Now. Exactly where I wanted to be.

Max pulled up my form-fitting athletic top, but when he hit my breasts, the skin-tight fabric didn't want to cooperate. The built-in bra was causing problems. I hooked my thumbs under the elastic strap and stretched it so it could make it past my breasts.

Max had stopped tugging when I'd taken over, and for a moment I was trapped—half-in and half-out of the top—with my arms extended above my head, my face hidden inside my stretchy top. "A little help, here," I said.

He hummed. "I think I kind of like this situation."

Since the fabric hid my face, he couldn't see me grinning like a fool. "You do realize that I can't touch you when my arms are trapped inside this thing, right?"

"You make an excellent point."

An instant later, he shucked me free and tossed the top to the floor. We both stripped off the rest of our clothes and then turned back to each other.

He stared at me, taking in every inch of my body, then slid off the sofa and dropped to his knees in front of me. I scooted back, but he grabbed me behind my knees and dragged me forward again, so my butt was almost hanging off the edge of the sofa. When I widened my eyes in surprise, he grinned.

"I've been dying to taste you. To hear you. The sounds you'd make when we were together always drove me wild."

My face softened with desire as I remembered the expertise of his tongue. "Who am I to deny a man such a long-held desire?" I leaned back and widened my knees.

He stared into my eyes, then slowly glided his hand up my thigh. At the juncture of my legs, he teased the outside of my opening, then tapped me slightly with the back of his hand. A few quick, light taps followed by some firmer ones.

My legs tensed and my knees tightened reflexively as I let out a combination of a gasp and a giggle.

"What are you doing?" I asked.

"If you can't tell, I'm doing it wrong."

"You definitely aren't doing it wrong." He did it some more, and the variation in rhythm and intensity drove me wild.

Desire overwhelmed me, making me tremble. He circled my clit with his thumb and then pressed on it, tearing a gasp of pleasure from me. He repeated the circling gesture with his thumb as he slid a finger inside me. A moment later, his lips touched me there, and the heat of his tongue against my clit drove me wild with need and want.

I grabbed hold of his thick, gorgeous hair, sinking my fingers into it and holding on for dear life.

"You have me exactly where I want to be," he said, pausing for only a moment before resuming the devastating motion of his tongue.

I couldn't respond. His words barely sank in, and I realized I was making whimpering and moaning sounds that would mortify me if I had even a shred of self-control right now.

I watched him with half-lidded eyes. He sat back on his heels and watched intently as he teased and touched me. He slid a finger back inside, then added a second one, stroking them in and out. "You feel so hot and slick. It's driving me crazy." He leaned in and did some wild flicking thing with the tip of his tongue that drove me wild and sent me squirming and moaning.

"You're so perfect." He leaned in and pressed his tongue hard against my clit as his fingers moved in and curved upward. I arched my back against the exquisite sensations and immediately shattered, my orgasm roaring through me.

I pulled my knees up against my chest as those delicious sensations continued to rock me, and I tossed my head from side to side. I wanted this to last, but I didn't know how much longer I could take it. As I tried to pull away, he eased his pressure and kissed the inside of my thighs, trailing kisses up one side and down the other.

"I want you inside me," I said. "Please, Max."

He pulled away and grabbed a condom from the box, ripping open the packet and rolling it in place. He rearranged me so I was lying on the sofa and then moved over me, tossing the back cushion to the floor as he settled between my legs.

He kissed my breasts, sucking each nipple into his mouth and tonguing it before moving farther up my body. He captured my mouth with his. His tongue danced against mine in a rhythm I'd never forgotten. No one could kiss like Max. No one could make my body sing the way he could.

He grabbed my leg behind the knee and lifted it higher, then used his hand to guide himself to my entrance. The sensation of him entering my body was perfect.

I slid my hands into his thick hair again, cradling his head. I felt him everywhere. Against my palms, in our kisses, in the press of his body against mine, and especially inside me, at our most intimate connection.

I met him, stroke for stroke. Push for push. The feel of him drove me wild. His thighs slapped against mine rhythmically. He shifted and pushed up on his arms, still pumping into me. I wrapped my arms and legs around him, holding him tight and grinding my hips against him.

"Sonya." He grabbed me around the waist and pulled me up with him so I sat astride him. He watched himself move in and out of me and then reached down and ran circles around my clit with his thumb. I let my head drop back as I rocked forward and back, matching his rhythm.

"You look amazing. Like a goddess." He sat up and buried his face between my breasts. The change in the angle also changed the pressure inside me. I felt myself shattering again as a second orgasm overtook me. Max stiffened as well. "God, I can feel you coming all around me."

He thrust hard, his orgasm overtaking him. His breath was ragged, and the tendons on his neck stood out as he threw back his head and gave himself over to his release.

The man was glorious. I loved seeing him this way. So satisfied. So joyful. And all because of me. Of us.

A matching joy filled me.

I watched as he mentally came back from wherever that orgasm had sent him. His eyes focused on me, and a delighted smile spread across his mouth.

He kissed me. Quickly. Perfectly.

"I'll be right back."

He stood, and I shivered without his heat pressing against me. He draped the blanket over me and left the room to dispose of the condom.

When he came back, he removed the rest of the cushions on the back of the sofa to give us more space, then climbed under the blanket with me and spooned against my back, holding me close.

I must have dozed off, because when I woke up, Max was gone. I could hear someone moving around in the kitchen. Max? It had to be. At least, I certainly hoped it was him, and not Emma coming home early from her sleepover. The thought had me pulling the blanket up to my chin.

A moment later, Max crept back into the family room wearing nothing but his jeans and a pair of sandals. When he reached the sofa, he began to strip.

"Where did you go?" I asked. "I missed you."

He slid under the blanket, facing me. "I pulled your car into the garage. I didn't want to give the neighbors anything to gossip about."

My mouth fell open. "I never even thought of that." I glanced at my watch, but it was too dark to see it. "What time is it?"

"Eleven."

"Not too late, then. I can't believe I was so careless."

"Would it be the worst thing in the world if people knew we were seeing each other?" He asked.

"Seeing each other is probably okay. Staying overnight isn't." I tightened my grip on the blanket. "I think I should go."

"I'd like you to stay, but it's up to you. If you want, you can wear one of my t-shirts in the morning so no one will see you wearing the same clothes."

I considered his suggestion. "I have a gym bag in my car with some things I can change into."

"I'll grab it for you in the morning and bring it to you. Along with a cup of coffee."

I sighed. "I'd nearly forgotten the way you used to wake me up each morning with a cup of coffee while I was still in bed. I really miss that."

He pulled me closer. "I've missed waking up next to you."

Tears sprang to my eyes. I'd missed him too, even though I'd refused to admit it to myself. Having him back was more than I'd dared to dream.

He stroked my back, cupped my bottom, and then slid his fingers to the cleft between my legs. "You're staying, right?"

I gasped in pleasure. "I am. You can have your way with me again, Mr. Ross."

"Thank you, Miss Gambit. I think I will."

A MEETING WITH THE PRINCIPAL

SONYA

I'd done it. I'd dropped my guard long enough to let Max back into my heart—and it felt right. In fact, it felt amazing.

It was as though the past five years had never happened. I was *supposed* to be with him. I'd known it back then, and now that truth seemed etched into my bones. Into my very soul.

The movers had arrived around noon the next day, so we'd had the morning to ourselves. It was almost as if we'd never been apart.

I'd stayed until late in the afternoon, but I had to head home to get ready for school the next day.

I'd be floating about six feet above the ground right now, except for one problem; my conscience. It kept me firmly tethered to the earth. By the time school rolled around on Monday, the damned thing wouldn't shut up.

I had a responsibility to Emma. To all my students. Was it ethical to be dating Max and also be his niece's teacher? I knew I'd never let my relationship with Max change how I treated her in the classroom, but other people might not believe it. Plus, that old scandal was out there—always threatening to come back to life, like a zombie in a horror movie.

I'd found out the hard way that what people thought about you could influence your life, even when what they believed wasn't true.

My worries scurried around in my brain like living creatures. Creatures that wouldn't shut up or give me a moment's peace.

Mid-morning on Monday, while my students were attending music class, I knocked on Cindy Goodfriend's office door. It was open, as usual.

"Hi Sonya, come on in." Cindy beckoned me. "What's up? I have about ten minutes before I need to leave for a meeting with the superintendent."

I hesitated. "I'm not sure how long this will take."

"Well, let's get started," Cindy said. "We can always meet again later if we need more time. Are you worried about the show?"

I turned and closed the door behind me.

Cindy raised her eyebrows. "You definitely have my interest."

I sat facing her across her desk and clenched my hands together. "It's a bit delicate," I began. "You know Max Ross is directing the show—"

"Is there a problem?" She focused, like a bloodhound on the scent.

"Sort of. The thing is—we already knew each other. In fact, we used to date."

Cindy didn't blink.

"Now that we're spending so much time together, things are starting to—" What? How did I finish that sentence?

"Get interesting again?" Cindy leaned forward, a sly smile tugging at the corner of her mouth. "I might be married, but I still have eyes. That man is gorgeous. Good for you."

I cleared my throat. That was unexpected. "The problem is that Emma is my student, and he's her guardian. Would I be breaking any sort of school rule if we were to…"

"You seem to have trouble finishing your sentences." Cindy settled back in her chair as I picked up a pen and flipped it over and over. "Just to be clear, our school district doesn't have any formal rules in place about teachers dating parents. It would be tricky since we'd have no way to influence the parent. Trying to control a situation like that would be awkward. That means you aren't violating any of our policies." She set her pen precisely in the center of her desk and met my gaze. "Of course, I'd expect you to show discretion since Emma is just a child, but Mr. Ross is her guardian, not me. What the two of you do *outside* of school is none of my business."

I sagged in my chair. "You have no idea how relieved I am to hear you say that."

Cindy tilted her head, assessing me. "Have you avoided getting involved with him because you're Emma's teacher?"

I squirmed in my seat. This was the hardest part of what I had to tell her today. The part that might get me fired. "There's something you should know that makes my situation even more complicated." I hesitated. "There's a chance keeping me on could cause the school district problems down the line."

Cindy frowned as she checked her watch. "You're right, this sounds like it's going to take a while, and I have to leave. I'll give you two options." She clicked to wake up her computer and open her calendar. "We can either schedule a meeting in two days to discuss the situation, or we can meet later this evening for dinner, and you can tell me about it then."

Easy choice. "Let's meet at Not a Yacht Club tonight at around seven. I'll fill you in."

"Sounds like a plan."

That evening, I found myself sitting in a booth, staring across the table at Cindy in openmouthed disbelief. "You're saying the district knew about my past all along and still hired me?"

Cindy ate another of the truffle fries we'd ordered. "I pulled your personnel file and read it before coming here. I found a brief paragraph about that old scandal, but it didn't raise any red flags with our hiring committee. The only details we cared about had to do with your performance at your last school. You had glowing reports from both the administration and the parents, and your students performed extremely well in their state tests. That's impressive for a new teacher. You should be proud."

"Those kids worked hard for me," I said, warming under her praise. "I didn't do it alone."

"You motivated them and helped them solve whatever problems were holding them back. As I said. Impressive. That's why you got the job."

Stunned, all I could say was, "Thanks."

"I have to admit though, if I'd known about the scandal sooner, I wouldn't have assigned Emma to your classroom. I also wouldn't have been so gung-ho on having her uncle co-direct."

I swallowed hard.

"It's too late to change any of that now. What's done is done. The last thing I want to do is yank Emma away from her classmates." She lifted her wine glass in a toast. "Here's to keeping the past in the past."

Relief washed through me as I clinked my glass against Cindy's. "Hear, hear."

30

WHEN "BREAK A LEG" GETS TAKEN TOO LITERALLY

Max

After a week of hard work, I'd finally unpacked the last box and hung the last painting. It was a relief to have everything squared away. I still hadn't located my antique clock and one of the television remotes, but they'd show up soon.

Despite the problems with the elevator on the day of the move, everything else had turned out even better than expected.

Sonya was back in my life.

Saturday night had been amazing. Being with her had almost taken me by surprise—but not quite. After all, I'd been trying to convince her to give me another chance for weeks. I'd simply needed to prove to her that she could trust me.

No small task. Not that I blamed her after keeping such a huge secret from her.

Having her in my life once again felt natural. It was as if no time had passed at all. We were back to reading each other's minds and finishing each other's sentences as if we'd never been apart.

I'd missed her. Missed our rapport. Missed her clever mind and gentle soul.

And now she was back in my life. *Really* back.

As I brewed my morning coffee, my phone rang. I grinned when I saw Sonya's name appear on the screen and swiped right to take the call. "Hi, babe."

"Hi, babe, yourself," she replied. Her voice was husky, and I could hear the smile in it. "Did I wake you?"

"Mmmm. I was having a good dream, too," I said, playing along. "Of you. I woke up, convinced you were lying next to me in bed. Imagine my disappointment when you weren't really there."

"Poor guy. It must be hard on you." Her husky voice drove me wild.

I groaned. "So hard. Hard enough to pound nails."

She chuckled. "Please don't tell me you say that to all the girls. It's a horrible line."

"Only you, sweetness. You bring out the bad boy in me."

"Bad is right," she said in that sultry tone I loved. "You know, I didn't call so early just to talk dirty with you."

"It doesn't sound that way from my side of the conversation."

"Focus, babe. I called because Crystal had an accident last night."

I stilled. "Crystal Falls? Our lead actress?"

"The very one."

"Is she okay? What happened?"

"A freak accident. The poor kid went roller skating last night and fell hard on her tailbone. She was in so much pain that they called an ambulance. It turns out she damaged the growth plate in her spinal column. I just got off the phone with her. She was in tears. She's going to have to wear a body cast for six weeks while her spine heals."

My mouth literally fell open. "You've got to be kidding me. That's horrible. Poor kid."

"She's pulling out of the show and wants Emma to step in since she's the understudy."

"Is she sure that's what she wants to do?"

"She was adamant. She's sore and achy and doesn't want

people staring at her on stage in the body cast. I told her we'd support her if she still wanted to play the lead, but she refused."

"The show is this coming Friday," I said. "That's a lot of responsibility for Emma."

"Today's Saturday. She has the weekend to get up to speed so she can step in for our run-through on Monday. I know she can do it. I have complete confidence in her."

I scrubbed a hand over my face. "I think I'll take a shower, make the banana pancakes I promised Emma last night, and break the news to her as soon as she's done eating."

"I can bring over some bacon to fry up if you'll make me some of those banana pancakes, too," Sonya offered in a wheedling tone.

"That's right," I said in a mock-forgetful tone. "You were always a fan of my banana pancakes."

"I know you haven't forgotten, so don't even try to pretend you did. You only mentioned them just now because you know I have no willpower where they're concerned."

"You see right through me. There's no fooling you, is there?"

"Not a chance," she said firmly. "Not with banana pancakes on the line."

"If you're here in thirty minutes, I'll let you have the first batch before I wake up Emma."

"Mmm. I'll be there in twenty."

I grinned. "It's a date."

As soon as we ended the call, I hurried upstairs and took a quick shower. I pulled on a pair of shorts and a t-shirt before padding back downstairs to the kitchen. I'd just started smashing the bananas when I heard a knock at the kitchen door. Sonya entered, holding a grocery bag.

"I brought bacon," she announced. She leaned in to kiss me, but then suddenly jerked back with a frown. She dragged her index finger across my cheek and came away with a shiny drop of banana goo.

She raised one eyebrow at me.

"Banana. One of the perils of making banana pancakes."

She stuck her finger in her mouth and sucked it clean.

My cock twitched.

"Not fair," I said, pulling her into my arms. "How am I supposed to make banana pancakes when you're doing erotic things with the ingredients?"

She rolled her eyes and shook her head. "You think everything I do is erotic. You even think I grade papers erotically."

"Only when you chew on the end of your red pen. I'm only human, Sonya. We mere mortals aren't equipped to withstand your blatant eroticism."

She poked me in the chest and then changed her mind and pulled me closer. "What am I going to do with you?"

"I have a list of suggestions if you're at a loss," I said, grinning. I pulled her into my arms. "First, there's kissing. I'm a big fan of kissing."

"Me too." She rose up on her toes and I kissed her.

I pulled back. "I tasted banana."

"Fresh off your cheek."

"If you'll give me a couple of minutes, I'll have your pancakes done."

"You drive a hard bargain."

"You said it, not me." I pressed my groin against her and then abruptly stepped over to the stove.

"I keep forgetting what a bad boy you are."

I grinned as I poured the perfect amount of pancake batter onto the hot griddle. "Maybe I'm hoping my teacher will decide to punish me one day." I waggled my eyebrows at her.

"You get worse and worse every day."

"And you keep teasing me with promises."

"Promises? What promises?"

"I seem to recall the promise of bacon. Where is it?" I pointed to the cast iron skillet heating on the stove. "It goes in here. You'd better get moving. Your pancakes will be done in a couple of minutes."

Sonya cut open the bacon container and arranged the strips in the skillet. A minute later, I flipped the pancakes.

"Those pancakes smell delicious," Sonya said, stepping up behind me and wrapping her arms around my waist, under my shirt, the temptress.

"Focus, Sonya," I said. "Grab a plate. These are nearly ready."

She moved directly to the correct cabinet, grabbed three, and then set them next to me. I was disappointed when she didn't wrap her arms around me again and instead picked up the tongs and began to turn over the strips of bacon.

I slid two pancakes onto a plate and then handed it to her while simultaneously plucking the tongs out of her hand. "You, sit at the counter and eat. I'll finish the bacon."

I swatted her bottom as she moved away, and she didn't even bother to scold me. She was too focused on her pancakes.

I'd already placed a bottle of pure maple syrup on the counter, and Sonya poured some over her pancakes before taking a bite.

She let out a decadent moan. "These are even better than I remembered."

"I've been hearing that sound from you quite a lot recently, but never in this context."

"Bad boy! So, so bad! You'd better watch out, or Emma's going to hear you. She's a pretty smart kid. She'll figure it out if you aren't more careful."

"You already know I think we should just tell her."

"And I already told you, I think we should wait until after school ends."

"That's months away. She'll be angry if we keep it from her that long."

Sonya let out a sigh. "I know, but I don't know how else to handle this. She's had so many changes to adjust to over the past couple of months. The last thing she needs is to worry about losing you to another woman."

"You make it sound as though she'd be jealous."

"I just don't want her to worry about another loss in her life." Sonya shrugged. "This has all been a huge adjustment for her."

"She'd never view having you in my life as being another loss. Besides, she's smart. She's going to figure it out on her own."

She let out another sigh. "I know. That's what I'm afraid of. What should I do about the whole 'conflict of interest' thing, what with me being her teacher? I wouldn't want to be accused of favoritism."

I held up my hands in mock defeat. "Fine. I give. I'll be your dirty little secret."

She scowled at me. "Dirty is right," she muttered. "What with that mouth on you."

I waggled my eyebrows. "I thought you liked my mouth on you." I slid two pancakes onto my plate.

She let out a moan of frustration. "See what I mean? You're as bad as a teenager. What are you, fifteen?"

"You certainly make me feel that way." I picked up tongs, plucked some bacon from the pan, and set it on a paper towel. "You know I only tease you because I love the way you react. If you really want me to stop, I can." I carried the bacon over to her. "Do you?"

She turned a sultry gaze on me. "Not on your life. I love the way you tease me."

I leaned down to kiss her but stopped when Emma's shout from upstairs interrupted me. "Uncle Max, are you making bacon?"

I closed my eyes briefly, then stepped to the doorway of the kitchen and looked up toward the staircase, but I couldn't spot Emma. "You bet I am!" I called back. "Miss Gambit just got here and has some news to share. You'd better get down here fast before she eats all the bacon and the banana pancakes. I've never seen a woman pack away so much food!"

I turned back to see Sonya scowling at me.

Emma's slippers slapped against the stair treads as she

barreled down them. "Hi, Miss Gambit," she said as she threw herself onto the barstool next to her.

I caught Sonya's eye and nodded, urging her to tell Emma the news as I slid my plate of pancakes and bacon in front of Emma and started cooking a third batch for myself.

Emma bit into a strip of bacon as she poured syrup on her pancakes.

"I have news," Sonya said. "I stopped by because Crystal called me this morning." She described the girl's roller-skating accident.

Emma's eyes went wide. "Wait a minute, wait a minute," Emma said, holding her hands up as though trying to stop Sonya's flow of information. "Are you telling me Crystal isn't going to be in the show?"

Sonya took in her shocked expression. "I'm afraid not. And you're her understudy. The good news is you have nearly a week to prepare."

"This is crazy." Emma squeezed her eyes shut. In fact, her entire body seemed to curl in on itself. "I've never even rehearsed one of her scenes."

"Don't freak out," I told her. "You have plenty of time to get up to speed. As part of the ensemble, you're in a lot of Crystal and Liam's scenes already, so you've heard them run their lines dozens of times. I bet you already know most of them. You probably remember their blocking for those scenes as well."

She frowned at me. "Maybe. But what about the scenes just between the two of them? I don't know those lines at all. Plus, the songs! I have to learn the songs too!"

"Eat your pancakes while we talk," I told her.

Emma poked at the stack and cut off a bite with her fork, but she didn't eat it.

I slid onto the barstool next to her and poured maple syrup over my own stack of pancakes. "I know it seems overwhelming to step into a big role like this when you look at the show as a whole, but you're more prepared than you think you are." I sipped my coffee. "After we're done with breakfast, I want you to grab your copy of the script and read through the entire thing. I think you'll be surprised at how much of her part you already know. I'm certain you can do this. I'll devote my entire weekend to helping you prepare. I bet you'll arrive at rehearsal on Monday brimming with confidence." I popped a bite of pancake into my mouth and let out a groan of pleasure. "These pancakes are amazing. Eat up, Emma."

She reluctantly took a bite. Then another. She didn't say anything more for a minute or so because she was busy polishing off her breakfast. By the time she was done, she looked calmer.

"I was thinking, we'll have a lot to celebrate once the show is over," I said. "Maybe we should plan something."

Emma's eyes lit up with interest. "Can Marley come over to celebrate? And maybe Miss Gambit?"

"Sure," I said. "I don't see why not."

"What about Liam and the others, though?" Emma said, her excitement dimming. "I don't want to leave people out."

"You make a great point," I said. "That sounds like a cast party. Sunday might be a better day for that. What do you think?"

"Can we do both? Friday and Sunday?"

"Sure. How can I refuse after you agreed to step into Crystal's role? We can do something small with just you and Marley and Miss Gambit on Friday night, and then have a big party on Sunday."

She frowned at me as though I'd just caught her in a trap, then let out a sigh of resignation. "Okay. It's a deal." She stood and rinsed off her plate in the kitchen sink. "It's not as if I have a choice. The show must go on."

"Thatta girl," I told her.

Emma turned and faced me, her shoulders square and her chin high. "If you need me, I'll be in my room, reading through the script." She tipped her head back, laid the back of her hand against her forehead in an attitude of despair, and swept from the room with long, graceful strides.

"She certainly has a flair for the dramatic." I grinned.

"You love it."

"I do. I think she's amazing. But then again, she's my niece, so I'm biased."

"You know," Sonya said. "It would help Emma to run through the scenes with some of the other kids. Marley and Liam live nearby. Do you want to call to see if they can rehearse here today?"

"Excellent idea."

"Their numbers are on the phone list I sent home. Liam's last name is Loxton."

"Thanks, babe." I leaned across Emma's vacant barstool and gave Sonya what was supposed to be a brief kiss—except that her soft, warm, maple-sugary mouth proved to be irresistible. My kiss turned deeper. I shifted off the barstool to get closer to her and cupped her face in my hands. God, but she was lovely. It took all of my willpower to pull away. "I'd better go make those calls. Stay right here." I kissed her on the tip of her nose. "I'll be right back."

I stepped into the living room and made the calls. When I came back to the kitchen ten minutes later, Sonya was just finishing loading the dishwasher and didn't notice me, so I slipped up behind her and wrapped my arms around her waist.

To her credit, she didn't jump or squeal. She simply leaned back against me, craning her head to one side to give me a kiss. I turned her to face me and pulled her firmly against my body. "I can't seem to get enough of you."

"I feel the same way." She slid her hands around my waist and tucked her palms into the rear pockets of my jeans.

I glanced toward the staircase. "We probably have another half hour before Emma comes back."

She cocked one eyebrow. "You aren't suggesting what I think you are—"

"That depends on how dirty your mind is."

She shook her head, giving me her best scolding-teacher look.

"You're incorrigible. I'm not about to get busy with you in the middle of your kitchen with Emma upstairs."

I grinned. "But if she wasn't in the house?" I hummed. "That gives me ideas for the future."

She smacked my chest with her palm. "You're so naughty."

"Why don't we go someplace a bit more private?" I suggested.

"I'm not going up to your bedroom. What if Emma saw me up there?"

"I have an even better idea." I grabbed her by the hand and led her down the hallway to my office, then closed and locked the door behind us.

She glanced around, taking in the space, but I didn't give her time to comment. Instead, I took her directly to my large desk, closed my laptop, and pushed it to one side. Then I picked her up by the waist to set her on the large, flat surface of my mahogany desk. "I told you about my plans for the house, but I happen to have left out the one I hold dearest."

Her eyelids fluttered, and she gave me a sultry look. "What might that be? As if I couldn't guess. I bet it has something to do with sex, right?"

I grinned as I spread her knees and stepped between them. "You're amazingly perceptive. You and I are going to have sex in every single room—with the exception of Emma's, of course."

She laughed. "Because that would be gross."

"Completely."

"And you've decided we should christen your office today?"

"I plan to nail you right here, with you bent across my desk."

She suddenly trembled and gripped me more tightly. Her cheeks blushed prettily, making her look absolutely gorgeous. "Nail me? Seriously? And if I don't agree?"

I leaned over and trailed kisses down the side of her neck. "I'm certain I'll be able to convince you, but of course, this will only happen if you're a willing and active participant." I grazed the side of her breast with my palm as I bent to take her mouth. She met my kiss with parted lips. Our tongues darted and tasted. I pulled her closer, and she let out a soft moan of pleasure that vibrated against my tongue.

She was absolutely delicious.

She dug her fingers into my hair as a barely perceptible moan escaped her mouth. She was trying to stay quiet, and the realization made me want to drive her wild with desire. But—right now we didn't have much time.

"Max?" She must have sensed my hesitation because she sounded confused.

I let out a low hum of satisfaction. "Are you enjoying this?"

"You're killing me," she said, her breathing coming in short gasps. "Do I need to remind you that we don't have all day?"

I stepped back, taking in her sex-glazed eyes. This was a sight I'd never forget for as long as I lived. "I like you this way."

Her eyes focused on me, losing that gorgeous haze. "Frustrated and sex-starved?"

I chuckled. "No. Well, yes. I suppose so. You look lusty as hell."

She gave me a slow smile. "I hope that means you're going to do something about it."

The doorbell rang.

Sonya's eyes widened. "Shoot."

I backed away from her, hating that this moment had to end, but we had a lot to do today to help Emma prepare for Monday's rehearsal.

I opened the front door.

"Thanks for coming so quickly," I told Renee and Marley Zerkowski.

A car pulled to a stop out front, and Liam opened the passenger door. Mrs. Loxton waved at me through the open driver's window. "I'll pick him up at six," she called out.

I waved back, and she drove away.

31

CRUNCH TIME!

Max

"Thanks for coming over," I told Marley later that afternoon. "I don't know what we would've done without you."

"I wish I didn't have to babysit," Marley said. "I'd rather stay. Should I come back tomorrow?"

"That would be perfect," I told her. "Stop by around ten."

"See you then," Marley said, then headed out the door.

"I can come tomorrow too," Liam said, "but I can only stay another hour today. We have tickets to the Penguins game."

Emma's eyes widened. "That sounds like fun."

Liam perked up. "Are you a hockey fan?"

"It's one of my favorite sports. That and baseball."

Liam looked at her with more interest. "Mine too. You know, my parents sometimes let me invite a friend. Would you like to come with us sometime?"

A broad grin split Emma's face. "That'd be great."

Sonya and I exchanged glances. Sonya mouthed the words, "young love."

My phone rang. I glanced at the screen. "It's Ford," I told Sonya. "I need to take this. Give me a minute."

She nodded, so I headed down the hall to the kitchen. "How's it going?"

Ford hesitated. "It's been better. I reached out to Raven about having her write a song for my movie, but she's not sure she's interested. She mentioned she might call you. I think she wants to get a feel about where the two of you stand before she agrees to anything. I wanted to send you her contact info so you'll recognize her number."

His words hit me like a blow to the chest, knocking the air from my lungs. Letting Raven get a foothold in my life again was the last thing I ever wanted. "Seriously? I have zero interest in talking to her. Can't you handle this without me?"

"I'm trying to. I just wanted to give you a heads-up. If you recognize her number when she calls, you won't get taken by surprise."

I let out a heavy sigh. That made sense. "Fine. Text it to me."

My phone vibrated, indicating I'd received a text message. Sure enough, it was Raven's contact info. I saved it under the name Nut-Job. "Does this mean you're actually considering having her compose something?"

"It's a strategic move. If I have a contract with her, she'll have a vested interest in the movie's success. It should keep her from sabotaging it by going after you or Sonya."

I shrugged. "Hard to tell. She's not always rational."

"Based on our recent conversations, she seems clear-headed," Ford said. "Sharp, too. I asked around. News is, she's stable now that she's clean."

People could change, couldn't they? Even so, this was Raven we were talking about. I suppressed a frustrated sigh. "Partnering with her seems like a needless risk, but this movie is your baby, not mine. Just don't say I didn't warn you when she does something that bites you in the ass."

Ford paused at that. "I think I'll add a penalty clause to keep her from saying anything that could hurt the movie. That should shut her up."

I cracked a smile. Finally, some good news. "That's an excellent plan. It might even work."

"I'll keep you posted," Ford said.

Distracted, I headed back to the living room. I hated that Raven had an inroad back into my life, but Ford might be right. A contract would put her on a leash and keep her from doing any further harm.

When I walked in, I found Sonya and the kids hard at work.

"Now that we've run through the entire show," she said to them, "I'd like to go back to the scenes with just the two of you on stage."

"Which one should we do first?" Liam asked.

"Scene five. The one where you just escaped with the Declaration of Independence and you're arguing with Emma. I want to make sure she knows the blocking."

The entire story was a spoof of the movie National Treasure. It was a fun story, and it tied in with the class trip to Washington the students would be taking at the end of the eighth grade.

"Take your places," Sonya told them. "You both enter from stage left."

Emma and Liam moved into position.

"Lights up," Sonya said.

The pair rushed onto the stage, arguing about the theft. Sonya watched for a minute and then said, "Stop."

They stopped mid-scene and faced her.

"Liam, when you say that last line, you're supposed to cross over to Emma and take her hands in yours. Try it again." She glanced at her script. "Emma, start with the line that begins, 'You've put me in an impossible situation.'"

"Got it," Emma said.

As soon as Liam moved back to his original position, Emma said, "You've put me in an impossible situation. I had nothing to do with the theft, but I could still end up in prison. I look just as guilty as you do."

Liam hurried toward her and took her hands in his. "You're a well-respected member of the senator's staff. No one would ever believe you're involved. But I promise, if things go wrong, I'll tell them you had nothing to do with it."

Emma snatched her hands from his and took a step back. "Don't be naive. We've been seen together. People know we're dating. Of course, they'll think I was in on it."

I tensed, reacting to the words. Emma spoke something true. People loved to assume the worst. Mostly because it made the gossip that much more scintillating. Only romances and musicals guaranteed happy endings. Real life never worked out that way.

So, why was I putting Sonya at risk? Darcy Falls had already confronted her. Eventually, she or someone else would start spreading that old rumor about Essie Harlow and Raven. Was the fact that Sonya and I were together again going to make things worse? It was. I knew it. Especially with Ford's plan to have Raven compose music for his movie.

I watched her. Could I give her up now, after being apart for so long?

My heart wrenched at the thought. I didn't want to leave her. I also refused to make a unilateral decision. If the risk seemed too great, we'd have to reach that conclusion together.

"Was that better?" Emma asked at the end of the scene.

"Much better," Sonya said.

"It's coming along great," I said. "Let's move on to the next scene. We have about a half-hour before Liam needs to go."

They worked through another scene, and then I brought rehearsal to a close. "It's almost six," I said. "Time to wrap things up for the day. Emma, you've made amazing progress. Liam, I can't thank you enough for sacrificing your Saturday."

Emma shot him a grateful look. "It was really nice of you to help."

Liam glanced down at his feet and shrugged. "No problem. I was happy to do it." He cleared his throat. "See you tomorrow. My mom just texted me. She's on the way, so I'll wait for her outside."

"I'll wait with you," Emma offered.

A pleased expression flickered across Liam's face. "Sounds good."

As Liam pulled open the front door, he said, "You know, Em, you're doing an amazing job. The show is gonna be great. I'm sure of it."

Emma's cheeks turned a rosy pink. "Thanks."

Liam shrugged. "No problem. The show must go on, right?"

32

SCENES BELONG ON STAGE

Sonya

I hurried out to my car in the teachers' parking lot after school on Monday to grab my spare charger. The last thing I needed was to have my phone die when a parent was trying to reach me.

I waved at Liam Loxton and his mom, Mary Lou, as they headed into the school wheeling the desk chair she was letting us use for the show.

A light-blue minivan I didn't recognize was parked next to my car in the teachers' lot. As I approached, the sliding door opened and revealed Crystal Falls. The poor kid wore a baggy pink sweatshirt—probably her mom's—over her body cast. She moved stiffly as she tried to climb out of the van. She lost her balance, and I reached her just in time to steady her and keep her from falling.

"Hey there, Crystal. You okay?"

She didn't meet my gaze. "Hi, Miss Gambit."

I closed the minivan door for her. "I didn't expect to see you here."

Crystal blushed. "Mom made me come with her today," she said under her breath.

"Are you picking up homework?" I asked.

Crystal opened her mouth to answer but was interrupted

when her mom came bustling toward us from the school, carrying a stack of books and papers.

Darcy Falls shot me a brittle smile, but her eyes shot daggers. "Miss Gambit, how thoughtful of you to help Crystal. We won't keep you. I can handle things from here," she said.

I felt my face flush with anger and embarrassment. I had been trying to help Crystal, and now her mother was acting like I was doing something wrong. I took a step back, my heart pounding in my chest.

"I hope you feel better soon, Crystal," I said, my voice shaking. I turned and walked away, my head held high, but my insides quaking.

The multipurpose room bustled with activity. The cast members were gathered in front of the closed bleachers, listening to Max. Liam and his mom were lifting the chair onto the stage, and groups of parent volunteers gathered around the edges of the room, working on various tasks.

Prisha Nathanson stood with a group of parents gathered around the costume racks. A moment later, some of the women wheeled the racks out into the hallway. Other parents were on the stage putting the finishing touches on some scenery. Mary Lou Loxton stepped out from the wings carrying a dining room chair, and others followed her with more chairs and a small table and began arranging them on stage, marking their locations with bits of tape.

Everything seemed to be working like a well-oiled machine. I exhaled, letting go of my lingering shame and frustration. I needed to stay focused on the rehearsal and not let Darcy Falls' snarky words get to me.

"Need any help?" I asked Prisha.

"Nope. I have everything under control," Prisha assured me.

"I can tell. I'm impressed."

Max joined us. "You've been amazing," he told Prisha. "I can't thank you enough for all your hard work getting things organized and running smoothly."

"We never could have done this without you," I said.

"Thanks. Can you make sure my professors know how pleased you are?"

"Absolutely!" I said. "I'll write a glowing assessment."

Prisha beamed.

Max checked his notes. "We need to get started. I'd like to run through scene six one last time before we do the entire show from beginning to end. There are a lot of entrances and exits in that scene, and I want to make sure everyone knows their cues."

Prisha nodded. "Stage manager!" she yelled. "Set up for scene six."

A tall, blonde woman hurried onto the stage and started directing the other parents working on the scenery. Some pieces were pushed upstage, but they whisked away the dining room furniture they'd just placed there.

I was surprised when Darcy Falls led Crystal into the multi-purpose room just as the kids started scrambling onto the stage. The moment Crystal's classmates spotted her, they jumped right back off the stage and ran to greet her.

Upon seeing everyone rushing toward her, Crystal froze in place, her eyes going wide.

"Careful!" Mrs. Falls shouted. "She isn't used to being in a body cast yet. She sometimes loses her balance. Don't make her fall."

Then why is she here?

I hurried to join them, and was relieved when Max came with me.

"I'm so happy to see you, Crystal," Emma said. "I've been worried about you."

"I can't believe you came in today," Marley said. "Doesn't your back hurt?"

"Yeah," Crystal said, her voice tinged with pain. "It aches, and this body cast is heavy and itchy. I wanted to stay home, but Mom said I had to come so I didn't miss rehearsal."

I shot a questioning glance at Mrs. Falls, which she ignored.

"Crystal, honey," she said, "you know that isn't true. You insisted on being here."

Crystal looked down at the floor. Everything about the girl's posture told me she wanted to disappear.

I stared at Mrs. Falls, perplexed. Why was she lying about her daughter? Was she cruel, or simply clueless? Did it even matter when the end result was the same?

"Would you like to sit down?" I asked Crystal. The poor kid looked exhausted. "You can use my chair. It has to be more comfortable than sitting in the bleachers."

Crystal shook her head. "It hurts to sit. On top of the whole damaged growth plate thing, I bruised my tailbone when I fell."

I frowned. Did Crystal's mom expect her to stand and watch everyone rehearse? Perhaps she needed to talk to me about something. "Do you have questions about Crystal's assignments?"

Darcy Falls looked at me like I was crazy. "Not yet. We haven't even looked at them."

Completely perplexed, I stared at her blankly. Then why had they come in here? "Have Crystal call or email me if she needs help."

Mrs. Falls gave a brusque nod.

Emma patted Crystal on the back, but looked startled when she heard the hollow thud of the body cast. She quickly stroked the girl's arm in a comforting gesture.

Crystal gave a tentative smile as she met Emma's gaze. Poor kid.

As much as I wanted to support Crystal, we couldn't keep standing here. I needed to get everyone back to work.

"All right. Places everyone," I announced. "We need to get through this scene and then we'll run through the entire show. We have a lot to do today."

The kids stampeded back to the stage, and I turned to follow them.

I was surprised when Crystal followed as well.

After she'd taken a few steps, I came to a halt. "Crystal, are you going on stage? I'm confused. You told me you wanted to drop out of the show."

"Mom says the show must go on," Crystal said in a hushed voice. "She said I can't just quit."

Max stepped closer to us. "It's okay, Crystal. Emma's your understudy. This is exactly why we *have* understudies. You're injured. We don't expect you to do the show when you're feeling so lousy."

Crystal's eyes filled with tears, and one fat drop rolled down her cheek. "So, I don't have to do the show?"

"Of course not," I insisted.

"Emma rehearsed all weekend to get up to speed," Max added. "You don't need to worry at all. She's got it covered."

"What's going on?" Darcy Falls asked as she bustled over. "Is there a problem?"

"Everything's fine," Max said. "We were just reassuring Crystal that she isn't letting anyone down by dropping out of the show. Her understudy can take over."

"What? That's ridiculous." Darcy looked genuinely offended. "Of course, she can do the show."

"Mrs. Falls," I said, "I don't think that's in Crystal's best inter-est. She wasn't even able to attend school today. You called the office to have me send home this week's assignments. She's obvi-ously in pain."

Darcy's jaw clenched. "My daughter made a commitment. I expect her to keep it. Besides, she's the lead." Her expression turned obstinate.

By this point, Darcy had managed to attract the attention of most of the adults in the room, and a few of them moved to join us, including Liam's mom Mary Lou Loxton, Marley's mom Renee Zerkowski, and the blonde stage manager whose name I couldn't remember.

With our audience growing, Darcy Falls raised her voice so everyone could hear. "You know what I think? This isn't about my daughter at all. It's all about giving little miss Emma Bachar preferential treatment. I know she's had a terrible loss, and I feel sorry for her, truly, but simply handing her Crystal's role isn't fair either. My daughter deserves to be in this show. She's worked hard, and it's wrong for the directors to take the part away from her."

Emma looked stricken. Her eyes sought Max's. "That's not true, is it? Does everyone feel sorry for me? Is that why you wanted me to take over Crystal's part?"

"Of course not," he said, his voice sharp. "You're the understudy. No one is stealing anything away from Crystal. She dropped out of the show because she was injured." He shot Mrs. Falls a furious glare.

Emma shot me a doubtful glance, clearly looking for corroboration, and that gutted me. Her chin quivered as she tried to suppress her tears.

Renee Zerkowski gasped and glared at Mrs. Falls. "How could you say something so hurtful about a child? Look at what you've done to her!"

As Emma's face crumpled, Max pulled her into his arms, and she buried her face against his chest.

Emma didn't need more trauma in her life. She'd already had too much. I wished I could erase that woman's words. Anything to keep Emma from being hurt this way. I'd dearly love to tear into Darcy Falls for hurting her, but I needed to remain calm, so things didn't continue to escalate.

"No one is taking anything away from Crystal," I said, my tone placating. "She called me Saturday morning to tell me she couldn't be in the show. I can tell she's in pain. I'd never ask a child to do something so taxing after experiencing the kind of injury Crystal did."

Renee Zerkowski reached out and touched Darcy's arm. Darcy flinched away, her eyes narrowing. "I know it's important for you to have her in the show, Darcy," Renee said, "but you need to let this go. Crystal just wants to go home and lie down. Emma has been her understudy for weeks. There's no preferential treatment going on, and you know it."

"There is," Darcy said, her voice rising. "It's obvious."

"Just because you were passed over for a role in high school, that doesn't mean that's what's happening here," Renee said, her voice hardening. "This situation is different. Crystal has been injured."

Darcy took a step back, her face flushed with anger. "I don't believe you," she said. "You're in on it too."

"I'm not 'in on' anything," Renee said. "I'm just trying to be honest with you. Crystal is hurt, and Emma is her understudy. That's the end of it."

Darcy shook off Renee's hand. "There is, too. I know there is." Darcy whirled and glared at me. "This is all your fault. You're kicking her out of the show because you're sleeping with Max Ross," she said with a hiss.

My jaw dropped. She was saying this here? Now? In front of Crystal, Emma, and all the parents? At least the rest of the kids were too far away to hear her.

Emma turned to face Mrs. Falls, dumbfounded. At least the girl wasn't crying anymore. In fact, she didn't look unhappy at all...just surprised.

Max narrowed his eyes at Mrs. Falls. "You need to watch what you say in front of my niece," he said in a clipped tone.

I was shaken, but I reached out to take Max's arm. I could tell he was angry, and I didn't blame him, but this situation was mine to handle. "I've got this," I told him.

Mrs. Falls's announcement might have thrown me, but I'd face it head-on.

I glanced around, taking in all the parents staring at us. "Max and I met years ago," I explained nervously. "We used to date."

"See? I told you?" Darcy said, her eyes glowing with malevolent glee. "They're sleeping together. That's the kind of person she is. A liar and a cheat."

"Well, I never—" Mary Lou Loxton said. She looked horrified.

My stomach fell at Liam's mom's reaction. I'd hoped everyone —well, it didn't matter what I'd hoped.

As I took in Darcy Falls's poisonous glee and Mary Lou Loxton's horrified face, it was as though they'd gut-punched me. My heart broke.

There was no place for me here. Not anymore. I'd faced this sort of condemnation five years ago, and now it was back.

I couldn't hold it together any longer. I turned and bolted toward the exit.

33

BETWEEN A ROCK STAR AND A HARD PLACE

MAX

Sonya had focused on Darcy Falls and Mary Lou Loxton. She obviously hadn't seen what I had—that none of the other parents were at all bothered by Darcy's revelation.

Mary Lou Loxton's horrified expression hardened, and she glared at Darcy Falls. "How could you speak to Miss Gambit in such a disrespectful way? Frankly, Darcy, I'm ashamed of you. You're an adult. You're supposed to set an example for your daughter. You aren't supposed to fling mud."

Confused, I suddenly realized Mary Lou's look of horror hadn't been about me and Sonya being in a relationship. Not at all. It had been about the way Darcy had announced it to everyone.

I moved to follow Sonya, but Renee Zerkowski stopped me. "I'll go to her," she murmured. "You need to defuse this situation before things get worse." She hurried off, leaving me wishing we could switch places.

Darcy's triumphant expression began showing faint cracks. Clearly, the mood of the group had shifted. Their looks of scorn were focused directly on Darcy Falls.

I glowered at her. "You have your facts wrong—"

"You've got to be kidding me, Darcy," the stage manager interrupted. "Have you no shame? No sense of decorum?"

Surprised, I realized our blonde stage manager was Mrs. Ewles, the former CFO of Lansdown Tech. She'd been a few years ahead of me at school. Right now, she looked as though she could tear apart Darcy Falls without batting an eyelash. I bet she kicked ass in the boardroom.

"How about if I start dishing up dirt from *your* past?" Mrs. Ewles suggested. "Believe me. I could. I know loads of stories. Who cares if a teacher is dating her student's uncle? Your past is much more checkered. Some of the stuff you did back when we were in high school was downright illegal."

Darcy flinched, but then straightened her spine under the other parents' angry gazes and scowled right back at everyone. "You're all blind," she snapped. "Can't you see that Sonya Gambit is actually that homewrecker Essie Harlow? She's the piece of trash who broke up Raven and Max. Aren't you worried about having someone like her in daily contact with your children?"

"I'm a lot more worried about someone like you," Mrs. Ewles snapped back. "You're the one causing a scene, throwing around ugly accusations, and interrupting the kids' rehearsal time."

"This ends now," I said, my voice cutting through the growing commotion. "Sonya had nothing to do with my breakup with Raven. That relationship was over before Sonya and I ever met. Those lies belong in the past. Don't try to resurrect them. Raven's drug-addled version of our breakup was a complete fabrication."

Mary Lou Loxton turned her sympathetic smile on me. "I figured out Raven was lying four years ago. Hadn't she just checked out of a drug rehab center when she made that nasty video about you and Essie? Not exactly your most reliable witness. Besides, your explanation made a lot more sense than hers did. Raven came across like a bitter ex."

Darcy Falls looked perplexed. "You're saying you'll take Essie Harlow's version of events over Raven's? Are you nuts? Even her own dad called her a gold-digger."

"I don't know Raven from Adam," Mary Lou said, "but Sonya Gambit has been Liam's teacher since August, and he says she's the best teacher he's ever had. That counts for a lot in my book. And that father of Essie's showed up in her life after abandoning her for fifteen years. I wasn't inclined to believe anything he had to say about her. It seems to me that you're just here to stir up trouble, just like he did, and I don't appreciate it. Besides, Max is standing right here, telling you the truth."

Mrs. Ewles put her hands on her hips and stared Darcy Falls down. "You're such a stickler about the rules these days. Did you forget that students aren't allowed to take part in after-school activities if they don't attend class?"

Darcy's mulish chin jutted forward an inch. "That only applies to athletes."

"You're wrong." Mrs. Ewles said. "I'll call Principal Good-friend now and she can explain the policy to you. In the mean-time, you need to leave. You're disrupting the rehearsal, and these kids need to prepare for Friday's show."

"You have some nerve." Darcy's face turned a deeper shade of red.

"Thank you," Mrs. Ewles replied with a feline smile. "It's served me well. Besides, I really don't like bullies."

Mary Lou stepped forward. "She's right. You've caused enough of a distraction for today. You need to go."

"You're embarrassing me, Mom." Crystal started wobbling toward the exit. "I'm leaving."

For a moment, Darcy stood glaring at the circle of women surrounding her. Then she let out a loud snort of disgust. "I'm calling the principal and getting this straightened out. This isn't the end."

Mrs. Ewles cackled. "You and your little dog, Toto." An image of the Wicked Witch from the Wizard of Oz threatening to steal Dorothy's dog popped into my head.

Some of the other parents chuckled. "Good one," one of them said.

"I'll walk out with you while you call the principal," Mary Lou Loxton said, ushering Darcy ahead of her.

Darcy whirled toward the door, complaining at the top of her lungs about ungrateful kids, and parents with their heads up their asses. Liam's mom picked up their pace and hurried them out of earshot.

"Thanks," I murmured to Mrs. Ewles.

"No problem," she said with a dismissive wave. "I enjoyed taking her down a peg. Darcy's always been difficult. I'm sorry she set her sights on Miss Gambit. That was unacceptable. I just feel bad for poor Crystal. That kid has it rough."

I glanced at the door, wishing I could go to Sonya. "I need to run this rehearsal. I'm not supposed to leave the kids unsupervised. Can you make sure Sonya's okay?"

Mrs. Ewles met my gaze and nodded. "She'll be fine."

Prisha had managed to keep the students up on the stage, but they were still rattled by the scene they'd just witnessed. Even though they hadn't heard Darcy's accusation, they could tell she'd been angry. Not only that but Miss Gambit had been upset and had fled the room in tears.

"Miss Gambit will be back soon," I reassured them. "In the meantime, let's get started."

As we ran through scene six, I kept glancing toward the door, but Sonya didn't appear.

It was a rough rehearsal. I had to keep feeding people lines they'd known by heart for the last two weeks.

Finally, Mrs. Ewles came back. "I spoke to Renee Zerkowski. She says Miss Gambit went home and wants you to handle rehearsal today. She said to tell you she'll call you later."

I hadn't protected her. Not being able to go to her left me feeling raw and inadequate. It tore my heart in two. I wanted nothing more than to go to her now.

When Mrs. Ewles headed backstage, Emma came down from the stage to talk to me, worry etched on her face. "Did she have news about Miss Gambit? Is she okay?"

I took a calming breath. "She'll be fine," I said, hoping I wasn't lying. "She had to leave for the day, but she says she'll call me later."

Emma looked worried. "I was afraid of this. Is she going to run away again?"

Panic pierced me. I hadn't even considered that possibility. Sonya wouldn't just disappear again, would she? I took a steadying breath. "Let's not jump to any conclusions. And let's not talk about it here. Later, kiddo. We have work to do here."

The rest of the rehearsal was rough. I was only able to run through about half of the show before the scheduled quitting time came around.

Emma waited until we were alone together in the car. She huffed out a sigh. "Everything that happened this afternoon was nuts. Miss Gambit didn't do anything wrong. Mrs. Falls was just being a bully."

I snorted. "You won't get an argument from me on that."

Her stomach growled. "Is dinner soon? I'm starving."

"It won't take long." I could put dinner in the microwave and then call Sonya.

Emma gestured toward my phone in the cupholder as I pulled into the driveway. "Can I borrow your phone to call Marley while you start dinner? My battery's dead"

"Make it quick. I need to call Miss Gambit as soon as possible, so keep it short." I pulled the car into the garage and shut off the engine. "Don't tell Marley what Mrs. Falls said. Right now, you and Crystal are the only students who know about her accusations. I'd like to keep it that way."

"Got it," Emma said as she peered down at the phone screen and scurried for the house.

I stopped in the kitchen and put the chili I'd made yesterday into the microwave, then went in search of Emma and my phone.

I found her up in her room. The door wasn't closed all the way, and I could hear her pleading with someone. "Please. You don't realize how bad things have gotten."

She wasn't talking to Marley. I could tell. So, who was on the other end of the line?

Suddenly I knew. I hoped I was wrong, but somehow, I knew I wasn't.

I shoved the door open and stormed over to where Emma sat cross-legged on the bed. I said nothing, but simply held my hand out for the phone.

Emma stared at me, a stubborn glint in her eye. She didn't move.

"Now, Emma," I said.

"Uncle Max wants to talk to you," she said, and passed me the phone.

"Hello?" I said, still holding out hope that I was wrong.

"Max, darling. I've missed you."

"Raven."

She rushed to explain that Emma had told her Essie and I were back together again and a parent was causing trouble.

I glowered at Emma.

She stared back, defiant.

"Tell me, Max. What can I do to help?" Raven asked.

"Don't do anything" I tried to hide the rising panic in my voice. The last thing we needed was Raven's "help." Knowing her, she'd bring an entire media shitstorm down on us. "I'm sorry Emma called you. Please stay out of it. Sonya's been through enough. She was hounded by reporters and your fans five years ago, she lost her job, and now she's afraid her entire life is about to fall apart again. If you turn the spotlight on her, you could ruin everything she's built here."

"Don't be so melodramatic, Max," Raven crooned, playing with me. "What on earth are you talking about? How did I ruin her life?"

I barked out a laugh. "You turned your fans against her. The reporters made her life a living hell. She got death threats, for the love of God. To top it off, you blamed your suicide attempt on our breakup and the fact that I'd been seeing her. You turned her into a pariah."

"You're exaggerating," she scoffed. "It wasn't all that bad. You know what they say, no publicity is bad publicity."

"Are you so wrapped up in yourself that you don't understand the impact you have on other people's lives? She was publicly shamed by your fans. They even started a hashtag called EssieIsASlut. That was entirely your fault. She had to legally change her name to escape those vultures. She changed her hair color to transform herself into someone who looks nothing like Essie Harlow so she could find a job and earn a living. Do us all a favor and stay out of her life."

"Max, I had no idea." Raven sounded genuinely surprised, which pissed me off even more.

"That's no excuse. You had power, she had none, and you used your power to destroy her in a fit of temper."

"I'm not that same person who did those things five years ago. I've changed, Max. You've got to believe me. I don't do drugs. I'm stable. I'm about to release my first album in five years. Your brother even wants me to write something for his movie soundtrack. Did he tell you? I've turned my life around."

Something in her plaintive tone almost made me feel sorry for her, but I held back. I couldn't forget what she'd done. I could, however, end this conversation. "Congratulations. On the album. On getting your life back together. On everything. But—"

"I owe you an apology, too," she interrupted. "I never should have been so bad to you when we were together. I know I lied to you. It was wrong. I don't blame you for leaving me. It was probably the smartest thing you could do."

Surprised, I dropped onto the edge of Emma's bed. I'd never expected to hear an apology from her. "I'm glad you got the help you needed."

"It's weird, you know? I used to feel so overwhelmed by everything that was happening to me. The climb to celebrity status happened way too fast. I didn't handle it well. It wasn't until I hit rock bottom that I realized my lack of control over my life was what really pushed me over the edge. After my little accident," she used her oft-repeated euphemism for her suicide attempt, "I worked with a wonderful therapist who helped me understand myself. It turns out I'm a bit of a control freak. I've hired two assistants. One of them is always with me to ensure everything gets done to my specifications."

I recalled the photos I'd seen of her and her "assistants"—two shirtless young men in black leather pants wearing dog collars. "Congratulations. I'm glad you found a process that works for you."

"That's all you have to say?" She bristled with irritation. "That sounds pretty damned formal and condescending coming from a man I used to be on intimate terms with. I don't think I like your tone."

I heaved a sigh. "Raven, I've had a rough day. I'm not in the mood for this. I'm not one of the boy toys you parade around on leashes."

"You never were any good at doing as you were told," she grumbled.

"So, we're done here, right? I'm sorry my niece called you. I'll make sure it doesn't happen again. Goodbye, Raven."

"Wait a—"

I didn't wait. I hung up on her and turned to glower at Emma. "Never contact that woman again. She's still as self-centered as she was five years ago. She'll only make the situation worse if she gets involved. It's her specialty."

She gave a heavy sigh, and finally looked contrite. "I'm sorry. I'm worried about Miss Gambit. I thought if Raven set things straight, everything would be fine."

"If that were possible, it would have happened five years ago. Believe me, I tried. Take my advice and keep Raven at a distance. Think of her as a stick of unstable dynamite. She'll take out everyone in her vicinity when she blows. I'm just glad she lives on the opposite end of the continent."

34

NO MORE BYSTANDERS

SONYA

A couple of hours after I ran out of the school, I pulled into the parking lot of the Not-A-Yacht Club. As I turned off my engine, my cell phone rang.

Max.

I hesitated, then grabbed it before it could go to voicemail. I didn't want to shut him out. Not again.

"Hi," I said. Brown leaves skittered across the restaurant parking lot. I lowered the visor to block the orange of the setting sun.

"Hey, babe." Max's deep voice vibrated through the phone and echoed straight to my heart. "How are you holding up?"

The knot of anxiety in my chest cracked wide open. Darcy Falls's outburst had targeted both of us today and I'd been worried he'd be angry about it. Instead, he was worried. About me. "Better, now that I'm hearing your voice."

"I'm glad. I would have called sooner, but I had to run the rehearsal and take Emma home. Rehearsal went as well as can be expected, considering Darcy's tantrum. The kids were a bit shaken, but we ran through more than half the show and nailed down the staging. Prisha pitched in to help, and the custodian locked up."

I pressed the phone closer to my ear. "Thanks for handling everything. I'm sorry about running out like that. If I stayed, I'd have said or done something I'd regret."

"I wish you'd stayed a minute longer. You have a hell of a parent fan club. They all sided with you. Mrs. Ewles is a badass and went toe-to-toe with Darcey. Liam's mom pretty much quick-marched her out of the school, and Renee cited some rule about kids not being allowed to participate in after-school activities if they don't attend class."

I stilled. "They did? I thought Mrs. Loxton was upset with me."

"So did I, but it turns out she was horrified that Darcy would stage a scene like that around the kids."

I ran through everything I'd seen right before I ran out and realized I might have jumped to conclusions. "What about Crystal? Poor kid. That had to have been so embarrassing for her." I paused. "Were the other parents upset?"

"With Darcy? They were pissed."

"No. I mean, how upset were they to learn about us? About who I really am?" I squeezed the steering wheel as I waited to hear the bad news.

"That's what I'm trying to tell you. No one is upset. Not about us. The person they're angry with is Darcy. I had the impression that some of them already knew you were Essie Harlow."

My mouth went dry. I was suddenly speechless.

"Are you there?" Max asked.

I forced myself to speak. "They knew?"

"Most of them, definitely. Apparently, you weren't as anony-mous as you thought you were. I don't think Mary Lou Loxton knew, but she might have been the only one who didn't. The only person who had a problem with your past was Darcy Falls."

"I can hardly believe it. Is that old story finally behind me?" Relief flooded me, and something else. I was filled with an impression of lightness. I had trouble identifying the emotion at first. Was that hope? Joy? "Have I been running away from a bogeyman?"

"I think this will blow over. It all depends on whether or not the news about your identity hits the ear of the wrong entertainment reporter. If it's a slow week, a news magazine like *Here's the Scoop* might decide to run with it, but under normal circumstances, I'd say you're safe."

The phrase he used made me hesitate. I felt a chill and realized that with the sun setting, it was getting cold outside. "What do you mean, 'under normal circumstances?'"

He took a deep breath. "Do you remember I mentioned that Raven's about to release her first album in five years? She's all over the news and social media right now, doing interviews and showing up on talk shows. That might make reporters more interested if an old scandal from her past reemerges."

The spark of hope I'd been fanning suddenly snuffed out. "That's it, then." My voice came out hollow and weak. "Darcy dropped her bombshell at the worst possible moment."

"Let's hope not," Max said. "With luck, nothing will come of this. Even if it does, we'll stand and face it. Together."

Something about his tone sounded like he was placating me and understating how severe the could be consequences. I'd been through this before. I knew exactly how devastating this could be.

"We?" I said, my temper flaring. "I didn't see you being chased around by Raven's rabid fans five years ago, being vilified on social media and getting death threats."

Max let out a heavy sigh. "I know you went through this alone last time, but it didn't have to be that way. It doesn't have to be that way now, either. I want to keep you safe, and I want us to show a united front. We need to stand together on this."

With the last light of the setting sun fading away, I blinked back the tears that threatened. I wasn't being fair, true, but I hurt, dammit.

My phone vibrated with an incoming text message.

"Hold on," I told Max.

I glanced down at the glowing screen. "I need to go. I'm meeting Lianna, and she just texted she's waiting for me inside."

He was quiet for a moment. "Don't leave things unresolved between us. We have more to discuss."

I hesitated. A heavy silence stretched between us. "We'll talk," I finally said, "but, I need to process everything you told me. I'll call you in a couple of hours."

"Promise?" He sounded uncertain.

My heart squeezed. He had reason to doubt me after the way I'd walked out on him five years ago. "Promise."

The moment I ended the call, another text message came through. This one was from the principal.

> Cindy: Mrs. Falls contacted me. To be clear, if a student is unable to attend school, they aren't permitted to take part in extra-curricular activities. That includes the show. School policy. I explained that to Mrs. Falls. She wasn't happy about it, but she's now aware of the rule.
>
> Me: Thanks for letting me know. We'll see if she shows up for class tomorrow.
>
> Cindy: Poor kid. Let's hope her mom doesn't force her.

The night was getting cold now that the sun was down. I tucked my phone into my pocket and burrowed into my coat as I hurried toward the Not-A-Yacht Club.

As soon as I entered the bar, Conner Gillette spotted me.

"Lianna mentioned she's meeting you," Conner said. "She's over there." He seemed distracted as he gestured toward a table in the corner. "I have something to take care of, but I'll stop by in a few minutes to say hi."

"Sweetie," Lianna said, rising to her feet when she spotted me. "I'm so glad you called." She gave me a hug and we sat. "I had Conner pour you some wine," she said, indicating the glass on the table.

"You're the best. Thanks for meeting me here."

"No problem. I had just left a meeting when you called, so I came straight over."

A pang of guilt hit me. "I'm sorry. I hope I didn't pull you away from something important."

Lianna fluttered her hand in dismissal. "Not at all. I solved a couple of tricky problems today, so I deserve to leave work at a reasonable hour and celebrate."

"What problems?"

"We had some process flow issues that were slowing down the new order system we implemented for a client, plus a couple of our support teams were understaffed. I had to juggle things around."

"Lianna to the rescue. Program manager extraordinaire."

"Thanks. But enough about me. You sound like you're in crisis mode. What's going on?"

"Direct, aren't you?"

Lianna smirked. "I'm a problem-solver. What can I say? It's my bag, baby."

I let out a laugh, then sipped my wine as I composed my thoughts. "You know about the whole thing with Raven five years ago. I think it's about to blow up in my face again."

Lianna lost the glint of humor in her eye and her face became tense. "What happened?"

"During rehearsal today, one of the moms outed me as Essie."

Lianna looked gratifyingly offended. "Seriously? What's this woman's issue? That gossip is five years old. Why bring it up now?"

My stomach tensed. I sipped my wine, looking anywhere other than at Lianna.

"Your relationship with Max did end five years ago, right?" Lianna asked, a teasingly suspicious glint in her eye. "Or is there something you aren't telling me?"

I folded my arms across my chest. "Things have changed between us."

Lianna settled back in her chair and stared at me. A satisfied smile tugged up the corners of her mouth. "And here I thought the reason you'd stopped calling me was because the show had taken over your life. Are you telling me it's because you've been getting busy with Max Ross?"

My cheeks grew warm, but I couldn't stop the smile that spread across my face. "Pretty busy."

Lianna's answering grin broadened. "You naughty girl. So, the two of you are a couple again?"

"It would seem so."

"Was he with you when the witchy mom revealed all?"

I nodded.

"How did he take it?"

"He was angry with her. Supportive of me. He seems to have calmed down now—I just got off the phone with him."

"That's good." Lianna looked satisfied with my answer. "Do you think he'll be there for you if things turn nasty again?"

"He made it clear he will."

"How about you?" She lifted one eyebrow. "Are you going to stand up for yourself this time?"

I stared back at her, not quite understanding what she was getting at. "What's that supposed to mean?"

"I'd think that was obvious. You let Raven stomp all over you five years ago. She's a vindictive you-know-what, but you never did anything to defend yourself. You never gave an interview. Never posted anything on social media. You just ran away and went into hiding. If you'd stood up for yourself, I bet things would have been very different."

"I'd wanted to—I even had something planned—but after that interview my dad gave..."

Lianna blinked her eyes and shook her head. "I'm so sorry, Sonya. Your father is vile, and it had to have been hard to deal with him on top of everything else, but you let *him* control the narrative, too. You never set the record straight and put *your* version of events out there."

I was stung by my friend's words. "Are you saying it's my fault? Are you trying to blame the victim? I expected you to be more supportive."

"I'm pointing out what you did wrong last time, so you don't make the same mistakes again," Lianna said gently. "Seriously, you need to stand up for yourself. Don't let this bully ruin your life. Weren't you talking about how bystanders need to stop being bystanders and take a stand against bullies? You need to follow your own advice."

"Except that I'm *not* a bystander. I'm the target."

"You know what I mean. Use the skills you bring to the table. Be the super-teacher I know you can be."

I snorted. "Right. Watch me corral unruly children with a single word. Calm parents with my laser vision. Stop bullies in their tracks."

Lianna leaned in. "Exactly. Stop bullies in their tracks. Use the stuff you learned in that anti-bullying program you were telling us about."

That finally got me thinking. I put my elbows on the table and rested my chin on my fists. "Bystanders," I repeated. "You make a good point. When you teach people to stop being bystanders and become upstanders, they can take away the majority of a bully's power. Why didn't I see this sooner? Raven is the bully. Her rabid fans are bullies too. But who are my bystanders?"

"Me. Max. Your students. Their parents. The other teachers. The school board. Our book club. Your friends." She paused and gave a low chuckle. "Raven's enemies."

I blinked. "She has a few of those. I think the woman managed to burn a lot of bridges when she flamed out five years ago." Then I shook my head. "I don't want to take that route, though. I might not like her, but I'd rather stick to the high road."

Conner came up behind me. "You take the high road and I'll take the low road, and I'll be in Scotland afore ye," he sang in that gorgeous tenor of his. "Whoever's got you looking so glum, let me at 'em," he added.

I smiled up at Conner, delighted by his beautiful singing voice. "Are you offering to take someone down for me?"

"Me? Never. I'm a lover, not a fighter," Conner said. "But if you need someone to charm them with great food and passable music, I'm your man."

"It's a deal," I said. Too bad his charm wouldn't work against someone like Raven.

"You still need to tell me what you're contributing to the feast on Thanksgiving," Lianna told Conner. "I want to make sure we have everything covered."

"Since Dante's making his caramel apple pie, I'll bring vanilla ice cream and whipped cream to go with it," he said.

"I'll make the turkey, the stuffing, and the gravy," Lianna said.

"With all my attention focused on the show this Friday," I said, "I nearly forgot Thanksgiving was next week. What do you still need?"

Lianna checked a list on her phone. "How about something with sweet potatoes or cranberries?"

"Can do. I'll find some good recipes and let you know what I'm bringing."

Last month, when Lianna had suggested we all have Thanksgiving together, I'd been thrilled to be included. After Mom died, my sister, Kendra chose to spend Thanksgiving with her roommate the last couple of years, so I'd been alone. Knowing I had someplace to be, with people who wanted me, made me appreciate this town and my friends even more.

A sudden presentiment of loss crept over me. I reached a hand to massage the spot over my heart. Would I still be living here next Thursday? I'd worked hard to build new friendships, and Sewickley already felt like home.

Thanksgiving. My friends. My community. My students. I'd have to abandon the new life I'd created if I let Darcy drive me away.

"I'm looking forward to having everyone over," Lianna said.

"I have a small house, but it has a dining room that's perfect for entertaining.

At that moment, I decided I'd be there too. Lianna was right. I needed to take a stand.

35

FINAL WEEK OF REHEARSALS

MAX

The moment Emma went upstairs to get ready for bed, I called Sonya. "How did everything go with Lianna?"

"Talking to her helped. She gives good advice." She yawned deeply. "I think I'm all talked out. I don't want to keep hashing over what happened." Her voice sounded strong. Confident. "I decided I won't let Darcy scare me off. I refuse to let her nastiness get to me."

"I like your attitude." I climbed the stairs toward my bedroom and noticed that Emma's door was closed. A light was shining from the gap beneath it, which was odd. Ever since we'd moved in, Emma had kept her door open. "Hold on a sec," I told Sonya. I knocked gently.

"Yeah?" came Emma's voice. She sounded subdued.

When I opened her door, I spotted her propped up in bed, reading. "Don't stay up too late," I told her. "You have a big week ahead of you."

"Okay," she said. "Sorry again about making that phone call."

"It's okay, sweetie. Love you."

"Love you, too." She set aside her book and turned off the lamp next to her bed, plunging the room into darkness. "Oh. I almost forgot," Emma added. "Miss Gambit's friend Miss Courtney is coming over tomorrow evening to run lines with me."

That took me by surprise. "She is? How did you manage to set that up?"

"She called and offered, and she said Miss Rose, the librarian, can come too."

I nodded. "Sounds good. Thanks for telling me. Good night again. Sleep well."

"You, too."

I backed out of her room and closed her door.

"I'm back," I told Sonya as I headed down the hallway toward my bedroom. I'd have privacy there and could tell her about Emma calling Raven. "Did you hear what Emma said about Courtney and Rose?"

"I did. They offered to help, so I gave them Emma's number. I hope that was okay."

"Absolutely."

"I heard Emma say something about making a phone call?" Sonya said, making the statement sound more like a question. "Why did she have to apologize for it?"

I dragged my hand through my hair. "Because she screwed up. She called Raven and told her what happened today."

Silence stretched between us. Finally, Sonya said, "I don't even know what to say. How did she get Raven's number? Why did she think it was okay to call? Did you stop her? Is this whole thing going to blow up?"

I heaved a sigh. "Ford contacted Raven about composing music for his movie, and he sent me her number in case she tried to call me. He wanted me to have her contact information in my phone so I'd recognize it if she called."

"And you didn't bother to tell me until now?" she snapped.

"I knew Ford wouldn't have her write a new score for him, so I decided not to bring it up. If the situation changed, I'd have informed you, which is what I'm doing now."

Sonya gave a frustrated sigh. "You can't keep secrets like this from me. It's what got us into trouble the last time."

I tensed. "That isn't fair. I'm not the one talking to her—Ford is." Then I stopped. "Well, I wasn't until today. When I took the phone away from Emma, I ended up having to speak to Raven. I was trying to do some damage control, and I think I was successful." At least, I sure as hell hoped I'd been.

"Tell me everything. What she said. What you said. Where you left things."

I ran through the conversation, making sure I included all the pertinent details. "I'm pretty sure she's going to stay out of it," I told Sonya, crossing my fingers for good luck.

I caught the sound of her quiet sigh of relief. "That went better than I would have expected."

"If it's any consolation, she sounded completely rational. Still manipulative—don't get me wrong—but not delusional."

Sonya made a sound of disbelief. "I don't know the woman as well as you do, so I'll have to take your word for it." She cleared her throat. "I heard from the principal. If Crystal isn't well enough to attend school, she can't be in the show."

"That makes sense. The kid has had a tough time of it. She looked miserable."

"Listen," Sonya said, "I have an American history lesson I need to review before I teach class tomorrow. Even teachers need to study. Can we talk later? I'm really beat, and I still have a lot to do."

The only time I saw Sonya for the rest of the week was during rehearsal. We were slammed with last-minute preparations for the show. Friday's performance was barreling toward us, and we had to be ready.

I would have loved to spend an evening with her, but we were all too busy. Sonya had papers to grade and schoolwork to attend to. I needed to help Emma stay on top of her homework. Plus, I had my own work to complete for Ross Film Productions. I had millions of details to address to get Ford's movie into production.

Courtney and Rose were lifesavers. I'm not sure Emma would have had her lines down if they hadn't come over to help. They also offered her their own opinions on the subject of Emma talking over Crystal's role. Their support helped her see that she was doing the right thing. Plus, their energy and enthusiasm helped bolster her enthusiasm.

I missed holding Sonya in my arms as we drifted off to sleep together. Funny, how quickly I'd come to need her in my life again. I missed her. I couldn't lose her again. I refused to even consider the possibility.

IT'S SHOWTIME!

Max

The November air was crisp and cool when I pulled my car into the school parking lot Friday afternoon, I spotted Sonya standing outside the building, talking with Principal Goodfriend.

Sonya wore a long-sleeved black top and black pants. The perfect outfit for working backstage and fading into the darkness. She looked sophisticated and sleek with her blond hair up in an elegant twist that bared her graceful neck.

Principal Goodfriend greeted me as I approached. "Thanks again for agreeing to co-direct the show," she said. "Sonya was just telling me what tremendous help you've been."

"No, I wasn't," Sonya protested with a playful glint in her eye. "I was telling you he saved the show, and I would've been lost without him."

Mrs. Goodfriend winked at Sonya. "I was trying to save your dignity."

"Too late," Sonya said.

"Don't let her fool you," I told the principal. "The show was a team effort. Sonya's becoming an excellent director. She knows exactly how to get those kids to snap to attention. And Prisha did a brilliant job as the producer. She made our jobs a million times easier."

"That's wonderful" Mrs. Goodfriend said. "I know you're busy tonight, so I won't keep you. I'll see you after the show."

Sonya watched her leave, then turned to me, shielding her eyes against the setting sun. "I'm nervous."

"The kids are ready. They'll be great."

"It isn't that. I have this sinking feeling Darcy will cause trouble tonight."

I raised one eyebrow. "I have the same feeling. She likes to grandstand."

Sonya smiled grimly. "We'll just have to shut her down if she tries."

Mrs. Ewles, the stage manager, came hurrying out the front door of the school. "Miss Gambit. I'm so glad I found you. Can you help backstage? The light we set up to follow along with the script isn't working. We could use a cell phone light in a pinch, but I'd rather not if we don't have to."

"I stashed some spare batteries back there," Sonya said as she headed to meet her. "I'll show you where they are."

I went in search of Emma in the classroom we were using as the hair and makeup room. She'd grabbed a ride with Marley and her mom because she hadn't wanted to wait another ten minutes for me to finish a phone call.

When I found her, she was already in her costume for the first scene. She pinched her bottom lip between her thumb and forefinger, a sure sign that she was nervous.

Renee Zerkowski, Mary Lou Loxton, and some other parent volunteers were scattered around the room helping the kids put on stage makeup or style their hair. The room smelled of hairspray and the flowery scent of makeup.

Emma's worried frown greeted me when I approached. "I wish we had another week to rehearse."

"I know, but you'll be great. If you forget a line, just roll with it. Like I said last night at rehearsal, the entire cast knows the show well enough by now that anyone can help if someone messes up."

Emma huffed. "I know all that, Uncle Max. This isn't the first show I've ever been in. It's just that I know I could do a better job if I had a little more time to rehearse."

"Take some time to center yourself and review the show in your mind," I suggested. "You'll be great. I'm certain of it. You have your lines down solid. You were even correcting Courtney and Rose last night when they were running lines with you."

Sonya stood in the doorway of the makeup room. "How's everything going in here?" she asked, glancing around. When her gaze caught on me, it stayed there.

"Miss Gambit," Marley called out, "can you help me with my skirt? Something's wrong with it."

Sonya broke our eye contact and went to Marley.

My brother, Ford stepped into the room with his fiancé, Mara Stellar by his side. Her blue-tipped hair fell in soft waves around her shoulders.

"Ford. Mara," I said, "it's good to see you. I'm glad you came."

"We wouldn't miss it for the world," Ford said. He tipped his head to one side to catch Emma's eye. "How you doing, Em? Ready for the show?"

Emma gave a jerky shrug. "As ready as I can be."

"Stay nervous. You can channel that energy into your performance," Ford told her.

She looked at him doubtfully. "Really? You aren't going to tell me to relax?"

"Would it work, or would it just annoy you?"

Emma smirked. "Good point."

I spotted my dad at the door and waved him over.

"Hi, Emma," he said, patting her shoulder gently. "You look elegant in that evening gown. All grown up."

"Thanks, Grampa Don," she said as she hugged him. "I'm glad you're here."

"Hey, what about us?" Ford protested.

Emma grinned. "You, too." She hugged him as well, then Mara.

Sin Bachar walked in with his girlfriend at his side. "Hey, can I get one of those hugs?" he asked.

"Sure thing, Uncle Sin." Emma darted over to him.

He crushed her in an embrace that made her protest. "Stop it. I can't breathe."

"I know the feeling," his girlfriend said. "Don't worry, though; I know CPR. I can revive you."

"This is my girlfriend, Miranda," Sin said.

"Nice to meet you," Don Ross said, shaking Miranda's hand. "Did Sin tell me you're both doctors?"

"That's right. We moved here together. We both managed to get residencies at the same hospital," Miranda explained.

"What kind of doctor are you?" Don asked.

"An anesthesiologist."

Ford let out a whistle. "Tough job," he said. "You see all sorts of surgeries. I bet it's a hell of a challenge."

"It can be," she said with a shrug, "but I love it."

"I want to introduce Miss Gambit to everyone," Emma said, and then darted away.

Emma grabbed hold of Sonya's hand and led her back to us She looked like she'd bolt if Emma let go.

When they joined us, Sonya stood next to me but kept her distance. She looked nervous as a girl who'd run out on a guy five years ago, breaking his heart, and was now about to meet his family.

"Miss Gambit," Emma said proudly, "this is my family." She ran through their names.

"Sonya and I are co-directing the show," I added.

Don glanced at me pointedly, then at Sonya. It was obvious he knew exactly who she was. "It's nice to finally meet you. Emma and Max have told me a lot about you."

Sonya seemed to catch on to the fact that he knew she was

Essie. She swallowed as she shook his hand. "Thank you, Mr. Ross."

"Call me Don."

Mara grinned. "I hear you're the newest member of my book group. I'm glad to finally meet you. Lianna sings your praises."

Sonya seemed to relax slightly. "She's such a good friend. Everyone at book group misses you."

"I hope to be there next month. Fingers crossed. Getting my new video game company off the ground has consumed me. Between that, my store, and Ford's movie, I'm swamped. I wish I could clone myself."

"Her brother wrote the comic book my movie is based on," Ford explained. "She's our subject matter expert on everything related to the story."

"Busy woman," Sonya said. "You make me feel like a slacker."

"Wild, right?" Mara said. "'Human sacrifice, dogs and cats living together... mass hysteria!'"

Sonya stared at her, confused.

Mara laughed. "That's a line from *Ghostbusters*."

"Give it time," Ford said. "You'll get used to her. She makes nerd references every chance she gets."

Mara elbowed him. "It was a movie reference. I chose it so you'd recognize it."

"A nerd movie," Ford amended.

"A great movie," Mara corrected.

Sonya watched the back-and-forth with a bemused smile on her face.

"Sonya," Don said, "from what I understand, you don't have family in the area. Would you like to come to my place for Thanksgiving? It's mostly the group right here."

"That would be most excellent," Mara said, her face lighting up. "You should come."

Sonya stared at my dad, stunned. "That's so kind of you, Mr. Ross."

"Don."

"Don," she said, agreeably. "Thank you. But I made plans to go to my friend Lianna's for Thanksgiving at around one."

"That's perfect," Don said. "You can come over to my place at six. I won't make you stuff yourself again. You can just hang out and watch us eat, or you can have a second dinner. Your choice."

Wily move on Dad's part, not giving her the chance to back out.

When Sonya glanced at me, I nodded, so she turned back to my dad and smiled. "Thanks. I'd love to come."

"Glad to hear it. I know you're busy right now. We'll get out of your hair so you can get back to your show. I'll talk to you later." Don turned to Emma. "Break a leg, kiddo."

"Thanks, Grampa Don."

"Say what?" Sin did a double take. "Did you just tell your granddaughter to break her leg?"

"You were never in any shows growing up, were you son?" Don asked. "It's bad luck to wish a performer good luck before a show. Instead, you tell them to break a leg."

"This is a strange family," Sin said as he followed Don out of the room.

After they left, Sonya still seemed off-kilter at meeting my family.

"My dad blindsided you with that invitation," I observed.

"A little," she said, pulling herself together, "but it was considerate of him. I'd like to get to know your family better."

I squeezed her hand briefly before letting it go. "I'd like that, too."

"Emma," Renee Zerkowski said. "It's your turn for makeup. Have a seat."

"Things look like they're running smoothly here," Sonya. "Let's go check on everything else."

At the door, we came face to face with Darcy and Crystal Falls.

I stiffened, but Sonya smiled at them in welcome and turned her attention to the girl in the body cast. "Crystal, how are you?"

"Doing a little better," she said. "Not as achy as I was."

"Crystal!" Emma exclaimed from across the room. "You're here! We're having a cast party at my house on Sunday afternoon, and I want you to come. Can you make it?"

Crystal looked surprised by the invitation. "Are you sure?" She glanced up at her mom's glowering face. "I mean, I'm not even in the show."

"But you were in the cast," Emma said from her chair. "That's all that matters. You should come. We miss you. The party wouldn't be the same without you."

Crystal's face lit up. "Sure," Crystal said. "If it's okay with my mom, that is."

A surge of pride filled me, tinged with melancholy. Emma always seemed to know the right thing to say—just like her mom.

"I still think you should have been in the show," her mother grumbled.

"You said you'd leave the decision up to me," Crystal reminded her. "I decided."

Darcy Falls crossed her arms and jutted her chin out mulishly.

"Please, Mom. I really want to go."

"Please," Emma chimed in.

"Please," said Marley. And Liam. And a chorus of other cast members.

Darcy's mouth fell open in surprise. "Well, if you feel so strongly about it, I suppose she can attend, as long as she's feeling up to it."

Interesting that in Darcy's mind, a party might be too much exertion for Crystal, but a week of rehearsals leading up to a show was fine. The woman was a mass of contradictions.

"I hope you enjoy the show," Sonya said as she turned to leave.

Darcy scowled at her. "That's hardly likely. With my daughter being replaced at the last minute, I doubt the show will—"

"Seriously, Darcy. Let it go!" Renee Zerkowski snapped as she planted her fists on her hips and stared the woman down. "Don't come in here and pick a fight right before the kids go on stage. You know better than that."

Darcy pressed her lips into a thin, furious line. Without another word, she spun on her heel and fled the room. Crystal just rolled her eyes and followed her out the door.

"Everything's fine, kids," Renee said. "Pre-show drama averted."

"I'm glad Renee was the one who shut her down," I murmured as we stepped into the corridor. "What I wanted to say wasn't nearly as diplomatic."

Sonya glanced back toward the classroom. "I can't believe Darcy would pick a fight right now. It was almost as though she wanted to sabotage the show."

I shrugged. "Maybe she did."

"Sonya. We found you," Lianna said as she waved from about thirty feet away.

Lianna stood with a group of women, one of whom was Scarlet Smith, the town's mayor. I recognized the others, although I didn't really know them very well. I'd met them through Mara and her comic book shop when they'd helped her with some signings and other events she'd hosted.

"Hi, Lianna," I said.

Sonya did a double-take. "You know each other?"

"You and Mara are in the same book club," I explained. "I met them through her."

Sonya smacked herself on the forehead. "Of course. How could I have forgotten?"

"Thanks again for running lines with Emma," I told Rose and Courtney. "Hi, Scarlet," I added. "It's good to see you."

"I guess you know everyone," Sonya said faintly.

"Since Scarlet's the mayor, we have meetings from time to time," I explained. "Ross Productions occasionally shoots in Sewickley."

"And because of that, we've been known to lock horns,"

Scarlet said, her bright red lips curling up in a smile. She narrowed her eyes at me. "When it comes to Sonya, I advise you to stay on all our good sides. We watch out for each other."

"Are you saying you're my posse?" Sonya asked with a grin.

I took in the women's stern expressions. "Thanks for the warning, but I think we're all in agreement when it comes to Sonya's happiness."

"I hope so," Lianna said. "It'd be a shame if we had to hunt you down and teach you a lesson." She kept her tone light, but her icy smile chilled me to the bone.

"Miss Gambit," Prisha said as she darted toward us, clipboard in hand. "The man in charge of the stage lighting is looking for you. There's a problem."

"That's my cue," Sonya said and hurried away with Prisha.

When I turned to face the women, I found them staring at me, eyes narrowed, faces grim. This pride of lionesses looked as though they'd tear me to pieces if I made the wrong move. "It was great to see you again," I said, edging away.

Scarlet smirked as though she could read my mind. "Later, Max. Give my best to your dad."

That woman was terrifying. With an uncle as a senator, it was no wonder that she was always attuned to the subtext in any conversation. She'd been raised to play the power game. She was always willing to flex a little political muscle if she believed the moment warranted it. She made it pretty obvious she'd do whatever was necessary to protect her friend.

Less than an hour later, Sonya and I stood in the wings as the theater lights dimmed.

She squeezed my hand and then took a calming breath. "It's show time."

"You just said the magic words," I said.

Sonya gripped a microphone and stepped onto the stage.

"Welcome to our fifth-grade show," she announced. The microphone gave a squeal of feedback. Sonya cleared her throat.

"First, I'd like to remind everyone to silence their phones. Also, no flash photography is permitted since it distracts the actors.

"As you know, our show tonight is a spoof of the movie National Treasure. It's my hope that learning a bit more about our capital city will make the students even more excited about their class trip to Washington at the end of the eighth grade. Judging by their enthusiasm today, I'm afraid they might be bouncing off the walls by the time the trip rolls around in three years."

The audience chuckled, warming to her.

"As some of you are aware, we had a cast change this week. Crystal Falls was injured and is unable to perform tonight. Her understudy, Emma Bachar, will be playing the part of Lydia Daring. Please give a round of applause to Crystal. She worked hard to prepare for the show and would have given an amazing performance."

The audience applauded warmly.

"Without further ado, I invite you to enjoy what our class has worked so hard to put together for your entertainment, *Treasure Hunt*."

As the audience applauded, Sonya exited the stage. As soon as the stage lights went down, the kids moved to their places. Since the cherry blossom scene was about to begin, I joined Ally next to the electric fan. The bag of cherry blossom petals sat open next to her.

"Hallo Herr Ross," Ally whispered, only taking her eyes off the stage for an instant to greet me. "Can I use extra cherry blossoms tonight?" She'd put her hair in tight braids to keep the fan from flicking it into her eyes.

"I think two extra handfuls would be okay. We don't want to overdo it, or it'll take forever to sweep them up."

"*Gut*," she said. "I mean, good." Then she grinned. "This is my favorite scene."

"Mine, too."

On stage, Liam and Emma were touring Washington landmarks, but tonight, Emma and Liam brought a different sort of emotional energy to the scene. I watched for a moment and realized it was fueled by the growing attraction between them. Back when Crystal and Liam had performed the pantomime, it had seemed sweet enough, but not particularly poignant—more like two good friends visiting landmarks. The only hint that the characters were romantically involved had come when they'd touched hands on the park bench and then looked away from each other to take in the swirling cherry blossoms.

Emma and Liam's energy was vastly different. The pair held hands from the very moment they came on stage. Their attraction was palpable, just as it needed to be for this scene to work. They were sweet together, I had to admit. Even so, something about what I was seeing bothered me at a visceral level. Since this romantic interlude was exactly what I'd envisioned, my growing unease was illogical.

As Emma and Liam approached the bench, Ally prepared for the big moment. As soon as they sat down, she released handful after handful of cherry blossoms. Emma's eyes danced with delight as the petals swirled around her. Then she turned and gazed directly into Liam's eyes.

The poor boy seemed to melt under her gaze. The pair looked completely besotted with one another, and I didn't think they were merely acting. My fatherly instincts roared into existence, and at that moment, I was enormously relieved I hadn't asked them to kiss on stage.

A moment later, the pair exited on the far side of the stage, giving me some time to get my emotions under control. Emma and Liam had done exactly what they were supposed to do. It wasn't their fault I was losing my shit.

As the crew set up for the next scene backstage, Sonya caught my eye. She tilted her head to one side, silently asking me what was wrong.

I gave her a tight nod, then flicked my eyes toward Emma and Liam. How had she picked up on my inner turmoil so easily?

She followed my gaze, looking perplexed, and then a slow grin slid over her face. When she looked back at me again, she wore a knowing expression and cocked a single eyebrow, making fun of me.

That put things into perspective. Sonya was right to tease me. I shook my head at my own overreaction, then shrugged it off.

The rest of the show ran smoothly. The kids hit their marks, remembered their lines for the most part, covered any mistakes so no one in the audience noticed, and put on a great show.

Senator Marley came on stage for her final scene. She was supposed to listen to Emma's explanation about the theft of the Declaration of Independence, forgive her for her involvement, and tell Liam and Emma the country considered them heroes for protecting the document from the would-be thieves. Emma was supposed to hug Marley, and Liam was supposed to shake her hand.

And that's exactly what they did…it all went smoothly, but then something new happened.

Ally fiddled with something backstage, and music started playing. Liam seemed to have been waiting for this, because he pulled Emma into his arms and started dancing with her, slowly turning them in place.

Emma looked startled by the unexpected change, but she went along with it. Ally turned on the fan, and a moment later, cherry blossoms fluttered across the stage, swirling around Liam and Emma.

It was sweet, yes. The audience loved it, bursting into applause—but when the pair exchanged a chaste kiss, my fatherly instincts flared to life again.

"Breathe," Sonya said, appearing out of nowhere and rubbing my back with her hand. "The good news is that they're only in the fifth grade. They're not likely to get into much trouble together at this age."

"Trouble?" My heart gave a thud at the thought of Emma in

trouble. "Please don't use that word when you talk about my niece and a boy." I rubbed at my chest. "It terrifies me."

She chuckled at me. "Buckle up, Max. You're in for a rocky ride. I hope her teen years don't kill you."

OOOH! LOOK! A MEDIA CIRCUS!

Sonya

Max and I barely kept pace with the cast members as they rushed down the long corridor to greet their adoring fans—namely, their family members. When the first student pushed open the door leading into the lobby, the crowd began to applaud.

"*Brava*!" Marley's dad shouted. "You were amazing."

The kids quickly dispersed into the throng, seeking out their parents like self-guided thermal missiles. Squeals of excitement and bursts of laughter filled the high-ceilinged room, and the sound reflected off the huge windows facing the parking lot, amplifying it.

"This is quite the scene," I commented, a little taken aback by everyone's excitement.

"I don't usually do shows with kids," Max said, grinning. "I have to say, their enthusiasm is contagious."

We were pulled from one group to the next as parents congratulated us on a successful show and snapped photos of us with their exuberantly grinning offspring.

From time to time, I caught sight of Emma and her family. Max stuck by my side as everyone congratulated us.

"Miss Gambit, can I get a picture of the two of us together?" Ally asked.

"Of course," I said. We smiled and posed for her mom. A few minutes later when I looked for Emma, I spotted her clutching multiple bouquets of flowers as she posed for pictures with her grandfather and uncles.

She positively glowed.

"Sonya, you did an amazing job," Cindy Goodfriend said, reaching out to shake my hand.

Tykera joined us. "No one would guess you had to fill in for me at the last minute. Thanks so much. I don't know what they would have done without you."

"It all worked out," Cindy said.

"I'm taking a leave of absence until after the baby's born," Tykera said. "I still feel lousy all the time. The doctor said that happens sometimes. Lucky me."

"We found a permanent sub to cover your class for the next few months," Cindy told her.

"Can you come with me, Miss Gambit?" Liam interrupted. "You too, Mr. Ross. My mom wants to take a picture." He led us over to her.

Mary Lou hugged me. "It was a wonderful show. Thanks so much for all your hard work."

"I couldn't have done it without parents like you," I told her. "Not to mention the kids. Liam in particular."

"You son's a talented young actor," Max said.

"I think so, too," Mary Lou said, smiling proudly. "And Emma was brilliant. She saved the show. Can I take a photo of both of you with Liam?"

"Of course." Max and I stood behind Liam and smiled while Mary Lou snapped a few photos.

"Let's get one with Emma," Liam suggested. He scurried away, and a moment later he was back with Emma.

"You two were so cute on stage together," Mary Lou said.

Max stilled, and Liam and Emma tensed, embarrassed.

I stepped between the two students and put my arms around their shoulders. "Smile for the camera," I said.

"Oh," Mary Lou said, "this is a great shot."

She held out her phone, and Max peered over my shoulder at it. Something in the photo's background caught my attention, and I leaned closer.

I tensed as I identified a television news crew entering the front door of the school.

"Max—" I said, trying not to panic. I scanned the crowd for the television cameras I knew I'd find.

He must have seen the same thing I had in the photo because he went on high alert.

I spotted the smiling face of a local television news reporter, Carol Perkins. Behind the gorgeous blonde was a man carrying a camera and lights. The reporter's smile flashed as she spoke to one of the parents who then looked around the room. He pointed directly at me.

Carol Perkins began moving toward me.

My stomach fell. This couldn't be happening. Not again.

I stared at the polished news reporter with a growing sense of dread. Maybe this moment was inevitable. Maybe if I'd stood up to Raven five years ago, her lies wouldn't still be chasing me.

As Carol Perkins cut through the crowd, people fluttered out of her way like pigeons avoiding a pedestrian.

Max stepped between me and the approaching piranha. "Head out the back way," he said. "I'll deal with this."

"No," I said, standing next to him. "These kids and tonight's show are my responsibility. I'm not running away. I can handle this. With luck, she's here to do a feel-good piece about tonight's performance. Maybe it's a slow news night."

Please, please let that be it.

Unfortunately, the glint in Carol Perkins's eyes kept me from believing my own words.

Movement out of the corner of my eye caught my attention. Most people were moving back to let the news crew through, but one person moved against the flow. Darcy Falls had set herself on an intercept course with the reporter, and she had a victorious gleam in her eye.

Max tensed as he spotted her too. "Darcy Falls looks way too happy right now," he murmured. "This has to do with Raven. I'm certain of it."

I had the sinking feeling he was right.

"Are you Sonya Gambit?" the reporter asked as she came to a halt in front of me. "I'm Carol Perkins with WZZZ-TV." The cameraman was edging to one side to record our conversation and pointed a blinding light in my face.

"I am," I smiled broadly. "Are you here to interview some of the students and their parents about tonight's show?"

"Is it true you're Essie Harlow?" Carol Perkins asked.

I froze. The hot lights made it hard for me to see anyone except Carol.

"She sure is," Darcy Falls said, coming to stand next to the reporter. "One and the same." She grinned with glee.

Ignoring Darcy, I focused on Carol Perkins. "If you aren't here about tonight's show, you need to leave." I pointed toward the door, feeling overly dramatic. "The students put on an excellent performance tonight, and they're the stars of the hour. You're creating a distraction and a nuisance. If you don't leave the school property, I'll call the police."

I glanced in the direction I was pointing, out the row of glass doors and into the parking lot, just as a limousine pulled to a stop out front.

The driver scurried around to open the back door, and a black above-the-knee boot slid from the back seat to step onto the side-walk. A skintight-leather-clad woman stepped out.

"Things just got worse," Max murmured into my ear. "Raven's *here*."

RAVEN'S TRUE COLORS

Sonya

I stared, frozen with shock, as Raven sauntered toward the front door of the school. From the spike-heeled boots, leather pants, corset, and—was that a riding crop?—to the self-aware gleam in her eyes as she fixed her gaze on the news van, the woman came across as calculated and predatory.

Raven. Her name suited her to perfection. Her waist-length black hair flowed around her like a cape and ended where her leather pants began. Her dark red and black corset was a splash of blood over her barely-there skintight black top.

The woman exuded control, dominance, and power. She knew it, too.

Savored it.

The bright lights illuminating the parking lot were shining down on Raven like spotlights. Two well-muscled and bare-chested assistants glided into flanking positions a scant step behind her. They wore matching skin-tight leather pants, black bow ties, and nothing else. Brave of them, considering the cool night air. This was Pittsburgh in November, not Miami Beach.

Carol Perkins and her cameraman abandoned me as they scurried toward the door. Were they hoping to find a great spot to film me and my nemesis as we finally had our epic face-off?

How could this be happening? Why had I stayed? Why had I let myself get ambushed again?

The determined look on Raven's face left no doubt as to why she'd come.

She was here to ruin my life.

Again.

My gaze darted around the room, searching for an exit. It wasn't too late to escape. Everyone was looking at Raven right now. I could slip away.

Disappear.

Run.

I took a step back but immediately bumped into a group of people crowding in behind me.

I turned to push my way through them and escape—until I realized I was standing face-to-face with Scarlet and the rest of my book club.

My posse. They literally had my back.

Not only that, but this particular gang of kick-ass women looked ready for battle.

Scarlet pulled her phone away from her ear. "We've got you," she said, her green eyes flashing with anger and determination. She stabbed her finger at the screen to end the call. "If that entitled prima donna thinks she's gonna come into my town and start causing trouble, she's got another think coming. I called our police chief and he's on his way. I've dealt with entitled jerks like her before. If Raven thinks she can steamroll over us, she's about to find out exactly how wrong she is."

Scarlet's self-assured attitude took the edge off my growing panic. When I took in the other women in my book club and the determination on their faces, my remaining panic evaporated.

This time, everything would be different. I wasn't alone.

I spotted Max's family right behind my friends, and they all looked wary as Raven approached, Don most of all. When he locked gazes with me, his expression grew determined. He gave me a quick, reassuring nod. That small movement made my heart swell with relief.

Max's family was there for me, too.

Max's warm hand slid into mine. "I'm with you, Sonya. We'll deal with her together."

I could do this.

I lifted my chin and headed toward the double doors. I wanted to confront Raven outside—I hated the idea of her coming inside my school.

My posse—now doubled in size—kept pace with me.

Two more television vans pulled up on the street. At least the drivers had the sense not to squeeze into the already-packed parking lot. The van doors slid open, and people piled out, racing toward Raven as the camera crews turned on their bright lights.

The savvy rock star paused and turned to take in the reporters streaming toward her. She gave a satisfied smirk as she turned to face the school again, just in time to see me and Max walk out the front door.

Raven's smirk suddenly morphed into a bright, calculated smile.

"Max, darling, how wonderful to see you again," Raven called out in a voice meant for everyone to hear. "And you must be Essie —or should I call you Sonya now? I understand you changed it."

Of course, she *had* to announce my name so everyone could hear it.

Raven didn't bother to hold out her hand in greeting. I didn't get the sense it was because she expected to be rejected, but simply because it wasn't in her nature.

"I've always been Sonya," I said. "Essie was a nickname."

"Isn't that just too cute? I suppose I should call you Sonya now, right?" Raven didn't wait for a reply but plowed ahead. She smiled. I could tell she was preening for the cameras as she posed with one long leg extended before her and her riding crop resting against it.

Raven kept her gaze fixed on me. "I did an interview a couple of hours ago with Lauren Harding. She's a reporter with *Here's the Scoop*. I'm sure you've heard of her. It's airing even as we speak." She glanced at the people surrounding us, gauging their reactions, and then turned back to me. "Lauren is known for her ability to draw out the people she interviews. I was surprised to hear myself revealing things—regrets—I thought I'd buried long ago. You, Essie, happen to be one of my regrets."

Raven reached out and took my hands in hers. I flinched at her cool touch, but I didn't pull away as she gazed into my eyes.

"I realized while talking to Lauren that even though I thought I'd apologized to everyone I'd hurt when I was in that horrible addiction spiral, I never apologized to you. Max's niece called to tell me about what you've been forced to endure. About how cruel people have been to you. You faced those attacks all alone. It must have been horrible for you. I didn't realize you'd even lost your job because of it."

"Two jobs," I corrected automatically. "Plus the death threats."

Raven's eyes widened. "That's terrible. I'm here to apologize to you for what happened, and for the part I played in it."

"I—" I halted, gobsmacked. I had no idea what to say. How to react. Was I supposed to smile graciously and let Raven off the hook? Did a few words make up for the evil this woman had spewed at me for so long? For destroying my life?

Raven released my hands and wrapped her hand around Max's upper arm. "I owe you an apology, too," she said, gazing into his eyes. "You spoke the truth when you said we'd broken up even before I went into rehab. I was wrong to call you a liar. The night you walked out, I knew we were over. Losing you made me hit rock bottom. It was what finally convinced me I needed to overcome my addiction."

Max's jaw flexed, and I could tell he was biting back a sharp retort. News cameras surrounded us. Carol Perkins seemed to be hanging on every word. He needed to choose his words carefully.

Tonight was turning into a reality TV show.

Raven smiled at the crowd, avoiding looking directly into the cameras. Wasn't that one of the tricks celebrities used to appear more authentic? To never look directly at a camera? Raven knew what she was doing.

Her fans might buy her schtick, but most of the people standing around us wouldn't. Sure, a few of the parents looked starstruck, but the majority looked skeptical—if not downright angry. They didn't believe Raven's act any more than I did.

"You know, Raven," Max said, stepping back so Raven had to let go of him, "I might have believed your apology if you hadn't orchestrated a media event. What did you do, call them from the airport when you landed to tell them you were coming here?"

Raven's mouth tightened, but she didn't respond.

"You're about to release your first album in five years," he continued. "That's why Lauren Harding was interviewing you, right? To talk about your comeback? Your apology comes across as self-serving. You could have made one at any time in the past five years and told the world that Essie Harlow had nothing to do with our breakup, but you didn't bother to do it until you saw a way to help your career. This media circus you staged turns your apology into a farce."

"You're wrong, Max," Raven said, feigning confusion. "Your niece called me, asking me for help. I'm here to set the record straight."

"Emma doesn't know you like I do. She still believes people will do the right thing because they're inherently good. And most people do. She'll learn soon enough that some people are only out for themselves. It'll only take a few manipulative people like you to destroy her faith."

The mood of the crowd around us shifted at this, turning angrier. Even the fans began to look doubtful.

Raven seemed to pick up on the change, and she took a shuffling step closer to her two bare-chested assistants.

I had a sudden flashback. Five years ago, when my father stood in front of the restaurant where I worked and told reporters

I was a homewrecker, I'd also sensed the crowd turning against me. When I'd seen so many strangers focusing their anger on me, I'd been terrified.

All I'd wanted to do was run. Disappear. Hide.

Now, as I watched the same thing happen to Raven, I didn't feel a sense of retribution. I didn't feel vindicated. Instead, I was filled with sadness. With sympathy.

I couldn't stand here and let Raven face all this anger alone. It wasn't in me.

I felt an overpowering need to de-escalate the situation, so I moved closer to her.

Three police cruisers pulled up to the school, and policemen came hurrying toward us. As they trotted closer, I recognized one who'd visited the school to promote good citizenship and positive police relations.

Chief Brown, the gray-haired police chief, approached us, one thumb hooked in his belt buckle. He focused his tight smile on Raven, seeming to ignore the crowd, but to me, it seemed deliberate. I'd bet he was acutely attuned to the mood of the people around us.

The chief tipped his hat back on his head. "I'd love to welcome you to our community, Raven, and of course, we're delighted to have you here, but I'm a little concerned about the distraction your presence is causing. If you'd be willing to move this media event down the street to the park, then I won't have to worry about the safety of our students. I'm sure you understand."

"But I—" Raven spluttered, holding her riding crop across her waist and flexing it nervously, "—I was just trying to apologize. Since I made my accusations against Essie publicly, I wanted my apology to be public, too."

"Which shows how magnanimous you are," Chief Brown said in a placating tone. "I just came from my house where my wife and I were watching your interview with Lauren Harding." He lowered his voice slightly and added, "My wife's a big fan of yours."

Raven nodded. "Please thank her for me," she said tightly.

"Will do." He cleared his throat. "I'm sure Miss Gambit appreciates you making an apology on national television. I have to tell you, I found that interview moving. It brought my wife to tears. Very touching. And you were right when you said your apology was overdue. But this?" He gestured toward the families standing in front of the school. "This doesn't strike me as being good for the children of our community. You're in the entertainment industry. You know what it means to upstage someone. Well, you're upstaging all these kids who worked hard on their show."

"In other words, you should leave," one of the parents yelled.

Raven's face crumpled and her hand dropped to her side, her riding crop dangling next to her high-topped boot. The woman looked crushed. Defeated.

She also looked completely confused.

I couldn't stand by and watch someone else get turned into an outcast. Not when I knew exactly how it felt. I took another step forward, determined not to be a bystander. "Raven, I want to thank you for your apology. You were brave to come here tonight without knowing how I'd react. That had to have been hard for you."

Raven's downcast eyes shot up to meet my gaze, and she searched my face. Whatever she saw there seemed to give her hope. "I truly *am* sorry," she said quietly—not even loud enough for the nearby microphones to pick up.

For the first time, I believed her. "Thank you," I said, just as softly. Our gazes locked for a beat, and she nodded.

I swallowed. "I think we should do as Chief Brown suggested and head to the park down the street."

"I-I—no." Raven tossed her glossy black hair over her shoulder and gave me a tight smile. "I need to head straight back to the airport. I'm flying to Los Angeles tonight and wanted to make a quick stop here to apologize in person. I'm sorry I created a spectacle."

Raven hesitated one last moment, then turned toward the waiting limo.

"Raven? Raven! It's me, Emma." Emma's voice came from the crowd as she pushed her way toward us.

Raven turned as her two shirtless assistants moved to flank her again.

Emma came to a halt in front of the trio, took in the bare chests and bow ties, raised her eyebrows, and stepped back.

Raven grimaced slightly and waved for the men to step back. "Don't mind them. They're my assistants. Dramatic, don't you think?"

"I guess." Emma cleared her throat. "Thanks for coming."

Raven smiled. "I'm glad you called to set me straight. You're a good person, Emma. You have a good heart. Try to stay that way."

In that instant, my heart softened toward her.

With that, Raven turned and climbed into her limo. It slowly crept forward as the people standing in the parking lot moved to let it pass. When the limo finally made it to the main road, it sped away.

The crowd started cheering. I wasn't quite sure if they were cheering Raven or her departure, but I joined in.

"Es-sie! Es-sie! Es-sie!" Lianna started chanting above the applause. I grinned when the rest of my friends joined in.

"Son-ya, Son-ya, Son-ya," a man's voice said even louder, changing the chant.

I turned to take in my small crowd of book-club supporters and found Max grinning at me as he chanted along.

It struck me. It had been him. He'd been the one to change the chant from Essie to Sonya.

Max opened his arms wide, and I stepped into them, wrapping my arms around his waist. My friends and some of the nearby parents burst into applause and let out catcalls and whoops of support.

"I'm glad I didn't run away this time," I murmured.

"Me, too," Max said, holding me close. "More than you'll ever know."

A moment later, Liam, Emma, and Ally came swarming around us, jumping and shouting, and flinging handfuls of cherry blossoms into the air. They'd brought the entire bag out with them and kept grabbing handful after handful and throwing them toward the sky.

It was breathtaking.

39

REWRITING HISTORY

MAX

An hour after Raven's departure, I sat on a barstool in my kitchen, nervously waiting for Sonya to arrive.

Emma set a small, dome-shaped cake in the center of the counter. We'd bought it at the Flamingo Bakery earlier that day. Sonya had mentioned once that she loved the Chocolate Bomb Cake they made. The dark chocolate glaze was covered with curls of white and dark chocolate.

Emma peered at the cake with her head cocked to one side. "Should we put candles on it?"

Those words hit me hard. Was she actually suggesting we light candles? She'd made a lot of progress over the past couple of months. I grinned. "Are you sure you want to light a bomb?"

She rolled her eyes. "You tell the worst jokes."

"Thank you." I examined the cake. "I kind of like it without candles. Besides, if Sonya tries to blow them out, those chocolate curls will go flying across the table."

"Good point."

A knock came at the kitchen door before it opened and Sonya came in, grinning broadly. She held a large cardboard box with a bright blue bow taped to the top.

"I sure hope that isn't a cake," Emma said.

When Sonya spotted the Chocolate Bomb, she let out a laugh. "That would be hilarious, but no."

Emma watched Sonya, a nervous expression on her face. A moment later, her chin quivered, and she ran to Sonya, hugging her like her life depended on it.

Sonya lifted the box high to keep it from bumping Emma's head, so I took it and set it on the table. It was a lot heavier than it looked.

Emma kept up her death-grip of a hug. "I'm so sorry I called Raven. It was a huge mistake. Uncle Max was right. She only cares about herself."

Sonya wrapped her arms around Emma's slight body. "Everything turned out okay. Your heart was in the right place. Besides, I think Raven might have finally learned her lesson."

"Does that mean you forgive me?" Emma asked, gazing up at Sonya with wide, hopeful eyes.

"How could I not?"

Emma gave her one last, tight hug, then stepped back. "That's awesome. You're awesome."

Sonya grinned, bemused. "Thanks. So are you."

Emma began bobbing up and down in excitement.

"What has you so wound up?" Sonya asked.

"The show. Raven. You. Plus," she gestured toward the countertop, "we got you that cake. Your favorite."

"You two feed me all of my favorite treats," Sonya said with a laugh. "A Burnt Almond Torte, a chocolate-filled croissant, and now a Chocolate Bomb Cake? You're spoiling me."

Emma could barely hold still. "The Burnt Almond Torte was better than it sounded. I'm dying to try the Chocolate Bomb. I have to say, this one has a better name."

"I'd be hard-pressed to choose one over the other," Sonya said, "but since this one's right here in front of me, it's currently my favorite by default."

"Your logic is impeccable," I said. As I turned to grab three plates out of the cabinet, the doorbell rang.

"I bet that's Marley," Emma said, darting for the front door.

I grabbed an extra plate. "Have her join us for some cake," I called out.

A moment later, both girls came barreling into the kitchen, laughter bubbling, feet pounding, and eyes flashing. "Can I spend the night at Marley's?" Emma asked.

I shrugged. "Sure, as long as her mom's okay with it. Besides, that gets me out of listening to the two of you giggle like schoolgirls for the next few hours."

"Hey!" Emma yelped. "We *are* schoolgirls!"

"Good point. Maybe that's where the expression came from."

Emma thought for a moment. "Guess so." She turned to Marley and then squealed with excitement. "Sleepover!"

My ears rang. "Are you sure your mom will be okay with this?"

Marley nodded like a bobblehead doll. "Mom says she'd prefer it if I stop talking her ear off and have Emma come over to listen to me."

I chuckled. "Let's fuel you up with some sugar and chocolate." I sliced into the bomb and began serving it.

"Wow." Marley's eyes went wide as I handed plates to her and Emma. "Is that chocolate mousse inside the cake?"

"And buttercream frosting?" Emma asked, swiping up a gob with her finger and popping it into her mouth. She hummed with pleasure. "It is."

Silence reigned as everyone ate. All I heard were forks sliding against plates and the occasional moan of appreciation. It didn't take long for Emma to finish hers off.

Sonya let out a moan of appreciation that sent a shiver of pleasure through me. "I think we have a winner," she said.

I had to give my head a hard shake to clear away the flood of erotic thoughts filling it and get my hormones back under control.

"Marley," I asked, then cleared my throat, "do you want to

take most of the cake back to your house? I'll keep a couple of pieces for me and Miss Gambit. You can have the rest."

"Yes-yes-yes!" Marley cried.

"I'll pack my bag," Emma said, scampering from the room with Marley on her heels.

I sliced off two pieces of cake and put them on plates before packaging up the bakery box.

Sonya looked sublimely happy perched on my barstool.

I teased her, slowly licking chocolate frosting off my fingertips.

That saucy grin of hers turned seductive.

I moved closer but stayed just out of reach. Torturing her—and me too. "What's in that box you brought? It's heavy."

She took in the distance between us and then smirked, letting me know she was onto my tricks. "What's wrong? Don't you trust yourself to come any closer?"

"I'm trying to be circumspect. At least—until Emma leaves."

"You're such a tease," she said.

An instant later, Emma and Marley came thundering down the stairs. I didn't envy Renee Zerkowski tonight. She'd be listening to those two squeal and giggle for hours to come.

On second thought, maybe I *did* envy her. There was nothing quite like being around Emma when she was this happy.

On third thought, there was nothing like being around Sonya when she was this happy, either.

Emma looked around the kitchen. "Where's the cake?"

"Right there," I said, pointing at the two slices I'd set in the middle of the counter.

"No way!" Emma protested. "You said you'd give us the rest!"

"After I saved some for myself. What can I say? I wanted a lot."

Marley's jaw dropped. "You didn't!"

Emma rolled her eyes. "Of course, he didn't." She stomped over to the refrigerator and yanked the door open. "He's making another one of his lame dad jokes." She snatched the bakery box from inside. "Here it is. All for us." She glared at me. "You can be such a guy sometimes."

"You say that like it's a bad thing," I said.

Marley laughed. "You're funny. I wish *my* dad was funny."

"My dad was pretty funny, too," Emma said. And just like that, her entire mood changed. "I miss him," she said, her voice husky. "Both of them. I wish they could have been here tonight to see the show."

"Me too," I said, meeting her gaze. "I don't know if it's possible, but if it is, I'm certain they were here in spirit."

Emma all but dropped the cake onto the counter before launching herself into my arms. Her little body slammed into my chest as though she was afraid I'd disappear if she didn't hold on tight.

She pressed her cheek against my shirt and in a muffled voice said, "Thanks for everything you do, Uncle Max. My life would all be a million times worse without you."

I kissed the top of her head. "I wish your parents were here too, Em. More than you can know. But I'm also thankful that I'm the one who gets to be your guardian now. You're a great kid. I'm proud of you, and I love you to the moon and back."

"See?" Marley said in an upbeat voice, clearly trying to cheer Emma up. "Your uncle is great. He always says the right thing."

"Don't say that. You'll only encourage him and his lame dad jokes," Emma said, pulling out of my arms just far enough to give me a wobbly smile.

I pulled her back into a big hug. "You know you love it."

"Dream on, Uncle Max." She poked me in the ribs, grinning as she stepped back.

She grabbed the cake box from the counter and handed it to Marley. "Can you take this while I carry my bag? I don't want to drop it."

"That would be tragic," Marley said, cradling the box in her arms.

"See ya!" Emma yelled as they went outside through the back

door. "Wouldn't want to be ya!" The girls' squeals of laughter were cut off when the door closed behind them.

"I'm not sure we should have given them so much sugar and chocolate," Sonya commented.

I raised my hands in surrender. "Too late now." I sidled closer to Sonya. "So, what's in the box?"

She grinned. "Impatient much?"

"Often."

She let out a long-suffering sigh. "You're worse than a kid. Were you this curious before Christmas growing up?"

"Worse," I said. "I snooped out all my dad's hiding places and knew exactly what I'd be getting even before Christmas rolled around."

She shook her head. "Where's the fun in that?"

I grinned. "It was loads of fun. Sneaking around. Knowing what everyone else was getting. It was a blast."

She narrowed her eyes. "Does that mean you know what I have in that box?"

I dropped the grin. "Nope. I had no idea you were giving me anything." I crossed my heart. "Promise."

She rubbed the back of her neck. "I planned this a while ago. I hope you don't think I overstepped or anything. I know how much it meant to you—" She stopped talking abruptly, looking nervous.

"Now I'm even more curious. Can I open it?"

She clasped her hands together and nodded. "Yes. You'll like it. At least, I think you will. Maybe."

"I know I will."

I pulled the bow off the top of the brown cardboard box and broke the tape holding it closed with a sharp yank.

Brown craft paper concealed the contents, and when I pulled it away, I revealed—my mantel clock. The one I hadn't seen since the move.

I shook my head. "I don't get it. This is my missing clock."

"I know how much it always meant to you, so I took it to a clock shop in Pittsburgh and had them repair it."

I stared at her in surprise for a moment. She simply stared back, her expression tense.

I gently lifted my clock from the box and set it on the counter. The dark wood gleamed. It looked perfect.

"Here," she said, handing me a silver clock key. "The repair guy said you should wind it right away and set the time." When our fingers touched, hers felt even cooler than the key. She must be nervous. "Is it okay?" she asked. "Do you like it?"

"I love it." I stroked the smooth wood of the case, admiring it. It gleamed with lemon oil. I opened the familiar glass door covering the clock face and slid the key into the first of the three holes to wind it. "I wanted to get it repaired, but I kept putting it off. Did I tell you this belonged to my great-grandparents?"

"Really? I didn't realize it was that old." She stepped closer to me.

"My great-grandfather bought it for my great-grandmother." I began winding the last gear. "It was one of her prized possessions. It was passed down to my grandfather. He knew how much I loved it, so he passed it down to me." I turned to her. "Thank you. This is perfect. I can't think of a more thoughtful gift."

I pulled her into my arms.

She laughed, delighted at my reaction as she draped her arms around my shoulders and kissed me. "I'm glad you like it."

"Love it," I corrected. I carried my clock to the living room and set it on the mantel.

I turned to face her. "Do you know when it broke?" I asked, pulling her back into my arms. "It happened the night you left. Those hands have been pointing at nine-seventeen for the past five years. Frozen in time at the moment you walked out of my life."

"What happened? How did it break?" Her hands stroked up and down my back.

I huffed out a breath and touched my forehead to hers. "I was stupid. After you walked out, I threw the remote across the room. It hit the clock and knocked it to the floor." I shook my head as it rested against hers. "I was such a fool that night. I wish I could go back and change everything. Do it over again and get it right."

She leaned into me, wrapping her arms around my waist. I tucked her close.

"It's done," she said. "Over. We can't go back and change the past. All we can do is move forward and make the best choices we can. There are things I wish I'd done differently too, but that's all in the past and we can't change any of it."

I draped my arm around her waist. "Are we back to where we were before all of that happened?" I stroked her cheek, loving the fact that I could hold her like this again. "Are we back on track?"

She closed her eyes, and I could tell she was savoring my touch. She covered my hand with hers, holding it in place against her cheek as she stared into my eyes. "I'm exactly where I want to be. Here. In your arms. I have my career, my friends, my community, and best of all I have you, too."

I pulled her close. "I love you, Sonya. You know that, right?"

Her tender smile nearly undid me. "I love you, too."

Was it that simple?

I pulled her over to the sofa. "Sit," I said, pressing her down.

When she sat, I dropped to one knee in front of her and took her hands in mine.

"What are you doing?" Her hand tightened around mine.

"Do you remember our last night together?" I searched her face, but she only stared back at me, confused. "I do. It's never far from my thoughts. When I came home, you were sitting on the sofa and I knelt in front of you, just like I'm doing right now."

She stared at our clasped hands in her lap. "I was watching Raven's video." She shook her head. "I was so angry. I hate thinking about that night."

"In that case, can I offer you a new memory?"

She narrowed her eyes. "Is that possible?"

"Think of it as an alternate memory. A what-if memory."

She frowned. "I can tell you're going somewhere with this, but I can't figure out where."

"I think you might like it if you give it a chance."

Her eyes held a playful gleam. "Fine. Proceed with your *'alternate memory.'*" She smiled, and her fingers twitched as though she was dying to make air quotes with them.

"Imagine this. Raven never made the video. I wasn't delayed coming home. I came home first and made dinner for you like I'd planned. Chicken cordon bleu."

She looked doubtful. "You didn't know how to make chicken cordon bleu back then, did you?"

"We're imagining. It sounds better than the spaghetti I'd planned."

Her eyes danced with suppressed laughter. "True. Go on."

"You came in from a long day at work to a room drenched in candlelight. Van Morrison was playing in the background. An excellent bottle of wine was open and waiting for you."

Her gaze softened. "Sounds better and better all the time."

"I was there, waiting for you. We had dinner. I pulled a Burnt Almond Torte from the refrigerator, and sitting on top of it was this."

She stared at me, then glanced down at the brown velvet box I held outstretched in the palm of my hand.

She froze. "Max? What's this?"

"My alternate ending." I held my breath, my heart hammering in my chest.

Her pulse jumped in her throat. She tore her gaze away from the box to look into my eyes, trying to read my soul. "Max, what are you doing?"

"I'm taking a chance. I'm trying to fix a five-year-old mistake. That's the way the night was supposed to have unfolded. I'm hoping, now that we're together and our lives are back on track again, I can fix this error as well."

She continued to hesitate.

My stomach flipped over a couple of times. Maybe I shouldn't have eaten that entire slice of cake. "Aren't you going to open it?"

Suddenly, tears began rolling down her cheeks. She took the box from my hand with trembling fingers.

When she flipped it open, her mouth dropped open as well. She gasped and covered her mouth with one hand. "Max, this is beautiful."

I glanced down at the blue stone. "It was my great-grandmother's. If you don't like the setting, we can have it redone."

She pushed me on the shoulder. "Never. It's perfect." She slid the sapphire onto her left ring finger. It was slightly loose.

I slid my thumb over it. "We'll have it sized to fit you."

"That, I'll agree to."

"Does that mean you'll marry me?"

"Of course, I will." She blushed. "Yes, Max Ross. Yes, I'll marry you."

THANKSGIVING

Sonya

The following Thursday, I peered up at Lianna's house from the street below. "I don't envy her this flight of steps to her front door," I commented, cradling the bowl of Orange-Cranberry-Walnut relish Emma, Max, and I had made last night. As I reached out to take hold of the handrail, the sapphire on my left hand glinted, catching my eye. I still wasn't used to seeing it there.

When Max grabbed the handrail, it wobbled. "This thing is dangerous," he said. "Lianna needs to get it fixed." He peered at the wet autumn leaves with consternation. "The steps might be slick. Take my arm."

It was such a small thing, but his thoughtfulness made my heart lurch. "Good plan." I let go of the handrail and wrapped my fingers around his arm instead.

The vibrant scarlet leaves in the row of bushes at the property's edge contrasted against the emerald-green grass dotted with shiny, wet, orange, and yellow leaves. I loved this time of year. Maybe that was part of why I'd always loved Thanksgiving best of all. No gifts to buy, just great food and family—or in this case, friends.

Of course, I'd had my share of dried-out turkey over the years, but I had no doubt that Lianna's bird would be cooked to perfection. Even if it wasn't, spending the next few hours with all of my friends would make this day priceless.

We made it to the top of the staircase without incident, and Max reached out to ring the doorbell.

I turned around to take in Lianna's stunning view of Sewickley once again. This was my reward for climbing that flight of steps. The town sat far below, framed by trees decked out in their autumn glory. I was a falcon perched atop a tree gazing down upon the quiet town. The light breeze blowing on the golden, crimson, and russet leaves sent them scampering.

Behind me, the front door opened with a burst of pressure and the delicious scent of fresh bread, apple pie, and sage. My mouth watered.

I turned as Gertrude gave a cheery greeting. "Welcome. Come in. Lianna is basting the turkey." She peered at the bowl I held. "What did you two bring?"

"It's my mom's Orange-Cranberry-Walnut relish," Max said. "Thanksgiving wouldn't be complete without it. We made it last night to give the flavors time to meld."

Gertrude's eyes sparkled. "Your mother's recipe? Isn't that sweet! I love traditions. That's why I made my yeast rolls."

I stepped into the foyer and inhaled deeply. "Are you baking them now? They smell amazing."

"Oh!" Gertrude said, her eyes going wide. "That's a sure sign that they're ready to come out of the oven. Let me go rescue them before they burn."

We followed Gertrude into the kitchen. Courtney, Rose, and Lianna gathered around the turkey sitting on the counter. Gertrude grabbed a pair of potholders and removed her perfectly golden yeast rolls from the oven. Now that I was in the kitchen, those amazing aromas hit me full force. Turkey, stuffing, rolls, oranges, sage, and a hundred other scents melded into a perfect one: Thanksgiving.

"Does it take three people to baste a turkey?" I teased. The three of them reminded me of Shakespeare's witches, gathered over a pot in the opening scene of Macbeth—except that this trio had dressed up to celebrate the holiday. All three wore pinafore aprons over their outfits. Lianna and Courtney had on stylish high heels to complement their dresses while Rose wore ballet flats with black leggings and a slim-fitting burnt-orange top.

Sexy witches.

"Three people means it will be done thrice as right," Rose quipped.

"I think the turkey is done," Lianna said. "The leg is wiggling nicely. Now it just needs to cool."

"That means we arrived just in time," I said.

Lianna turned and wiped her hands on her frilly 1950s-style apron before wrapping me in a hug. "I'm glad you're here. You can put your coats upstairs on my bed." She looked past us. "Where's Emma?"

"She spent the night at her friend Marley's," I said.

"The Zerkowskis are having an early dinner, too," Max added. "Emma asked to stay and eat with them, and I said it was okay. We'll all be together later today when we have our second dinner at my dad's place."

"I'm sorry she couldn't come," Lianna said, "but she'll probably have more fun with her friend. I'll be doing a double Thanksgiving today too. I have to head over to my parents' place later."

"Apparently, it's all the rage this year," I said.

The doorbell rang as Max shrugged out of his coat.

"I'll get the door," I said. I set the bowl of relish on the counter and took Max's coat with a wink. "I'll take this upstairs while I'm there. Two birds with one stone."

I shrugged out of my coat as I headed for the door. When I pulled it open, I found Ford and Mara on the porch. Mara held a large baking dish in an insulated bag.

"We brought the twice-baked mashed potatoes," Mara announced. "Are you the gatekeeper?"

My response was immediate. "Are you the key master?"

A surprised grin split Mara's face. "Awesome! You got my *Ghostbusters* reference."

"What can I say? After I missed the reference at the show last week, I watched the movie again. I thought it might come up, and I was right."

"Aw," Mara said. "Aren't you the best!"

"Come on in. I was about to take our coats upstairs. Can I take yours, too?"

"Sure; thanks," Mara said, shrugging out of her leather jacket and revealing a red, white, and blue Wonder Woman dress. Her blue-tipped brunette hair curled inward, framing her face.

"You look adorable," I said as I took the jacket. "I love what you're wearing. Very patriotic."

"This?" Mara looked down at her dress. "I'm a big Wonder Woman fan. I tend to wear comic book themed-clothes a lot."

"What, no compliments for me?" Ford teased.

"Nice jeans," I said dryly. I glanced at Mara, and in a falsely hushed voice asked, "Is he always this needy?"

"Hey, I resemble that remark," Ford protested.

"I'll meet you both in the kitchen after I drop these off upstairs," I said. I trotted up the staircase and found Lianna's pale lavender bedroom, where I added the coats to the growing pile on her bed. I paused. I liked it here. The room was nicely balanced and had good feng shui.

Back downstairs, I found that Conner had arrived. He set his beautiful dessert on the counter.

"What kind of pie is that?" I asked.

"Caramel apple. Dante made it. He's been on a baking frenzy lately. I helped him with the latticework crust."

"Is that caramel drizzled on top?"

"Sure is." He held up a grocery bag. "Can I stash the ice cream in the freezer?"

"Over there," Lianna said, pointing toward her stainless-steel fridge. "There's plenty of room now that all the food is about to go on the table. I want to thank all of you for bringing some of your favorite dishes today. It made my job a million times easier."

Lianna pointed toward two bottles of wine and a tray of glasses on the counter. "Help yourselves. There's more wine in the dining room."

"Having Thanksgiving dinner together was an inspired idea," Rose said. She twisted the corkscrew into one of the bottles. "This is so much more fun than the lonely Thanksgiving I had last year." She yanked, and the cork came free with a pop.

"I couldn't agree more," Courtney said. "We should make this an annual thing. Maybe a different person could host each year."

"What a marvelous idea," Gertrude said. "Thank you, Courtney. You always think ahead."

Courtney looked pleased by the compliment.

"Can we host next year?" Mara asked, glancing at Ford. At his nod, she grinned in delight.

"Sounds good to me," Lianna said.

Rose poured herself a glass of wine, sat on one of the barstools, and pulled her large tote into her lap. "Is everyone here who's supposed to be here?" she asked as she rummaged through her purse.

Lianna glanced around the room. "Max, Sonya, Ford, Mara, you, Gertrude, Courtney, and Conner. That's it. We're all here."

Rose lifted her glass and took a deep swallow. "Good. I wanted to show you all something. It was news to me, but maybe some of you've already seen it." Rose glanced at me and then pulled a copy of *Here's the Scoop* out of her purse and set it on the counter.

I tensed at the sight of the magazine's masthead. That rag had hounded me for so long, I'd probably never shake off my instinctive aversion to it. I glanced at Max.

His arm encircled my waist reassuringly. "Breathe," he murmured in my ear.

He knew me so well.

A yellow post-it note stuck out from the magazine, like a

caution sign. Rose opened *Here's the Scoop* to the marked page as she cleared her throat.

"'Raven Reaches Out. Today, rock star Raven announced she founded a new charity, Stand Up to Cyber Bullying. The foundation's goal is to assist victims of social bashing and cyberbullying by providing financial assistance for psychological counseling and legal fees. 'People who have been systematically targeted by online trolls and cyber-bullies need help, both with getting their harassers to stop and with facing the aftermath. This foundation will offer assistance, both with getting people in touch with those who can help and with covering the expenses associated with providing that help. I decided to spearhead this because I'm ashamed of the part my thoughtlessness played in instigating a cyberbullying campaign against Essie Harlow. At the time, I never considered how my privileged position of power could influence people and unintentionally convince them to torment her.

"'In an effort to atone for my thoughtlessness, I created this foundation to help make sure this doesn't happen to anyone else. Anyone who finds themselves in a situation similar to Essie's can reach out to us and get the help they need.'

"Raven has announced a benefit concert, and all proceeds will go to fund her new foundation. She plans to organize another, larger event in one year and invite other musicians to take part."

Rose stopped reading and looked up from the magazine to peer at me with a worried expression. "Did she tell you she was doing this?"

I took a deep breath and then exhaled. It felt good to be in the know for a change.

"As a matter of fact, she contacted me on Monday to make sure it was okay to mention the name Essie in her interview. I told her yes, but that she should keep my current name, as well as Max and Emma's, out of it. I think she really does regret what happened. This new foundation sounds like a fantastic idea. It could have helped a lot five years ago."

Max leaned closer and kissed my temple.

Courtney's eyes seemed to light up, and she nodded at us approvingly. "I still haven't congratulated you on your engagement. The fact that you found your way back to each other is pretty damned amazing after everything Raven did to drive you apart."

"It's like a fairy tale," Rose said. Her eyes sparkled with romantic mischief as she tucked her magazine back into her purse. "An evil witch drove you apart and you ran away, but you persevered, escaped from the forbidden forest, and found your way back to each other. Then they all lived happily ever after. The end."

Lianna rolled her eyes as she smiled. "You're a goof, Rose. You should write books. You're always making up stories."

I glanced around the room at the happy faces of all my friends. "I'm lucky to have you all in my life."

"We feel the same way about you," Mara said. "I'm so glad you and Max are back together again."

I glanced over to see her staring at me with a well-pleased smile. I cocked my head. "You know, we need to coordinate this whole wedding date thing. Max and I haven't set one yet. With two weddings, we wanted to check with you first because we don't want any conflicts."

Ford cleared his throat. "We haven't set a date yet. I'm trying to talk Mara into having a destination wedding. I think it'll help keep the paparazzi away."

Mara leaned against him and wrapped her arm around his waist.

"My idea is to charter a plane and fly the entire wedding party to some quiet island," Ford continued. "I was hoping for next spring. That will be just before we start filming, and I don't want the wedding to turn into a media circus."

Mara's eyes widened as though she'd just been struck by inspiration. She released Ford and then reached out and snatched up my hands. "I just had the very best idea! Why don't we have a double wedding?"

I tensed.

She must have felt my reaction because she squeezed my hands even tighter. "Don't say no. You're as leery of the paparazzi as we are. Probably even more so. Just think of it. We could say our vows far away from any prying eyes."

The idea sounded like a dream come true. An island? No reporters? I glanced at Max, but he just shrugged in a whatever-you-want sort of way.

What *did* I want?

This. Precisely this.

I started grinning like a deranged person, but I couldn't stop myself. "This is the perfect solution. The thought of planning a big wedding that would impress all of Max's Hollywood connections was starting to freak me out. Escaping to an island is my idea of perfection. Besides, I'm happy to turn most of the decisions over to you and go along with whatever you want. I hate entertaining."

I yanked Mara into a bear hug. "You're brilliant! I love it." Then, I pushed Mara to arms-length and peered into her eyes, searching for any misgivings. I couldn't find them.

Mara grinned delightedly. "You might regret that when you get a wedding cake with Clark Kent and Lois Lane as the cake topper."

"Bring it on." I shrugged. "As long as the cake tastes delicious, I'll be happy."

Mara fluttered her palm over her chest. "A woman after my own heart. Let's get together later and look at our calendars to pick a date."

"I bet our guests will be happy about it, too," Ford said. "Max and I will probably invite a lot of the same people. This will make it easier on them."

Max's phone rang. "It's Emma. I need to take this," he said, stepping away.

Mara turned to Ford. "Are you sure a double-wedding okay with you? I didn't even run it past you before I asked Sonya."

"Whatever makes you happy is okay with me." Ford kissed the top of her head.

"Lianna?" Mara said. "Can you point me toward your bathroom?"

"At the top of the stairs. You can't miss it." Lianna hefted the enormous turkey from the roasting pan and set it heavily on the serving platter. "As soon as I finish making the gravy, we can eat." She grabbed a bowl from the cabinet and started scooping out the stuffing from inside the bird. "I'm banishing all non-cooks from the kitchen. Anyone who needs to wash their hands can go upstairs to do it."

"I can scoop out the stuffing while you make the gravy," I volunteered.

Lianna handed me the spoon. "Thanks."

The delicious scent of thyme, sage, and—sausage?—struck me. "Does your stuffing have sausage in it?"

"Sweet Italian sausage. It's my great-grandmother's recipe. She was from South Carolina. It has grits in it, too."

"Grits!" I stared down at the heaping mound of stuffing in the bowl. "That must be why the stuffing isn't dry."

"It's a good thing I have an empty stomach," Conner said with a grin. "I'm starving. Want me to carry the turkey to the dining room?"

"Only if I can trust you not to steal a bite," Lianna said as she turned on the gas burner and set the roasting pan over the flame.

Mara reentered the room. "What did I miss? It looks like dinner is almost ready. Is there anything I can do to help?"

"Build me a first-floor bathroom?" Lianna quipped. "I hate having to send guests upstairs to use the restroom. What if someone can't manage the steps?"

Conner laughed. "Then they'll never walk in your front door in the first place. That's a hell of a staircase you have out there."

"You need to fix the railing," Max said. "It's wobbly."

"It's on my to-do list. I also want to move my laundry room up here from the basement. I hate carrying baskets up and down from the basement."

"Hire my brother," Courtney told her. "Gillette Construction is the best in town." She broke off a corner of the crust on the Caramel Apple pie and ate it.

"Hey," Conner complained. "No stealing bites. Lianna said so."

"He's at the top of my list of contractors to call." Lianna tasted the gravy before she added salt and pepper. "I should have the money set aside by the time spring rolls around."

"Don't put off contacting him," Courtney said. "Kincaid always has multiple projects going on."

As Lianna carefully poured the hot gravy into a serving container, she announced, "Dinner's ready. Can you all carry something into the dining room?"

A few minutes later, we were all seated at Lianna's long table. Three chairs were on one side, and four were squeezed in on the other, the last one at an angle next to the head of the table. There were so many platters and bowls of food in front of us that the poor table should be groaning from the weight.

The nine of us squeezed in, with Conner claiming the small corner spot next to Lianna.

Lianna stood at the head of the table in front of her golden-brown turkey and rested her hands on the back of her chair. "Since this is our first Thanksgiving together, I'm starting a new tradition. We'll go around the room and have each person share something they're thankful for. Don't cop out by saying something vague and non-specific. Give me something from your life this year. Dig deep." She glanced at Mara, who was seated to her right. "You go first."

"That's easy," Mara said. "I'm thankful I found Ford."

"Ditto," Ford said, grinning at her.

"New rule," Lianna interrupted. "No dittos. Ford has to come up with something different. That goes for all of you. No repeating what someone else said."

Ford scowled at her. "Fine. I'm thankful I stumbled upon *Ghost* in Mara's comic book shop so I could turn it into a movie, and that Mara is back to doing video game design and development."

"Nice," Lianna said. "A double. And congrats on your movie. Now you, Sonya."

I took a breath. "First, I want to say I'm thankful Max and I are finally back together again after five long years apart."

Lianna tapped her chin. "That's a bit like Mara's, but I'll let it slide since it was so specific."

"There's more. I'm also grateful that Raven stepped forward and is trying to address the damage she did five years ago. She might be late with her apology, but I still appreciate it."

"Brava! I love it." Lianna looked across the table at Max, who had taken the seat at the foot of the table. "Max, it's your turn."

He glanced at me and seemed to hesitate. "I'm thankful Emma is alive and well and living with me. Losing Hailey and Barry was horrific, but I'm grateful we still have her."

The room fell silent. The pressure of Max's loss pressed on my heart, rendering me unable to speak. Our gazes met and locked. I could read all the loss and heartache there, but also all the love. All the hope.

"To Emma," Ford said, breaking the silence.

"To Emma," I said along with the others. I raised my glass in a salute and then took a deep swallow of wine.

Gertrude hesitated for a moment. "I suppose it's my turn. I'm thankful I found this wonderful book group. You all make me feel young again." She glanced at Rose, who sat next to her. "You're the one who posted the notice about the group at the library. Thank you for that."

Rose cleared her throat. "It was my pleasure." She looked around the table. "I'm thankful all of you are my friends, and for my job as the librarian for the teen section. After growing up in the foster system, having people I can count on means a lot to me." She gave a wistful grin. "Max, Ford, are you sure you don't have another brother lying around somewhere? I'd like my own happily ever after."

Everyone chuckled.

Ford squinted his eyes. "I'll have to send Sean your way the next time he's in town."

Rose blushed. "I was joking. I totally forgot you even *had* another brother."

"That doesn't surprise me," Max said. "He's almost never in town." He gave Rose a wink. "But I'll introduce you the next time he's around."

Rose tried to hide her flaming face by taking a gulp of wine.

Courtney cleared her throat. "I'm thankful my research has had a breakthrough using a new drug combination. I'm using one of our drugs along with one from a competitor."

"How would that work?" I asked, confused. "How can you use a competitor's drug?"

Courtney winced. "Right now, I just buy it off the shelf. Now that we know this combination has merit, our legal department has to begin negotiating with them. That's the tricky part, but if we come to an agreement, we might end up with an excellent cancer treatment." She glanced at Conner. "What about you? What are you thankful for?"

He tipped his head from side to side like a clock pendulum. "It seems a bit banal after you brought up the whole curing cancer thing, but I'm thankful I moved back to Sewickley and my restaurant is a success, knock on wood." He tapped on the table leg, then looked up at Lianna. "We're back to you. What are you thankful for this year?

"I'm thankful my divorce from Paul went smoothly and that I've been able to move on with my life." Lianna looked around the table. "Also, I want to thank each of you for all of your help these past few months. You've been incredibly supportive.

"To friendship," Lianna said, raising her glass for a toast.

"To friendship," we all chimed in, clinking glasses.

"Time to dig in," Lianna said. "If we keep toasting, our feast will get cold." She took a spoonful of the twice-baked mashed potatoes and passed the serving dish to me. The others followed suit, passing around various bowls and platters.

Mara drizzled gravy on her turkey. "Lianna, how are you adjusting to being single? Is it a big change?"

Lianna gave a soft huff of laughter. "Life without Paul is remarkably similar to life *with* Paul since he traveled all the time. We were lucky to see each other two weekends a month. Not a lot has changed except that I'm living in a different house."

Gertrude raised her glass. "Good riddance to the man."

"Hear, hear," Mara said, reaching across the table to clink glasses with Gertrude.

Conner leaned back in his chair. "Long distance relationships are rough. I don't know how Dante does it. With Angelina in Central America working for Doctors Without Borders, they rarely see each other. He flew out to visit her last night since we're closed over the Thanksgiving holiday. I guess the good part for me is that with both of us being effectively single, we can devote all our time to growing our business. Not a Yacht Club will be opening a kayak rental area next spring."

Ford raised his yeast roll slathered in Orange-Cranberry-Walnut Relish in a mock toast. "Here's to your kayak rental business. May it be a rousing success." He bit into his roll and then closed his eyes in bliss. "Damn, this is good. For me, this will always be the taste of Thanksgiving."

"Lianna, thank you again for keeping up with our weekly dinners," Gertrude said. "I so enjoy the time we spend together."

"So do I. But, I've been thinking. I really need to find you a man," Lianna said. "Someone you can cook for and fuss over. I can tell how much you enjoy it."

Gertrude scowled. "Don't be silly, girl. I'm perfectly content. Why would I want some man messing around in my life and trying to change things?"

I sat back, happily absorbing the conversation, the ambiance, and the companionship swirling around me. I'd come close to running away from all of this only a couple of weeks ago. I'd nearly let my fear of Raven and those social media bullies scare me away. Thank goodness I hadn't, because I would have missed this moment. This gem of a day. This perfect slice of life.

Max peered at me. "Happy you stayed?"

I widened my eyes. "What? Are you reading minds now?"

"Of course. Didn't I tell you that was one of my superpowers?" he teased with a wink. "You looked so perfectly happy, it was the logical conclusion."

"Hey, you stole my line," Mara interrupted, clearly eavesdropping. "I'm the one with superpowers."

"I'm happy to be here," I told everyone. "I wouldn't have missed this for anything."

Max's pale blue eyes crinkled at the corners as he smiled at me.

"I'm especially happy I found you again," I added softly. "You're the best part of my life now.

We lingered at the dinner table, laughing and talking, but once we were all done, everyone pitched in to clear the table and clean up. Lianna put away the leftovers, Conner took care of rinsing, Gertrude loaded the dishwasher, and the rest of us carried plates in from the dining room.

After I dropped off an empty bowl I paused near the kitchen doorway to watch everyone bustling around, chatting and cleaning.

I loved this. Loved that I finally had a place to call home. That I'd finally stopped running. This community was exactly the sort of place I'd always dreamed of being a part of.

My emotions overwhelmed me, and I had to turn away from the scene and step back into the dining room to gather myself.

Max was here, picking up a nearly empty bowl of twice-baked mashed potatoes from the table.

I grabbed him by the elbow to waylay him. In a low, earnest voice I said, "I want to do this again with you next year. Every year."

"You do?" He glanced back into the kitchen to take in all our friends and smiled. "This has been fun."

I shook my head in frustration. "That's not what I meant. Not exactly. I mean, yes, I want to have Thanksgiving with everyone again, but I want more. I want to create traditions with *you*. I want to be with you every day. I want to build a life with you and make our own memories together. I want us to stand side by side as we embrace our future."

"That's exactly what I want. You can see it too? Us building a life together? Having children? Raising them here among our friends and family? It's everything I want." The corners of his mouth lifted. "I guess it's a good thing we're getting married."

I moved forward to kiss him and bumped against the empty bowl he held.

He laughed, set down the bowl, swept his arms around me, and pulled me into him. "No obstacle can come between us."

"Not even twice-baked mashed potatoes," I teased. I moved in for a kiss.

"Break it up, you two," Ford said from behind me. "No PDA."

I turned in time to see Mara steal up behind him.

"Yes, PDA," Mara said, poking Ford in the ribs. Then she yanked him to her and kissed him soundly.

Max cupped my cheek in his hand and gazed into my eyes. "'Before I met you, I was lonely, but now I'm where someone loves me best of all.'" Then he leaned in and kissed me.

I melted into him. "I'll always love you best, my wild thing."

Maybe my life really could end in a happily ever after.

CHICKEN PICCATA

Level: Moderate
  Prep Time: 15 min
  Cooking Time: 25 min
  Total Time: 40 minutes
  Serves: 4

Ingredients:

- 2 large skinless, boneless chicken breasts, butterflied (cut in half lengthwise so you have 4 thinner pieces)
- Salt and black pepper to taste
- Flour, for dredging
- 6 tablespoons butter, divided
- 5 tablespoons olive oil
- 1/3 cup fresh lemon juice
- 1/2 cup chicken stock
- 1/4 cup brined capers, rinsed
- 1/3 cup fresh parsley, chopped

Directions:

1. Pat the chicken dry with a paper towel. Salt and pepper it to taste. Dredge chicken in flour and shake off any excess.
2. In a large skillet over medium-high heat, melt 2 tablespoons of butter and 3 tablespoons of olive oil. When heated, add 2 pieces of chicken and cook for 3 minutes. When the chicken is browned, flip and cook the other side for 3 minutes. Remove and transfer to a plate. Cook the chicken in batches if necessary and add more butter and oil if needed. Remove the chicken from the pan and set aside.
3. Without cleaning the pan, add the lemon juice, stock, and capers. Bring to a boil, scraping up the brown bits from the pan for extra flavor. Taste and adjust the seasonings if needed.
4. Return the chicken to the pan and simmer for 5 minutes.
5. Place chicken on a serving platter or individual plates.
6. In the skillet, add the remaining 2 tablespoons of butter to the sauce and whisk. Pour the sauce over the chicken. Garnish with parsley.

BLACK CHOCOLATE COCONUT ICE CREAM

Level: Easy (requires an ice cream machine
    Prep Time: 5 hours or overnight to freeze the bowl
    Cooking Time: 10 min
    Chilling Time: 1 hour
    Churning Time: 20 min
    Additional Freezing Time: 1 hour
    Total Time: 2 hours 30 minutes
    Serves: 4-6
    Ingredients:

- 2 cups full-fat coconut milk
- 2 cups condensed coconut milk
- 2 tablespoons arrowroot starch (arrowroot is better than cornstarch which doesn't freeze well)
- 2 tablespoons honey or maple syrup
- 2 teaspoons vanilla extract
- 3–4 tablespoons activated charcoal powder
- 3 tablespoons cocoa powder

Plus:

- Bag of ice

- Carton of salt

Directions:

1. Freeze the freezer bowl for at least 5 hours, or overnight.
2. In a medium-sized saucepan, on medium-low, mix the milk, condensed milk, starch, honey, vanilla extract, cocoa powder, and charcoal. Do NOT boil.
3. Pour the mixture into a bowl, cover, and place it in the fridge for at least 1 hour before making ice cream.
4. Assemble the ice cream-making machine according to its directions, adding the ice and salt. Turn on the rotating freezer bowl.
5. Pour the chilled ice cream mixture into the freezer bowl and churn for 15–20 minutes or until it reaches a "soft-serve" consistency.
6. If you're like Dante and you like thicker ice cream, pour the soft ice cream into a freezer-safe container, cover it, and freeze it for about 1 hour.

TWICE BAKED MASHED POTATOES

Level: Moderate
   Prep Time: 20 minutes
   Cooking Time: 1 hour 15 minutes
   Total Time: 1 hour 35 minutes
   Serves: 8
   Note: Can be made in advance
   Ingredients:

- 5 pounds Yukon Gold potatoes, peeled and cubed
- 1/2 cup butter
- 1/4 cup milk
- 8 ounces of cream cheese, softened
- 1 onion, grated
- 1 egg
- salt and pepper to taste

Directions:

1. Preheat oven to 350 F (175 C).
2. Lightly butter the inside of a 2-quart casserole dish.
3. Boil a large pot of lightly salted water.

4. Add potatoes. Cook until tender but firm, about 15 minutes; drain.
5. In a large bowl or stand mixer, mash the potatoes with the butter and milk. Beat in cream cheese and onion. In a small bowl, beat the egg with about a cup of mashed potatoes, then mix it with the rest of the potatoes and season with salt and pepper. Transfer the mixture to a 2-quart casserole dish.
6. Bake for 1 hour. Potatoes should be puffy and lightly browned.

CARAMEL APPLE PIE

Level: Moderate+

Prep Time: 30 minutes
Cooking Time: 1 hour
Total Time: 1 hour 30 minutes
Serves: 8

Ingredients:

- 1/2 cup white sugar
- 1/2 cup brown sugar
- 1/4 cup water
- 1/4 teaspoon cinnamon
- 1 pinch salt
- 5 Granny Smith apples - peeled, cored, and sliced
- 1 pastry for double-crust pie

Directions:

1. Preheat oven to 425F (220C).
2. In a saucepan over medium heat, mix together butter, white sugar, brown sugar, water, cinnamon, and salt. Bring to a boil, remove from heat, and set aside.

3. Roll out two pie crusts: A 9-inch crust for the bottom of the pie and a 10-inch circle for the lattice on top. Put the 9-inch crust into the pie plate and pour in the apple slices.

4. Cut the second 10-inch crust into 8 (1-inch) wide strips. Weave the pastry strips into a lattice pattern. Fold the ends of the lattice strips under the edge of the bottom crust and crimp to seal either with your fingertips or with the tines of a fork.

5. Pour the butter-sugar mixture over the pie and completely coat the lattice. The sauce will soak down into the pie through the crust.

6. Bake for 15 minutes. Reduce the heat to 350 F (175 C) and bake for another 35-40 minutes. The crust should be golden brown, the filling should be bubbling, and the caramel on the top crust should be set.

7. Note: Allow to cool completely before slicing.

CRANBERRY ORANGE WALNUT RELISH

Level: Easy

Prep Time: 10 minutes

Total Time: 10 minutes

Serves: 10 small servings or 5 medium-sized servings

Note from Sheridan: This is my grandmother's recipe. She was raised in South Carolina and this recipe was handed down in our family. It's a big hit at our house, so I usually double the recipe.

Ingredients:

- 1 navel orange (seedless if possible)
- 1 (12-oz) bag of fresh cranberries, rinsed
- 1/2 cup sugar
- 1/8 teaspoon cinnamon
- 1/2 cup chopped walnuts

Directions:

Option 1: With Kitchen Aid grinder attachment (my preferred method)

- Prep: Wash the oranges. Cut them into quarters and remove the seeds, the center white section, and the stem end. Do not remove the peel.
- Grind: Run the cranberries and orange sections through the KitchenAid grinder.
- Stir in sugar, cinnamon, and chopped walnuts.
- Chill, covered, for at least 2 hours to allow flavors to develop.

Option 2: With a food processor

- Prep: Wash the oranges. Cut them into quarters and remove the seeds, the center white section, and the stem end. Do not remove the peel.
- Mix: In the food processor, pulse the cranberries with the orange sections, sugar, and cinnamon until it's well blended.
- Stir in the chopped walnuts by hand so they don't turn into goo.
- Chill, covered, for at least 2 hours to allow flavors to develop.

FOR MORE INFORMATION
ABOUT BULLYING

If you'd like to learn more about bullying, its effects, and what you can do when confronted with it, visit the following sites:

https://www.stopbullying.gov/
https://bullybust.org/
https://en.wikipedia.org/wiki/School_bullying

BIBLIOGRAPHY

Contemporary Romances

The Way to a Woman's Heart series - the **Coming Home** trilogy

Slow Simmer
Here's the Scoop
From Bitter to Sweet

Coming in 2024
The Way to a Woman's Heart series - the **Destination Wedding** trilogy

Too Much On My Plate
Say Cheese!
Turkish Delight

Historical romances

Gambling On a Scoundrel

Secrets and Seduction series:

Lady Cecilia Is Cordially Disinvited for Christmas
(A prequel only available through my VIP club)

It Takes a Spy…
Lady Catherine's Secret
Once Upon a Spy
My Lady, My Spy
Along Came a Spy

ABOUT THE AUTHOR

I'm Sheridan Jeane, and I write the **Way to a Woman's Heart** series of romcoms set in Sewickley, a small town near Pittsburgh. These books all feature my favorite things: food, books, family, and friends.

You can also check out my exciting Victorian-era romances from my **Secrets and Seduction** series. They're filled with spies, intrigue, and tender, sensual moments.

More about me?

I'm the daughter of an artist/art-therapist/professor mother and an opera-loving/computer engineer/do-it-yourself father. Growing up, I assumed parents routinely converted their garages into well-stocked art studios complete with potter's wheels, kilns, and every color of paint under the sun. Didn't every second-grader learn how to weld or nail shingles on the roof of the 2-car garage their dad built? And what about all those after-opera cast parties? Weren't they run-of-the-mill too?

No?

Go figure!

That probably explains my quirky outlook on life.

Visit me at www.SheridanJeane.com